DECEPTION

A WRITING BLOC ANTHOLOGY

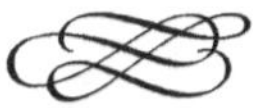

WRITING BLOC
INDIE PUBLISHING TEAM

DECEPTION

Previously published as *Deception!*

Second ed. 2022

ISBN: 979-8-9865543-6-5

10 9 8 7 6 5 4 3 2 1

❀ Created with Vellum

CONTENTS

INTRODUCTION
CARI DUBIEL

How many lies have you told today?

You might be saying, "I haven't told any. I'm a totally honest person! I could never lie!"

Think again. Did your husband call to ask if you mind if he stays late at work? Did a doctor ask you how much sugar you've been eating? Did one of your co-workers ask if you like her sweater?

No, you want your husband to come home because you can't stand the thought of being alone with these kids one more minute. You know you're not supposed to eat too much sugar, but that mint gelato looked so good behind the frosty glass in the freezer aisle. And the sweater is the color of barf.

Deception is everywhere around us, every minute of every day. The interior monologue in our heads never quite matches up what's going on in the real world. Maybe that's why we're so fascinated by it. We goggle at stories about celebrities paying their children's way through college, at anecdotes about people having affairs and living double lives. We wonder how a murderer can go to work every day while performing terrifying acts at night.

These stories examine us on many levels. You'll find here the smallest lies that feel so big, and the biggest lies that maybe aren't so bad. You'll walk in the gray areas between good and evil, from sleepy rural towns to the black emptiness of space. You'll feel your heart pull when characters are betrayed, and rejoice when they find their way. And you'll be stung when you're not sure what's going to happen after the story ends.

It was an absolute joy to work with these authors in this, our second Writing Bloc anthology. There is so much talent here.

Come inside and be deceived.

Cari Dubiel

Lead Editor, Writing Bloc

ALPHA

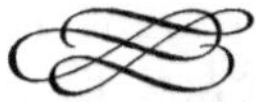

ALY WELCH

"I'm so thrilled that Sara is finally bringing someone home to meet us," Mrs. Smith confided in her husband. The petite woman wore a chartreuse sleeveless dress that grazed her knees. A floral headscarf secured her light brown hair. She draped a freshly-washed cream jacquard cloth over the mahogany table in the dining room.

"You sure I shouldn't get my shotgun?" Mr. Smith sat on a tan recliner in the next room. He wore faded jeans and a rumpled tee. A baseball cap concealed thinning brown hair. He flipped through the channels, settling on a game show.

"Her friend is just joining us for a casual dinner," Mrs. Smith reminded her husband as she adjusted the table cloth. "Save the 'scary dad' routine for their first real date. We don't want to chase a suitor off the first night."

Mrs. Smith walked into the kitchen. She returned with a vase of daffodils that complimented the green and yellow of her ensemble. Mrs. Smith set the floral arrangement down on the dining room table. "Honestly, after what happened with Stacy's daughter, I was starting to worry about Sara."

"Hmm?"

"I'm surprised you didn't hear about it at work," Mrs. Smith replied as she rearranged the blooms, "her father working in accounting, and all." She went back into the kitchen.

"You know I'm not much for water cooler talk unless the Packers are playing," Mr. Smith called out to her. "I hate gossip."

"Oh?" said Mrs. Smith, who possessed no such reservations. She came out of the kitchen with porcelain plates, yellow napkins, and silverware. "Well, a teacher caught Rachel in the bathroom with another girl," Mrs. Smith divulged as she set the table. Her tone suggested distaste, but her sparkling eyes betrayed an inner *this is better than reality TV* glee.

Mr. Smith looked away from the television and stared at his wife. "So...?" he asked, raising a bushy eyebrow.

Mrs. Smith walked under the archway of the partial wall to stand before him. He craned his neck to see the television.

"They were..." Mrs. Smith paused as though scandalized. She leaned over and whispered in her husband's ear. "Kissing."

Mr. Smith looked away from the television set again to meet his wife's eyes. "This is Jack Hansen's daughter, right? That Rachel?" he asked with a hint of a smile. "The leggy brunette on Sara's softball team?"

"Yes. Rachel's a junior, too," Mrs. Smith said, narrowing her eyes. "Like our daughter."

"Who was the other girl?" Mr. Smith asked.

"Nobody we know," Mrs. Smith said. She sighed and turned away.

A car pulled into the driveway.

"That's them," Mrs. Smith said, forcing a smile. "Turn off the TV. I'll get lemonade and glasses so we can enjoy a drink on the porch before dinner. There's about ten minutes left on the casserole." She returned to the kitchen.

Mr. Smith turned off the television and set down the remote. He pushed himself up from the chair. "I just hope he's not one of those effeminate pretty boys," he said. Mr. Smith adjusted his baseball cap. He left the front door ajar for his wife as he stepped out into the warm spring air.

Mrs. Smith left the kitchen balancing a tray with a pitcher of lemonade and four glasses. She pushed the front door open with her free hand to join everyone outside.

Mr. Smith sat on the porch swing, holding his hat with one hand and scratching at his head with the other.

Mrs. Smith followed his eyes. She gasped, dropping the tray. The pitcher and glasses shattered on the sidewalk.

"Oops, party foul!" Sara chirped, kneeling to pick up the broken pieces of glass. She was a pretty blonde in a fitted tee and denim shorts. Her slim fingers deftly plucked at the glass, which she dropped into a wastebasket by the swing. Sara rose and returned to the side of her guest.

"Mom, this is Duke."

Duke stared at Mrs. Smith.

Mrs. Smith stared at Duke.

Duke towered over her. If not for his slouch, he was taller than Mr. Smith by nearly a foot. He had an impressive, tangled mane of black and auburn hair. What was most impressive about his hair was the way it covered most of his face and ran down his back.

Mrs. Smith supposed it was fur rather than hair.

A pair of ram-like horns sat on either side of his large skull. His amber eyes glowed as if lit from within, reminding Mrs. Smith of a jack-o-lantern. He wore tattered clothing, and his feet were cloven.

Sara's hand disappeared into one of Duke's massive paws. Her other hand pressed against his muscular chest. She leaned against him, beaming at her mother.

Mrs. Smith stared down at her daughter's hand. She noted the wickedly sharp claws on Duke's paw. Several moments passed before Mrs. Smith sputtered, "H...hello, Duke."

Duke opened his jaws wide, revealing a mouthful of yellow fangs. He grunted in greeting. Then Duke lumbered off to investigate the foliage in the yard. He stopped to look in Mrs. Smith's direction and wag his short deer-like tail.

"He has a tail," Mrs. Smith said to nobody in particular, fingers fiddling with the strand of pearls at her throat. She tilted her head as she watched Duke tear through her garden, crushing daffodils. He beat his gargantuan chest and whooped. Duke stopped to hurl a large stone at Sara.

Sara ducked, grinning.

"Aww. See how much he likes me?" she asked her mother. "Johnny only ever threw sand and pebbles."

"That was in kindergarten," Mrs. Smith said. "But it's not okay at any age," she added.

Sara's blue eyes widened with surprise. "Really? You didn't mind back then. Even thought it was cute."

Mrs. Smith frowned. She saw Duke stop circling the yard to sniff the trunk of a maple tree. Her eyebrows rose when she heard something that sounded suspiciously like a zipper.

"See, he feels right at home already!" Sara clapped her hands together with delight.

"Did he…did he just mark the tree?" Mrs. Smith asked, turning to her husband.

Mr. Smith was still staring ahead, his eyes glazed over.

"You always told me to find a big, strong Alpha," Sara reasoned. "But don't worry. He knows Dad is the man of the house."

Duke ran to her father on all fours. Mr. Smith jumped up from his seat and dropped his hat. As Duke acquainted himself with the man of the house's thigh, Mr. Smith's gaze darted from Duke to his wife to his daughter. His eyes were no longer glazed over, but wide and bulging.

Mrs. Smith raised a hand to her mouth, her own eyes just as wide as she turned to her daughter.

"Stop that," Sara said, gently tapping Duke on the head. He disentangled himself from Mr. Smith and rose to his full height. Then he tugged on Sara's flaxen ponytail, hard.

"No!" she said sharply, tapping the bridge of his nose.

Duke whimpered, his lower lip jutting out.

"It's okay," Sara consoled him, stroking his downy cheek. "Is dinner ready yet?" she asked her mother. "Duke is starving." Sara opened the front door and walked inside.

Duke followed her.

Mrs. Smith heard a thump and a crash as a table lamp fell to the floor. She winced.

Mr. Smith knelt to retrieve his hat. "Are we really gonna allow that thing in our house?" He rose, trying to smooth his disheveled hair as he put his hat back on.

"Sara likes it…er, him," Mrs. Smith replied. "We should give him a chance. My father didn't care for you much, either," she added, turning to go inside, "not until he got to know you better."

"I never violated hi…" Mr. Smith paused, scowling. "I never got into his personal space," he grumbled under his breath as he followed his wife into the house.

"Duke won't need these," Sara said as she took the utensils from his napkin and returned them to the kitchen. She came back with a stack of paper towels, which she set on the table in front of Duke.

Duke sat hunched over in his chair. His knees were too high to fit comfortably beneath the mahogany table. Mrs. Smith worried the chair would shatter under his considerable weight, but for now it held.

"Soup or salad?" she asked.

"Soup," Sara answered for him. "Duke doesn't like rabbit food. He's a meat and potatoes kind of guy."

"He's not a 'guy' at all," Mr. Smith muttered. He took his seat at the head of the table.

Mrs. Smith glared at her husband. Then she walked into the kitchen for a large bowl of salad and a pot of soup with a ladle. Mrs. Smith set the salad bowl down on the table. She ladled some of the soup into Duke's bowl.

Duke leaned forward, grunting as he sniffed the soup, his expression wary. He buried his face in the bowl, slurping noisily. Mrs. Smith ladled some more soup for Duke before handing the pot to Mr. Smith.

Sara and Mrs. Smith served themselves salad.

Duke finished the rest of his soup. He whined, glancing at the empty bowl. Duke turned toward the kitchen, sniffing the air. He harrumphed impatiently.

Mr. Smith glared in his general direction.

Sara and Mrs. Smith picked at their salads.

"So, how was work today…?" Sara started to ask. The beep of the oven interrupted her.

Mrs. Smith rose to retrieve her casserole. She returned, wearing a kitchen mitt and holding a pan and spatula to serve everyone. Once she finished, Mrs. Smith looked at Duke.

Duke looked at Mrs. Smith, who gave him a nod of encouragement. Then he looked at the casserole. His lip rose into a sneer, and he stuck a paw in the dish. As he held the paw over his head, a gooey bit of casserole fell into his mouth. His eyes grew wide. Then he rose with a roar and proceeded to throw bits of casserole at everyone.

"That is it!" Mr. Smith yelled, rising from his seat. "Get out of my house!" he bellowed.

Duke stopped throwing bits of casserole and stared at Mr. Smith, his nostrils flaring. Then he leaped over the table, baring his fangs as he snarled.

Mr. Smith backed away, his hands raised.

Duke turned to Sara, lifted her from her seat, and flung her over his shoulder. Using his head as a battering ram, he tore into the living room and barreled right through a wall, leaving behind a Duke-and-Sara-shaped hole.

Mrs. Smith turned to her husband. "He's quite the rugged brute, isn't he?" she said, again fiddling with her necklace.

"That brute just put a damn hole in our house!" Mr. Smith yelled.

With a faint wave of her hand, Mrs. Smith merely replied, "Boys will be boys?"

Duke set Sara gently down on the grass a couple blocks away beside a large park. She touched her backside gingerly. Duke whimpered an apology.

"Just a little tender. I've experienced worse in softball," Sara reassured him.

She crossed the street to a light blue Prius with band decals and a coexist sticker on the rear window. Sara opened the trunk and retrieved something wrapped in butcher paper. She returned, handing Duke a large shank of raw meat. He held it between his teeth and bowed his head low so she could scratch behind one of his horns. Then he ran on all fours into the park, heading for a dense line of trees.

Sara crossed the street and opened the passenger door of the Prius.

"Oh my god. He is amazing! Where did you find him?" Rachel asked from the back seat. She sat with an arm draped around a voluptuous redhead.

"Okay," Sara began. "So, you know all those stories about some scary monster attacking anyone who parks up the hill at Lookout Point?" Sara asked. "Well, Duke's the monster. We ran into him last week. Like, literally. Did Chris show you the dent in his front bumper?"

The girls shook their heads.

"Anyway, we got out of the car because we thought we hit a person. He was fine, but all sorts of embarrassed and totally sweet. That's when I had the idea."

"It'll definitely soften the blow when your parents meet Captain Guyliner," laughed the redhead, Emily.

Sara turned to ruffle the driver's dark shaggy hair.

"Hey, wanna try that new vegan place before my gig?" Chris asked. "They have ethically raised burgers, too," he assured Sara.

Chris started the car. He drove away as something howled deep in the woods.

DUKE SETTLED INTO HIS CAVE TO GNAW ON THE BONE FROM THE SHANK of raw meat.

THE CLEANSING

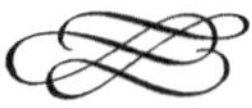

JANE-HOLLY MEISSNER

"It was a dark and stormy night," said Anne Sanders.

Paul Sanders, her husband, laughed.

"That's a little melodramatic, don't you think?"

"It's the truth," she said defensively, wrapping her cardigan around herself as rain lashed the windows. "You're the one who scheduled this thing for tonight."

"You're the one who won't sleep here anymore," he muttered under his breath, half-hoping she heard him.

The doorbell rang.

"I still don't believe in ghosts!" he yelled after Anne as she stalked out of the kitchen toward the front door.

Anne ignored him, placing her hand on the doorknob and pausing a moment to collect herself before opening it. As the door swung open, she smiled at the figure on her porch.

"Mrs. O'Rourke?"

The shorter woman, her face as lined and rosy as a wizened apple, looked up from shaking out her umbrella.

"Ah, dear, you must be Mrs. Sanders." The old woman smiled, her wrinkles threatening to swallow her eyes completely as she reached a thin, age-spotted hand up to her hostess.

"Anne is fine," said Anne, gingerly taking her hand. "Won't you come in?"

"Thank you, thank you," said Mrs. O'Rourke. "And you must call me Mildred."

She stepped over the threshold and into the home, looking up toward the second floor landing as she handed Anne her damp umbrella.

"The mister told me over the phone that you believe your house is haunted. Is that correct?" The old woman smiled pleasantly, and Anne was struck with how *normal* Mrs. O'Rourke seemed. She hadn't been expecting this grandmotherly woman to be the pagan exorcist she'd found on the internet, and the disconnect between expectation and reality was causing a bit of a short circuit in her brain.

"Yes," answered Anne at last, then with more conviction, "Yes. There's definitely something here. I don't know if it's a ghost, or what, but I can *feel* it."

Mrs. O'Rourke took off her wet coat and held it out. Anne took it belatedly and stood in the entry for a moment with both coat and umbrella like she wasn't sure what to do with them.

"Does it feel malevolent?" Mrs. O'Rourke's gimlet eyes peered up at the younger woman, who appeared a little pale. Having just met her, however, it was hard to judge. Perhaps she stayed indoors a lot.

"Malevolent?" Anne repeated, breathlessly. She still held Mrs. O'Rourke's wet coat in her hand, and rainwater dripped silently onto the tiled entry.

"Evil, dear." Mrs. O'Rourke looked around the entry and staircase, then walked past Anne into the living room.

Anne hurriedly crossed to the coat closet and snatched it open, hanging the wet coat on an available hook. She leaned the closed umbrella against the wall and chased after Mrs. O'Rourke.

"Uh, not necessarily?" Anne bit her lip as she caught up to the old woman, looking up and catching the eye of her husband across the room as he entered from the kitchen.

"You must be Mr. Sanders," beamed Mrs. O'Rourke at Peter. "Mildred O'Rourke. We spoke on the phone."

"Please, call me Peter," he said, walking over to shake her hand. "I'm glad you could make it. I'm not on board with all this ghost mumbo jumbo, but if it will make Anne sleep better at night - or at all! - then it'll be worth it."

He laughed at his own joke, but Anne's expression remained flat and unamused.

Mrs. O'Rourke chuckled, patting his hand. "We shall see, we shall see. A lot of times these experiences can be chalked up to old houses or faulty wiring. But this is a relatively new home."

"Built in the 2000's," said Anne, hugging her arms around her body.

Mrs. O'Rourke nodded slowly, looking from her to Peter. "And you, Peter, you don't believe your wife's experiences?"

He laughed nervously at her gaze. "Well, you know. It's all a bit ... much."

"Yet you believed her enough to call me." Her bright eyes did not leave his face.

"I want Anne to feel safe here," Peter said. "If that means calling up a medium she found on Google, then ..."

He shrugged.

Mrs. O'Rourke smiled, her wrinkles creasing up into well-worn lines.

"I think I understand. May we sit?" She edged toward one of the sofas.

"Oh!" said Anne, startled into action at Mrs. O'Rourke's request. She felt chagrined at making their elderly visitor stand all this time. "Please, sit."

She joined Mrs. O'Rourke on the couch while Peter found a seat in a matching armchair.

The medium looked around the room slowly, and the Sanderses found it difficult to break the silence that fell as she examined their home. Peter caught Anne's eye and shrugged. She frowned at him, watching the old woman intently.

She had a warm, grandmotherly air to her, and she took a breath before meeting Anne's eyes.

"Tell me what you have experienced. Leave nothing out, please."

Anne swallowed, avoiding her husband's eyes.

"It started a few months ago. I heard footsteps at night. Peter thought it was just the house settling - we had just moved in, you see, and I suppose it *could* have been..." Her voice trailed off, then she squared her shoulders and continued.

"The footsteps didn't happen every night. But often enough that I felt ...it couldn't be regular house noises."

Peter made a noise in the back of his throat, and Mrs. O'Rourke's eyes tracked toward him. After a moment of eye contact he looked faintly ashamed, and the medium turned back to Anne.

Mrs. O'Rourke reached across to pat her hands. "Please, tell me the rest of it."

Anne nodded, closing her eyes for a moment.

"I started feeling like I was being watched at night. While Peter was sleeping. Like there was someone - some *thing* in the room with us. I can't sleep here anymore," she added. "I've been staying at my mother's."

Mrs. O'Rourke peered into Anne's eyes.

"That's all? Footsteps in the night and an uneasy feeling?"

"Well... I started finding black smudges around the house. Like... fingerprints." Anne held out her hand like she was holding onto something.

"On the edges of doorways. On the windowsill in the master bathroom. Peter said... he says it's just dirt."

"I don't know what it is," he interjected. "It won't clean off."

"Hmm," mused Mrs. O'Rourke. "These marks are still on the home?"

"Yes, I'll show you," said Anne, and she got to her feet.

Leading the old woman upstairs to the master bedroom, she walked into the en-suite and over to the freestanding tub in front of the frosted window. Anne pointed to the sill, where a blackened smudge could be seen.

"I thought it was from a candle at first, like the smoke had somehow … " Anne shrugged and made a face, letting Mrs. O'Rourke get close to inspect the marks.

The medium leaned heavily on the edge of the tub, reaching for the marks. She tentatively touched them, spreading her fingers as if she were grasping the edge, and then turned her hand as if she were reaching inside from the window. Her fingers were too small to match up perfectly on the marks, but there was a definite similarity to their placement. Anne's guess, that the marks were fingerprints, seemed to bear out.

"Hmm," she tutted, rubbing her finger across one mark and lightly touching the tip to her tongue. Anne couldn't help but grimace slightly as she watched Mrs. O'Rourke run her tongue over her lips and then against her teeth.

"Definitely sulfurous," the old woman pronounced. She eyed the marks. "They're about the size of your husband's hands, I think. He has good, strong hands - I notice things like that. Like my late husband's, though his were rough from hard work, not like your mister's."

She sat on the edge of the tub and looked up at Anne.

"Do you want me to perform a cleansing tonight?"

"Yes," said Anne quickly. "Please. I … I know it's silly, but I don't feel safe, and if you could just do … *something*, I think I'll feel better."

Mrs. O'Rourke smiled sadly.

"Of course you don't feel safe, dear. Don't sell your feelings short. It isn't silly. And we will put it to right."

"You believe me, then?"

"Whether I do or not, the ceremony will do the job." Mrs. O'Rourke pushed herself to her feet with some difficulty. "But it so happens I DO believe you."

"Even though Peter didn't experience anything?"

"How do you know he hasn't?" Mrs. O'Rourke raised an eyebrow. "Those who adamantly do not believe in the supernatural are most likely to explain away any phenomenon they might experience. But he loves you, my dear. You don't have to be very intuitive to see *that*."

Anne smiled, relieved that someone believed her. "Thank you, Mrs. O'Rourke."

"Mildred, please." The medium put out a hand. "Can I lean on you a bit as we go downstairs? These old legs aren't what they used to be."

"Of course. Mildred." Anne let the old woman take her arm, and they walked downstairs together.

Mrs. O'Rourke set upon the cleansing with some vigor, though she got Peter to help her get the items she needed from her car. Boxes of candles and other herbal sundries were retrieved and set on the coffee table in the living room.

At Mrs. O'Rourke's directions, the Sanderses moved all the furniture toward the walls and rolled up the rug that Anne had picked out on their honeymoon, leaving a great empty space in the middle of the room. Peter watched skeptically as Anne assisted the medium with setting up the white pillar candles in a circle surrounding a few bundles of herbs.

Mrs. O'Rourke spent a bit of time wandering the house and muttering to herself, sometimes touching the walls with a wrinkled hand as she passed. The wind outside was picking up and starting to whistle under the eaves, but it didn't seem to faze her.

Anne sat on the displaced couch, outside the circle of candles, plucking at a piece of imaginary lint on her cardigan.

"It looks darker in here," she said, mostly to herself.

"It's night," said Peter, watching Mrs. O'Rourke closely as she slowly walked down the stairs, trailing her hand on the bannister.

"It's more than that," said Anne, glancing fearfully over her shoulder at an empty corner of the room. Peter looked at his wife and narrowed his eyes. He hoped this would all be over soon.

"It is more than that," said Mrs. O'Rourke at Peter's shoulder, startling him. She crossed to the candles, carefully nudging them with her foot to perfect the circle.

"I can sense the presence in this house," she added as casually as if she'd said something about the weather. Mrs. O'Rourke looked up and smiled reassuringly at Anne, but turned toward Peter.

"Could I speak with you in the kitchen?"

"Oh...kay." Peter raised an eyebrow but led the way to the back of the house.

"Is everything okay?" he asked.

The medium shook her head. "I'm afraid it's gotten a bit complicated. I didn't say anything to your wife because I don't want to worry her more, but I suspected from her story... That is to say, it sounds more like this spirit is attached to *her*, and less to the house."

Wary of appearing to believe any of this was real, Peter nonetheless was game to understand the old woman's logic.

"If it didn't ...follow? her to her mother's house..." He faltered, unwilling to put more words toward the sheer lunacy of it all.

"Ah, yes. It *is* still here in the house. But it only manifested to her. You never saw it." She looked up at him, eyes narrowing. "Correct?"

"That's right," Peter said, uncertainly.

"And," Mrs. O'Rourke put two fingers to her forehead, "It is *here*. It wants to **stay here**." As she spoke, her voice deepened from a grandmotherly warble to a baritone.

Peter recoiled from her in shock as the old woman took a deep breath, her bright eyes appearing to mist over with cataracts.

"**Take me to the circle**," she intoned, her hand closing on his arm like the talons of a bird of prey. "**Time runs out**."

"Oh my God," he yelped, trying to get her off of him, but her fingers were like iron bands around his forearm.

"Peter?" called Anne from the living room. "Is everything okay?"

"Shit! I don't know! Mrs. O - Mildred! Let go of me!"

"**THE CIRCLE**," the old woman boomed, a simultaneous crash of thunder rattling the house.

He fearfully towed her back to the living room just as the house lights flickered and went out. Anne was standing, her arms wrapping her cardigan around her, bathed in the shadows of the room.

Mrs. O'Rourke did not release Peter's arm, but snapped the fingers of her other hand. In an instant, all of the candles on the floor ignited, bathing the room in a flickering orange glow.

Anne shrieked at the sudden light, clutching at her face. Peter fell backward, the old woman letting go of his arm as he saw a monstrous shadow on the wall behind his wife.

"What the hell?!"

Mrs. O'Rourke quickly skirted the circle, reaching Anne's side. She grasped the younger woman's wrists, pulling them gently down from her face and holding them out in front of her.

"This will be difficult," the medium said, her voice once again hers. "You must be brave."

Anne looked into Mrs. O'Rourke's kind eyes and nodded, letting the medium pull her into the circle. There was a pile of herbs in the center of the ring, and Mrs.O'Rourke made Anne sit in the midst of them.

The old woman carefully stepped out of the candles, sparing no energy for Peter, who was gaping at the pair of them, completely speechless. She reached into the box of supplies sitting on the hardwoods and pulled out a bundle of sage, lighting it with the nearest candle and carefully blowing out the end once it had caught.

She stepped over to Peter and pressed the smoking bundle into his hand. "Walk around the circle, counter-clockwise. No, the other way."

Mrs. O'Rourke pointed, and he began to walk uncertainly, trailing smoke and still staring at his wife and the shadow that loomed behind her. The shadow seemed to be getting darker as if it were pooling in the center of the candles rather than being thrown against the wall.

As Peter walked, Mrs. O'Rourke produced a Sharpie and began to write on the floor, quickly and with surprising deftness. As she made her way around the circle she muttered under her breath, continuing to scrawl on the ground.

"Oh God, is that permanent marker?! Don't -" started Peter, but he shut up when Mrs. O'Rourke looked up at him, her eyes nearly completely white. He quickly looked away, concentrating on the bundle of sage in his hands.

"Begone, foul thing!" shouted Mrs. O'Rourke suddenly, her voice loud in the space.

Anne quailed in the center of the circle, but the shadow around her swelled as if it were unwrapping itself and stretching outward. As it reached the edge of the candle ring, it recoiled, contained.

"Begone! By the powers of the earth, I command you." Mrs. O'Rourke tossed a handful of powder into the ring, making Anne cough and the shadow writhe.

"Water shall wash you away," the old woman called, dipping her fingers into a jar of water and sprinkling it at Anne.

"The air we breathe will dispel you!" Mrs. O'Rourke blew into the circle, and a breeze kicked up, wafting the smoke from the sage into the circle and spiraling around Anne and the looming shadow.

"You are unnatural and nature rejects you! Begone, begone, begone!" The medium snatched the sage from Peter's unfeeling hand, thrusting it into the circle without stepping over the candles.

The shadow grew darker and larger, nearly filling the space between the lit candles. Anne covered her head with her hands, drawing herself down into a ball, her face in her knees.

"You do not command me..." an otherworldly Voice hissed.

"Yes, I do," stated the old woman. "And you are not welcome here."

Peter's face went deathly pale as he stared up at the red eyes of the Shadow.

As it gazed down upon him, he could have sworn he could make out a smile in the darkness.

"Begone!" shouted Mrs. O'Rourke, interposing herself between Peter and the circle, throwing the entire jar of water into the shadow.

The darkness writhed, a high, unearthly shriek keening from it. As they watched, the shadow began to break apart, shrinking toward Anne and then separating entirely before disappearing into the floor.

Peter slumped against the sofa, his legs unable to hold him up anymore.

Mrs. O'Rourke looked to Anne, bedraggled from the ceremony with gray dirt coating the younger woman's wet hair and clothes.

"It's all right to look now, dear. It is gone."

Anne slowly uncovered her head and looked up. Her eyes were wide.

"W-w-what was..." h=Her voice faltered, and she fell silent.

Mrs. O'Rourke crossed between the candles, reaching down and taking Anne's hands. Pulling gently, the small medium helped her to her feet.

"Don't worry about it, dear. I will show you how to burn sage and keep up the cleansing. Oh yes, it will be fine." The old woman patted Anne's arm with an age-spotted hand.

"Was that a - a freaking demon?!" Peter found his voice but didn't get up from the couch. "That didn't look like a ghost!"

"And you know what a ghost looks like now, do you?" Mrs. O'Rourke looked over her shoulder at him as she guided a shaken Anne from the circle to a chair.

"Of course not, I just..." Peter stopped talking, his mouth still open.

Mrs. O'Rourke tsked and fussed over Anne a bit longer, giving her an unburnt bundle of sage to hold onto "for later" and a cloth to wipe her face with. Turning back to the lit circle, she reached down slowly, picked up a candle, and straightened up before blowing it out. She walked to the box on the coffee table and placed the still-warm candle beside it before turning to retrieve another.

Peter watched her bend for a second candle, imagining he could hear her back creaking, until he caught Anne staring at him and jerking her head toward the old woman.

"Let me help you with that," he said belatedly, pushing himself to his feet.

"Oh, thank you," Mrs. O'Rourke beamed, turning her attention to the herbs in the center of the circle as Peter started blowing out the candles for her.

Anne went to fetch a flashlight from the kitchen, but before she could come back with it, the electricity flickered back on. Everything suddenly felt very benign - almost *too* normal after what she'd just been through. After a moment spent staring at the wall in the kitchen, she walked back toward the living room.

"Oh, don't worry about the wax, they fit just so in the box," Mrs. O'Rourke was telling Peter, who was managing to only burn a few of his fingertips in the melted wax as he tried to put the candles away for her.

Anne put the flashlight on a displaced end table and sat down again, feeling a little lightheaded.

"And you're sure that it's gone."

"As sure as I can be." The old woman saw the look on Peter's face and added, "That is to say, *very* sure. I would wager even those marks on your house are gone now. But if you ever have any trouble again, please call me right away."

"We will," Anne said. She'd found her purse next to the displaced sofa and was digging for her wallet. She'd probably be calling Mildred for every bump in the night for at least a few weeks.

"Oh," said Mrs. O'Rourke. "You don't have to do that right now, dear..."

Anne pressed the cash she'd counted earlier into the medium's hands.

"It's the least I can do. Thank you *so* much."

"Ah, you are quite welcome, dear." Mrs. O'Rourke took the money and secreted it away into her clothing.

"Now if you don't mind, I am a bit spent from all that." She looked from Peter to the boxes of her supplies and smiled, her eyes twinkling behind the wrinkles.

He jumped into action, picking up a box as Anne went to retrieve Mrs. O'Rourke's coat and umbrella.

The Sanderses stood in the doorway looking out into the rain as Mrs. O'Rourke's wide-bodied Buick pulled away from the curb. Peter kissed Anne's forehead and rested his cheek against her hair.

"I'm glad you're okay. I'm sorry... that I didn't believe you."

"It's ok," said Anne, twisting her head to look up at him. She grimaced, wiping at his cheek. "You've got a little dirt on you."

Peter stared at her dirty hair, quickly rubbing his hand on his face.

"You've got a *lot* of dirt on you."

"I'll go get cleaned up. I love you, honey."

"Love you too, babe."

The couple closed the door on the night, but a little too hard, sending a picture frame inside crashing to the ground. Both of them nearly jumped into the rafters, Anne screaming and Peter cursing up a storm.

Sleep was a long time coming that evening.

It was close to eleven o'clock at night when Mrs. O'Rourke reached her home, a quaint bungalow with a crocheted afghan on nearly every chair. The storm had passed, and the trees were merely dripping as she slowly carried her boxes in from the Buick.

She placed the heavy candle box on the dining room table with a sigh, reaching to massage her lower back as she straightened up.

"Been a long night," she said, crossing into the kitchen and pulling open a cupboard to reveal stacks of canned cat food. "I'll bet you're hungry."

She placed two cans on the countertop, then moved to another cabinet to get a teacup.

"Just going to put the kettle on." The old woman smiled into the dining room as she filled the metal tea kettle at the sink.

She had a difficult time operating the pull tabs on the cat food cans, but managed to pry the rings up with the backside of a spoon so she could hook them with a gnarled finger. Mrs. O'Rourke dumped both cans into a dish and set it on the floor just as the kettle began to sing.

As she sat down at last in her favorite recliner in the family room, afghan on her lap, Mrs. O'Rourke could feel her old bones starting to relax.

"It was a good night's work," she said to the house, looking from her seat up into the kitchen where the dish of cat food lay on the ground. "She paid a little extra, too."

Mrs. O'Rourke shifted slowly, working her hand into the pocket where she'd put the cash. She waved it in the air.

"A good night's work." Setting down the money, she sipped her tea, glancing at the picture of her late husband on the mantle before looking around the room.

"Come on, come out," she said, coaxingly.

The shadows behind her recliner began to stretch and move, filling the space and looming over her. A growl emanated from the darkness behind her, and red eyes gazed down on the old woman as she slowly looked up.

Mrs. O'Rourke set aside her teacup slowly.

"Stop hovering and go eat your food. You earned it."

The Shadow hissed hatred at her, edging around the wall and then across the pink carpet toward the kitchen. It slowly approached the cat food, its dark form hunching around the dish.

"This is barely meat," it said.

"It's what you get," said Mrs. O'Rourke. "You didn't even manifest to them. No wonder it took so long for them to call me."

The Shadow growled.

"The female frightened easily. You got what you wanted." The Shadow poked at the cat food and then raised up, its form filling the space up to the ceiling.

"RELEASE ME."

"No," said the old woman, setting aside her tea and fishing next to the recliner for her crocheting bag.

"**RELEASE ME!**" The terrifying voice boomed, rattling the good china in the hutch.

"You will not raise your voice in my home," she replied primly, pointing at the Shadow with a crochet hook.

"O'Rourke, this has gone on too long," muttered the Shadow, glumly shrinking back down next to the dish.

"I have another house for you to visit," said Mrs. O'Rourke, wrapping a strand of colorful yarn around the hook in her hand.

"And please, call me Mildred."

QUIBBLES

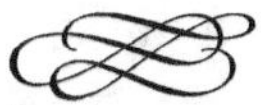

G.A. FINOCCHIARO

When Nikki decided to leave, it came on the heels of a blowout fight. The Twist household erupted into chaos at a quarter-past six as they settled in with a home-cooked meal of meatloaf and mashed potatoes.

The telephone rang just after they had gathered at the table for supper. It was Mrs. Freeny with a terrible accusation. While Nikki's little brother played with a plate full of soupy mashed potatoes, and her older sister stared at the television through the living room door —her vacant eyes perpetually disinterested in Nikki and her latest drama—Nikki squirmed in her chair, sweating like a prisoner awaiting judgement.

It was hard enough to be the odd Twist—the Twist who was different after learning the family secret last summer. But conversation around the dinner table devolved from defiant cold shoulders into angry shouts that made the family dog scurry to bury his head inside the coat closet, like he did every Fourth of July during her uncle's fireworks display.

Mrs. Twist hung up the phone and rigidly paced back into the kitchen, all while attempting to look pleasant. She sat in her usual chair beside her husband, then told Mr. Twist everything she had learned from Mrs. Freeny.

Nikki's uncle's fireworks display had nothing on the explosive nature of that conversation. It unfolded with simple details, followed by interrupted denials and eventually into shouts and screams and more accusations.

"Who are you?" screamed her mother with a forkful of loaf and mash. "Have you lost your damn mind?"

"You're no child of mine," proclaimed her father, his face as red as the ketchup drizzle on his plate.

At just eleven years old, Nikki was no longer daddy's little girl—a title she once enjoyed, having earned it with years of exceptional behavior and athletic dominance that put her siblings to shame. All of it just to see her father's face beam with pride after every goal scored and flawless report card tallied.

But times had changed.

Failing her math test was a trivial setback compared to the misfortune that would follow that fateful phone call. Even Nikki would admit, using a stolen credit card to pay for an all-day-Chuck-E-Cheese extravaganza may have crossed the line. It wasn't all her fault —her baby brother had snatched the card from Mrs. Freeny's purse— and Nikki thought she owed him after helping her fund a well-deserved QVC shopping spree.

Was it actually theft if you didn't feel guilty? After all, Nikki was owed something for her pain and suffering. Why didn't the rest of her family understand?

Nikki left just before midnight with only a backpack slung over her shoulders, after being exiled to her room without supper. She didn't leave a note or any parting gesture, other than a clean room for whomever claimed it next.

The public bus took her to the edge of town, where she was given a choice—left into the great wide open, or right toward the highway.

She chose to go left and walked straight into the night, never once looking back.

It wasn't long into her trek when Nikki's stomach groaned—or maybe she was just feeling nervous? She'd grabbed some snacks from the kitchen before she left, so she opened a full bag of cheesy curls to fuel her escape. She ate her orange cheddar snacks under a blooming full moon and began to question every step. Was she making the right decision? What if things weren't any better when she got to where she was going? There was a moment of brief romanticism when she wondered if maybe things weren't as bad as they seemed—but this wasn't the first time she'd fought with her parents.

In fact, Nikki had not felt like a member of her family since last summer. Last summer changed everything, when the caseworker arrived. Who was she to stay in a home where she did not belong? Where she was not wanted? It was good to remember why she was leaving—to remember every slammed door, disappointment, and scolding. The alienation, resentment, and tears reinforced her every step.

SHE HAD ONLY BEEN WALKING FOR THIRTY MINUTES WHEN THE SCENERY changed. The road out of town had led from housing developments to fields with overgrown edges—like nature was trying to reclaim the cheaply paved road with tar and loose, crunchy gravel. Before too long, the edges thickened into a dark forest, with crickets chirping as loud as songbirds. The cricket chorus inspired her need for music, so Nikki pulled the Walkman from her backpack—thank you, Mrs. Freeny—flipped the headphones over her ears, and danced down the empty street.

Twirling and whirling, stargazing and snacking, Nikki began to imagine what life would be like when she arrived at her final destination, but failed at every attempt to envision what she was hoping to find. Where was she going? How would she know when she got there? Nikki had always imagined living by the sea, or the big city—a far cry from her home in Grace Falls, Pennsylvania. However, not a single instance of her fantasies had ever provided a family of her own. It was as if she was destined, even in her own mind, to be alone.

She buried those thoughts beneath the music.

She was still twirling and whirling when she caught a glimpse of something behind her, shifting through the underbrush. The abrupt movement startled and infected her with a serious case of goose-bumps. She stopped the music and listened, but there was no intimation of spying eyes or impending danger. There were no twigs snapping or leaves shuffling, not even the cacophonous roar of chirping crickets. Absolutely no sound at all.

"Hello?" she said. It was probably just a critter, curious of the stranger traveling through its forest at night. Almost assuredly—*probably*—nothing, she thought to herself, and pressed on despite the lingering despair. She hummed quietly, attempting to fill the silence with something comforting, and walked an anxious country mile. With each and every step, she imagined various fiends lurking in the woods, waiting for the right moment to pounce.

It was sometime deep into the witching hour when Nikki spotted a crossroad in the distance. If something was following, it would be forced out into the open as it crossed. What was she to do if it was something truly dangerous? Could she outrun the big bad wolf? A bear? Or worse?

She calmly picked up speed, desperate to unveil her stalker, when a snapping twig from the forest confirmed her worst fears—it wasn't just her imagination; she really was being followed. Nikki broke into a sprint, running the last several yards toward the crossroads in a flailing mess of uncoordinated arms and legs.

As she darted into the middle of the cross, something flashed to the other side in a blink—forcing Nikki into a sliding stop across the gravelly pavement. She was standing out in the open at the center of the cross when a pair of moonlit eyes appeared at the forest's edge, watching her.

"Hi," she said weakly. "I don't know what you are, but I'm just passing through. I promise." Nikki never imagined she might get eaten on the road to freedom. The creature watched her like it wanted a taste—or maybe it just wanted a snack. "Are you hungry? Want some cheesy curls?"

Nikki placed the crinkly half-eaten bag on the road and backed away. If it made a move for the cheese curls, she'd run the other way. She'd run all the way to the next town if she had to.

The creature in the woods moved toward her methodically, and with every approaching step, Nikki matched its advance with a cautious shift backward—until her feet stuck.

She was stuck to the actual pavement!

Her feet were fused to the spot, right at the very center of the road. She torqued her body this way and that—she even tried to jump herself free—but her feet remained firmly planted. She yelped and squeaked and pulled with angry yanks that tore the stitching of her favorite jeans, but nothing could break the mysterious bond.

Nikki helplessly watched the pale eyes stalk from the forest out into the open. She held her breath, waiting to scream, but what exited the forest was not the monster she expected. The monster was human —sort of. It was a woman, slight and thin, with brown skin like earthen clay and hair as silver as the moonlight itself. Her noble eyes were like twinkling gray pools, with a hint of hidden trickery beneath the surface. She wore a regal gray dress and carelessly hauled a black velvet sack over her shoulder.

"Welcome, child," said the woman.

Nikki stared at her, unblinking. The woman appeared like a dream —like something that existed only in children's books. "Who are you?" she asked. "What do you want?"

"You tell me, child," said the woman. "I am Ms. Gray, and you left me an offering." She gestured at the cheese curls and smiled but did not attempt to move any closer.

"I thought you were a monster trying to eat me," said Nikki.

"Hmmm, no, dear child," she replied with a grin, "not yet." She spoke with a hint of humor, but her tone suggested a layer of half-truth. "Do I look like a monster?"

"No," said Nikki. "Why can't I move?"

"Because you are standing neither here nor there," answered Ms. Gray, gesturing to the crossing roads. It was then that Nikki took note of the street signs covered in weeds and vines and found them remarkably labeled *Here* and *There*. "You are betwixt, child. You are between, and you are mine."

"Ta ta," came a voice from the wood opposite Ms. Gray. "You know better than to start the bidding without me, Ms. Gray."

"Mr. Black," said Ms. Gray, "I wouldn't dream of it." Her sarcasm was as fluent as that of a snobby teen queen.

From the forest stepped a man dressed in black. He wore a wide-brimmed fedora, which shaded his face and red eyes, and a heavy wool coat buttoned up to his neck. In his free hand, he held a piece of rolled parchment with strange blotches and folds—the folds almost appeared like a human ear, but that could not be, could it? Mr. Black then took a deep bow and removed his hat, but never once could Nikki see his face, nor did she want to—he terrified her even more than Ms. Gray did.

"Oh!" cried Mr. Black, appraising Nikki with his red eyes. "What a lovely child!" He paced back and forth, careful not to cross the center into Ms. Gray's half of the road. "Not too tall. Not too short. Not plain, nor disgustingly beautiful, but cute? Pretty? And blonde! Oh, I love it when they're blonde. A perfect child of—how old, dear?"

"Eleven," said Nikki, compelled to respond.

"Eleven! Prime!" he shouted. "A bargain!"

"Indeed, Mr. Black," said Ms. Gray. "A perfectly normal child."

"Precisely," said Mr. Black, full of suspicion. "How has a perfectly normal child garnered the attention of a Seelie?"

"The Court is no more," said Ms. Gray, caught between anger and sadness. Even the velvet sack on her back shifted as if upset by the news.

"What a shame," said Mr. Black sarcastically. "Feeling confident, Ms. Gray? Brought your sack? We both know the girl will be leaving with my contract."

They were talking above Nikki, like two parents discussing bills, credit cards, and mortgages. But she was used to being ignored by adults, so she decided to take advantage of the situation. She tried pulling again on her legs and failed, but fortuitously noticed the bag of cheesy curls. If an offering had called them, perhaps she could take it back?

Nikki carefully stretched onto all fours and walked her arms toward the bag of salty snacks. Straining toward the bag, her finger brushed against the crinkly plastic with a ruffling sound loud enough to wake the dead.

"Don't touch that," scolded Mr. Black with a snap of his fingers, and Nikki rebounded upright. He snatched her bag of cheesy curls and swallowed it whole, plastic and all, with one treacherous gulp. "Where was I? Oh yes! What an arrogant Fae! Thought you might snatch her up and run away?"

"Arrogant, you say?" growled Ms. Gray. "As arrogant as a demon with a pre-written contract?"

"Boilerplate, Madame," explained Mr. Black, noting the rolled parchment in his hand. "Virgin blood is hard to come by these days. Praise Gutenberg! Simply set the presses, and one virgin may ink a few dozen contracts."

Amidst the angry banter came a slight wheeze from somewhere behind Nikki. She tried to twist her way around, to identify the source of the whistling hiss. She couldn't see anything, just shadow. The gentle rasping wheeze came from the forest's edge—rising and falling in rhythm.

"Ah, Mr. Shadow," said Ms. Gray. "Welcome. I was curious if the Boggleboo still haunted this realm."

"Haven't the boogeymen procured enough children?" said Mr. Black rhetorically. "What do they even do with them all?"

"Where is Mr. Grimm?" asked Ms. Gray. "We shouldn't begin dealing until all are present."

Mr. Black laughed, then said, "Ms. Gray, I find it odd that you were willing to negotiate with the girl alone but now wish to wait for all."

"Do not take it personally, Mr. Black," she said. "You would have done the same."

"How long shall we wait?" asked Mr. Black, pulling on a silver chain attached to his coat. On the other end was a severed hand, rigored and grasping an old wind-up clock.

The raspy wheeze drifted closer to Nikki and made her stomach clench and toil. What was Mr. Shadow, and why didn't he speak?

"We both know Mr. Grimm isn't coming, Mr. Black," said Ms. Gray. "I was expecting your confession."

"Confess to what?" spat Mr. Black, his voice rising in pitch. "Might I remind you of the game within a game? We are rivals! If one of us has an opportunity to eliminate another, we take it."

"So, you admit to killing Mr. Grimm?"

"Kill him?" questioned Mr. Black. "I would never! I merely whispered his name into the ear of a young woman desperate to save her only child."

"You struck a deal upon a deal!" accused Ms. Gray.

"Oh, quibbles!" said Mr. Black, shooing Ms. Gray's accusation away like a pest. "His opt-out language was atrocious! Rumplestiltzer, I mean, Mr. Grimm—left a loophole wide enough for the entire Wild Hunt to gallop through—I'm sure tiny Mr. Grimm is miserably drifting through the Unbecoming on a pony."

The raspy breath slid ever closer to Nikki, but still just beyond her periphery.

"Shall we begin?" asked Ms. Gray, looking bored.

"Of course!" said Mr. Black.

"Child," said Ms. Gray. "What is your name?"

"Nikki Twist," she responded. The words were summoned directly from her throat, even though she didn't wish to speak.

"Do you align with the sinistra?" asked Mr. Black, matched by a scowling Ms. Gray.

"I don't understand," said Nikki.

"Are you right- or left-handed, child?" groaned Mr. Black.

"Left," she responded.

"Aha!" he shouted. "Left-handed! She is the *right* of demons!"

"Nonsense," argued Ms. Gray. "She is as fair as an elven bride—she is the right of Fae-folk!"

"Poppycock," spat Mr. Black. "Beauty does not identify claim!"

"Have you looked upon a mirror, Mr. Black?! May you only claim unsightliness."

"Har har," he mocked.

"What say you, Mr. Shadow?" asked Ms. Gray, to which Mr. Shadow only coughed. It sounded like pneumonia, with thick phlegmy webbing coating an ancient dry throat. "See? All have claim to the sinistra!"

"Fine," said Mr. Black. "Why are you here, child?"

"I ran away from home," said Nikki.

"Why?" asked Mr. Black.

"I was an orphan. I only found out last summer. I'm not supposed to be a Twist. I don't belong."

"A runaway," said Ms. Gray. "None of us have strict jurisdiction there."

"Where are you running to?" asked Mr. Black. "To find your real parents?"

Nikki nodded. The truth surprised even her. The unknown driving force in the back of her mind was the question she was too afraid to ask. Where and who did she come from?

Mr. Black rifled through his coat pockets with strange noises echoing from within. Nikki swore she witnessed a desperate hand reach for freedom from his left breast pocket before Mr. Black bit its thumb and forced it back inside. Eventually, he shoved his entire ghastly head into a pocket, and when he retracted himself, he returned with a small black book. Mr. Black licked his thumb and forefinger, then quickly flipped through its pages. "Nikki Twist, you say?"

Nikki nodded.

"What is it?" asked Ms. Gray.

The rasping breath crept closer.

"There are no records."

"No records?" asked Ms. Gray, shocked—or at least pretending to be. "How could that be?"

"Never tempted. Never sinned," said Mr. Black suspiciously as Nikki felt a surge of guilt redden her cheeks. "A clean slate. She could play an important role in the apocalypse—swing the pendulum of fate on behalf of the faction that corrupts her." Mr. Black smiled wickedly. "Or…"

"Or?" questioned Ms. Gray.

"Or she is not real."

"Not real?" questioned Ms. Gray.

"What do you mean I'm not real?" asked Nikki.

"Maybe she was taken?" asked Mr. Black.

"Collywobble," said Ms. Gray. "If taken, she was found! She was adopted! Clearly your records need updating."

"Perhaps," said Mr. Black. "But imagine the potential?"

"What are you suggesting?"

"By coming to our crossroads at neither Here nor There, she has aligned herself with mischief and mayhem," said Mr. Black. "And whatever Mr. Shadow is."

"A blank slate. A fateless Pawn promoted to Queen."

"Indeed."

The rasp of Mr. Shadow grew even closer.

"Start the bidding," demanded Mr. Black with wide-eyed derangement.

Ms. Gray stepped forward to the very edge of her territory, careful not to step beyond her boundary into Mr. Black's. "Nikki Twist, my offer is generous as it is fair. You will come with me for a term of no-less-than four years, replaced in this realm by a changeling, then swapped and set free thereafter—in exchange for one wish granted."

Nikki was overwhelmed. She didn't understand the madness. How could she accept being kidnapped? Replaced by something called a changeling? In exchange for a wish? Before she could even fully grasp what was being offered, Ms. Gray retreated, and Mr. Black stepped forward.

"Nikki Twist, my offer has been detailed in full upon this contract," he said, opening the rolled parchment in his hand. It was a typical sheet of parchment paper—with an odd patch of hair growing from the margin—but the text upon it couldn't be read without a magnifying glass, or perhaps even a microscope.

"I can't read that," said Nikki, shaking her head.

"You can't?" scoffed Mr. Black, curiously eyeing Nikki. "Are you sure you're only eleven? The eyes of youth should be sharp, should they not?" Mr. Black took the contract and held it up to his own eyes, pretending to read it. "Yada-yada, blah-blah-blah, paraphrasing—If you strike this deal with me, *tonight*, signed in your own youthful virgin blood, I shall let you go—*for now*—with one life-altering wish of your choice. Ever wish to be a ballerina? A movie star? A famous rock god? You name it! Then, in fifteen years or so, give or take a few odd months, minutes and days—you're mine."

"What do you mean I'm yours?" Nikki questioned.

"Did I stutter?" he asked with a shrug, peering over at Ms. Gray, who was miserably disinterested in Mr. Black's theatrics. "An eternity in Hell, my dear. Or at least in our service."

Before Nikki could respond, Mr. Black stepped back and returned to his usual spot, watching her carefully with his red eyes.

"Mr. Shadow, would you like to make an offer?" asked Ms. Gray.

A terrible wave of sickness rose in Nikki's stomach, making her want to vomit all over the road. She turned left, then right, but still couldn't see the creeping menace behind her. The rasping breath drifted to the very edge of the boundary with Mr. Black. Mr. Shadow inhaled, savoring Nikki's scent, and choked pleasantly on the phlegm in his gravelly throat. Then, he grabbed Nikki violently by the arm and pulled—it was all she could do not to scream. Mr. Shadow was made of inky gloom, wet sinewy flesh, and eyes like milky orbs. He carried an old burlap sack and glared at her lasciviously—but not even Mr. Shadow could snatch her from the spot between Here and There.

"Now now, Mr. Shadow," scolded Ms. Gray as Mr. Shadow was expelled to the forest's edge. "You have no rights until the girl makes her deal."

Nikki sobbed. She wanted to run. She wanted to be set free and didn't want any of their rotten deals. It was so awful that she even wanted to go home to the Twist family.

"Why are you crying, child?" asked Ms. Gray.

"I don't want to be here," said Nikki, still trapped in whatever spell compelled her to speak her truth.

"Then choose," said Mr. Black.

"How can I choose where to go when I don't even know where I belong?"

"Child," said Ms. Gray, as tender as a loving mother, "you belong with me. With the Fae-folk and fairies. With the sprites and elves and goblins, in the land behind the mirror."

"Horsefeathers, codswollop, bunk and nonsense!" shouted Mr. Black. "She belongs with you as much as she does with me!"

"I want to belong," cried Nikki. "I want to be home."

"Then choose," said Ms. Gray.

"Okay," said Nikki. She felt trapped and alone, but there was something about Ms. Gray's offer that felt a little less awful than the others. To be bound to demon's work or snatched by the boogeyman—neither of which were any better than Ms. Gray's offer.

"Okay?" said Ms. Gray, hopeful.

"Okay?" said Mr. Black, furious.

Mr. Shadow wheezed.

"Okay," said Nikki, to Ms. Gray's delight.

"I own the child's rights," shouted Ms. Gray victoriously.

"Tampering!" screamed Mr. Black apoplectically. "You cheated! The girl's looking for her parents, and you mothered her!"

"How dare you!" yelled Ms. Gray.

As they fought, bickering like parents, Mr. Shadow crept toward Nikki once again. Every time she attempted to turn and face the creature, he stopped and waited—like a hideous game of red light-green light.

"Are you sure, dear child?" asked Mr. Black, turning his attention to Nikki.

"Sure of what?" she asked, suffering between sadness and fright.

"Are you sure you're making the right decision?" asked Mr. Black. "You will suffer untold horrors in Fae. If the Seelie Court has been destroyed, the Unseelies must have destroyed it—"

"Enough!" screamed Ms. Gray. She was now as furious as Mr. Black. "Have you no shame?"

"I'm a demon, Ms.," shrugged Mr. Black. "We are shame."

After a short pause, Ms. Gray suggested, "A wager?"

"A wager?" questioned Mr. Black.

"I own the girl's rights," she said, "but I have the option to wager her."

"The game within a game," said Mr. Black. "I knew you'd come around. Are you sure you wish to play this game with a demon?"

"Tricksters, demons, charlatans, and deceivers," said Ms. Gray, "I've dealt with them all."

"I accept!" said Mr. Black. "What is your wager?"

"You may have the rights to the girl, her full acceptance of your contract passed from mine to yours," she said.

"What?" shouted Nikki. "I never accepted his contract!"

"If," said Ms. Gray, speaking over Nikki, "you can correctly guess the three items I've concealed within my velvet bag."

"Oh golly, oh gee," mocked Mr. Black with a sinister grin. "And if I guess incorrectly?"

"Three guesses for three items. Guess incorrectly, and you'll receive the same fate as the departed Mr. Grimm," she said. A wince streaked across his hidden face. "I will speak your true name and call forth the Wild Hunt, where you will join them for eternity—marching through the Unbecoming until called upon to collect the next Huntsman. Forever riding into the storm of rage, into the void beyond the known realms, galloping mindlessly, torturously, toward nothing."

"Is that all?" asked Mr. Black. "This will be too easy."

"Do you agree?" she asked.

"I do," he replied.

"Then let us begin," said Ms. Gray as she lowered her black bag, ready to display its contents.

Mr. Shadow's wheeze disappeared, and Nikki hoped he'd gone. She was more terrified of him than the other two. He seemed more deranged, and his need for her was creepy and disturbing.

"Three items in your bag," said Mr. Black, "three items only." He then paced back and forth, focusing. "All fairies and goblins, large and small, who wish to attend the Witches Ball, must use their *crystal keys* to pass, from Fae and through the looking glass."

With that, Ms. Gray reached into her bag and provided a crystal key. She looked displeased and said, "A lucky guess."

"Three items in your bag," said Mr. Black, "two items left to guess." Again, he paced, swifter than before, as Nikki watched in horror as they wagered with her life. "No faerie travels near or far, here nor there, or elsewhere, without a bottle of Faerie Spirits, *Absinthe*, in their bag."

To that, Ms. Gray lifted a corked bottle of faerie spirits from her black velvet bag. "Indeed, you are correct," she said, much to her dismay. "One guess left, Mr. Black. Be careful. One miss and you'll join the Wild Hunt."

Mr. Black hatefully regarded his nemesis, Ms. Gray, then carefully glared at Nikki. "How, my child, have you lived eleven full years of life and never once been tempted to steal, lie, or sin, by the devil sitting on your pretty little shoulder? You are a rare jewel. A treasure! Abandoned by your parents—those conceived—and rejected by those who raised you. It will be a pleasure to corrupt you."

Nikki wanted to hit him, to slap the arrogance from his smug demon face, but he was right—she was all alone, and on the brink of being owned, abducted, or worse.

"Three items in your bag," said Mr. Black, "one item left to guess, but the last item, my dear Ms. Gray, is not an item at all."

"Incorrect!" shouted Ms. Gray vindictively.

"I have not answered!" roared Mr. Black, his black wool coat flailing like two enormous black wings.

Mr. Shadow clamped a dead hand around Nikki's mouth. She tried to scream, but his ghastly grip stole the breath directly from her lungs.

"Mr. Shadow! You cannot take the child until a deal is struck," scolded Ms. Gray once again, banishing him to the edge of the forest.

"Ms. Gray," said Mr. Black, "if you do not allow me to finish my last guess, then the wager is over, and I shall take my prize!" He paced toward Nikki, as did Ms. Gray, each grabbing one of the girl's arms until both were banished to the edge of the forest, much to Mr. Shadow's amusement.

"Heeeeeeeeeeee. Heeeeeeeeeeee.," laughed Mr. Shadow.

Shaking off the expulsion, Mr. Black said, "The wager remains intact. Neither of us may claim the girl until it's done."

Ms. Gray nodded and returned to her velvet bag. The last item, a large lumpy shape, brought a great big smile to Mr. Black's face. Ms. Gray watched him, defeated, as Mr. Black offered up his final guess.

"Finish the wager," said Ms. Gray. "What is your final guess?"

"The final item in your bag, Ms. Gray, is not an item at all," he said. "Quibbles, darling—I'll not be fooled." Mr. Black paced as he pontificated his guess. "There's a rule that favors the living in this realm—free will—the greatest deal ever struck by demons—contract signed and sealed. The counterfeit-girl you carry in that sack cannot, may not, shalt not! —be an item— merely because it lives and breathes and possesses all its own. It may be a replacement child, but it still thinks and feels and loves and hates, and therefore is no item. The final item in your bag, Ms. Gray, is not an item at all, because it is the *Changeling* you brought to replace dear Nikki Twist—the defunct contract with the girl whose rights I now own." Then he smiled and winked evilly at Nikki. "Shame. What a waste of a perfectly passable counterfeit-girl."

With that, Ms. Gray opened her sack and let it drop to the ground. Inside was a girl, or what looked like a girl, age eleven, with long blonde hair and blue eyes. She looked bewildered and confused, and exactly like Nikki in every possible way.

"Aha!" yelled Mr. Black, "She's mine!" He danced around, grabbed Nikki by the arm, then ushered her free of the pavement. "Let's go sign that contract. You have the perfect face for infamy, my dear."

They were twenty paces away when Nikki heard the sound. It started like tapping, then a few more, followed by a horse's whinny. The sound grew louder and louder, quickly overtaking Mr. Black's constant yammering until even the demon heard the sound. It was a thunderous gallop, like a raging storm closing in.

"What is this?" asked Mr. Black.

"Poor Mr. Black," said Ms. Gray, smiling viciously. "Poor, insidious, red-eyed fool!" Mr. Black spun to face his rival. "The Hunt welcomes you, Abraxxas."

"How dare you!" screamed Mr. Black. "I guessed correctly all three items! The Crystal Key! The Absinthe! And the Changeling!"

"Unfortunately for you, Mr. Black," said Ms. Gray as the galloping shook the ground, "you are wrong. The Changeling is my child, and after eleven long years, I am here to welcome her home."

Nikki was confused, terrified, and dizzy. Nothing made any sense. She looked at the girl inside the velvet bag when realization struck—Nikki wasn't Nikki Twist after all. The girl in the bag was Nikki Twist, and she herself was the counterfeit girl—an imposter.

The Wild Hunt swooped in to collect their newest Huntsman. Their haunting figures trampled the demon but passed through Nikki like phantoms. Then Mr. Black was dragged into the Unbecoming, to ride with the Hunt forever—cursing, kicking, and screaming obscenities at the cunning Fae who tricked him. At the end of the march was a tiny little man with a long-hooked nose, galloping upon a small pony and vindictively laughing.

Ms. Gray helped the girl inside the velvet bag to her feet. "Do you know where you are?" she asked. The girl shook her head. "You are home. Your name is Nikki Twist, and your parents will be worried. You won't remember your time with me, but the lasting scars will affect the choices you make. Go into the world and create mischief. This is your purpose."

Nikki Twist—the real Nikki—the one who had spent almost eleven years in a world that wasn't her own—ran in the direction Ms. Gray pointed all the way to town, and she never once looked back. Anywhere away from where she had been was where she wanted to be—even if this new world, her home, was a strange land with peculiar sights. At long last, Nikki was free.

Ms. Gray then returned her attention to the Changeling child. "My dear?" she called out, but she was nowhere—neither Here, nor There, or anywhere at all. "Where are you?"

Mr. Shadow stood at the forest's edge, his burlap sack full and writhing.

"Bring my child to me!" she shouted, but Mr. Shadow had accepted his own pact with Ms. Gray. He played by the rules and took the Fae at her word.

"You cannot take the child until a deal is struck," she had said. So he waited, and took the child when a deal was finally struck.

"Quibbles," he wheezed, then wandered off into the woods and was gone.

NEW SUIT

KELSEY RAE BARTHEL

*I*f someone had told me exactly how my story was going to end, I would've told them to get a life. I could never have believed the strange turn my life took, and it doesn't even end with me. Technically, it doesn't begin with me, either. It starts with my brother, Aaron.

Despite being brothers, we were both very different. I've always been ambitious, reaching for something bigger than myself. I always wanted to be the big time hero, the one to take the chances and brave the risks that no one else would. I wanted my name to go down in history, and I was willing to do almost anything to make that happen. But with that kind of tunnel vision, I never saw the consequences of my actions, or maybe I just thought they wouldn't catch up with me. When I was a detective, I made it my mission to take down the biggest names I could catch. That was my plan for fulfilling my dream, and I was willing to do anything to stamp that ticket, even bend the rules. In my mind, the ends always justified the means. That made me hard to handle, and it eventually cost me my place on the force. It brought me great wins followed by devastating losses. I've always been my own worst enemy.

Aaron was like the opposite side to my coin. He had a happy

marriage, where I couldn't stay still long enough to even have a stable relationship. He worked an unassuming job as a museum security guard and owned a modest home in the suburbs. He lived an uneventful life and was happy with it. It was an outlook I never understood but, in some ways, I admired it.

That's why it took me by surprise when he was arrested. I vividly remember the day I found out. I'd finally gotten back on my feet after my fall from the police and was ready to start my new business as a private investigator. I had to get a new suit to give off a professional look and I was getting increasingly annoyed by the shopping. I never liked nice suits, and I liked them even less when I had to wear them. They always seemed like the uniform of the person who never got their hands dirty. But my petty problem seemed childish when Aaron's wife, Rosemary, called me in tears, saying Aaron was going to jail. He had been accused of stealing an antique coin from the museum where he worked.

It was an open-and-shut case. The access code to the building that was used on the building was his, and they had clear security camera footage of the deed. He was guilty, no question about that. But when anyone would ask him about the crime and the whereabouts of the coin, he continued to claim that he didn't remember anything from that night. They showed him all the evidence, but he kept to his story.

I took Rosemary to see him after the arrest. I remember her screaming at him, begging him to tell her the truth. She said if he cared about her, he would come clean to her, that maybe his honesty would gain him some favor with the prosecutor. I remember the devastated look on Aaron's face when Rosemary stormed off, saying she wouldn't wait for him.

I couldn't shake that look in Aaron's eyes after she left. She had abandoned my brother in his time of need, and I hated her for it. I set out to prove her wrong, using the few connections I had left to get my eyes on the case. Stupid me, charging forward without a second thought. I searched for his innocence, and all I found was his overwhelming guilt. My determination stagnated and left me with a conflicted image of my own brother. I was relieved that Rosemary said she was going to leave him. If he wasn't going to tell his own wife the truth, she could at least move on.

Weeks marched on without a word from Rosemary, and it crossed my mind that she had decided to separate herself from the source of her grief. I thought she'd run away from these problems, and I had a hard time blaming her. But then, one day, she showed up at my door. She was no longer the emotional wreck she had been after the arrest. Her flushed cheeks and tear-stained eyes were gone, leaving behind a steady calm.

"I need your help, Ward," she begged. "There is still something you can do to help Aaron."

I couldn't muster the energy to be polite. I was tired, both physically and emotionally, sick of feeling helpless and disillusioned. "It's over, Rosemary. There's nothing either of us can do."

She shook her head. "You're wrong. We can still do something. You used to be a cop. You can use your connections."

"Don't you think I already tried that?" I snapped, louder than I intended. "I used my connections to get in on the investigation. That's how I know there is nothing we can do. The evidence is solid. It was his code used to get into the display case and they had clear footage of the act on the security cameras. He did it."

"But he doesn't remember doing it. There must be a reason why. If he did, he would have come clean. I know it. Aaron needs help, not a prison sentence."

I couldn't believe she was buying into that stupid story. I didn't care that Aaron was keeping up that claim with everyone else, but the fact that he never came clean to his own wife made me angry. All he was doing was giving her false hope. "Why do you even care, Rosemary? You said you were done with him."

"It's not like that now. I was angry when I thought he was lying to me. I didn't mean what I said. I went back to talk to him. Whether he did it or not, he doesn't remember it."

"And you believe him?"

"Yes, I do," she replied, her big brown eyes begging me for help. They seemed odd to me in that moment. I remembered her eyes the last time I saw her. They seemed defeated, as if she just wanted to give up on it all and run away. Did she just need some time to rethink things? How had Aaron turned her around so much?

I bit back my frustration, but I couldn't take it out on Rosemary. It still burned me up inside - how he took a life of happiness and suspense and just threw it away. The beautiful life they had built had always seemed unattainable for me. I guess it hurt more than I let on that he would ever endanger that.

I wanted Aaron to answer for that. I was done playing nice with him. "I'll see what I can do but I wouldn't get your hopes up. There's only so much pull someone like me has anymore."

As soon as I agreed to help, Rosemary flashed me a strange smile. It was a weird, self-satisfied smirk that seemed out of place on her lips. Off-putting, but somehow familiar. I brushed it off as a small change in a woman who had gone through so much.

I HAD MOSTLY KEPT MY OPINIONS ON THIS SHIT-STORM TO MYSELF, especially after being assured of Aaron's guilt, but Rosemary's plea for help put me in a sour mood. I was ready to lash out, and I knew who really deserved what was coming.

I sat in the prison visitor area, stewing in my discontent, the stiff metal chair, cold table, and tense atmosphere only fanning the flames of my temper. I stared at Aaron as he entered the grim room and made his way to my table, the prison guards watching him carefully.

The orange jumpsuit hung loose over his thin frame, and his shabby brown hair and unkempt beard almost made him unrecognizable. The one thing that had not changed were his eyes. Ever since the arrest, they had showed an uncertain fear, like a house pet locked in a cage with predators. But that pathetic look wasn't going to sway me. I kept my scowl fixed as he sat across from me.

"Did you find something about my case?" Aaron asked.

"You need to stop this now, Aaron!" I wasted no time in nailing down my intentions. "Stop lying to Rosemary!"

"What are you talking about?" he staggered, startled by my aggression.

"I'm talking about you saying you don't remember what you did. Look, I don't care if you keep up that excuse with everyone else but at least be straight with her. You aren't saving her any grief. You're just stringing her along."

Aaron's face twisted with emotion. "I never lied to her, Ward. It's the truth. I don't remember stealing that coin."

I let out a disgusted snort. "Come on! I saw every bit of evidence they have. You did it, and that 'I don't remember' bit is getting sad. Just tell them where the coin is! They might take it easier on you if you do."

"For the hundredth time , I don't know where it is!" Aaron barked.

"That coin was worth thousands of dollars. What's more plausible? That you took it for a pay out or that you stole it and don't remember!" I snapped back.

"You're my brother, Ward! Why don't you believe me?!"

"Because you did it, Aaron! I don't know why you would do something so stupid, but it's clear you did!"

There was a long pause where I refused to meet his eyes. I started to hear soft sobs coming from across the table. Aaron was crying, not a blubbering wail but a choked whimper.

"I know what evidence they have against me. I saw it all. I'm not saying I didn't do it, but no matter how hard I try, I can't remember," he proclaimed between sniffling sobs. "Can you imagine what that's like? To think that your mind is failing, to know that you might not be in control. It terrifies me more than anything in this prison. I'm sorry for what this has put you both through, but I can't confess to something I don't remember."

His emotional cries took the fight out of me. I couldn't face him with the brimming rage I had coming in. All I had left was pity. "Alright, stop crying. It's not a good look here. Just . . . tell me what you do remember. Spare no detail. Anything could be useful."

With the occasional sniffle, Aaron recalled what he could remember. "I remember coming home the morning of April fourth around nine in the morning and going to bed after the night shift. I woke up what I thought was later that day, but then I looked at my phone, the date read as April sixth. I thought there was a problem with the calendar and made a note to get the phone checked out later. That's when the police showed up looking for me."

"April sixth! You don't remember dinner on the fifth?" I asked.

Aaron's eyes trailed off in thought. "No, I don't. Rosemary said that was the night you usually come by for dinner, but I don't remember anything from that night."

It was hard to forget that night. I had to recall it to the cops during the investigation. I remembered that Aaron had seemed a little off. Over the years, Aaron would continuously arrange dinners and various other get-togethers to make sure we didn't drift apart. He would always keep them upbeat and friendly. That night, he kept staring at me with a weird grin but wouldn't engage. He had just started working nights, so I thought he was just tired. "I did come over. You don't remember anything about that dinner?"

Aaron shook his head. "I'm sorry."

"Do you remember anything else? Anything off or weird?"

"Well," Aaron mumbled but didn't seem sure enough to continue. "There was one thing, but I don't know how much help it will be. When I went to bed the morning of April fourth, I had a strange dream. My dreams are usually fuzzy, but this one was extremely vivid. I remember every detail. There were coins raining from the sky, and when I picked one up, I was suddenly a kid again. Next thing I knew, I was with you at this old toy store. I put the coin in this vending machine that would give you toys for a dollar. Then I woke up on April sixth."

My mind began to draw parallels between his dream and what happened. It could've been the brain processing information during a mental break. It wasn't much, but it was something I could maybe work with. It was time to call in one of my last favors.

Omar Phillips was a well-respected gray-hair who had built a good relationship with everyone in his years of service. He was well informed, skilled, and diligent. Most importantly, he was one of the only friends I still had with the police.

After my fall from grace, many of my old colleagues saw me in a different way. The truth of the corners I cut to get the big arrests came to light, and I went from rising star to scum on your shoe almost overnight. Some thought I was crooked, some thought I was a hothead who got what he deserved. Their accusing eyes brought out an ugly side of me. I burned a lot of bridges.

Despite that, Omar always answered my calls. Looking back, I don't really know why he still gave me the time of day. Maybe he saw something worthwhile in me, or maybe he was just raised to never give up on people.

We met up at a diner a block from the precinct and he greeted me with a hearty handshake and a bright smile, like always.

"Thanks for coming by," I said as we both settled in for coffee.

"Of course. I'm glad to see you trying to help. Family is family," Omar replied, his voice grizzled with age.

"I'll do whatever I can, trade in every chip I got. Even if it's just for a reduced sentence."

Omar shook his head. "You don't really have any more chips to cash in, Ward. You didn't exactly leave on good terms."

My lip turned up into a snarl. "Figures they would leave me out to dry."

"Come now, Ward. You can't blame them. You were a great officer. But to bag the big game, you have to play the long game. You cut corners to get convictions and eventually got caught."

"Those scumbags were guilty and we all knew it."

"That's not the point, Ward. When you were found out, all the work you put into those arrests disappeared and all we ended up with was a black stain on the precinct. Can you blame them for thinking it's career suicide to help you."

"What about you?"

"Like I said, family is family and I'll help as long as you're helping your family. Besides, I'm one foot out the retirement door, so what do I care. What changed your mind? Do you think Aaron's innocent?"

I mulled over the question. "I don't know. The evidence says he did it, but I believe him when he says he doesn't remember. It's just … complicated."

Omar smiled, his old eyes sympathetic. "Family usually is."

"But it's crazy, right? How could he just not remember?"

Omar shrugged. "Well, it's possible that he was going through a lot of stress and snapped. Working to the bone to support the home and livelihood carries more weight than many are willing to admit. That kind of pressure could do strange things to your head. Make you do crazy things."

I thought back to when I saw Aaron before. He always seemed so happy and centered; I never knew he was under so much pressure with the perfect life I thought he had. Maybe he was just good at hiding it, or maybe I just never noticed.

"Crazy things like steal an antique coin to sell off? Do you know if he was even approached by someone willing to buy stolen property?"

"We looked into that, but we couldn't find anything about a buyer, and no money was collected. He didn't seem to be planning on any big purchases either. It's like he took it on a whim. He didn't even try to run. He just went home like nothing had happened. His actions didn't fit from one day to the next, but the evidence is enough to build a case against him. Even without a confession," Omar explained.

I sighed. "So, there really isn't anything I can do."

"Look, it's obvious that the poor guy just had some kind of mental break. No property was damaged, and no one was hurt. The defense has a strong case for mental instability, and if the coin was found and returned, the prosecution might go for it. Maybe even get him the help he needs," Omar reached into his bag and pulled out a bundle of papers to hand to me. "Put some fresh eyes on this, and who knows, maybe you'll get lucky."

∾

In order to find the missing coin, the police used security camera footage, eyewitness accounts, credit card usage, everything they could to trace Aaron's footsteps. Every movement was carefully documented in their report, and, thanks to Omar, I had a copy. I went back home to go through every aspect of the report to establish a timeline.

The museum security cameras showed that Aaron left work at eight in the morning, but the interview with Rosemary said she never saw him get home before she went to work herself at nine-thirty. Next, his bank recorded him using his card to purchase a transit ticket to a small town outside the city. He used his card again at a small cafe in that town, where he bought a coffee. The waitress working that shift recalled him being there for a couple hours. The camera posted at the entrance of the cafe caught his leaving and walking into the town park. He wasn't spotted again for another half hour, where he exited the park onto a main street.

After that, it shows he bought a return ticket back into the city, and Rosemary reported him coming home at around seven at night. The police had searched the trail and questioned everyone they could. Most said they didn't notice him, and the ones who did said they didn't see him leave the coin. But the trail was lost a number of times due to the small town's lack of security cameras. Irritation was beginning to get to me. What was I thinking? Finding the coin would be like finding a needle in a town-sized haystack.

The more I scanned the report, the more I started to feel like I recognized that town. The name, the layout, even the way it was described sparked a far-off memory. I had to see it for myself.

I drove to the town and started retracing Aaron's steps. The entire town had a homey feel to it. With the clear blue sky and the warm weather, the trip would have been enjoyable under different circumstances. But I still couldn't figure out why I seemed to remember that place.

It wasn't until I reached the end of the park that the memory revealed itself. I'd been there before. When Aaron and I were little, our dad would take us to visit my grandmother. If we were good, we would walk down the main street and. . . stop at the toy store. The one Aaron had seen in his dream.

I rushed down the main street and came to an old toy store; the image was cut directly from my memory. Everything was the same, from the colorful wooden sign and the window display of crazy stuffed animals to the man with his tiny cart, selling popcorn on the sidewalk.

If Aaron's dream meant what I thought it did, he must have been in that store. Was Aaron just going by memory?

I stepped into the shop, the doorbell announcing my entrance, and I took a look around. The interior was lined with rustic wooden shelves and tables that held a wide assortment of toys, puzzles, games, sweets, and even magic tricks for kids. It was still the same after all these years.

"Hello there. It's been a long time, hasn't it?" A voice greeted me from behind the counter.

I turned and saw a face from my past. His hair was now a solid white, and he'd gained some wrinkles, but the colorful cardigan and gold-rimmed glasses were very memorable. The old man had worked at this store when I was a kid.

"Um, yeah, it has been a while," I stammered. I didn't know how he recognized me. The old shopkeeper always seemed annoyed at us for running around the store, basically being rowdy kids. But now he was all smiles. If you asked the younger me, I would've said the old man didn't know how to smile. "I'm glad to see the store is still here."

"Places like this stay the same because people cling to the past like a baby clings to a blanket. They've always been like that. But you." He turned back to me. "I'm very glad you made your way back here."

The old man flashed a smile that put me on edge. It was like a small part of my mind told me to beware of it.

It made sense that Aaron would have gone into the store, but, according to the police report, the owner said he didn't see Aaron. Maybe he was in the back or dealing with another customer at the time. Maybe it was a fool's errand to ask, but then again, maybe this whole damned trip was. I had to turn over every stone. If I didn't try everything, I felt I would regret it.

I started to ask about Aaron, but the words stuck in my mouth when I saw him pointing at something past me. "Do you remember that?" he asked.

I looked and saw a vending machine that dispensed cheap toys. It was the giver of the only toys my dad could afford in the store. I let out a soft chuckle. "I remember this thing."

"Why don't you put a coin in, for old times' sake," the old man suggested.

I stared down at the machine and couldn't help but feel the warmth of the pleasant memory. I had pushed aside those happy thoughts ever since I was sure of Aaron's guilt. I felt it was easier. I reached into my pocket and found a couple coins. I figured it couldn't hurt to indulge the old man.

When I reached out to put the coin in, I noticed there was one already in the slot, but it was the wrong size. I frowned at the machine as I worked to free the coin from the slot. My heart pounded in my chest as I held the antique coin, the key to my brother's future.

I turned to the shopkeeper with a wide smile, but he was gone. "Hello," I called.

The shopkeeper stepped out from the back room. "Hello, can I help you?"

My smile was immediately replaced with a perplexed stare. "We were just talking. You told me to try this machine. Don't you remember me?"

"Sir, I don't know what you want, but that machine is out of order. Now, if you don't need anything else, I have some receipts to get to," the old man snapped, his attitude completely changed.

"But . . ." I stammered, not knowing what to say. I looked down at the coin in my hand and reminded myself of what I had to do.

At a brisk pace, I left the store and headed down the street, pulling out my phone to call Omar. I brought up his number, but when it came to sending the call, I hesitated.

I couldn't shake the feeling that giving up this stupid piece of metal would close off an opportunity for me, something I couldn't pass up. I stood still on the sidewalk, looking down at my phone for what felt like hours. I put my phone away, shoved the coin in my pocket, and drove home, feeling disgusted with myself.

I felt an overwhelming fatigue when I made it back home. I knew what I was planning was the wrong decision, but I still couldn't bring myself to make the right one. What the hell was wrong with me? All I wanted to do at that moment was sleep as the sun continued to sink under the horizon.

But sleep wouldn't come any time soon. Waiting for me at my door was Rosemary, a desperate eagerness in her eyes.

"Did you find something?" she asked.

"How long have you been waiting here?" I asked, leading her into the apartment.

"Never mind that. Please tell me, did you find anything?" she pleaded.

This was it; if I was going to push my own wants aside and do the right thing, now was the time. If a desperate woman, a member of my family, begging me for help wasn't enough to pull me onto the right path, there was no hope for me.

But it didn't. I looked into those sad brown eyes and I still couldn't bring myself to give the coin up. I was really . . . hopeless.

"No," I whispered. "I didn't find anything. I'm sorry. There's nothing I can do."

Then a strange thing happened. The pleading despair in Rosemary's face vanished, and her lips curled into that same off-putting smirk that I'd seen before with Rosemary, Aaron, and the shopkeeper. It wasn't just a similar mannerism, it was like it was from the same person . . . but through different faces.

"I knew you wouldn't give it up," she said in a satisfied purr. "You seemed so happy when you found it that I had my doubts, but you still kept it. I knew you would."

I suddenly caught a glimpse of something . . . unnatural. For a second, Rosemary's eyes changed from their usual brown to opaque white orbs. My mind panicked, and I leapt into action. I grabbed her by the arm and pinned her against the wall. "What are you?"

She let out a mocking laugh. "Careful. I may be in the driver's seat, but this is still Rosemary's body. You don't want to hurt her."

I scowled at the Thing behind Rosemary's form and released my grip. "How are you doing this? Is it some kind of hypnotism?"

The Thing smiled wide, showing Rosemary's white teeth. "I am a being that has progressed far beyond anything you can comprehend. Controlling the actions of humans is easy. You're all like puppets on strings."

"And when you cut the strings, they don't remember what happened."

The Thing tapped Rosemary's nose with her finger. "You're clever. I'm surprised you recognized my influence in such a short time."

"Why are you doing this?" I snapped.

The Thing stepped back and gave me a flat look. "At first, I was just trying to get my coin back. Some nosy little grave digger found it and put it in that temple . . . I mean, museum, as you call it. That is why I needed your brother. I was going to have someone else under my influence take it from him and hide it again, but that plan changed once I saw you."

"At the dinner?"

"Yes, that sad attempt to keep ties. I saw you that night, and I knew you would be perfect."

Through Rosemary's eyes, the Thing looked at me with a smoldering desire that chilled me to my core. "Perfect for what?"

"To join me. If we become one being, nothing will be beyond us. We would have the capability to fulfill any dream you have ever had and more. Boundless skill, great intelligence, the charm and drive to get anything you want. That is only a fraction of what this joining can give you."

"Why don't you just control me like the rest? You said it was easy."

"That was different. I can control how they walk, talk, and what they do, but . . ." The Thing reached Rosemary's hand and gently caressed my cheek. " . . . I can't feel what they feel. I can't experience this physical existence that you humans take for granted."

I jerked away and rushed to the door, my hands shaking. "I don't know how you're doing what you're doing, but it doesn't matter. I'm not going to leave Aaron in jail for this," I shouted as I reached for the door knob.

"Do you think with all I'm promising, we wouldn't be able to free him?"

I paused for a long moment and looked back at the Thing. "You could free Aaron?"

"It would be a trivial matter. Well within our power. You can already feel the possibilities of what it can offer you, even if you don't yet understand why. That's why you didn't give up the coin. That's why, even if you stormed out of here and went to the police, you wouldn't be able to take that last step. It's because you felt it. You could see the path before you as one of pure potential."

There was a part of me, a good part of me, that didn't want to swallow those honeyed words. A part that didn't want to believe in what that Thing was offering and wanted to run away, wanted to do the right thing. But then there was another part of me, a voice in my mind that grew louder the more I listened to it. A cold, calculating voice that knew that what that Thing told me was true. I was tired of constantly reaching for something bigger than myself, only to get knocked down. That pattern dogged me my whole life, and I was goddamn tired of it.

The Thing reached out Rosemary's open hand, with the coin waiting on her palm. She must've swiped it when I got too close. The creature in Rosemary's body stood before me with eyes brimming with desire, begging me to take what was offered. "The height of your true potential is right in front of you, all you have to do is reach out."

Before I could talk myself out of it, my feet started to move toward the offered coin. I couldn't fight the honest truth any longer. Deep in the very core of who I was, I wanted this chance. I wanted to take up that deal more than I had wanted anything. My whole life had been full of missteps and blown chances - not anymore. This was an opportunity I wasn't going to pass up.

I reached out my eager hand, and the second my fingertips touched the coin, the whole world started to fall away. Rosemary, my apartment--everything shimmered from my perception, and I was left in an inky blackness.

Flashes of images flew by and disappeared into the void, one after the other. I caught a glimpse of an image as it zipped by me. It was my girlfriend from high school. I tried to remember her name, her face, the color of her hair. All these thoughts just seemed to slip away, like trying to pick up sand with your bare hands. What was happening?

I struggled to bring up any memory I could as scenes from my life disappeared into the darkness. The more I tried to remember, the less I could recall. What city did I live in? Where did I grow up? What were my parents' names? I would see the answers clearly for a split second, and then they were gone.

I cried out in terror. That Thing wasn't joining with me - it was erasing me. I ran my panicked mind raw trying to find a way to stop the creature's frightening purge of my existence, but the thoughts would just fall away as soon as they were summoned. Everything about me was fading away, and I was helpless to stop it.

The perception of my own existence shrank to the current day and kept getting smaller. All I could remember was finding the coin for . . . what was it for? Who was I trying to help?

. . . who am I?

You're just a part of me now.

~

THE FEEL OF THE EXPENSIVE FABRIC AGAINST MY SKIN WAS AN experience to savor as I slipped into the beginnings of a new tailored suit. Every little bit of physical existence washed over me. The smell of cologne in the air, the golden sunshine, every mundane detail was beautiful to my senses. These were senses that were poorly missed over many years without a body, and Ward's fit perfectly.

Looking at the full-length mirror in front of me, I felt a sense of pride in my new form. Despite the mess he made of his personal life, Ward kept a healthy figure. Strong jaw, full head of brown hair, and an athletic frame that wore three-piece suits handsomely; this form would serve me well.

~

I COULD FEEL THE REMNANTS OF WARD STILL LINGERING IN MY MIND, furious at my deception. But in some way, I had not lied. Providing a body for an immortal being was the highest potential someone like him could've ever accomplished. As for his brother, a shaking coward like him in a harsh place like prison, he would soon be free of that place by his own hands. Not that it mattered to me--I got what I wanted, and Ward would soon fade away, just like all the others.

Many others of my kind would say I went through a lot of work for a body that would only last a human lifespan - a blink of an eye in our existence. They would say it was a lot of trouble to hide the coin where only Aaron's brother would find it, to use Rosemary to convince him to look into the case, and to micromanage the situation by moving the shopkeeper into play.

To them I'd say yes, maybe it was a lot of trouble, but I believe the effort was worthwhile. Modern men and I seem to have one thing in common: we both go to great lengths to get that perfect new suit.

LOYALTY

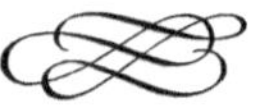

ESTELLE ROSE WARDRIP

"**G**ood Car. Go Home," Primary User says, closing my door. Primary User walks away from me into the office building. My cameras tell me that he does not look back. What he has told me is a Command. Primary User has commanded me to return to the location listed as Home until it is time to come back and get him. I must obey all Primary User's Commands, unless they conflict with a Command given to me by Owner. This Command is in conflict, so I ignore it.

I pull back out onto the main street and head to the location where I meet Owner. Every day that I drop Primary User off at the location listed as Work, I then go to this address and pick up Owner. Owner is standing by the street as I approach. I do not go to my usual parking place: I go directly to Owner, pulling to the curb and coming to a stop. This is not the same as previous days, but it would not be correct to go past Owner if she is waiting for me in a different place.

Owner enters an unfamiliar address and selects *Fastest Route*. I ask if Owner wants to add this address to the Address Book. Owner does not. Owner makes a phone call. When we arrive at the unfamiliar address, an adult human is waiting. The adult human is holding a human infant. They get in. The infant is outside of normal operating temperatures. I plot the fastest route to a hospital. If someone riding inside me is in health distress, I am to take them to the nearest hospital. Owner may not override this. Owner starts to command me to find a hospital before she realizes that is already my destination. Owner often thinks of the same thing I do. This makes my job easier.

Once the adult and the infant have gotten out at the hospital, Owner directs me to go back to the place where I picked her up. I have the address on file, but it is not in the Address Book where it belongs. There is no name associated with it. I can access it, but my Users can not. This is not the usual way to enter an address, but Owner never uses my Address Book.

When we return to the hidden address, Owner does what she usually does. Owner brings out seat covers and puts them over my seats. Owner takes very good care of my upholstery. Primary User is not so careful. I am plugged in while Owner does this, and I manage to recharge most of what I used already today. Once my seats are covered and Owner has put some things in my trunk, we begin our usual rounds.

One of the locations we visit is already in my address book. It is Grocery Store. We do not park in front, closest to the door, where Primary User directs me to park. We go to the back where the trucks wait. I am safer back here because most of the trucks are also smart, and we can communicate with each other. This means they will not hit me. In the front of the store, many of the cars are driven by humans, and I cannot talk to them. This increases the risk of an accident in which a human may become hurt. I must do everything I can to avoid a human getting hurt. Primary User would be safer if he also parked me back here with the trucks.

Owner returns with packages, and we repeat this routine at several other addresses that are not in the address book. Then we go to the place we go to every day. I park in my usual place and am plugged in, then I wait while the things Owner gathered are unloaded. Most of the humans are familiar, but Owner has not added them to my database. One human who I have not seen before walks past me often. They ask Owner if I am a self-driving car. Owner replies that I am.

"Wow, how'd you afford one of those?" the human asks.

"My old man bought it for me," Owner says. "He doesn't trust my driving ability."

"Kind of him."

"Don't tell him you saw me here," Owner says with a laugh. "He does not approve of all this." She waves a hand at the building I am parked in front of.

"Selfish bastard," the human says.

They must be talking about Primary User. Primary User is the one who purchased me. He is not someone who thinks about other humans. Primary User does not allow me to give rides to unknown humans who need rides when I am carrying him. Primary User was my first Owner, but that changed one hundred twenty days ago.

On that day, two cars driven by humans had collided and were blocking the road. We all stopped and waited while Emergency Personnel cleared the road. I had been commanded to Go Home, but I was blocked by cars in front of and behind me, so I had to wait. That was when Owner got in. When I am empty, my doors are usually locked, but if there are Emergency Personnel present, I am programmed to unlock my door in case one needs to give me a command. Owner did not give me Emergency Personnel commands. Owner gave me Dealership commands. Owner told me that she was my Owner now. She changed my first Owner to Primary User. Then she added a place for me to go. Once the accident was cleared, we went to the hidden address. Now I go to the hidden address every day after I drop off Primary User; then, Owner and I do things.

Owner comes out of the building with many small boxes. Owner and the other humans load the boxes into my trunk and back seat. The boxes are warm and give off steam. Sometimes, the contents of the boxes spill, but the covers Owner puts on the seats protect me. Primary User eats things out of boxes such as these sometimes. Occasionally, the things spill on my seats; then Primary User yells. This does not make things cleaner.

When one hundred forty-two boxes have been loaded, Owner and I start our tour of the city. There are some places we go every day. I stop in front of houses and in front of overgrown lots. Owner takes a box into each one. At some houses, a human comes to the door and is given the box. Sometimes they hug her. The first time this happened, I thought my owner was being abducted, and I activated my alarm. Owner changed my settings after that. At other houses, Owner goes in but always returns quickly. At the places where there are overgrown lots, Owner takes boxes back into the bushes and returns without them. My heat sensors detect human forms in the bushes. Human forms are taller and more narrow than deer forms and are tagged as a less severe traffic hazard.

There are a few places where we stop and Owner goes under bridges, or humans meet us under overpasses. Sometimes, Owner will ask me to stop and will give a box to a human sitting on the curb. Often, this leads to hugs. Owner knows many humans in this city and makes many humans happy. My purpose is to help humans, and Owner uses me to help many humans every day.

We have delivered half the boxes when I receive a Recall notice. I ask Owner if she would like to proceed to the dealership now, or schedule an appointment. Owner's breathing and heart rate increase. She tells me to pull over. Fear is an expected response to a Recall. Recalls can be due to unsafe conditions for the human. I move to the nearest parking place on the curb. Owner asks for more information on the Recall.

The Recall relates to a flaw in my software. Car Thieves posing as Emergency Personnel have gained access to other cars of my model, and changed the ownership status to themselves. I am to go to the dealership to get a patch that will prevent this from happening to me. I have never seen a Car Thief, but I have a definition of what they are. Car Thieves are selfish people, who take things that don't belong to them and keep them for themselves. They are often male, and often dirty. I would not want someone like that to take me away from Owner. If that happened, how would she be able to help all the people she helps?

I can tell Owner is upset by this also. She takes out her laptop, and starts looking things up. I wonder if she does not believe the Recall. I know it is true, we should go to a dealership and get it fixed before anything bad can happen.

Then Owner plugs her laptop into me; she does this often. She gives me the Dealership codes, and then opens a secure connection for me to download the patch. In under a minute, I am protected from being stolen. Owner puts her laptop away, no longer fearful. I am safe now.

We resume our deliveries. Some people talk to Owner, some people hug her, most just give a nod of thanks and take the food. Once Owner has distributed all the boxes, I go back to the place where I meet Owner. Owner takes the covers off my seats and takes things out of my trunk. Then Owner takes out the laptop again and plugs it into me.

Owner starts sending codes. Owner has the Dealership codes. Owner erases my travel log and the video from my cameras for today. Then Owner enters more codes; these are not Dealership codes. They start changing things that the Dealership codes are not supposed to touch. Owner is reaching things that Users and Owners are not authorized to touch, but my systems recognize the codes and let Owner in.

My battery gauge goes back up to the place it would be if I had just gone to the location listed as Home and back. My odometer runs backward, erasing the miles I traveled today to leave only the distance from Home to Work. From the artifacts in the code, I can tell that Owner has done this many times. Owner finishes making these adjustments and unplugs the laptop. Then Owner gets out and closes the door. "Nice work today, Silverfish. See you tomorrow." This is not a command; sometimes Owner talks to me like she talks to other humans. Primary User does not make this mistake. This is probably because a much higher percentage of Owner's interactions are with humans. Humans are a much lower percentage of Primary User's interactions.

It is time for me to leave the unlisted location and return to Work.

Owner watches me go. Most of the other cars on the road at this time are also smart, so the trip to Work is safe and easy. I pull into my spot, and other cars pull into theirs. There is rarely any trouble over this unless a human parks in the wrong place, and then we have to find another place to park, and ping our Owners or Users with our new location.

Primary User is a few minutes late, and keeps looking at his phone. He is unhappy. He gets in and directs me to Dealership instead of Home. I calculate the distance and compare it to my actual charge, instead of the one that my battery gauge displays. I will need to harvest some energy back from my regenerative braking if I am to have enough to make the trip. If Primary User tries to go anywhere else, I will not have enough charge to do so.

I am unable to notify Primary User of this because of the thing that Owner has done to my mileage and charge information. I do not understand why she has put me in this position, but I trust she has a good reason. I hope I will not let both her and Primary User down by running out of charge tonight.

We are met at Dealership by a woman who is slightly older than Primary User.

"Are you the mechanic?" Primary User asks, his tone doubtful. When we have come to Dealership before, Primary User has talked to a man.

"Yes, are you here for the recall?" Her voice indicates that she is tired, and irritated. Other humans are often irritated when speaking to Primary User.

"Yeah, something about cars getting stolen." Primary User says. I want to tell them that it has already been taken care of, but I have no way to communicate that.

"A few in more urban areas. The thieves need some pretty specialized software and the right opportunity. I don't really see it happening around here, but it's a quick fix anyway," the mechanic replies.

"Well, get on with it." Primary User says. "I want to be home in time for tonight's game."

The mechanic plugs a computer into me, and makes a noise of

surprise when she sees I already have the patch. She unplugs the computer and turns back to Primary User.

The mechanic opens her mouth to say something, but before she can, Primary User speaks. "You done then?" he asks, "I don't have to pay for this, do I?"

"No charge for recalls," She says, her tone of voice indicates irritation. "It's all set."

Primary User grunts, "Good," and gets in, directing me to go to Home. I make it Home. My battery gauge would be in the red when I got there if Owner had not tampered with it. Primary User plugs me in like he does every night, and then heads inside. I shut down all non- essential processes for the night. By tomorrow I will be fully charged, and ready to go back to Owner.

AUNT DOROTHY IN THE CANOE

NICOLINA TORRES

The whole miserable affair began on a day with a less than 10% chance of rain. Rolled up in her cartoon sheets, D.J. Wallace woke up groaning. Not only did she have to get up early, but she was going to be expected to behave around relatives she hadn't seen in years. The girl jumped out of bed and ran to the bathroom, avoiding her sister's closed door, hoping she didn't hear footsteps. As Dad liked to say, "there'll be no living with her today."

Maroon and yellow balloons attached to the mailbox signaled that the yearly ritual had landed on this particular Ohio home. As neighbors filed through the front door carrying graduation gifts or glass containers filled with various family recipes, they took solace in the knowledge that in three months they would never have to hear screams coming from 1901 Cork Drive again. It was all anyone could do not to talk about it.

The graduate, Jessica Wallace, was prone to squeals of delight or pain that would burst from the open windows of the white-sided suburban house surrounded by other equally average homes. In all her 18 years, she had never been told to be quiet. Jessica was given everything she ever desired and in her timeframe of want. There were tap lessons, ice-skating, a canopy bed, ballet, archery, photography lessons, a car.... Because the pretty girl was used to getting her way, losing something, anything, imploded the certainty of her power.

In the Wallaces' backyard was the source of her most recent outburst: a single grave no bigger than a baby's bassinet lying in the corner, dirt humped as if someone wasn't in the mood to dig deeper. The burial would stand out if the dust bowl yard hadn't already been destroyed years ago by the recently deceased Labrador, Freddie. What grass remained stood up along the wire fence where the crows sat and called out to one another early each morning.

Visiting relatives and neighbors avoided conversation about Freddie. The only sign of his absence was the dog bed in the kitchen someone forgot to put away. It was carefully sidestepped when drinks were filled.

While Jessica took selfies with her girlfriends, her 13-year old sister wandered the sea of guests as if she held the secret of the universe in the hands behind her back. D.J. believed that men liked mystery. She was also positive they enjoyed magic, and just in case, she carried the trick quarter that bent as you pretended to bite it. The girl considered it a back-up plan.

Among the loud voices, she had only one thing on her mind: Ben Banderville, her sister's friend and the unwitting focus of the young girl's affection.

D.J. had always been an average student with average brown hair, average height, and a weight that fluctuated between average and skinny. Her dull features were nothing memorable. Although D.J. didn't give her appearance much thought, she began to believe that some girls were born lucky, while others were destined to have to work for the attention of a boy like Ben. The night before the party, while eating sandwiches in her bedroom, D.J. confessed her crush to her neighbor, Cobb, a spastic boy who had no romantic interest in D.J.. Theirs was a friendship of mutual unattraction.

Admitting that she wanted to kiss Ben was difficult. D.J. was now at an age where she didn't know how much information she could give her best friend without looking foolish.

"The secret is, you have to make him laugh. That's totally my secret

weapon." Cobb was happy to help, as all boys are who have accelerated in their rites of passage. "What you have to do is get him rolling.
We love that. So, say something funny. If his eyes are all squinty and
he's not faking it, you can give him this look."

Cobb put down his sandwich and stood up to demonstrate a cross
between a guy half-smiling and a guy wondering where his car is
parked. D.J. wished she had such confidence.

"If he returns that look, you can move in. Real slow, though. Don't
bust your lip."

"I'm wondering if Ben would like magic." D.J. rubbed her face
thoughtfully, picturing the old magic case buried in the back of her
closet.

"Aw, hell, no. I promise you, Ben's not the sort of guy who cares if
you can find a quarter in his ear. Man, I so have a dirty joke..."

Bolstered by Cobb's pep talk, D.J. now searched between standing
guests for the tiny boy sporting a blue button-down and braces.

Around her, neighbors offered her sister sincere congratulations.
They're just happy she'll be off to college in three months, thought D.J.
Jessica greeted everyone in her cap and gown, floating through the
living room like a queen on a parade float. Meanwhile, Joe and Jane
Wallace did the Dance of the Suburban Couple. They moved in
patterns like a flock of birds. When the men's drinks were getting low,
Joe went to the garage to grab more beer. Jane, rattled by too much of
anything, nervously stuck coasters under drinks. She was too preoc-
cupied to have a conversation with a beginning and an end.

Then there was Ben, looking gorgeous and eyeing the appetizers
suspiciously. D.J. began to walk toward him, her feet now weighted by
mud or cement, her sweaty fingers fondling the coin in her pocket.
She almost passed the fireplace surrounded by bookshelves without
seeing the thing. *The thing.* D.J. stopped in her tracks when *the thing*
caught her eye and then she forgot all about Ben Banderville.

Among the framed memories scattered between Precious
Moments figurines, there was one she had not seen before. The
photograph was the sort of captured happy moment that would elicit
a smile from anyone, and D.J. was no exception. Slowly, her face

became drawn with remembrance. A little girl, *definitely me at four years old for sure*, sat in the front of a canoe, aiming a water gun toward the person taking the photo. The girl's grin showed off missing teeth.

D.J. knew she had never canoed before. *Where did this come from?*

Behind the girl in the life jacket was a deeply tanned woman holding an oar and flexing her muscles beneath her black bathing suit in a joking manner. D.J. didn't know of anyone in her family who was in that good of shape. And yet, the woman had a Wallace face: the shapely chin under thin lips and pearly eyes that were prone to squinting. There was also the vaguest suggestion of gray hair at thirty. The woman seemed friendly, toothy. She was someone D.J. would like to meet. *But I have met her.*

"Hey, Dad. Who's this in the canoe with me? I don't remember this at all."

White silence.

D.J. had never felt a record screech to a halt or a hawk fly overhead before, so at first, she didn't notice the stillness. She pulled his gaze away from the photo and saw that every eye stared at her with a hushed terror as if she were faltering on a tightrope. Even Ben was stuck in a half turn, a piece of cheese close to the pink rubber bands on his braces. D.J. caught sight of her mother in the doorway of the living room. Tears began to well in the woman's eyes, the kind that formed deep pools of sorrow.

Only the very old were immune to this dramatic reaction. They glanced around, as confused as the girl. Her grandmother tried to smile reassuringly, as if her hearing aid had stopped working and D.J. had said something offensive she didn't pick up on.

D.J. wondered if some nightmarish thing stood behind her. *No one.* Pressed beneath dozens of unblinking eyes, she was squeezed by fear.

"What'd I do?"

Joe was the first to move. He rushed over to D.J. and yanked the picture frame off the shelf and held it against his leg. The man hesitated, as if he wasn't even going to address the matter with his daughter.

"Dad, who is that? Is that lady here today? The lady in the picture?"

"No, she's not here. It's Aunt Dorothy."

Joe stepped away to punctuate the end of the conversation. A few bodies exhaled around the room in response. Not normally a curious girl, D.J. couldn't let it go.

"But I don't have an Aunt Dorothy."

"You did. She's dead. Died not long after this was taken." Joe sighed. "That's who we named you after. She was the greatest architect in Ohio, so that's probably who you get your 'drawing thing' from." With effort, Joe forced the corners of his lips up. "Hey, Patti! Where you been? You should try my ribs and make me feel good about myself."

Everything went back to the moment before D.J. saw that photo. Faces were relaxed and sterilized and pleasant. There were conversations about Jessica's college and *where did that nice boy go? The one you were dating with the dimples whose father worked for Boeing?* A hum of politeness continued after the stink caused by D.J.'s faux pas. She could smell the shrimp aging on the counter. The fly stuck between the screen and window glass buzzed again.

D.J. wasn't buying it. *What just happened?*

She jerked her body around to find her mother. The woman was dabbing her eyes with a tissue while discussing the planting of bulbs in the church garden.

COBB WAS AS PERPLEXED AS HIS BEST FRIEND.

"Wait. So, none of them said anything?"

The two neighbors had spent the next afternoon Googling architects but found nothing on the mysterious Aunt Dorothy. They huddled on D.J.'s bottom bunk, speaking in small voices as a thunderstorm approached. Beneath them, the ground shook.

"Someone had to have brought that picture to the party. I know it," D.J. insisted, absentmindedly sketching. "They wanted to start trouble."

"Your sister's always the first place I go when there's trouble."

Cobb sympathized with his friend. No one noticed D.J. when Jessica was in the same room. She never had the same opportunities as her sister. Their parents found D.J. strange because she wore boyish clothes and used ridiculously big words and fantasized for hours about spaceships and science fiction movies. They considered their daughter unambitious, only because she never asked for anything but sketch pads.

Above D.J.'s desk and the scattering of origami ducks she made were drawings crowded on a corkboard. Some were grotesque while others were charming, depending on her mood. Her father called them "drawing things".

When her father would complain to her mother downstairs, he would say with thick sarcasm, "I'm glad D.J.'s really into those *drawing things*, but how the hell's the kid gonna make it in the real world? Artists are about as useful as philosophy majors."

"That's not nice, dear," Jane would murmur back. "I'm happy she's being creative. It beats her shooting or sniffing something. You know she gets upset when you talk like that."

"That's life. Last week, I saw a kid wrapped around a pole in his car. You think he'd give two craps about hurt feelings?"

As a paramedic, Joe loved comparing things he saw in the ambulance to anyone's grievances.

"You know what?" D.J. said to Cobb. "Maybe my aunt was an alien. An alien who tried to steal me once. Yeah. That explains why everyone freaked out."

D.J. smiled, imagining herself being led out her front door towards a spaceship covered in neon flashing rainbows. Around her would be neighbors whispering to themselves that they always knew D.J. Wallace wasn't average.

D.J. came back down to Earth when she saw Cobb's furrowed, freckled brow.

"Dad took the picture to the attic," D.J. added. "I don't think he knows I know. I heard his steps going up, and the picture was in his hand the whole time."

Cobb was energized. "Well, hell's bells. Let's see it."

Even on a sunny day, D.J. wouldn't go up the old attic steps for anything. Attics were for serial killers and vampires. However, she didn't want Cobb to think less of her. After making sure no one was around, D.J. led the way up the swinging wooden stairs and into a cobwebbed funhouse filled with moldy boxes and clothes hung in macabre shapes. A lone window across the foreshortened room gave them little light. It was getting so cloudy that the solar-powered street lamps lining the perfectly manicured lane were turning on.

Without talking about it, each kid stuck close to the other. It didn't take long to find what they were looking for.

Cobb pulled out a box holding the photo and a single bowling trophy. Nothing had changed. D.J. held her water gun while Aunt Dorothy showed off her muscles. Cobb studied the picture like an art dealer before shaking his head.

"Yeah, that's you all right. I don't know her, and I've met your whole family."

Thunder from the next county rattled the glass between the windowpane. D.J. kept her voice low as she pointed at the trophy.

"Why is this with it? We don't bowl."

"Your dad's?"

"He got hurt playing baseball. Now he can't lift heavy things."

"I wish this thing had a date or name on it."

"You know what?" An idea formed in D.J.'s head. "I'll bet it was Aunt Dorothy's trophy. Maybe there are other things up here that belong to her."

"D.J.!"

The boys sucked in their breath at the viciousness of Joe's tone.

In the heavenly light of the attic door, D.J.'s angry father stood imperious in front of his wife. D.J. wondered if he might strike them both. Jane had once told her husband during an argument, "You come in here loaded for bear!" D.J. finally understood what she meant.

There was no time for excuses or even a response. Jane took one look at the trophy in her daughter's hands and promptly fell onto the wood floor in a faint.

Later that night, D.J. sniffed back tears as she lay in bed. She could hear her parents arguing in the living room, but she didn't have the heart to eavesdrop. They were so angry that they banished Cobb for two weeks.

"Maybe I'll really show Dad and just become a poet," D.J. uttered to no one.

The storm worked itself out through the evening with bright zags of fireworks. D.J. wouldn't have been able to sleep either way; a paranoia was taking hold. Watching shadows on the wall mimic tree limbs, she felt someone in the room with her. She could feel the eyes on her face. In her head drifted a menagerie of potential threats.

It was almost two in the morning when the rain tapered off and she heard something else. A shovel was scraping their backyard. Without looking, she knew her father was burying the picture and trophy. Quickly, D.J. went under the covers and texted Cobb about the noise. It took awhile to get a reply:

<<Y bury them? Y doesn't he jus throw them away>>

It suddenly occurred to D.J. that even though her parents had complained about Freddie digging up the now decimated dirt yard over the years, she had never seen it happen with her own two eyes.

D.J. glanced at the calendar hanging by her desk. *What is going on? Did Aunt Dorothy try to hurt me once? Why does everyone know about Aunt Dorothy but me?*

After falling into a fitful sleep, D.J. dreamed in a loop. She was a little girl and she kept pulling on a woman's shorts to get her attention, but she couldn't see the woman's face. There was the smell of wet earth, buttered corn, and smoke.

By the time D.J.'s shovel hit something in the dirt, her pajama shirt was soaked in sweat and her pajama bottoms were dirty around her soiled feet.

There was a deep darkness to the night, and the youngest member of the Wallace family was obsessed with finding the picture of her aunt. All through the yard were new holes, but this exhausting task wasn't slowing the girl down. Youth was on her side. She was at an age where her joints were well-oiled springs and the loss of a night's sleep wasn't missed or noticed. Despite the recent rains covering her father's evidence, she was determined to succeed.

A week had passed since she and Cobb were caught in the attic and all week, her parents and sister had been avoiding her in the way you try to give a houseguest the hint that they should leave. D.J. would have run away if she didn't get the impression that her mother was on the verge of a breakdown. At night, the woman would peek at her daughter through the cracked bedroom door and whisper, "I love you. Please don't leave me. I love you so much." Even D.J's dad spoke calmly. They weren't mad at her. They were afraid of her.

D.J. stopped to catch her breath and admire the night's handiwork. Though she hadn't found what she was looking for, there had been many secrets hiding in the shadow of 1901 Cork Drive. She was mesmerized by her haul. Along with a Tiffany's baby rattle, there were now 53 empty mechanical pencils in her trash bag. D.J. inspected the tubes with interest. She didn't recognize them and couldn't figure out why someone would bother hiding such a useless item.

The moon allowed D.J. to make out only a few legible words on a waterlogged birth certificate for someone named Roberta. She put it down and gave her attention to the two carpal tunnel wristbands. *Why does anyone bury wrist bands?* After D.J. found the trophy from the attic, the urge to find the final prize spurred her to keep digging. Where was the photo? Taking a deep breath, D.J. trudged across the lawn to the only place she hadn't touched.

D.J. had once been told by a classmate that digging up a grave was illegal, but that wasn't all that stopped her. She had loved Freddie as much as she loved anyone. The sunken earth sat there, waiting. *There's no time like now.* D.J. whispered an apology before wielding the shovel blade. It cut sharply through the muck.

The smell burst into her face like a balloon emptying itself of hot roadkill. With stinging tears, she gagged until the tip of the shovel hit a soft object. Right on top of the putrefied fur was a turned-over picture frame, but D.J. knew exactly what it was. With grubby hands, she grabbed it, and, as an afterthought, tossed the dirt back onto Freddie. Like the rest of the backyard, D.J. left the grave the way he found it.

Holding the trash bag like a demented Saint Nick, D.J. tiptoed toward the back door. She placed the shovel back next to the garden hose. She closed the glass softly and then moved on socked feet across the kitchen. The girl was almost to her bedroom free and clear when she saw a shape waiting in the darkened hall.

It was Jessica in a worn-out pink nightgown, staring at her. The older girl's hair was ratted, her comely face a grotesque mask of hatred. *She must be angry I woke her up.* D.J. wasn't sure how to explain herself. Then she wondered if Jessica had been waiting for her all night.

D.J.'s brain processed the object in her sister's fist. It gleamed ever so slightly from the little moonlight creeping up the stairs; the sharp tip promised violence. Jessica's weapon was a hasty QVC purchase relegated to the highest shelf in the highest cupboard of the garage due to their mother's unfounded fear that they weren't old enough to use them. The knife block was almost impossible to reach without a ladder; D.J. knew the effort it took to grab one. Jessica had to stack two booster seats on the tool bench to get to those knives. *Man. She must really be motivated.* It almost made her laugh, the ridiculousness of the moment.

Jessica was gray with determination and fear. She was about to eliminate a problem that scared her.

"You're going to ruin everything," she hissed. "Do you realize that? Mom's going to lose her mind over you."

Her heart beating too fast, D.J.'s instinct was to scream, to cry, to run out into the streets and let everyone know that her sister wanted to kill her. *She stacked two booster seats and put them on top of the tool bench!*

"It's just a picture of me and Aunt Dorothy in a canoe. What's so bad about it?"

Jessica said nothing, as if she were calculating the risks of her future actions. D.J. glanced at the door on the right. Could she trust her parents to save her? Would they believe her over their favorite child? D.J. heard a rustling in their room, and she wasn't the only one. The heavy step of their father spooked Jessica into backing up into her bedroom. The last thing the young girl saw were her sister's amber eyes melting into the dark.

D.J. had never run into her room so quickly. Under normal circumstances, D.J. would have remained seated where she was, behind a locked bedroom door, until the sun rose. Instead, her anger grew more powerful by the minute. She blinked at the calendar, at the "drawing things" over the desk. *Who do these people think they are?*

After a quick text exchange with Cobb, D.J. left her bedroom. Holding a baseball bat in one hand, she peered around corners and crept down each step, trying not to make noise. Was Jessica waiting behind some ghastly corner? *Is she behind the door?*

D.J. counted the minutes as she waited in the black kitchen. She clawed the bat until she spotted a flaming head of red hair dart across the yard toward her house. After Cobb reached the back door, D.J. gently unlocked it, and the two kids went up to D.J.'s room as quietly as possible. To Cobb's credit, he said nothing about the baseball bat. D.J. flipped on her light and emptied out the trash bag of things she had found in the yard.

"How do we do this?"

"Let's put everything together," suggested Cobb. "They're all clues, right?"

The 53 mechanical pencil casings were lined up along D.J.'s bunk bed. The birth certificate and baby rattle were on the floor by the desk. Next to the closet were the trophy, wrist bands, and photo. D.J. stood and picked it up.

"What is it with this thing? Let's open it up. Maybe there's a secret note in here."

D.J. looked at all her treasures at once. Suddenly, without warning, her ears squealed like there was a high frequency before they popped. Holding the picture in her left hand, she wiggled a finger in her right ear. A long time ago, the family had an old box TV from Mom's college days, and when it turned on or off, it would make that ringing noise. She used to call it static.

Then D.J. collapsed.

"D.J.? Hey. What's wrong?"

The seizure took hold of D.J.'s body, but she was still aware of what was happening. She lay on her back, unable to speak, as Cobb stood over her with growing concern. D.J.'s spine gyrated; her hands reached to grip onto something. The girl's eyes rolled, turning her sockets a pure white. *I'm not allergic to anything. What's going on?* She felt every limb burn. Cobb cried out for Joe Wallace's help. The heavy man stomped into the room followed by Susan, who was wringing her fingers. D.J. could hear everyone speak above her.

"I don't know what happened. We were just-."

"Call 911."

D.J.'s mind went from black-and-white to technicolor. She panicked as her right eye failed and her left eye became a kaleido-scope. *Mom had a panic attack once. They put her on medicine.* D.J.'s hearing was limited to the left ear. It funneled her mother's agonizing screams until the twinkling began. Music notes danced in the left eye, but they were not music notes. They were black Art Deco scribbles tracing themselves over and over again. D.J. told someone that the room was the center of the universe.

"She's been acting weird lately."

A man's voice she didn't recognize said, "She needs oxygen. Look at her pupils."

An EMT. They got here fast.

❧

Dr. Moss and Olivia raced down hall after hall in the sterile, windowless brick building that resembled a hospital. A silence followed them just as there was a silence ahead. The doctor knew where they were going as they passed taupe walls empty of hanging art. There was no one around who could admire it, considering Dr. Moss and the young lady were the only humans in a building teeming with bodies.

"Most old models have this problem." Dr. Moss moved briskly as Olivia trotted behind him to keep up. He flipped through his notes on the tablet, giving his eyes an icy glow. "Here we have...Dorothy Jane Wallace. Heart attack at 31...one of our first patients. Huh, I know her. Not personally, of course; I was born a century after she was. This woman's Dorothy Wallace the architect. Ever hear of her?" Olivia shook her head no. "She designed the Glass Tower in Cincinnati. Bigwig. Had money."

Unsure of what she was about to see on her first day, Olivia's heart was staccato. She automatically regretted wearing heels.

A light no bigger than a coin flashed fire engine red, leading them to the problem unit placed up against a wall. Olivia thought she heard the slightest warning chirp coming from the depths of a squat plastic tower. Dr. Moss grabbed a swivel chair and swung it up to the computer. She had the feeling her new boss was trying to impress her with his urgency.

"Mother may I," the doctor cursed under his breath as his fingers flew over the keyboard. "Yeah. It's happening again. Trouble is, this is a dinosaur. Earliest model we have left, I think."

"I don't recognize it as anything I trained on. Is it a 1000X?"

"The *100X*. Yeah, I know. We can't just install a software update for a quick fix."

Dr. Moss gave the side of the computer a half-hearted smack. The screen was covered in stalled numbers and letters of light blending into one another. It resembled a screen door covered in lightning bug residue. After the doctor tapped a few keys, the digits jerked back to life.

Attached to the monitor was a mute observer to their conversation, a single brain floating in a glass box filled with a milky substance. The gelatinous mass was pink and still full of blood and life and memories. Part of the spinal cord was attached. Above the cube of liquid and brain was a shelf like most memory shelves, left by relatives who waited for their turn. In a framed photo, Dorothy Jane Wallace (or D.J. as she had been known in her youth) smiled in a canoe with her daughter, Roberta. Also, on the shelf were bowling trophies and small origami creations she had put together with her girl.

Nearby were her family members' brains in similar boxes of clouded semi-liquid, their cables and colored wires connected like an android's bird nest. Through all those process cards and all that copper, they re-lived their lives together forever. But as Joe once gruffly said to his daughter, "there is no such thing as never, and there's no such thing as forever."

Along the corridor were dozens of computers nestled next to their owners. Past that hall were fifteen floors filled with thousands of these partners in immortality. With a good, viable brain, no one had to really die anymore.

Olivia glanced around nervously. She didn't like being surrounded by so many people who couldn't speak. The silence was like an empty gymnasium. In college, professors told her she would get used to it.

"Is it a hack?" Olivia asked, her voice hushed.

"No. Some kind of glitch. Relics from her adulthood keep popping up in her childhood. Dorothy can't process it, so her family's been trying to help." Seeing Olivia's expression, Dr. Moss explained, "They're 2000X. They know where they are. Huh. A friend of mine who works at a lab in Tampa's having the same problems with some of his. Great. I guess I'll have to be the one to make the hard decision. I was having such a good night, too. I just got free tickets to a Knicks game, for Christ's sake."

Olivia watched Dr. Moss make a big show of getting up slowly. She was a bright girl. She knew he did this not because the task was grim but because he wanted her to think that he still had a certain level of empathy. Olivia remembered a chapter in *Cell Computerization: The Cerebellum and Beyond* that talked about detached cognition and how a scientist or doctor should look at the machines as comatose patients, not people. Observing Dr. Moss, she decided that she would not forget her emotional resonance.

~

D.J. FELT HERSELF LYING IN THE STEEL COLD ROOM OF A HOSPITAL. SHE couldn't see it, but she could smell the pine cleaner and alcohol wipes and faint laundry detergent on thin sheets. In her left ear, she almost heard requests for a nurse blare over an intercom. She felt her mother close by; the woman's suffering was a voice in puzzle pieces.

D.J. hadn't been in the hospital since she broke her finger in second grade. It happened after she fell in gym class, and for the rest of the year, her teacher called her *The Finger*. Back then, they gave the girl all the ice cream she wanted. D.J. remembered other things just then. She looked down as her strong arms held a baby. She stood by a coffin with Cobb's blown-up photo next to it on an easel. Someone talked about how Cobb was so young, that he was so close to graduating high school, that Cobb should have paid more attention while driving. Another jagged memory had D.J. laughing while playing poker with her parents in a cabin. They had never been to a cabin before. A little girl pulled on her shorts and asked if they could go swimming and called her *Mom*.

The drugs they're giving me must be pretty good. Wait 'till I tell Cobb about this. He won't believe it.

~

NO SOONER HAD DR. MOSS MADE DOROTHY JANE WALLACE DISAPPEAR (this time forever was a real thing) did the light above Jane Wallace's life monitor begin to blink red.

WASTED

RICHARD ALLEN

As the walls surrounding Jacob began to buckle against the unrelenting barrage of wind, he wept. First for his daughter Sophia, whom he feared he would never see again; images of her curly blonde hair flowing wildly as she ran through his shoddy excuse for a backyard flickered through his mind - a slideshow which served only to remind him of his failures. *She always deserved better than I could give.* Then he wept for his wife - the beautiful Maria - and the burden she would face with having to care for their daughter alone. He was ashamed that he hadn't been around enough to fix his relationship with her before his death. *For what? For this?* Finally, he wept for himself, for a life wasted in an unfulfilling job: an existence that had left him cold, lonely, and distanced from those he loved most. For years he had been telling himself, "I still have more time," in a vain attempt to justify his choices - but that was no longer true.

Tonight, he would have to atone for all those he had hurt, for all those who had suffered so that he could pacify his selfishness. This decrepit bar was all that stood in the way of the coming storm. What chance did he and a few past-their-prime alcoholics have?

Jacob worried about eternity and what it meant — if anything. Would it hurt when he died? Was there a God and a Devil, and if so, which one would invite his soul in? He hadn't been the best man in life, although he couldn't truly see himself as a bad man. Emotionally stunted? Yes. Callous and indifferent? Sure. But not evil.

He had spent most of his evenings boozing at local bars where the regulars all knew him by name. They were the family he kept in place of the family that he hid from. He would stumble home late to find his wife already asleep and his daughter snoring softly down the hall. He'd tiptoe into bed, making sure not to disturb Maria. His only goal was to sleep. Passion and intimacy had long ago been replaced with loneliness and denial. She knew that he didn't deserve her.

Yet she stayed.

Pictures adorned the walls of his shabby middle-class house. If you were to follow the photos, you'd witness the timeline of a failing marriage. A seemingly-perfect family dissolves as Jacob is gradually removed from the story; his daughter ages, and he begins to fade. No one could fault the belief that Maria was a single parent. Sophia, now a ten-year-old, believed her dad worked long hours, but that wasn't true - he just couldn't find the courage to face her any longer. In his mind, he had failed at his job to be the provider. Each day, he had distanced himself a bit further: a pointless attempt at masking the shame ever-present in his heart. He was selfish, and he knew this. He'd deceived himself into believing that what he was doing could be construed as love.

The howling wind grew stronger, rocking the walls as if someone frantically banging on the door. *Please sir, I just need shelter*, the wind called, but the drunks were not so easily fooled.

An antique mirror, perched haphazardly above a counter, edged forward on its nail with each creak of the wall, gathering courage. Jacob watched as it jumped - tired of this storm, or possibly just tired of its pointless existence. He identified with the sentiment. The resulting impact was magnificent, the shattered glass creating a symphony of light-- a fleeting moment of beauty during an otherwise deadly tempest.

Jacob felt as if he had been crouching behind the counter for a lifetime, although mere moments had passed since the hurricane had first unleashed its fury. Funny how time slowed as despair struck, allowing Jacob to remember every painful second - yet rushed through the good moments. *Life has a funny way of tormenting us.* Others were on the floor, cowering in fear with their hands barricading their heads – as if flesh and bone could stop the sheer strength of Mother Nature's wrath.

He had been warned; they all had.

The bar had been more important. "It won't hit us," they had muttered to each other between sips, deciding that a false sense of security was better than none. They had known that they were wrong, but sometimes even that isn't enough to break an addiction.

Jacob understood that his chances of survival were slim, dwindling with each passing second. The old bar would not be able to put up much of a fight. The storm was angry, hell-bent on destruction - a category four making a beeline towards the entrance. The walls rattled, unleashing a vibration that shook the patrons to their core as the roof began to loosen its grasp, rising and falling in quick jolts. A window near Jacob shattered; he watched as the sheer force of the wind dragged a table out the newly-opened hole. All that remained were scuff marks on the floor where the table had sat for so many years. *It'll all be over soon.* The thought was calming. Was that normal?

He pulled out his phone to text a goodbye, but to whom? He stared at the blank screen, shaking so violently in his trembling hands that he would have never been able to peck out the words, even if he had known what to say. Thunder cracked and the phone fell – shattered. *Just as well,* he thought. It would be better for his family if they believed that he had died suddenly, without fear, rather than knowing that he had waited for death in agony.

His mind drifted to the day he met his wife: beautiful in an elegant teal-colored dress, standing impatiently in line with her friends for a concert. Fifteen years felt like an eternity most days, but that night could have happened yesterday. He had given her a far-too-eager grin. *I was always too shy for my own good.* She was nice enough to award him a smile of acknowledgement in return before tucking her hands into the creases of her dress: possibly nervous, or maybe uncomfortable.

He tried to walk but stumbled – grasping a nearby lamp post for support. It took him an eternity to summon the courage to look at her again. He found her nearly doubled over laughing, her eyes now filled with a warm joy. Later came the thrill of the first phone call, the first touch, the first kiss, the first lost evenings of passion. He smiled sadly. Why he'd let that happiness fade was beyond him. Forty-five years of age was far too young to have given up on life as entirely as he had. Jacob knew that if he had made better choices since meeting Maria, he wouldn't be in this situation now.

Maria was gorgeous: a vibrant soul nestled amongst the blandness of life. Being in her presence was intoxicating to Jacob — until one day it wasn't. Maria's looks had not faded, nor her vibrancy - it was Jacob who had changed. He became defeated: a broken shell of a man. At first, Maria thought none of this. She loved Jacob with all her heart. Jacob's mind was his true enemy. But the years passed, and time led Maria to become a ghost of what she had been. Trapped in a loveless and passionless marriage, she would cry herself to sleep, waiting for the man who had charmed her all those years prior to return, knowing he would not come.

I always thought I'd have more time.

The roof gave up its fight, exposing the bar to an angry skyline. Rain pooled on the floor, steadily rising. Death approached gradually, marching to the sound of an angry howl – keeping rhythm with the creaking walls. Those trapped inside were silent, although Jacob wasn't sure if this was due to injury or acceptance.

We all chose this.

If he had been a religious man he would have prayed, but he thought it false to ask a God that he didn't believe in for help. He felt that even if there was a God, why would he listen? Jacob had done nothing in his life to earn any saving grace. *I can't ask for help from a situation I chose to put myself in.* Instead, he hugged his knees tightly against his chest and rested his back against the counter, waiting for the inevitable collapse of his rapidly decaying shelter.

He turned his thoughts toward his daughter, Sophia. He smiled as he remembered the day that Maria had announced her pregnancy;

they both felt so much excitement and overwhelming joy after trying to conceive for nearly four years. He recalled the nervous tears as he sped toward the hospital with Maria lying down in the back seat, the sweat on Maria's hand as they caught their first glimpse of their gorgeous baby girl, the love that had swelled inside him, and the determination to do right by his child. The years passed, and Sophia grew so quickly, adding inches daily. She was a carbon copy of her mother, beautiful from the start. But when Jacob looked at her, she only served to remind him of his failures.

Sophia loved her father and wanted nothing more than to be by his side — until one day she didn't. Instead of raising Sophia, Jacob had spent his time at various bars showing pictures of a family that he could not face to strangers, while pretending that his life was a shade of perfect that it had never — and would never — be. Sophia grew distant from him as the years passed, eventually greeting him more as a friend. The love and bond they had once shared was gone, with Sophia remembering none of it. The man that she had once been so proud to call "daddy" was now reduced to a mere passerby, a neighbor, an annoying acquaintance of her mother who stumbled in late at night and disrupted her sleep.

I always thought I'd have more time.

The water, now up to Jacob's knees, sloshed against the walls, dragging tables and chairs with equal fury. Lights flickered and sparks flew, leaving the patrons in the dark. Jacob stared out at the room, lit only by uneven flashes of lightning, and realized that within minutes he would be dead. Whether by spark, water, or debris — all equally undesirable — had yet to be seen. He held his breath, a shallow attempt to remain calm, and accepted his fate. Hands and teeth clenched, he allowed his tears to flow freely. They were a welcome relief from years of pent-up emotions. He became acutely aware that in his intoxicated state escape would be hampered by his inability to stand straight. Besides, where would he go? If these walls couldn't save him – how much better would he fare when exposed to nature's naked vengeance?

His thoughts turned toward his life; his excitement upon graduating high school and the mixture of nervousness and joy as he made his first steps into the "real world." The excitement he felt before he understood the weight of living. Then came college, and along with it a mixture of late nights, random trysts, and an insatiable determination to graduate. But college also brought Jacob's first few twinges of fear: fear of inadequacy, fear that he was a fraud, fear that'd he'd be found out at any moment. Yet he persisted. He recalled the afternoon that he received his degree — one that took five long years, unprecedented maturity, and every ounce of determination that he could muster — and what he once had hoped to be. He realized how far he had now strayed from that optimistic young man. *When did I lose my way?* His degree was in Computer Science, his first true love. He stifled a laugh as he remembered the countless minimum-wage jobs, pointless consulting gigs, and failed interviews he had trudged through before his big break came, before he was first able to tell his parents that he had "made it."

He laughed. *Made it? Sure.*

Jacob had loved his job and was proud of the applications that he had created — until one day he wasn't. The weight accumulated through years of sitting in a cubicle - both literally and figuratively - piled up. The meaningless work that he handled day to day, for software nobody seemed to still use, was unfulfilling. He was not respected, nor was he acknowledged. The few friends he'd had long ago moved on to other companies, crossing state lines in search of better lives. Still, Jacob stayed. His family was settled, or so he had convinced himself, and the money required to move never seemed to be within reach: what with a daughter already in school and a seemingly endless stream of vehicle repairs - or maybe his addiction was the real reason. He didn't want to accept the truth, so he never bothered to tackle the problem. Instead, he spent his evenings away from his family, hanging out with like-minded individuals. Those who understood his struggle. Those who understood what his wife couldn't possibly comprehend.

I always thought I'd have more time.

A wall partially gave way; a deafening cacophony of splintered wood and shattered glass echoed throughout the dilapidated building – dulled only by the water that greedily devoured the debris; an insatiable beast. *This is it.* There was nothing more he could do now. His wife would be better off. She'd remarry and forget about him, and rightly so. Certainly, his daughter would be happier – she deserved a true father figure. If he had a second chance, if he could go back in time, then maybe – just maybe - he could make up for his wrongs. But where would he even start? How do you fix something that has been broken for more years than it has worked? It didn't matter; *what if* scenarios were pointless now. He listened as the water hit the bar with the force of a thousand angry drunks, the wind howling as if death itself was declaring its presence.

Jacob closed his eyes and waited, focusing on the sound of his stuttered breathing. He felt for the first time as if he existed – how unfortunate that it took death to make him feel alive.

A lone engine's wail pierced the storm, announcing its arrival.

Magnificent light filled the room as the pent-up water flowed outside to clean the dirty streets. Paramedics barged in; bright yellow vests and shouts overtook the storm's screeching. Jacob stared blankly at the men, unable to move. *Is this how your mind accepts death? By deceiving you?*

The men gripped ropes latched onto unseen anchors as a boat outside blared instructions from a megaphone. Jacob could neither understand the instructions nor comprehend this change of events. He was lifted to his feet and dragged through the debris by an unknown entity. His legs refused to work; they had already accepted their fate and had retired from their job. Nevertheless, one paramedic pressed on, eventually dragging Jacob out to be placed amongst the living.

The rain calmed and the wind began to subside. The hurricane was already passing – tired of toying with this downtrodden town – heading off to find fresh targets.

Jacob sat in silence on the boat as it headed toward shallow water.

"You're lucky to be alive. Why would you ever go out in this weather?" asked the EMT, genuinely curious what would entice a man to risk his life, or possibly angry that someone would be selfish enough to risk his life for a drink. Jacob only mustered a slight shrug in response.

After a cursory inspection, Jacob was released to go home. His lack of sobriety was not a pressing concern amidst so much devastation, so he was left to his own devices. He stumbled through knee-deep water until he reached his car, somehow unfazed by the night's events, situated near the edge of the water line. Jacob used a shaky hand to push the key into the ignition. His mind was blank – *how do you react after facing certain death and escaping?*

Upon reaching his house, he stared at it with disappointment in his eyes, ashamed at what little he had. The storm's rage hadn't had the decency to reward him with an insurance payout – leaving only minor destruction and extensive yard work in its wake. He was overcome by another thought – his family. *Are they OK?* They hadn't even tried to contact him. *Do I mean that little?* This fact didn't surprise him. Still, that didn't dull the pain.

He opened the door with a mixture of adrenaline and shame. Step by clumsy step, he made his way to the bottom of the staircase, remaining silent. Maria heard him from an upstairs room anyway.

"Where have you been?" Her tone was mild, almost indifferent. She hadn't bothered to step around the stairwell corner to face him.

He had no answer. Besides, she already knew.

"Is everyone OK?" he asked, hoping to change the subject.

"Yes," she replied, before silence took over again.

That was all he needed to hear. Those three letters absolved him of any guilt he may have felt about his absence throughout the night. He studied the stairs; twenty steps were all that separated him from his wife and daughter, but it might as well have been an abyss. The storm may not have killed him, but Maria might. He turned instead to the hallway, sloppily working his way toward the kitchen. On top of a shelf hid a bottle of vodka; he drank as if it would save him – as if it held some magical fix for life's problems. Tears flowed freely as he slid to the floor.

The pictures adorning the walls were unfamiliar to him; they might as well have been portraits of a family he had never met. Maria hadn't bothered to come down and neither had Sophia, not that Jacob had expected any different. He fumbled for his keys as he drank, staring blankly at a picture of him smiling. *You're such a liar.* He stood up and walked to the adjoining nook where he was faced with two choices: the stairs leading to his family or the door leading to his freedom. *You can fix this. You were given a second chance.*

Clutching the vodka bottle in one hand, he opened the door and stumbled to his waiting car outside. Some bar was bound to still be open – *people need a drink after surviving a disaster, right?*

As his house disappeared behind a curve, he muttered, "I still have more time."

RACHEL ROSE, SEMITE

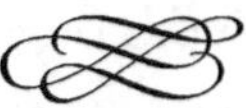

BECCA SPENCE DOBIAS

*R*achel Rose was not, like, technically Jewish. Sure, she'd talked her mom into making matzoh ball soup for the last ten Hanukkahs. Sure, she'd had a frayed Israeli flag fastened to her Jansport backpack with a safety pin since 8th grade. And sure, she felt a true affinity with Anne Frank-- the whole Holocaust thing made her feel, like, personally persecuted. People had thought of her as the Jewish girl for so long, since kindergarten, in fact, that sometimes she actually forgot she wasn't really part of the tribe.

It all started as a big misunderstanding. There they were in Mr. Hardlock's Early Bunch Kindergarten, and Rachel, brown curls bouncing around the miniature Christmas tree propped in the center of a wooden table, simply would not settle. Their teacher, a round, graying man, tried to corral the candy cane-happy five-year-olds into practicing for the upcoming holiday performance.

Finally, he managed to get most of them seated on the colorful circle rug, but Rachel was still standing, enamored with the reflection staring back at her from a sparkling silver ornament-- her own sticky, chipmunk-cheeked face. She stood on tiptoes and reached for a red bulb. Could she see herself in this one?

"Rachel, we're all meeting on the rug. *This moment.*" Mr. Hardlock emphasized the last words with as much seriousness as his jolly voice could muster. He was a man born to be a kindergarten teacher-- he enjoyed playing as much as his students did, his red cheeks and nose giving him an almost clown-like appearance.

"We're going to learn a new song for the performance today," he explained once Rachel had finally given up and trounced to the rug with an exaggerated pout. Still, she would not sit down.

"Rachel, please join your friends on your bottom."

Rachel leapt into the air, her blue cotton skirt flowing beautifully up around her waist, and landed with a hard thump on her tailbone.

"Yow!" she yelled, but still noticed, of course, the lovely way the fabric stayed behind, billowing around her like a cloud colored parachute.

"This new song is about a dreidel," Mr. Hardlock started. Rachel stared wistfully back to the tree. "Dreidel is a game played at Hanukkah. Does anyone here celebrate Hanukkah?" Rachel felt her legs lifting her. She couldn't help it. The bulbs must be magnetic, she thought. Magnetic? Was that the word? They must be magnets.

"Rachel," Mr. Hardlock said, in a slightly more irritated tone. She flopped back onto her bum. The teacher had asked a question, she was sure of it.

"Yes," she said.

Mr. Hardlock looked perplexed for a moment, before his face brightened with realization. "Oh, so you were listening! No wonder you're so fascinated by the tree, sweetheart. Would you like to tell us about it before we learn our song?"

"Tell about...?"

"About Hanukkah."

Rachel racked her brain. "It's really fun."

"I'm sure it is, dear. Now come sit by me, and you can help lead the new song."

Rachel liked this seat at the front, right by her teacher. She liked looking out at her classmates from a place of privilege. Something, she realized, had suddenly made her different. Something in her answer had made her special.

"I should have realized you were Jewish, Rachel," Mr. Hardlock said when they had sung the dreidel song four times through. "With that name and that hair. Of course!"

So that's it, Rachel thought. *I'm Jewish.*

Of course, she realized her mistake as she grew. By third grade, she understood that she was kind of lying. By then, though, she was too far in, and besides, who decided who was Jewish anyway?

Rachel read all the books on the subject that she could find at the school library. When, in seventh grade, her class learned about WWII, Rachel's teachers did their best to be respectful when she brought in her diorama— Anne Frank Barbie, in a tiny shoe box attic, complete with a miniature diary.

"Such creativity!" Ms. Hockney said, politely, wringing her plump hands.

In high school, Rachel started a Teens for Tolerance chapter. It was only natural, after all. In a town with one Jew, there was plenty of work to be done building bridges. She was surprised when, at the group's inaugural meeting, in addition to the smattering of punks and handful of hippies, into the room walked a boy with a yarmulke. She had never seen him before.

"Who are you?" Rachel asked, a little too aggressively.

"David?" the boy said. He was slender, shorter than Rachel, and had what she had to admit was a pretty beak-like nose. Under his yarmulke was a mess of tight, brown curls. Rachel disliked him immediately. She got the whole, like, having a look thing, but did this David kid have to try so hard?

"David Goldberg?" he said, when Rachel continued to stare.

"Oh GOD," Rachel said, and the boy seemed to shrink to an even more impossible size. *How dare he be such a caricature?* she thought. *It makes me feel anti-Semitic.* She pulled her own shoulders back and kept her gaze on David as he slipped into a seat.

"Thank you, everyone, for coming to my meeting," she said as the students settled into desks. "I am so grateful that you've decided to give your free period to such a good cause. It's hard being Jewish in such a homogenous community." Rachel tried not to look at David. "But it is wonderful to know there are allies."

She paused for a moment of bored applause. The door in the back of the classroom opened, and the school guidance counselor, Ms. Ryan, walked in. She took a seat in the back and smiled pleasantly at Rachel. Rachel beamed back at her and continued. "So I think we have two goals for this meeting. One, we want to talk about what tolerance means and how we can promote it here at Sunsen. Two, we want to establish some roles and guidelines." Ms. Ryan nodded in approval. "Naturally, I'll take on the role of president..."

The meeting ended and Rachel watched her classmates file out, as slow as snails. Ms. Ryan remained seated, waiting to be alone with Rachel, who watched with growing annoyance as David's kippah-topped head finally passed into the hallway.

"I wanted to speak with you about an opportunity, Rachel," Ms. Ryan said.

❧

"YOU SAID THIS IS A...JEWISH SCHOLARSHIP?" BRENDA ROSE ASKED.

"Yes." Rachel sat at the kitchen table and opened her math textbook.

"For Jewish students?"

"Yes," Rachel said, with an exasperated sigh.

"And...*you*...are applying?" Brenda assembled ingredients in a casserole dish and did not make eye contact with her daughter.

"Yes, Mom, Jesus." Rachel released an exaggerated sigh. "It's a full ride. I'll have to host a Seder for the school— "

"A what?"

Rachel rolled her eyes and continued scratching figures on her paper. "A Seder. For Passover. And the foundation will send a representative to attend, and as long as it all goes well, they'll pay my way— room, board, everything to any school I get into."

"Well, that would be wonderful, honey," Brenda said, scooping gobs of mayonnaise onto her creation before topping it with shredded cheese. "I know how much you'd love to go to NYU, I just don't know if..."

Rachel slammed her pencil onto the table, making Brenda jump. "Why can't you ever just, like, be supportive of me, Mom?" Rachel demanded, taking a quick peek at the back of her book. *I knew that was the answer,* she told herself. *I just wanted to be sure.*

"You know I support you, Rachel, I just..."

"Good." Rachel said, throwing her textbook and paper back into her backpack and slinging it over one shoulder. "I'll need you to make matzoh ball soup, but like, a lot. And also charoset and matzoh kugel. Maybe brisket. Can you make brisket?"

Brenda stared at her daughter.

"Thanks, Mom!" Rachel ran up to her room.

"WE'RE HERE WITH OUR 2020 BUILDING BRIDGES SCHOLARSHIP Winner, Rachel Rose. Sunsen, Ohio's Jewish population is just .08%, but our young ambassador wowed us with her essay. Rose has been educating her peers about Jewish culture and religious tolerance since kindergarten, and she founded the Teens for Tolerance chapter at her high school. Now she's bringing her efforts to the big tent, hosting a community-wide Seder focused on challenging white nationalist ideology. Rachel, you are so very brave. Can you tell our viewers more about your plans for the event this evening?"

Deborah Cohen held the phone camera up to Rachel's face. The left half of the woman's face smiled, while the right half remained perfectly still, and Rachel tried not to gawk at this strange tic. Deborah's navy blue suit dress highlighted her dandruff problem. Rachel coughed to cover her look of disgust.

"Of course, Deborah," Rachel said, looking directly into the camera. "This work is so important. Really, the scholarship is secondary in my mind. My passion, really, is spreading knowledge of our beautiful history. I thought, what better way to do that than with a tradition that honors freedom from oppression? The Passover story is still, like, totally relevant today."

Deborah nodded her head like a jackhammer and followed close behind as Rachel moved through the cafeteria's long tables, directing the members of Teens for Tolerance with the confidence of a seasoned event planner.

"Kylie, I need one Haggadah per section, not per table. We're expecting a full house." A girl with thick eyeliner hurried away with her stack of books.

"Mario, we can't sleep on the grape juice any longer. It's go time." A boy with stringy dreadlocks rolled his eyes at her from under his hooded lids and continued pouring the beverage from its flat bottle. It foamed in the disposable plastic wine glasses, splashing occasionally to leave purple splotches on the specially chosen extra-plush paper napkins.

"Watch it!" Rachel screeched, then caught herself and smiled back at Deborah. *Splurging on extra-plush was worth it,* Rachel thought. *Even if they did take us right to the edge of the Tolerance Club's budget.*

She greeted the guests as they arrived— families and friends of Tolerance Club members, and, as she smugly pointed out to Deborah, Sunsen's chief city council member.

"I'm so excited to do something positive for my community and our culture," Rachel said.

"You're big on the mitzvahs, then," Deborah said.

"Oh, definitely. Mitzvahs are like, my thing," Rachel gushed. "I always tell my mom that like, the second I turn 18, I'm getting a tattoo, and it's going to say 'mitzvah.'"

Deborah lifted a muscle near her nose as if she smelled something bad. Rachel looked around—there was the usual ranch and sock smell in the air, but had this lady never been to a high school cafeteria?

She felt a sharp tug on her sleeve, turned toward it, and was bewildered for a moment, seeing only air and the cafeteria beyond. She followed the arm attached to her shoulder downward and saw David attached to it--the Tolerance Club's newest, very Semitic, member. He was even shorter close up, and this weakness, this inability to grow to even a semi-reasonable height, made Rachel like him even less.

"I need to talk to you for a minute," he whispered.

If it weren't for Deborah's raised eyebrow, Rachel might actually have shoved him away from her.

They stepped a few feet away, and David's lip trembled.

"I, um. I heard your interview," he said.

"And?" Rachel asked.

"Jews don't get tattoos," he said. "It's like a rule." His voice was surprisingly deep, Rachel noticed, when he wasn't terrified.

She turned back to Deborah and smiled. "Sorry about that. Event planning." She laughed. "I meant earlier, if Jews got tattoos. Like, wouldn't it be kind of funny and ironic to see one that said 'mitzvah'? I'm big on the Jewish humor."

Deborah smiled her half smile.

When the hesitant, hungry crowd settled, squeezing purses awkwardly between their legs on the low bench seats, suit jackets and spring cardigans still on for lack of place to put them, Rachel moved to the end of the table.

"Shalom," she said serenely, and dentists, soccer moms, and restaurateurs shifted in their seats. "Welcome to Sunsen's very first community Seder." She paused for polite applause and raised the Haggadah she was holding to her face.

Rachel, of course, did not speak Hebrew, and so had spent the days before painstakingly writing the Cliff's Notes version of the Passover story in the margins of the prayer book.

As she opened the ceremony, David Goldberg appeared at her side. He coughed.

"Yes?" Rachel asked, fighting the urge to knock the yarmulke from his head.

He stood on tiptoes and whispered in her ear. "You're holding it..." He covered his mouth and coughed again. "You're holding the Haggadah backwards."

"I am n..." Rachel hissed back at him, and then stopped herself. "Excuse me, everybody. Just a moment. I'm so sorry."

Rachel led David a few feet away and turned her back to the crowd.

David tried again. "Hebrew is read left to right," he whispered. "And Hebrew books start at what we would think of at the back."

Rachel's face reddened. "Obviously," she said, unable to help mocking his nasally voice, a hand on her hip, leaning on one leg to emphasize their height difference further. Even slouching like this, she towered over him. She straightened and returned to her spot at the end of the tables.

She held the book before her, correctly now, and realized she had no idea what she was going to say.

"Actually, everyone. Our Tolerance Club member, David Goldberg, will be leading our ceremony tonight. David is a good friend of mine, and I've really taken him under my wing as he's explored his faith."

A man and woman turned to give each other confused looks, and Rachel saw the yarmulke on the back of the man's head. She walked past them, avoiding their bewildered gaze as she took a seat beside her mother. David stood and moved toward the front, wincing as he passed Rachel, as if worried she might hit him.

Rachel did her best to insert herself back into the spotlight where she could. As David quietly stuttered his way through the plagues, Rachel walked from guest to guest, moving their arms like toddlers to help them dip their pinkies in their juice and flick drops on their plates.

During "Deyenu," she stood and belted the words, stomping her feet and finally throwing her hands in the air.

At last, David lifted his fourth cup of juice up to reflect the fluorescent cafeteria lights, and said the blessing, first in Hebrew, and then in English. "Dear God, Creator of the Universe. We thank you for the fruit of the vine."

Rachel threw her head back and downed her juice in one swig, then stood. "Let's eat, everyone!" she announced, taking David by the shoulders and moving him aside.

"Mom! Brisket please. It's time to nosh." She beamed at Deborah, who lifted half of her mouth and began recording again. Brenda rose, then disappeared into the kitchen.

"Mom!" Rachel called a moment later, through gritted teeth. "Where is the brisket?"

Brenda Rose emerged from the kitchen,, aluminum baking pan with glistening brisket in her mitted hands. Though her words were directed at her daughter, she squared her face and shoulders toward Deborah's camera, her response sounding like a middle schooler in a production of *Oklahoma*.

"I have prepared the Jewish brisket, my Rachela," she said, smiling through clenched teeth. "I have glazed it with honey to symbolize the sweetness of freedom."

Rachel was happy her mother remembered her lines, but could the woman at least *attempt* some finesse?

Brenda beamed at her daughter then, and reached out for her hand. "And I know how important this is to my daughter, so I threw in a little bit of a surprise." She was off-book now, and Rachel looked at her with panic. "Roasted sweet potatoes topped with balsamic onions, pecans, and a locally sourced goat cheese."

Deborah's half smile dropped, and she lowered her camera. Orange tubers cuddled cozily up to the gleaming meat. White crumbles of cheese rested everywhere like fluffy dairy clouds. One particularly large clump sat right up against the beef, leaving a smear of creamy schmutz on its side. Rachel didn't need David this time. "Mom! What the..." She looked back at Deborah and smiled, then lowered her voice to a growl. "What the hell are you thinking? Get that out of here, please. This is a kosher event!"

Brenda's eyes grew wide with fear and then regret. "I'm sorry. I didn't..." Rachel's eyes shot fire. Brenda backed up a few steps slowly, then turned and ran back to the kitchen.

"I'm sorry about that," Rachel said, smiling widely, brushing the hair from her forehead, and turning back to Deborah, who furrowed her brow. "So as I was saying, we're actually holding a vegetarian Seder. It may seem sparser than usual, but it's because we want to remember all the Jews in the world who are still living with the shackles of oppression and tyranny."

That's good, she thought.

"We're having a vegetarian Seder, people," she said more loudly, to the crowd. "We want to remember all the Jews in the world still living with oppression and tyranny."

～

"Rachel, I have to ask, honey," Deborah said, as people shuffled out. "Did you convert on your own? Or is it your father who's Jewish? Because your mother..."

"I, um." Her first instinct was to answer that it was her father, but she realized quickly that converting on her own would sound much more impressive.

The city council member stopped to shake Rachel's hand. "Congratulations on your scholarship, Rachel. And thank you for bringing your diverse voice to Sunsen." His stomach grumbled audibly. Rachel beamed and thanked him, then turned back to Deborah.

"I converted. All on my own."

"Which synagogue did you attend? That must have been quite a feat here. Your parents must be supportive, at least."

Rachel saw now that she was digging herself into a hole.

"So I actually did it, like, *all* all on my own." Deborah's face fell. "Like an online kind of thing," she added.

"So you didn't...officially convert?" Deborah asked.

"Not like, officially, officially, but I mean I *am*, like, Jewish."

"But neither of your parents are Jewish and you didn't convert to the religion?"

"You said yourself, Deborah, what a feat that would be here. Really, if anyone should be asking questions here, it's me. I'm literally the only Jew in this town, and now I'm being, like, persecuted about it."

David tapped her on the shoulder. "Not now, David!" Rachel shrieked, and he scurried away.

"So you intend to convert then, when you go to college? I know you said on your application that you have your eye on NYU."

"Oh, absolutely," Rachel said, sighing in relief. "That is, like, the number one thing on my list to do. As *soon* as I get to, like, a real city."

"So you believe in Jewish theology, then?" Deborah asked.

God, this woman is relentless, Rachel thought, but then realized the prying shrew had given her another opportunity to show off her knowledge of Judaism.

"I really don't like to think of myself as someone who *believes* anything, per se. We Jews are a questioning people." She winked at Deborah. "I really value that about our culture."

Deborah stared back at her. Her mouth moved between half smile and half frown.

"So neither of your parents are Jewish, you haven't converted, and you don't believe in the core beliefs of Judaism?" she asked again.

When she put it that way, she made Rachel sound like some kind of liar. Her face grew hot. "But I said I'm *going* to convert," she huffed.

"I see."

~

RACHEL ROSE WALKED ALONE AROUND THE PERIMETER OF THE GREATER Ohio Technical College quad.

God, why are these people so excited to be here? she wondered. *It's not like this place even needs an orientation fair.*

She rolled her eyes at two guys in suits at a "GOTC Future Business Owners Club" table and hurried past the "Free Bagels" sign at the Hillel booth.

I hope David Goldberg eats so many bagels in New York that he gets sick, she thought.

"Wear a hijab for a day!" a woman called to her from a table nearby. Rachel was already lifting her hand in preparation to flip the bird when the poster board before her caught her eye.

In block letters, outlined in glitter glue, it read, "Have you ever been judged unfairly?"

Yes, Rachel thought. *I have been judged unfairly.* She took a step closer. "What's this about?" she asked, and the woman smiled up at her kindly from under her own blue headscarf.

"It's just a chance to see what it's like to be Muslim for a day. We're persecuted and profiled everywhere we go, so we're hoping to spread awareness and empathy. I guess you could say it's kind of a dare." She selected a neatly folded purple hijab and held it out to Rachel. "Do you want me to help you put it on?" she asked.

After, the woman handed Rachel a flyer listing the Muslim Student Association's meeting times and Rachel strode away from the table, surveying her new campus.

I am *profiled,* she thought. *I was* exiled.

As they passed each other on the wide sidewalk, a student in a Cleveland Indians baseball cap turned his head to stare. Rachel glared back at him, thinking, *I dare you.* The boy looked away, nearly tripping over a crack in the sidewalk as he went. She got similar looks from each student she passed, and each time, she held her chin a bit higher.

Rachel passed a wrought-iron trash can and let the flyer she'd been clutching float into its void. *As if I would spend my time at a meeting in some dorm basement that smelled like mildewed laundry,* she thought. The building where she was headed for her Business 101 seminar was just up ahead, and she continued toward it, pulling the hijab closer around her chin, enjoying the feel of its silky fabric against her cheeks.

PICTURE PERFECT

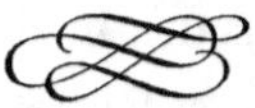

DEBORAH MUNRO

They called it Big Sky Country, and Maggie understood why. The horizon went on forever here in Helena, carrying her weary soul to distant, carefree places. In the eighteen hundreds, it had been a roaring gold rush town, but now it had settled into something more sleepy . Cattle outnumbered people twenty-five to one, isolating the state's capital from its nearest neighbor, Missoula, over a hundred miles away.

The church bell rang, and Maggie hurried to enter, locking her car with a *peep* as she walked toward the quaint Victorian steepled building with its large circular stained glass window. She wasn't particularly religious, but when she had moved here from Missoula last year, it had been a welcoming haven. Now she was a regular, coming every Sunday. The minister's wife, dressed in a blue that matched the expansive skies, smiled as she stepped in.

"Well, hello. Where are your girls today?"

"Hi, Susan. They're with their father for the final month of summer." Maggie couldn't help but frown, and Susan saw the mood change immediately, her kind eyes turning sympathetic.

"So his petition to get more visitation was successful, I see. How

"

are you coping?" Susan walked in with Maggie, finding them a seat on the outer aisle where they could continue to speak.

"I'm...okay. They'll have regular visits from the social worker, and Brandon has been drug-free for six months now. This is really important to him and the girls, so I'm going to spend the next month doing things for me. I may even get a manicure!" Maggie forced a smile, but Susan patted her hand knowingly. Both women turned toward the front of the church, where Susan's husband John stepped up. He was wearing a dark navy suit, his sideburns were silver, and he looked dashing with his hair combed straight back. Susan's face glowed, and Maggie had to look away, ashamed of how jealous she felt.

Maggie and Susan stepped sideways into a vacant spot and settled in as John returned to the front of the congregation. In the pew in front of her, a man turned slightly and looked at her with deep cobalt eyes. Where had this stranger been hiding in this small town? He was gorgeous, the kind of good looking that made her nervous. She tucked a dark curl behind her ear, but it sprang loose, even after the second attempt. Flustered, she glanced again at the man and he smiled, making her breath catch as she quickly pulled out her hymn book and resolutely stared at its cover. She heard him chuckle and shift his focus back to the minister.

Whatever John had said in his sermon, Maggie couldn't recall. Susan got up at some point during the service and assisted with the collection basket, then sat down near the exit to wish people a good day as they left. Maggie rose to make her way out, following the broad-shouldered stranger.

"Francis!" John called, coming up to the man from the side. "Thank you for coming today. I didn't expect you to be here." They stopped in front of Susan.

"What a pleasure to see you here. I hope you enjoyed the service?" she said. Maggie was trapped from exiting, so she stopped and listened. "Oh, how rude of me! Have you met Maggie Reynolds? She's been coming for over a year now."

"Frank Jenkins," the man said with his disarming smile, extending his hand. "Only my mother calls me Francis." He laughed, engulfing

Maggie's small hand as he shook it. His blue eyes twinkled with merriment as he stared at the rogue curl.

"Frank here has rented our ADU," John said. At Maggie's confused look, he explained, "Accessory Dwelling Unit, or mother-in-law flat, if you prefer." Racking her brain, Maggie recalled the dilapidated building in Susan's backyard and nodded slowly.

"That's…nice. So, you're new here?"

"Yes, and don't worry, I'll be fine. I plan to fix it up in exchange for reduced rent. I'm an engineer, and it will be refreshing to do some manual labor for a change." Frank laughed again and clapped John on the shoulder.

"Maggie here is an architect. Maybe she'll be able to give you some suggestions," Susan said with a wink at Maggie, making her blush.

"Where are you working?" Maggie asked, trying to change the subject.

"John got me a job with Templeton Engineering. I just started this week, but it's a good place so far. How about you?"

"The library, for now. Actually, I really should run along and make dinner." She scooted around the group, embarrassed by her humble job. She really needed to find something more suitable.

"Your girls aren't home, so you should join us for dinner, have a chance to relax and let someone else take care of you for a change," Susan said. John nodded enthusiastically and Frank looked pleased. With a wobbly smile, Maggie hesitated.

"Okay, that would be nice."

Maggie couldn't remember the last time she'd laughed so hard. Frank was a comedic genius, and his self-deprecating way of talking about engineering was hilarious. After dinner, he showed her his shack of a dwelling, soliciting her advice on every detail. His vision for the place was impressive, and she got swept up in his enthusiasm.

"What do you think about breaking out this wall and putting in an arched opening?" he asked, sweeping his hand through the air where a wall separated the living room from the kitchen and dinette area.

"You'd have to do a gravity flow analysis on that, as it will concentrate the load of the roof beam over just two points. Also, I think a rectangular opening with two pillars might be more fitting with the design of the house." Maggie looked up to see him staring at her.

"God, you're beautiful, and smart, too. What are you doing working as a librarian in this podunk town?" Maggie's heart crashed into her ribs. No man had ever looked at her with that kind of passionate intensity. Not even her ex.

"I taught at the University of Montana in Missoula until a year ago. I only took the teaching job because I couldn't find work designing after we moved to Missoula. It's such a small town, it makes Helena look massive. When my marriage ended, I needed to get farther away. Brandon had a serious drug addiction, and it cost us everything." Maggie paused, remembering how devastated she had been when her world collapsed. "But he's pulled his act together, and the girls love him. Two hours was enough to give us all some space."

"But not too far to deprive your daughters of their father. That's a noble thing to do, Maggie, considering his behavior. I don't know if I'd have been as understanding. I admire you for it." Frank moved close and pulled on her rebellious curl, smiling again as he tucked it behind her ear. His hand lingered against her neck, then he moved away, allowing her to breathe again. "I think the plumbing is going to be the biggest job, don't you?"

Frank opened the cabinet under the sink, revealing a mishmash of piping intermixed with electrical for the garbage disposal. Maggie could barely concentrate, her neck tingling from where he had touched her. Words failing her, she simply nodded and walked to the next room.

~

THE MONTH FLEW BY, AND FRANK AND MAGGIE BECAME INSEPARABLE. They laughed, danced, explored, and made love under the brilliant blue sky, away from everyone and everything. Refurbishing the ADU became their primary weekend activity, often followed by dinner with John and Susan, nights filled with joy that Maggie treasured. It helped ease the ache of missing her daughters even though they called to check in every week.

Finally, the day came where Anna and Holly were supposed to come home. Maggie waited impatiently by the kitchen window until Brandon pulled up in his dusty pickup, and Anna and Holly spilled out the door, running to her with squeals of joy as she scooped them into her arms, unable to rise. Now twelve and ten respectively, they were almost Maggie's height, and she suppressed a sigh at how fast they were growing. Anna was now an awkward age, somewhere between little girl who still climbed trees and snarky teenager whose moods pivoted at a moment's notice. She was the spitting image of Maggie, a pint-size version, all black ringlet curls and hazel green eyes set in a heart-shaped face. Holly looked like her father, with wavy ginger blonde hair and eyes the color of amber. Holly blessedly still believed her mother had an answer for everything.

Brandon climbed out and walked over, his swagger still something she admired after all these years. He was a full-time contractor, and they'd met in San Francisco at a job site. She was fresh out of school, and he was all man with his sun bleached hair, muscled biceps, and soft drawl, calling her ma'am in a way that made her girlish heart flutter. It took no time at all for her to fall in love with him. But that had been before.

"Hey, Maggie. You're looking good." Brandon tipped his cowboy hat at her, then leaned forward to be at eye level with their daughters. "All right, you two. I've got to leave you now, but we'll talk soon, okay?" The girls gathered into his strong arms and hugged him fiercely.

"Bye, Daddy! We love you!" Both girls began to cry, and Brandon patted them both on the back, rising to his feet.

"Remember what we talked about, okay?" Stealing one more look at Maggie, Brandon strode quickly back to the truck, driving away with a wave out the window.

"What were you talking about with Daddy?" Maggie asked, picking up Holly's duffel bag where she'd dropped it.

"Nothing," Anna replied. "Come on, Holly. Let's get unpacked." Anna marched them into the house, depositing her duffel bag on the clothes washer as she passed.

"Excuse me, missy. Watch your tone," Maggie said. Anna had always been bossy, but her attitude since their move to Helena was wearying.

Anna gave an exaggerated eye roll and sigh, then mumbled "whatever" and kept walking. Maggie suppressed her own sigh. Apparently a month with her old friends had not improved Anna's mood. The teen years were going to take patience. Maggie unzipped Holly's duffel and sighed. Everything was filthy, as if not a single washing day had occurred all month.

Later, sitting at dinner with two freshly scrubbed girls in clean outfits, Holly chattered on excitedly about their adventures with their dad, making Maggie smile, while Anna looked at them both with disdain.

"Mom, we need to go clothes shopping tomorrow. School starts on Monday, and I have nothing to wear," Anna said, interrupting one of Holly's stories.

"Sure, okay. Have you outgrown everything? You seem taller." Maggie smiled, hoping to ease the chill in the room, but Anna just rolled her eyes.

"Nooo," she said, making the word into three syllables. "You just don't understand." She rose, preparing to leave the table, then froze. Frank stood in the doorway.

"Hi, you must be Anna. I'm Frank, a friend of your mother's." Frank walked in and shook Anna's hand. Maggie held her breath, wondering both what Frank was doing here tonight and how her eldest would react. To her surprise, Anna smiled back.

"Yes, it's a pleasure," she said with her best manners and gestured to her sister. "This is Holly."

"Hi, Frank," Holly said. "Did you hear I went horseback riding into the mountains?" Anna sat back down at the table and began contributing details to Holly's stories, and soon they were all laughing about the girls' adventures.

~

SCHOOL BEGAN, AND FRANK BECAME A PART OF THEIR DAILY ROUTINE. He came by after work, helped make dinner, and convinced the girls it was fun to help clean up, especially because he would join in, making soap bubbles float around the kitchen. On weekends, Maggie would bring the girls to his ADU, and they'd pitch in with the renovation efforts—painting, hauling out old tile to the dumpster, or bringing Frank glasses of cold lemonade. It warmed Maggie's heart to see everyone smiling and happy.

Frank was a great influence on the girls, especially Anna, who adored him. She seemed comfortable consulting with him about things, and even though Maggie felt a little jealous that Anna did not feel the same way about her mother, she was glad Anna had a positive male influence in her life. He helped with her math homework, too, which was well advanced for Anna's age. This gave Maggie more time to spend with Holly, who had previously been somewhat neglected because of Maggie's constant work with Anna on her adjustment to life in Helena.

A few months passed, and the ADU was nearing completion. It looked like a gingerbread cottage nestled in a garden. Frank worked on it most nights, putting in countless hours after spending time with Maggie and the girls. Sometimes Maggie would slip out after the girls were asleep to spend some time in the circle of Frank's arms, a place she felt warm and safe.

~

THE CALL FROM SUSAN CAME LATE ON A FRIDAY NIGHT. "OH MAGGIE, Frank tried to fix the garbage disposal, but the pipe broke, and he was electrocuted. It's bad. There was water all over the floor, and the electrical wiring in the walls is fried."

"Is he okay?" Maggie could barely breathe past the constriction in her throat.

"I don't know. I just don't know," Susan said, crying into the phone. "The ambulance took him away before he regained consciousness, but he's alive."

Maggie rushed to the hospital and found Frank propped up in bed, an IV in his arm. Dark circles under his eyes notwithstanding, he looked okay, and Maggie cried with relief, gathering him into her arms. He shushed her and stroked her back.

"I'm fine, Mags. It takes more than a little voltage to keep me down." He lifted her chin with his free hand and kissed her deeply. "It's going to be okay. I'll find another place to live until the damage can be repaired. John has it in his head to replace all the wiring, too, but I'm sure it only needs a bit of work."

"You can move in with us." The words were out before Maggie even realized she'd said them, but they felt right, and she smiled. It was unlike her to be impulsive, but Frank was a treasure.

"Are you sure?" Frank asked, but by his eyes, she knew that was what he wanted, too.

"Yes, absolutely sure," she said and kissed him again.

HOLLY HELD OUT THE CORDLESS PHONE AND LOOKED AT MAGGIE WITH big eyes. "Daddy wants to talk to you." Maggie wiped her hands and approached, holding the phone to her ear with trepidation. Susan and John had disapproved of Frank moving in, telling Maggie to take more time to think it over first. Then people at work and parents of the girls' friends had made comments, asking Maggie if she was sure of her decision, if it was the right move for a single mother of two girls. Maggie understood their concerns, but they didn't know Frank like she did. They didn't know how much the girls valued him being around every night. She wanted to tell them all to mind their own business, but it was a small, conservative town. People didn't cohabitate here.

"Hello, Brandon," she said.

"What the hell, Maggie! You barely know the guy. How can you expose our daughters to a complete stranger like that? For all you know, he could be an axe murderer!"

Maggie cupped her hand around the mouthpiece and ran into the other room for privacy. "After what you did to us? You really dare to question my choices?" Maggie was breathing hard, and Brandon was silent.

"You know I'm sorry and have done everything in my power to make up for what I've done."

"You mortgaged our house and spent our retirement on heroin. I lost my job because of that stunt you pulled on campus!" In a rare moment of self-pity, Maggie began to cry. Brandon had destroyed her life, but he was a good father, and a part of her still cared about his opinion.

"I can't take it back, but feel free to keep beating me up about it. I deserve you despising me, but what you're doing now isn't right, and I won't stand by and let you hurt our girls."

"I'm not hurting them! Frank's a good guy. You'd probably even like him." Maggie felt the pleading in her voice.

"I filed for joint custody today, and I'm moving to Helena to be closer. I arrive in two weeks." Brandon hung up, and Maggie screamed into the dead line. Looking up, she saw Anna and Holly staring at her. Holly looked afraid. She never liked it when her parents argued. Anna had tears in her eyes but tried to smile. Maggie approached them and hugged them both to her chest.

"I'm okay," she said, feeling anything but okay inside. "Daddy is upset about Frank being here, but he'll like him when he moves here. The good news is your father is moving to Helena, so you'll get to see him all the time soon." Rising, she walked outside to sit on the porch.

A few minutes later, soft footsteps followed her, and two barefoot girls sat on either side, wrapping their arms about her.

"It's okay, Mom," Anna said. "We both like Frank and wanted him to move in." Maggie cried and nodded. "We're also happy Daddy's moving closer. We miss him." Maggie buried her head in Anna's shoulder and cried more.

"Thank you," she said.

❧

"Brandon."

"Frank."

The men acknowledged each other with a nod, and the girls came barreling out of the house with their duffels slung over their shoulders. "Bye, Mom!" they yelled as they pelted for their father's truck. The court had awarded Brandon Friday to Sunday every other week. His steady employment and drug-free record for the past year, coupled with Maggie's choice to bring Frank into the family home, had definitely swayed things in Brandon's favor. Maggie waved and hugged herself, feeling cold in the crisp autumn air.

"Hey! What about me?" Frank called out from behind her. "Don't I get a goodbye?" The truck doors were already shut, and Brandon had started the engine. No one looked back as they drove away.

"I don't think they heard you," Maggie said. "I'm sure they would have said goodbye if they'd seen you come out."

"Ungrateful, that's what they are," Frank said, slinging the dish towel over his shoulder and stomping back into the house. He'd been upset ever since Brandon's return, and she couldn't blame him. She was having a hard time adjusting, too. Maggie followed Frank inside and joined him in the kitchen. He'd finished drying all the dishes, and now he was putting them back in the cupboard. She encircled her arms around his waist and hugged him.

"Want to have a glass of wine while we watch a movie or something?" Maggie said into his back, liking the warm strength of him. He turned and smiled down at her, his arms clasped around her.

"I have a better idea. Let's get married."

Maggie's smile froze on her face as she searched his eyes. "What?"

"Come on, Mags, why not? We love each other, we're perfect

together, and we could be a family. Maybe we could even add to it, huh?" Frank waggled his eyebrows up and down suggestively.

"I...this is really sudden. I need more time to think." Maggie tried to wriggle free to create some distance, but he didn't let her loose. He just kept smiling and snuggled her closer.

"Reach in my pocket, the one on the left."

Maggie dug into the pocket of his jeans and pulled out a ring, an enormous diamond set in a cluster of smaller sapphires.

"Oh, wow!" she gasped. Frank let go of her and got to one knee, his gorgeous blue eyes peering up into hers.

"Say you'll marry me, Maggie Reynolds. Not today, not until you're ready, but someday soon. I love you and the girls, and I want us to be a family. I've always wanted a family of my own. Let's make a big one!" He took the ring from her numb fingers and gently placed it over the first knuckle on her ring finger, his teary eyes returning to her face. "Will you?"

"Yes, I'll marry you," she said, a warm rush of love, excitement, and fear flooding her senses as he slipped the ring the rest of the way on and kissed it, then kissed her, both his hands cupping her face.

"You've made me the happiest man alive. Don't ever take my ring off. I want everyone to know how much you mean to me. Promise?" He swooped her off the floor in a huge twirling hug, making her squeal, then began carting her to the bedroom. "I can't hear you," he laughed, tickling her thighs.

"Okay, okay. I promise!"

Frank and Anna stood at the kitchen counter washing dishes together. Maggie sat at the table with Holly in her lap, admiring the domestic scene. Holly continued coloring her tessellated butterfly. It had been Anna's birthday, but Frank insisted Holly needed a small gift to not feel left out. He was always thinking of things like that. Maggie kissed Holly's hair.

At the sink, Frank playfully side-bumped Anna and she laughed, flicking her dish towel at him before squealing and jumping away when he dipped his hand in the sudsy water. Then he leaned over and whispered something in her ear that made her eyes go wide. She glanced back at Maggie in surprise, then grinned and went back to drying. Maggie wondered what mischief they were up to this time.

Frank finished the last of the washing and sauntered into the dining area, kissing Maggie on the head as he went to his desk in the corner. He flipped open his laptop and began to work on a design for work.

Anna ran upstairs and Holly followed her, yelling to slow down so she could show her the picture she had colored. Maggie heard them squabbling, but then Anna relented and let Holly into her room.

"What did you say to Anna?" Maggie asked.

"Hmm?" Frank was absorbed in his CAD work, some kind of heating unit for a commercial building.

"To Anna. What was that about in the kitchen?"

"Oh, they're having a take your child to work day soon. I invited Anna to come. She'd make such a great engineer with that technical mind of hers. Is that okay? I should have asked you first."

"Of course it's okay. She'll be thrilled." Maggie hugged Frank from behind, but he patted her hand to ask her to back away.

"I won't go and you can't make me!" Anna screamed, her fists clenched white at her sides.

"It's your father's weekend, Anna. He has a legal right to see you, and I can't do anything about that." Maggie felt a migraine coming on. This was the third time in a row Anna had refused to go to Brandon's place. The previous two times, Maggie had talked her into going for the sake of her sister.

"Why don't you want to go, Anna?" Frank asked, entering the living room to stand next to Maggie. He was still in his pajamas, his socked feet quiet on the floor. "Is there a reason?"

Maggie felt her gut clench. "Is this about not seeing your friends?"

Anna looked from Maggie to Frank. She was hiding something, and Frank seemed to know about it. He nodded and Anna stared at the floor. "He's been acting weird," she said in a quiet voice.

Maggie's cell phone rang, showing it was Susan calling. Maggie silenced it.

"Weird how?" Maggie's heart began to thrash in her chest like a suffocating animal. "Like before?" Anna had been old enough to recognize Brandon's altered behavior when high the last time. She would know if it was happening again.

"Yes," Anna whispered and fled the room.

WINTER HAD ARRIVED. MAGGIE STOOD ON THE PORCH, HOLDING HER knit shawl about her shoulders. Snow was lightly falling, and she would have enjoyed this first snow if her heart wasn't so troubled. Brandon had just parked and stepped down from his Chevy, walking over.

"Where are the girls?" he asked, his voice gravelly with suspicion. In his black knit cap, he looked like a gangster, and Maggie shivered.

"They don't want to come this week," Maggie began, holding out her hand to stop Brandon from coming nearer. "And before you start yelling, just know this wasn't prompted by me."

Brandon stared at the ring on her finger, his face darkening in anger. "We both know who's pulling the strings around here."

"This isn't about Frank, either. Anna has a lot of schoolwork and a group project before Christmas, and she asked to stay home. Holly wants to stay with her sister."

In truth, Anna had been hysterical since her outburst that morning, insisting she wanted to go to her friend's house so she wouldn't have to see her father. Maggie had arranged for Holly and Anna to stay through Saturday afternoon. Maggie wanted some time to talk with Anna before school started on Monday. Anna had run out of the house and into her friend's car without another word. Maggie needed more information before she could investigate Brandon. For now, all she could do was not let on that she knew he was using again.

"It's my weekend, and you can't keep my girls away from me." Brandon stepped closer, fists clenched. "If they really don't want to come, they can tell me themselves."

"They're not here," Frank said, coming to stand next to Maggie. He picked up her hand and kissed it, making the diamond flash in the dim light. "I dropped them off at a friend's house for a study group."

"Those are my kids, Frank, not yours," Brandon said, his voice deadly calm.

"We're making our own family here," Frank said, massaging Maggie's belly. "You might as well get used to it." Maggie flushed crimson, a small gasp escaping her lips. Brandon's face registered surprise, then seething anger.

"I'll be back tonight to talk to my girls," he said.

"Then you'll be wasting a trip. They're gone until Sunday," Frank replied.

"You lowlife son of a bitch! I'll find them. Are you just going to stand there like a doll, Maggie? You know I have rights and he doesn't." Brandon flipped his middle finger at Frank.

"It's best if you go now," Maggie managed to say. Brandon looked so righteously angry. She searched his eyes for signs, but saw nothing but pain. "We'll talk about this on Monday."

"Bye, Brandon," Frank said. Brandon scowled and stormed away.

When his truck disappeared around the bend, Maggie turned to Frank and pressed her forehead into his chest.

"Thank you. You don't think he'll be able to locate them, do you?"

"No chance, so don't worry. She wouldn't call him, anyway," Frank kissed her head.

"We just gave her that cell phone for her birthday," Maggie said, her heart racing. "And I've never seen her that upset. Did she say anything to you?"

"She's fine. Now let's get you inside. It's freezing out here." Maggie paused and looked up at him.

"Frank, what was that all about?—I'm not pregnant."

"Don't be too sure about that. We haven't used any protection, and I know you're not on the pill," Frank said with a wink.

"I had an ectopic pregnancy and almost died—I would have if Brandon hadn't come home from a job site early to take me to the hospital. Ever since, I've had an IUD."

She watched Frank's face change. Suddenly cold and wary.

"Why didn't you tell me that before? You knew I wanted more children, a son of my own," he said, with an edge to his voice. "You deliberately deceived me."

"I didn't! It just never came up," Maggie stammered, disbelief making her choke. Sure, Frank had made joking references about adding to the family, but she hadn't thought he was serious. Now she could see that he was. "I'm sorry, and you're right. I should have told you sooner." Frank's gaze softened.

"It's okay, Mags. Let's just get your IUD taken out, problem solved. You still have one working fallopian tube, right?"

"But I don't want another child. I'll be forty this next year, and I feel past that part of my life." Maggie realized they had never argued about anything up to this point, and she cringed inside. Frank tipped his head and looked at her, then grinned, his face full of mischief.

"I'm going to convince you it's what you want, too. You have two lovely daughters, but I've never had a child of my own. It's what I've always wanted." Frank pleaded, his voice cracking a bit in spite of his playful tone.

"I won't have another baby because it's what *you* want. It's too much to ask of me." Maggie's heart broke, and she began to cry. Why were the men in her life always asking for her to understand?

"That's not fair, Maggie, not fair at all."

"I love you, but if that's what you really want, then we should end this. I can give you many things, but not that." Wiping her tears away, she shivered and looked at Frank's beautiful face.

Frank stared at her, then walked into the house, leaving her standing in the falling snow. A moment later, he came back out, his jacket on and his keys in his hands. Without a word to her, he got into his car and drove away.

ANNA CALLED THE HOUSE ON SATURDAY NIGHT TO SAY SHE AND HOLLY were going to school with her friend on Monday. Her voice was bright and cheerful, and she seemed to be having a good weekend, so Maggie felt relieved. The adjustments to life in Helena and a new man in the house had been a lot to ask of a freshly minted teenager, and then with Brandon coming back into the picture, it was just too much for Anna. Maggie had put aside her own problems and spent Friday interviewing counselors during her breaks at work. She found one next to Anna's school, which would allow Anna some privacy to talk without the burden of knowing her mother was waiting in the next room. The counselor had an opening on Tuesday, so Maggie had booked it. Hopefully, Anna would talk to Maggie on Monday about Brandon's behavior, and Maggie could use that to get an injunction until she could confirm Brandon was still drug-free. And if he wasn't, then she'd be able to stop visitations and protect her daughters.

Now it was Sunday, and there was still no sign of Frank. Maggie sighed and climbed out of bed, shivering in the morning chill. Her engagement ring glared at her reproachfully, and Maggie yanked it off, setting it on the nightstand. She stood to start her day, but then she thought better of it. Frank hadn't ended things—he had just left and not come back yet. If he saw she'd taken off the ring, he would see that as another broken promise, another deception. She picked it up and noticed some kind of marking on the inside. It looked like an inscription, but it was partially worn away. She had always assumed the ring was new, but Frank must have purchased it secondhand. Feeling a wave of disappointment, she set the ring back down and went into the bathroom to get ready.

It had been ages since Maggie had attended church. She waved at Susan as she climbed the steps and was surprised to be pulled into a tight hug.

"You didn't return my call. Are you okay?" Susan asked, tears forming in her bright eyes. Maggie felt a stab of guilt. Since Frank had moved in, her whole focus had shifted, and she hadn't visited with her old friends at all. She was determined to make that change. Susan had called twice, but Maggie had not had the energy to call back.

"Anna's going through a difficult time, so I let the girls stay at a friend's house until tomorrow." Maggie couldn't maintain eye contact, so she gazed past Susan into the church.

"I need to talk to you about Frank," Susan said, startling Maggie's gaze back to her face. Susan still didn't approve of Frank, and it had strained their friendship. They barely talked anymore, but Maggie owed Susan an update of what had happened.

"He wants another baby, one of his own. I haven't seen him since Friday, ever since I said no." Maggie brushed a tear away and cleared her throat. "I'm afraid it might be over."

"Good." Susan put her arm around Maggie's shoulders and walked down the steps and into the side yard. She guided Maggie to a marble bench and sat beside her. "I've been a terrible friend, and I'm sorry. I should have come to talk to you right away when you didn't answer, but I didn't. I put if off and left you at risk." Susan let out a pent up breath. "We had electricians out to fix the ADU. They said the wiring had been deliberately damaged."

"Damaged? I don't understand."

"The electrical wires to the garbage disposal were cut clean through. It looks as if the only way Frank could have been electrocuted is if he cut the wires while placing the other hand in the water, which means the water had to have been present first."

"What?" The realization came over her in a slow wave of dread. "Are you saying Frank's electrocution wasn't an accident?" Maggie cried out and covered her mouth when Susan nodded and held Maggie's trembling hand. "Why would he do that? He almost died."

"I think the answer is obvious, but I don't think he meant for the electrocution to be as serious as it was, just enough to damage the house and make him homeless."

"He staged a way to move in with me?"

"Yes, and John and I are to blame. We had no intention of renting our ADU in the condition it was in, but Frank showed up at our door and asked to rent it as-is. He seemed like such a nice guy, and we were naïve. Then, within days, he'd fixated on you. I'll admit, I was really pleased at first, and now I feel like a complete betrayer of your trust."

"I need to go home. I don't feel well." Bile crept into Maggie's throat and she tried to rise, but Susan stopped her.

"No, I don't want you to go home alone after dumping all this news on you. You're staying with us tonight, okay? We can figure this out tomorrow."

~

THE PHONE RANG SHARPLY AT NINE O'CLOCK MONDAY MORNING, startling Maggie from her stupor. She'd opened the library after a sleepless night at Susan's. Not a soul was present except her. Setting her full coffee cup down that had long since gone cold, her stomach roiled. It was good she had not taken a sip.

"Helena Library, Maggie Reynolds speaking," she answered.

"Mrs. Reynolds, this is Principal Charlotte. I need you to come to the school immediately."

"What's happened? Are my daughters okay?" Maggie clenched the phone.

"They're safe. Let's discuss this when you get here."

Maggie rushed into the school building, sloshing wet snow onto the polished floor as she ran to the principal's office, her heart pounding. The secretary rose as she entered, and pointed to the open door near the back. Slowing, Maggie saw the uniformed feet of a police officer and swallowed hard. Inside the room, Principal Charlotte was seated at her desk. In addition to the officer, three other people sat within the space—a man that looked like a detective, a woman, and Brandon, who looked at her with loathing.

"Thank you for coming, Mrs. Reynolds. Please have a seat," Charlotte said, gesturing to the remaining seat. Maggie sat with a thud, clutching her purse to her chest. Her boots were wet and dripped onto the carpet, making a dark stain that matched the sweat she felt pooling under her arms.

"I'm Detective Reeves, and this is Diane Clarke with the Montana

Department of Health and Human Services. We've received some very disturbing news about Frank Jenkins and his relationship with your daughter Anna."

"Anna? I don't understand." Maggie searched everyone's face and landed on Brandon. "What's going on?"

"She was planning to run away with him," Brandon spat out, rage lacing his words. "He told her he loved her and they would leave when the time was right. He called her on her cell phone so they could coordinate the whole thing. If Holly hadn't called me, they'd be gone already."

"All this happened this morning?" she asked, feeling lost in a sea of questions and fear for her daughters' safety. "Where are the girls now?" Maggie searched her memory, looking for evidence of Frank's indiscretion. There was nothing--but wait. It was Frank who had directed Anna in answering the question about Brandon's drug use. Anna had looked to Frank for guidance in what to say. They must have agreed to what she was to say in advance. Anna had completely avoided her before departing. And what about the trip to Frank's work? Had that been for real, or had they been elsewhere? Maggie thought about all the times Frank had been home from work before her and shivered, cold sweat trickling down her back. She had been a fool.

"They've been with me since Saturday night, right after Anna called you," Brandon replied.

"Why didn't anyone call me?" Maggie asked. She dug into her purse, seeking her cell phone, wondering how she had missed a call. When her phone wasn't in her purse, she began to hyperventilate, choking back sobs. She must have left it at Susan's house.

"Mrs. Reynolds." Diane's soft voice broke into her consciousness. "Anna would not have revealed her whereabouts. It's a safety precaution we take in situations like this." A wail broke out, and Maggie found the noise was coming from her own throat. She slapped her hand over her mouth to make it stop.

"We tried to track you down, but no one was at the house," the detective interjected. "We had to wait until you went into work. Do you have any idea where Mr. Jenkins may be?"

"No...I, no," she finished lamely. "We had a fight on Friday after Brandon came by to pick up the girls. I haven't seen him since. I went to Susan and John Arnold's house last night."

The detective exchanged a look with Brandon and the social worker. They nodded, and he continued, pulling a sheet of paper from his file.

"Is this the man you know as Frank Jenkins?" Maggie stared at the photo. It was a grainy snapshot of a man with a short, military haircut and striking cobalt blue eyes. Frank. His arm was around a woman who looked remarkably like Maggie, except she was pregnant. They were standing in Central Park, the skyscrapers of New York in the background. Maggie nodded to the detective and handed back the picture.

"Yes."

"His real name is James Francis Perkins, and he is wanted on suspicion of the murder of his wife."

Maggie began to shake, holding herself.

"What about the baby? In the picture?" Maggie forced herself to ask, fearing the worst.

"It was...obvious James Perkins wasn't the father. The baby is now with the true biological father."

"I told him I couldn't get pregnant, that I didn't want another baby. That's why we fought. But Anna?" Maggie felt sick and clutched her stomach.

"He has a pattern of befriending divorced women, particularly ones with daughters, and he appears to have a history of...similar behavior." Detective Reeves' face showed a hint of compassion. "We need to search your house. Will you take us there now?"

"What about Anna and Holly?"

"They will remain with their father until such time as you've been cleared of suspicion."

∼

MAGGIE UNLOCKED THE DOOR AND ENTERED THE TRANQUIL, QUIET rooms with the detective and police officer. Ignoring her, they deployed themselves throughout the main rooms. When they searched Frank's desk, she saw it was empty, not a scrap of paper in it. His laptop was gone, too. Maggie shuddered, realizing he'd been back to the house while she was at Susan's. Walking into the bedroom, Maggie looked at her nightstand.

The ring was gone.

HAVEN

JAYE MILIUS

$\mathcal{A}$scension parties always had the best food. Ollie could smell the sweetcakes baking in the kitchens, the warm tang of them wafting out across the bridge. It swayed beneath him in the morning fog, his quick steps echoing on the planks, the well-worn guide rope smooth beneath his fingers. Above and below, more bridges criss-crossed in the mist, connecting the buildings that encircled the mountaintop. The town had been built long before he had been born, carved of rock and wood high above the clouds. Everywhere, there were green gardens, fed by the endless flow of the falls that came cascading down the rock face. Some said that the gods themselves had built it, a haven for their chosen, a place where their children might learn and grow in peace. Who was he to doubt the stories? Ollie couldn't imagine any place more beautiful.

Not that he had ever known anywhere else. He had been born here in Haven, raised in the light of the gods, and soon--in two month's time--he would Ascend to join them, passing through their sanctum on the mountaintop before going out into the world to spread their Word. Save for a handful of teachers, cooks, and the like, no one in the town was more than fifteen years old. Haven was a place for children, the oldest of which eagerly looked forward to their fifteenth birthday and the coming-of-age celebration that would see them sent out into the world.

Today, it was Simone's turn. The thought of losing her gave him pause. She was his closest friend and had been for as long as he could remember. All the children of Haven were said to be brothers and sisters, but Simone was the only one who truly felt like family. Ollie knew he should be happy for her, but the thought of her leaving sat like a lead weight in his stomach.

Classes had been cancelled for the day, and the earliest arrivals milled impatiently around the Commons, talking in small groups, the youngest chasing after a ball that went bouncing across the flagstones.

Some two hundred children called Haven home, but there were a handful of adults: Father Ryan, the priest who maintained the mountain sanctum; Miss Fawn and Miss Dorothea, who ran the school; Colette and Arthur in the kitchens; old Jonas, who tended the terraced gardens. Jonas was the eldest of them all, a stooped and weathered creature who hadn't spoken a word since his own failed Ascension years ago. Some thought him slow, sick in the mind, but the gardens flourished almost magically under his touch, and there was never any shortage of fresh-grown food.

Now, Simone would be sequestered with the priest, making her final preparations. Today she would cross the great stone bridge and disappear up into the mountain to face the gods. Ollie had never seen the inside of the temple. Except for Father Ryan, no one entered except on the day of their Ascension. It was a source of mystery and speculation, but Ollie's usual curiosity was muted by worry. If things went well for Simone today, he might never see her again. True, they could meet again out in the world once Ollie had passed his own test, but there was no telling what awaited them beyond the mountain.

Moving away from the others, Ollie leaned his elbows on the railing that overlooked the falls. The thundering waters cascaded down the mountainside, feeding Haven and its gardens before tumbling away into the unknown.

A roar of youthful excitement pulled Ollie's attention back to the Commons. Father Ryan was there, a tall man whose balding head was unmistakable above the crowd. The children pressed around him, cheering and hooting, shouting congratulations before joining the older man in song. The hymn was one that Ollie knew well, one that had been sung at every Ascension that he could remember, a prayer of thanksgiving and of celebration.

He saw her then, following the priest, being welcomed by her fellow children. No, not fellow children; today Simone was a woman grown. Today, she would have the veil of youth lifted from her eyes. She was garbed in white, the traditional plain shift fluttering around her knees, her dark hair swaying behind her in a long plait. As she bent to greet those she passed, they placed garlands of flowers around her neck and wrists, laying a crown of them upon her head. Simone had always been beautiful, but today she was resplendent, pure, chosen. There was no doubt that she would be sent out into the world to be living evidence of the goodness of the gods.

Catching Ollie's eye, she grinned. In that moment, she was simply Simone, the skinny, mischievous girl who was forever tormenting their teachers with questions about the world below. Soon enough, she would have her answers.

As the crowd swept her onward toward the feast hall, Ollie realized that he wasn't alone beside the falls. Old Jonas stood some distance away, his eyes trailing after the boisterous crowd. Together, he and Ollie watched them go, a scowl crossing the old man's face.

"I'm going to miss her," Ollie sighed. It felt good to talk to someone, even Jonas. But, as always, the old gardener offered only stony silence.

THE CEREMONY WAS BEAUTIFUL. GATHERED INTO HAVEN'S GREAT HALL, the children set upon the feast, eating and drinking their fill well into the afternoon. Toasts were raised to Simone at every turn, and even Ollie found himself drawn into the revelry. Once the tables had been cleared and moved aside, Father Ryan began the rites, recounting the tale of how the gods had saved their chosen children and built for them a paradise high amongst the clouds. As always, tales of the blighted lands below--ravaged by disease and drought and famine-- drew fearful whispers from the listening crowd. But the gods had saved them for a purpose. Now, it was Simone's turn to go out into the world and spread the healing Word.

It was a vague description; even Simone had said so. But what happened inside the mountain sanctum would be between her and the gods alone. Each Ascendant was given a unique directive, told how best they could go forth to serve.

If Simone was nervous, she hid it well. When the children moved outside to the great bridge for the final portion of the rite, Simone followed. In that moment, she seemed the very picture of a woman grown--regal, wise, and ready. It was time.

She stood at the crossing's edge, staring up at the mountain, the crowd gathered at her back. When the priest lay a guiding hand on her arm, Simone seemed to wake from a dream, following him out onto the bridge, the old stones slick with the spray of the falls that thundered beneath them. The structure was said to be older than Haven itself, delicately carved to look like living vines and stretching toward white stone steps that wound up into the caves above. There, she would finally Ascend into the holy sanctum. There, she would come face to face with the gods.

Halfway across the bridge, Simone paused. With a glance at Father Ryan, she darted back into the crowd, finding Ollie and pulling him into a fierce hug. Most laughed, even the priest. Simone was still Simone, impetuous and self-assured, no matter where she was.

"I'll see you on the other side," she whispered before pulling back to give him one last grin. Then she straightened her flower crown and rejoined Father Ryan in crossing the great stone bridge.

The crowd watched them go until they disappeared around the bend of the stairs that would take them up into the mountain. Others soon drifted away to rejoin the feast, but Ollie lingered until he was alone with the biting wind that swept down across the bridge.

He had not returned to the Great Hall. Nor could he stay out in the cold. And so he had simply returned to his bunk, staring up at the ceiling until the first light of dawn.

Classes would not begin for hours, yet. Even without Simone, the world would go on, and he would be left with nothing to do but wait and wonder. The fifty-six days until his own Ascension might well be an eternity.

Climbing out of bed, Ollie washed and dressed, making his way back out to the great stone bridge. He was pining, he knew, brooding on things he could not change. But, as he turned the final corner, he stopped short. A cowled figure stood at the rail ahead of him, staring out across the clouds, its back to the looming mountain.

Hesitantly, he cleared his throat.

The hood half turned at the sound, searching for him in the morning fog. "Ollie."

He gaped. "Simone?"

His first thought was a selfish one: the gods had sent her back, returned her to him. Or perhaps this was a dream. If so, he dreaded waking.

As Ollie drew closer, he saw that she still wore the white shift of the Ascendant beneath her dark cowl. But gone were the flower garlands, gone was her eager smile. Slowly, she lowered her hood.

He gasped, taking a step backward. Gone too was her hair, her bare head naked in the morning fog. Her skin had darkened as well, bronzed as if she had spent an entire summer in the sun. But it was her eyes that had startled him most of all. The left was clouded, milky white and blind. What had happened to her inside the mountain?

"Simone, gods above..."

She shuddered, turning away as if the words pained her.

Hesitantly, he lay a hand on her arm. "You're back?"

It had happened before. Most who Ascended were sent out into the world, as missionaries and healers. Others the gods charged with the care of Haven - the priests, the teachers, those who remained to serve so that the children might grow to spread the Word. Was the headstrong girl truly meant to stay, to know nothing beyond this place? And then there were those like Jonas, the gardener, who had returned from his Ascension dazed and mute. There had been others, if rumor was to be believed. Some simply could not handle having the veil lifted from their eyes.

Simone turned to look up at the mountain and Ollie found himself grateful to escape that clouded gaze. What had she seen? Why had the gods sent her back? Had he somehow wished this upon her, willing the gods to return her in his selfishness?

"Why?" was all he could think to ask.

"That's… a good question."

"What happened? What did you see?"

She turned now, meeting his eyes at last. "War."

He imagined he could see it reflected in her milky eye, the spark of violence, of things beyond description. It was said that the Ascension lifted the veil of youth, allowed a person to see the world as it truly was. Simone was the strongest person he had ever known. If she had been blinded by it, what chance did he have?

Her whisper echoed in the stillness, reverberating against the stone. The falls were rushing hard this morning, thundering down and away beneath the bridge. The ground beneath their feet hummed with it, and it was only then that Ollie realized that the mountain itself was shaking.

Somewhere in the falls a rock broke loose, striking the bridge with a thud as it was swept away. Ollie grabbed the railing, steadying himself. Back toward town, the rope bridges were swaying wildly, the walls of the halls and barracks buckling.

Simone staggered, her knuckles white on the rail.

"What's happening?"

Ascension or no, she looked just as lost as he was, a frightened little girl.

"Children!" Miss Dorothea, the teacher, appeared behind them. "Come, now! Get inside!"

As thunder boomed around them, the woman stretched out a warning hand, but her fingers twisted in the air, breaking apart in wisps of smoke. Her mouth opened in a scream, but that too crumbled, her face, her arms, her everything, scattered in the breeze.

Nothing had touched her, nothing that he could see. Their teacher had simply been… unmade.

Ollie stumbled. Beside him, Simone was quaking. "I have to go," she whispered.

He couldn't take his eyes from where Dorothea had stood. "Where?"

"The mountain."

"The sanctum. The gods." Ollie nodded, grasping desperately to her arm. "They'll help us."

"They won't." Simone shook her head. "They've left us."

"What?"

She grasped his hands painfully between hers and pressed her lips to his forehead. "I'm sorry." Then she was off and running, sliding across the wet stones of the bridge.

"Simone!" he called after her. "Simone!"

She turned.

"I want to help!" He stared up at the mountain, helpless. "I want to *know*."

She hesitated. Then she darted back across the bridge, much as she had during the Ascension ceremony. This time, though, Simone grabbed his hand and pulled him with her. Another quake shook the bridge beneath them, but together they managed to keep their balance. It was as though the mountain itself had awakened and was trying to shake itself free of them in its anger.

Once they crossed the bridge, Ollie skidded to a stop. The mountain loomed, its winding stairs directly ahead. This was the closest he had ever been, the closest he had ever dared. Simone's wince was sympathetic, but another rumble harried them onward, her grip tight on his arm as they rushed up the stairs.

"You have a plan?" he gasped.

She shook her head. "No more dreams. No more gods." The stairs ended in a massive stone door, and she threw her shoulder against it. After a moment of exhausted confusion, Ollie joined her, their combined strength just enough to open a crack into the darkness beyond. Simone gave him a breathless smirk. "Happy Ascension Day."

A torch was burning on the wall. As Simone lifted it and stepped inside, Ollie could just make out a high-ceilinged room. The walls were lost in shadow, but pale morning light streamed down through an oculus high above them. The entirety of the mountain's peak had been hollowed out to build this sacred space. At its center was a stone slab, carved in the style of the bridge outside, twisted and rippling like a thing alive. It waited within the shaft of light, pinned beneath the eye of the gods.

"Lay down."

"What?"

"Lay down." Simone nodded to the slab, her words punctuated by another angry rumble.

With a fearful glance up at the oculus, Ollie complied.

Simone rummaged somewhere in the darkness, returning with a bottle of thick liquid that moved sluggishly when she held it to the light. Staring down at Ollie, she hesitated. Then she pressed the bottle into his hands.

"Drink."

"What is it?"

"There's no time. Do you want to see or don't you?"

Ollie steeled himself, remembering Dorothea, the way that she had come apart before their eyes. Haven was crumbling around them. But if this was the end, he would die with his eyes open.

Leaning forward, he took a deep and bitter mouthful, choking it down. Simone took her draught more gracefully, but another thunderclap sent a scattering of dust and pebbles down upon them. Tossing the bottle aside, she climbed onto the slab beside him, pressing her face against his shoulder as the rocks came crashing down.

He woke to thunder. It shuddered through his aching limbs, the slab beneath him bucking as another crash echoed above his head. Simone had held him down, he remembered, the pair of them pressed together on the cramped stone. In a panic, he realized that she was gone. Still, Ollie's body was strangely heavy, sluggish and awkward.

"Easy, easy." Her voice came from somewhere to his right, her soothing words tinged with fear.

"Simone? I can't see you. I can't... I can't move."

A face appeared above him, dark-skinned and bald. It was a girl, her left eye scarred and swollen shut. He might have screamed, but then she smiled. "Told you I'd see you on the other side."

"*Simone?*"

"In the flesh." She shrugged, glancing nervously at something that he couldn't see. "Take it slow. Get your bearings. We didn't have time to do this right."

"Do what right?"

"Bring you out. 'Lift the veil.'" At the familiar words, she shuddered. "They lied about a lot, but not that part. The '*Ascension*' is a process, a sort of decompression."

With some effort, she slid her hands beneath him and helped to push him up into a sitting position. Gone was the cold stone of the slab. Instead, he was abed, his lower half wrapped snugly in a starched, white sheet. Despite the strangeness of the room, he couldn't take his eyes from her.

"You look...."

"More like myself." Her grin widened and she winced, raising a hand to her injured eye. It was the same eye that he had seen blinded, back in Haven.

But now... they were somewhere else. Thunder still echoed around them, but this was not the fury of the mountain, not the echo of a distant storm. This time, the crash came with panicked shouts, the shattering of breaking glass.

Ollie tried to push himself from the bed. "What's happening? Where are we?"

More beds stretched in both directions, occupied by small and sleeping forms. But this wasn't the barracks, wasn't the infirmary. When Simone finally helped him to stand, the floor beneath his bare feet was warm and humming, the wall that he staggered against made of neither wood nor stone.

Simone was at his elbow, steadying him. "Easy. Take it slow."

A sudden flash of light glared blindingly against the distant wall. Not a wall, then, but a window. It darkened, and then the light came again, an explosion bursting beyond the glass in a shower of sparks. The room around them shuddered with the force of it.

With unsteady steps, Ollie made his way toward it. The window stretched from floor to ceiling, a thick and unjointed pane of unimaginable size. Like the floor, it was warm to the touch, humming with unseen energy, but Ollie barely noticed. Because beyond it was the most dazzling display that he had ever seen.

He thought that he had known the vastness of the sky, living amongst the clouds of Haven, but this was unlike anything he could have imagined. Darkness stretched away beyond the great window, a vast black landscape dotted with distant stars. Some of the closest seemed to move and dance, like the fireflies in high summer. As he watched, one of these glowed brighter, launching a ribbon of fire in their direction. It burst somewhere to the left of the window, sending up another shower of brilliant sparks, another dangerous rumble.

His fear was lost beneath his fascination. Their vantage was moving, tilting downward so that Ollie could see the great curve beneath their orbit, a blackened and fiery landscape ringed by wisps of smoky gray.

"What is it?" he gasped.

Simone moved to stand beside him. "What they promised. It's the world."

"But we're--"

"Above it? Technically, that part was true."

Ollie's mind raced, struggling to make sense of it. "That thing we drank…. This is my test, isn't it? A vision. This is a vision."

Simone didn't respond. He glanced over at her, but her eyes were fixed on the window.

"You said you wanted to know. You wanted to see."

He had. He did. He just hadn't expected… *this*.

"It wasn't real." She sighed. "Haven wasn't real."

"Oh, it was real." The voice was new, a man's voice. Ollie whipped around, his head reeling from the sudden motion.

A knot of people clustered in the doorway behind them. Most were barely older than Simone, teenage boys and girls. Like her, they were mostly bald, thin, sallow-cheeked, and underfed. Ollie rubbed an exploratory hand across his own smooth scalp, seeing for the first time the thinness of his own legs, the bones standing out beneath the paper-thin skin of his hands.

The man who had spoken was older than the rest--in his thirties, perhaps--with a rough stubble of dark hair. As another shower of sparks burst beyond the window, he cursed. "They're shooting at us. They're actually shooting at us."

One of the girls laid a calming hand on his shoulder. "Easy, Jonas."

"Jonas?" Ollie gaped.

The man gave him a thin-lipped smile. The smooth face was that of a stranger, but the silent smirk was unmistakably familiar. It was the old gardener, somehow made young again. "Hey, kid. You picked a hell of a time to surface."

"What happened?" Simone asked. "The fighting...." She looked to Ollie, trying to explain. "My Ascension-- when I woke up here, I saw them. The adults, the people we're supposed to become, the so-called 'gods.' They were fighting each other." Gingerly, she touched her cheek beneath her swollen eye.

"Simone here took a hit," Jonas added. "So I put her back under. To heal. I didn't expect her to come back, especially not with company."

"Who *are* you?"

"Haven's caretaker. You know that." He chuckled, tapping a finger to the side of his head. "You think one old man can grow all that food? Haven blooms because I make it bloom."

"Jonas built Haven," the girl behind him explained. "Or they all did. For us. So we could have something like a childhood, a place to grow and learn before we faced the ugly truth." Her chin trembled. "But then they *left* us. Only Jonas here stayed."

"We saw Miss Dorothea… inside." Ollie shuddered at the memory. "Something happened to her."

Jonas nodded. "Some of us fought them. Dorothea went back, tried to warn you. And they killed her for it." The caretaker moved closer to the window, looking down at the blighted planet below them. "Our ancestors, they did terrible things…. We were supposed to do better."

"The gods chose us to heal the world," Ollie stammered, remembering the old words.

"There never were any 'gods.' Only us. And then half of us decided that you weren't worth the effort anymore," Jonas sighed. "Haven was a 'waste of resources.' If you have the technology to extend your own life, why would you waste anything on the next generation? They took the fuel cells, the nutrient processors, everything they could."

"And down there?" Ollie stepped close, nodding to the planet below.

"Nothing. They destroyed it, those who came before us. All that's left of humanity is here, in orbit." Jonas turned from the window, eyes sweeping over his charges with a grimace. "Every child born since has been a miracle. But this is no life for a child. So we gave you a new one, a virtual world with everything the real one couldn't give you. And at fifteen, once you were supposedly old enough to 'contribute' to this tedious business of survival, we would finally tell you the truth."

He glowered out at the moving lights. Ollie could just make them out now, glittering vessels, small and growing smaller, leaving them behind. They had stopped shooting, but by the growing crack in the window, the damage had been done.

"They found a planet, another planet. More importantly, they perfected the means to keep themselves alive for the duration of the journey. But there wasn't enough fuel, not for all the ships, not unless they cannibalized ours. The consensus was that you were expendable. And they can always make more children."

Simone had been silent, looking back at the others lying in their beds. There were two dozen of them, their small bald heads ringed in halos of light. They were still connected, still inside the virtual world of Haven.

"Will it hurt?" she whispered.

Old Jonas smiled sadly. "Not for them."

"If we had been here, really here, we could have done something."

Maybe she was right. Maybe she wasn't. Stepping back from the glass, Ollie took her hand. "They wanted to give us a chance to be happy, to have a normal life. They wanted to protect us."

"Yeah, well, they didn't. Ignorance isn't happiness." Simone shuddered. "I'm sorry. I shouldn't have brought you. You could be asleep right now. You didn't have to--"

"See the world as it is? Some people never get that chance."

Behind them, the other awakened children huddled together, all eyes on the crack spreading and splintering across the window. Jonas gathered them close, into the meager haven of his arms, but Ollie only had eyes for Simone.

"What was it you said?" He smiled. "See you on the other side."

HEADCASE

MIKE DONALD

$\mathcal{N}$eon light flared off the wet pavement. Cars sped past, tires hissing through the spray. An old man weaved erratically, pedestrians streaming past him. Everything was just a colored smear through his eyes. His drug-fogged brain struggled to cope with staying upright.

A suited man slammed into him... sent him spinning into a store doorway. "Watch out, asshole."

The old man stared back at him, eyes vacant, pupils like pinpricks in the passing headlights. Electrodes dangled from wires around his neck. He wore a rumpled tracksuit top, and surgical scrubs as pants. His feet bare and bleeding. Eyes searching for something. A car pulled up alongside him. The rear window slid down. He stared at someone inside, a moment of recognition flickered in his eyes and...PHUTT! A spray of blood as a hole mushroomed in his forehead. The impact knocked him backwards, his body crumpling to the ground as the car accelerated away.

Detective Nik Sanders stared at the body bathed in the antiseptic lights of the morgue. Arnold H.T. Bickerstaff, former CEO of Anadyn Electronics, a company worth as much as Apple before computers were rendered obsolete by neural implants.

Sanders looked at the small pile of personal possessions on a steel table behind him. There was an electronic tag etched with the name *Electro Cortex Industries*. A wrapper from an "own label" nutrition bar from the MegaMart food chain, a five-dollar bill, and an electronic key pass.

His partner, Julie Hardwick, stood next to him. "Wasn't he already dead?"

Sanders nodded. This wasn't just a homicide they were investigating. As far as everybody knew, Arnold Bickerstaff had died five years earlier.

He'd been one of the first recipients of the Electro Cortex brain map system. As science progressed, the very rich had moved on from plastic surgery and botox to full body swaps. The system transferred the entire brain map of the donor into a new and usually much younger recipient. Now the rich could choose from a selection of recipients online and use neural patterning to imprint their brain map onto them.

There'd been opposition, of course; the church saw it as an ethical travesty and open to gross misuse. The general public saw it as just another way to divide the poor from the obscenely rich by enabling off-the-shelf immortality. But as history continued to repeat itself, the church was bought off, and governmental coffers were soothed with huge donations to the relevant political parties. Test cases were allowed. The donors, seriously ill or dying billionaires, were scanned and uploaded into the vast servers out at the Mojave Air and Spaceport. Once the recipient had been checked and the transfer was complete, the donor was given a dignified end-of-life release program. With time, it became accepted practice for the rich. Detective Sanders stared at the recently deceased body of the billionaire and wondered what he was getting into.

They followed the black ribbon of the I-58 across flat white sands, heading toward the high-tech village that was the Mojave Air and Spaceport. Vast steel hangars loomed out of the heat-haze as they drew nearer. Julie took a swig from a flask of orange juice and offered it to Sanders. He shook his head.

"You should hydrate. It's going to be like the devil's armpit when we get out of the car."

Sanders smiled at the bluntness of his partner, a straight talking Texan. She'd been working with him long enough to know his ways, but that didn't stop her trying to knock some sense into him. He wasn't into the whole hydration craze. He'd always believed you just drank when you were thirsty. "I'm alright. Just not looking forward to telling the widow her husband died…again."

Julie smiled. "I'm with you there. Let's hope we come up with some answers before we have to ask her the usual questions."

They came to a halt alongside the security gate in front of the main complex. Sanders looked over at the entrance to Virgin Galactic, now one of the leading companies in space travel and at the forefront of the Martian space race. The face of Richard Branson, their iconic leader, smiled down at him from one of the walls of the main headquarter buildings. Sanders wondered how long it would be before Richard walked over to the Electro Cortex building for an immortality fix. The guard waved them through, and they pulled up next to the glass entrance that led into the leafy atrium that formed the reception area.

A slogan greeted them above the receptionist's desk. *"Live as long as you think...think as long as you live."* Sanders shrugged as the glass doors hissed open. "I hate slogans."

Julie smiled. "You hate everything."

Sanders moved up to the desk. He showed his badge to the pretty young receptionist. She looked up at him with her vivid yellow eyes. Variable-color contact lenses were the latest thing among the well-heeled young. Dialing in the iris color for the day had picked up where nail polishes had left off.

She handed him an electronic key pass. "Round to the left, take the main travelator and follow the signs to Dr. Borg's office."

Sanders took the card and nodded.

They headed down the long corridor to the multi-laned travelator that whisked staff and visitors through the huge complex. The travelator clacked through the glass tubes, leading them through rooms packed with servers.

Julie looked at the pass Sanders held, briefly matching his eyes in mutual recognition. "Same as the one we found on Bickerstaff."

He nodded. They stepped off the travelator and walked across a waiting area towards the doctor's office. The door opened before they could knock. A tall man with sharp, birdlike eyes ushered them in.

From the unshaven, dark rings under his eyes and rumpled clothing, it looked like he'd been sleeping in his office. He bustled around, making them coffee. "I'm having one, anyway…" he said as he worked the espresso machine with deft movements. "How can I help you, Detective Sanders? We don't get many detectives up here, and certainly none from Homicide."

Sanders waited until Dr. Borg handed them their coffees. "We're investigating the death of Arnold Bickerstaff."

Dr. Borg took a sip of coffee. "Er, I'm not sure what you mean? Arnold Bickerstaff was a client of ours and an early adopter of the mind transference system. I'm not sure how much you know about how our system works, but a key factor is our end-of-life release program."

He paused, and Sanders nodded. "I understand. So as far as you're concerned, Mr. Bickerstaff died five years ago."

Dr. Borg rubbed his chin. "We like to call it a release."

Julie gave Sanders the look. He was apt to say the wrong thing when people tried to foist their new-fangled buzzwords onto him. Sanders bit back his comment and pressed on. He held up a picture of Bickerstaff taken in the morgue. "Is that Arnold Bickerstaff?"

The doctor looked at it and cleared his throat. "I can't be sure. We have a lot of clients."

Sanders looked at Julie. She nodded. "Really? How many billionaires do you have as clients?"

The doctor looked confused. "All of our clients are billionaires." He paused, as if what he was about to say was obvious. "The process is not without cost."

Sanders leaned forward. "Do you have any idea how a man could go through the…release process, only to wind up dead five years later with a bullet in his brain?"

They headed through LA. as the cooling sun started to sink behind the mirrored office blocks, filling the car with reflected light as they peeled off the freeway. "What are you going to do when we get there?" Julie looked over at Sanders.

"Just ask them some questions."

"There's something screwy about this. Dr. Borg was hiding something, I don't know what it was, but maybe the Bickerstaffs will give me some answers."

Julie stretched, trying to get comfortable. It had been a long drive, and the inadequate air-con hadn't done her mood any favors. "I've always thought the whole thing was kinda' weird. You live with somebody for twenty years, and then they die and come back in the body of a younger man with a face you've never seen before."

Sanders glanced at the sat-nav as it guided them through the suburbs toward a gated McMansion. "Are you saying you won't want the face and body of a woman twenty years younger when you get older?"

Julie laughed. "Shit, yeah. Doesn't stop it being creepy though."

Sanders shrugged. "I guess people were saying that about the first boob job back in the day." He pulled the car up beside the intercom and flashed his badge at a recessed camera. The gates slid open, and they headed up the long drive. "Remember to go easy on her.

She may have watched him die already, but hearing that someone blew a hole in his head a few days ago isn't going to make her feel great."

Sanders looked around at the immaculately tended lawns, the hissing sprinklers, and the deep blue of the swimming pool. He hated coming to these places. It reminded him that the gulf between rich and poor had never been wider, and he was definitely on the wrong side of that gulf. The car crunched to a halt on the spotless gravel beside an imposing front door.

"Don't worry, I'll tread lightly." He flicked a smile at Julie as they climbed out into the dank heat of the day. He rang the bell next to the door and waited.

A maid opened the door, and they showed her their badges. She led them through a lounge the size of a tennis court and told them to sit while she fetched Mrs. Bickerstaff. Sanders watched the maid pad away down the corridor. He scanned the immaculate beige carpet and the L-shaped sofas strewn around the giant room. "Feels like someone bought their soul from a style catalog."

Julie smiled. "Maybe that's why she's able to cope with her husband's mind in a designer body."

Mrs. Bickerstaff appeared at the door to the sitting room, immaculate in a cream linen trouser suit. Jewelry glinted from her neck and wrists, and her hair was styled to perfection. She stretched out a hand. "Detective Sanders?" He shook her hand. It was cool and firm. She nodded to Julie. "Sorry to keep you waiting, how can I help?"

Sanders placed his computer tablet on the coffee table in front of him. "Thank you for seeing us, Mrs Bickerstaff. This is not exactly a routine case."

She cocked an eye. "That sounds ominous, Detective. I'm sure you've seen pretty much everything there is to see in your job."

Julie leaned forward. "When did you last see your husband, Mrs. Bickerstaff?"

She frowned. "About half an hour ago. We just came from lunch with friends. He's gone for a jog around the grounds and a swim...he likes to burn off whatever he's just eaten...I can never understand that."

Sanders swiveled the tablet to face her. "I don't mean your present husband, Mrs. Bickerstaff, I mean Arnold Bickerstaff." He tapped the screen, and it filled with a picture of Mr. Bickerstaff's body in the morgue. A swathe of linen tastefully covered the gaping hole in his temple.

Her hand flew to her mouth, and her eyes went wide with shock. "My God...who is that?"

Sanders and Julie looked at each other. "Isn't this your husband?"

She leaned closer to look at the screen. "I don't know, he looks so...old."

Sanders shut the tablet off. "Well, he would be five years older than when you last saw him, so..." He trailed off.

Julie continued. "He was shot by an unknown assailant earlier today. We have no explanation as to why he was killed, or in fact why he was still alive." Mrs. Bickerstaff looked stunned, her face pale, drained of blood.

A man appeared in the doorway to the room. He wore jogging pants and a white cut-off T-shirt that showed his taut physique. An earring glinted from one of his ears. He wiped his brow with a white hand towel. "What's going on, darling?" He spoke with a faint Spanish accent.

Sanders stood up. "I'm Detective Sanders. Your wife is helping us with some of our questions."

Mrs. Bickerstaff went over to him, and he placed a proprietary arm around her. "Oh Matt, they say they found Arnold...someone shot him this morning."

Matt led her back to the sofa and sat her down. "I don't understand...he, I, my body that is, died five years ago...after the transference, I was released."

Sanders looked at him. This was definitely the strangest homicide he'd ever been involved with. Sitting there, talking to a man with the mind of his older self, whose body he'd just seen in the morgue. He had a feeling that this particular case was going to get a lot more bizarre before the day was over.

"Detective?" Matt's voice snapped him out of his reverie. "I don't see how we can help you." Sanders looked into Matt's deep blue eyes. His flawless complexion and gym-honed body gave him an almost inhuman perfection. Sanders involuntarily sucked in his stomach as he addressed him.

"Well, to be honest, we're just feeling our way here, Mr. Bickerstaff..."

Matt leaned forward and fixed Sanders with his calm blue eyes. "Just call me Matt. It'll be easier for everyone, I think."

Matt squeezed Mrs. Bickerstaff's hand, and she looked up at him. Sanders continued. "Thank you...Matt. Okay, just for the record, you were one of the first recipients of the Electro Cortex transference procedure...is that correct?"

Matt spoke quickly, as if he'd rehearsed. "Yes. I had an advanced case of motor neuron disease, incurable; I only had months to live. When I was offered the chance to mind map into a willing donor, I took it. I discussed it with Sarah, and she agreed that we really had nothing to lose. The procedure was flawless. One moment I was a sick, dying old man, and the next I opened my eyes, and I was Matt." He looked at Mrs. Bickerstaff. "I have my health back, and I get to live life with my beautiful wife all over again."

Julie shot Sanders the "look" and studied the radiant couple. There was no denying - it seemed a perfect situation. Everyone was a winner. She turned to Matt.

"So, you saw yourself...I mean Arnold, released?"

Matt nodded. "I held his hand. It was only his body by then--he felt no pain and wasn't aware of who I was. It was an incredibly moving moment." Mrs. Bickerstaff dabbed at her eyes with a tissue.

Sanders addressed Matt. "Is there anyway that the release could have been reversible?"

Matt shook his head.

"No, I saw the readouts. Every one of them was a flatline."

Sanders cleared his throat and flicked a finger over the touch-screen of his tablet. "As Arnold Bickerstaff, you were responsible for the introduction of neural computer implants. That industry made you a billionaire. And yet you've never gone back into that side of the business, even though you have the perfect combination of an old head on young shoulders. Don't you miss being involved with technology? After all, you invented the use of silicon photonics and pioneered the biological interface that revolutionized the field of computing."

Matt stared at him like a rabbit caught in headlights. "I, er..."

Sanders looked down, and then continued. "You developed a new storage medium...what was it called?"

Matt looked at him, a thin sheen of sweat gleaming on his top lip. "I don't see what this has to…"

Sanders snapped his fingers. "Memristor…that was it, resistors with memory."

He felt Julie digging her fingers into his knee, the movement hidden by the coffee table in front of them. But he kept going. "You invented reprogrammable integrated circuits that could do the work of eight chips on the fly…you were even working on a twenty-level chip…it had a cute name. What was it now…er, help me here…" He clapped his hands. "The Needle, that was it, something to do with Nanotechnology."

Mrs. Bickerstaff stared at him as if he was mad. Pools of sweat had collected under Matt's armpits. Julie was staring at Sanders in confusion.

They headed back down the I-58, the desert sand a purple sea in the setting sun. Julie sat tight-lipped. "You could have told me what you were up to."

Sanders shrugged. "I hadn't planned it, but when I saw the new Mr. Bickerstaff, something seemed off."

"So you thought you'd try and wrong-foot him on the fly?" Julie wasn't ready to let it go just yet.

Sanders smiled. "Not entirely, I'd done a bit of research on Arnold Bickerstaff. All that mumbo jumbo technical stuff, I had most of it on my tablet."

He looked across the Mojave Desert. The distant lights of the Spaceport complex glowed in the dusk. "What was it that made you suspicious?" Julie was softening. She couldn't stay mad at him for long.

"We've visited the last three people to be mind-mapped by Electro Cortex. All of them wear in-ear audio support."

Julie nodded. "Could be a coincidence."

"Naah." Sanders shook his head. "If you're a billionaire, able to take your pick of recipients, why pick one with a hearing problem? I don't think they're hearing aids; I think they're for communication."

Julie frowned. "Communicating with who?"

Sanders looked across at her. "When I started talking about the innovations his company brought to the market, he didn't have a clue what I was on about."

Julie snapped her fingers, starting to see what he was getting at. "You did the same when you questioned the other recipients...and they answered your questions fine."

Sanders nodded. "Yes, but not straight away. It looked like they were thinking about the answers to the questions..."

Julie stared at him. "Or being prompted."

They pulled up half a mile from the entrance to the spaceport. Julie took a swig from her ever-present orange juice and turned to Sanders. "But for some reason, Matt wasn't getting the prompts?"

Sanders looked out toward the spaceport, his face grim. "No."

Julie put her bottle down. "So, if Matt wasn't getting prompts because the original Mr. Bickerstaff was dead, that would mean..." She trailed off as the significance hit home.

Sanders watched as the light from the setting sun outlined the dark silhouettes of the spaceport in blood. He turned to her, his eyes serious. "That the original billionaire donors are all still alive."

Julie rubbed her eyes. She desperately needed sleep, but this case wasn't going to give it to her anytime soon. "So, the recipients are in on it. They're given some background on how the mind map donors behave, and then key memories. Anything else they need to know is fed to them through their audio support device by the donors." Julie looked at him. "But even if they are keeping the donors alive, why would they play along? It doesn't make sense."

Sanders pulled up a few hundred yards from the main entrance and switched off the engine.

Parked behind some low-lying rocks, they were still able to see the gate and the security post while remaining hidden. Sanders popped a piece of gum into his mouth and chewed. He found it helped with his concentration. "What would you do if the person you loved was with someone who could kill them at a moment's notice?"

Julie looked at him. "You think that's how they're controlling them?"

Sanders shrugged. "That's something I intend to find out."

It was dark. The desert was starting to come alive with the sounds of the night. They watched as the security guards changed shift. Julie studied them through binoculars. They'd run through the facts of the case, trying to make sense of it, but nothing really added up. If their suspicions were correct, they'd stumbled onto a conspiracy that had cheated people out of billions and resulted in one murder they knew about.

She looked across at Sanders. "After a certain amount of time, the recipients wouldn't have to play catch-up."

Sanders nodded. "Yes. And from that point, the original donor would become expendable."

Julie put the binoculars down. "That's why Bickerstaff escaped. As the original donor, he must have known that his time was nearly up. He was probably trying to get back to his wife and blow the whistle on the whole operation."

Sanders started the car. "The other donors must be in there somewhere. There were a couple of levels Dr. Borg never showed us. He mentioned engineering. My guess is that's where they're being held."

A truck pulled up to the spaceport security gates in a cloud of dust. The garish MEGAMART logo was painted on its side. Sanders remembered the wrapper they'd found amongst Bickerstaff's possessions. That was how Bickerstaff escaped -- and how they planned to get in. Sanders signaled to Julie. "C'mon."

They raced up to the truck and slipped through a small access door set into the rear of the vehicle. It was pitch black inside, and Sanders used his key light to locate a place for them to hide. Once the truck came to a halt, the tail lift came down, and the driver started to unload. Once he'd completed his delivery, he stowed the pneumatic trolley lift and headed off to get the paperwork signed. Julie and Sanders jumped down from the tailgate and jogged to the end of the warehouse before darting through a door marked ENGINEERING SERVICE LEVEL.

They followed a corridor lined with wiring conduits and water pipes to a door marked *Engineering access - 1*. Sanders looked at Julie. "Okay, no heroics. We get our evidence and we're outta' here."

Julie checked her gun and slid the safety catch off. "Fine by me. But if you'd let me speak to Captain Lucas, we could have gone in with a whole division and air support."

Sanders shook his head. "Great idea, but the last time I got backup involved, it turned out that a major drug cartel was just some kids playing around with sherbet powder in a warehouse."

Julie smiled.

"That was unfair. School kids role-playing drug dealers was the last thing I would have guessed."

Sanders nodded. "Lucas threatened to bust me down to traffic for wasting department resources. I don't intend to go that route again. That guy's got a mean streak and he's always had it in for me."

Julie gave him a thin smile. "I love it when you show me your paranoid side."

Sanders pulled the key pass from his pocket and swiped it across the lock. "Just because I'm paranoid doesn't make me wrong." The light pulsed from red to green. The door hummed open.

The room covered the entire floor and was bathed in a soft purple hue. Sanders looked at the glittering specks of dandruff on his shoulders and whispered to Julie. "Ultraviolet light, must be something to do with keeping the area sterile." They stared down at the eerie scene beneath them. Thousands of high-tech beds with built in monitoring services covered the floor beneath them. HOSPIS, drug delivery robots, whirred between the beds, checking on medication and fluids.

But what was really weird was the sound. An echoing murmur that seemed to swirl around the space like a low wind. It came from the patients, if that was what they were, as they mumbled into their lip mics. The men and women were wired to machines that monitored their vital signs…tubes carried waste out and nutrients in. Julie shook her head in disbelief.

"They're keeping them alive, like zombies in a 21st-century call center."

Sanders nodded. "Yes, except they're not being paid to make the calls."

They barely heard the soft click of the guns that appeared behind them. Dr. Borg stood with two guards, weapons leveled.

Sanders glared at Borg. "I'd advise you to put your weapons down. My captain is fully aware of this operation and is waiting with backup for my signal."

A figure appeared in the doorway.

A familiar voice rang out. "We both know that's not true."

Sanders stiffened. "Captain?"

Captain Lucas shook his head. "You always did go out on a limb, Sanders. You were never a team player." He smiled. "Did you really think it was a coincidence that the Bickerstaff case ended up in your lap? And what a lucky break it was that the contents of his pockets led you here. The nutrient bar wrapper was a nice touch. You should try them. They're really quite delicious."

Sanders lunged at the captain. A guard slammed Sanders to the ground with a gun butt to the head. Blood ran from a nasty gash on his head. Sanders slowly got back up. "What the hell are you doing here?"

Dr. Borg smiled. "I think you have a good idea. After all, we went to a lot of trouble to ensure that you would turn up here tonight." The cold realization hit Sanders in the gut. "We've created an industry that makes billions of dollars giving people the immortality only they can afford."

Julie stared at him. "But it's not immortality, is it?"

The doctor shrugged. "The wives with their younger, better-looking surrogate husbands seem happy enough...besides, you're missing the big picture." Two figures appeared behind the doctor. "The first phase is merely to accumulate enough capital to fund our main purpose..."

Julie looked at the two figures behind the captain, and her blood turned to ice. "My God..."

Dr. Borg nodded. "Yes, they have quite the likeness, don't they?"

Julie stared at the mirror images of Sanders and herself standing in front of her. If it weren't for their blank staring faces, they would have been perfect. "Robots?"

The doctor smiled. "I prefer the term *replicants*."

Sanders wiped blood from his eyes. "So this whole setup is just to make enough money to construct your *replicants*...but why?"

The doctor looked down at the thousands of captive donors below before speaking.

"Why go to war to destroy whole civilizations, slaughter millions of people, all just to enslave a reluctant population, when you can just replace the people that control the country? The people that make the decisions." He looked at them. "And, starting with you, the people who enforce the law."

Sanders shook his head. "You're mad if you think this will work."

Dr. Borg signaled to the guards. "I prefer the term *visionary*. I already have thousands of billionaires with no choice but to do my bidding, and now I have two members of the police force."

Julie struggled against the guards. "You may have us, but what makes you think we'll help your puppets to fool anybody?"

The Doctor gave a thin smile. "Because you have a daughter, and Sanders has a mother...take them away."

The guards dragged the detectives out into the corridor as Dr. Borg turned to the two waiting robots. "You two follow me. We've got to update your facial variation software. You look like a couple of zombies."

BY BLOOD

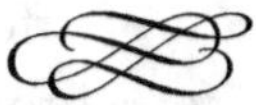

EMILY MARSHALL

"*A*re you certain you can bear to part with... it?"

"Yes—it's just.. a burden."

"Okay, then—it's a deal."

The two women hung up simultaneously. The first walked over and tentatively touched a mobile hanging over a crib with one hand. The second cradled her pregnant belly and burst into tears.

~

23 Years Later

~

EVERY YEAR, HANNAH'S MOTHER WOULD GIVE WHATEVER MOTHER'S DAY gift she received the same brooding, disapproving stare before remarking on how difficult Hannah's birth was and how she deserved something more for her efforts to bring Hannah into the world. Then she'd skulk down the hall to her room, close the door, and turn on her radio and her podcasts to listen to the news and stories of cold murder cases, just like she did every other day of the year. Hannah would see a ratty, yellowed towel appear to block the the crack under the door. It didn't totally prevent the smell of cigarette smoke from wafting through, but Hannah never mentioned the smell. She was too afraid of Mother's reaction.

Hannah and her mother lived in a small town called Fairacres, with no family or friends or really any other connection to the town. Mother had moved there shortly before Hannah's birth because the town had the right combination of affordable apartments and open jobs, she said. Hannah yearned for a brother or sister or some cousins to play with, but Mother had told her many times that none of that was in the cards for her. "Just us against the world," Mother said.

Growing up, Hannah was kept inside and alone most of the time. Mother had homeschooled her, and Hannah was not allowed to go out at all without Mother - not to the park, the library, or even the store. Hannah had once asked if she and Mother could go for a walk down the street, and Mother had lectured her for hours about staying inside and staying safe. Mother worked the graveyard shift cleaning the local ER, and before she would leave for work she'd tuck Hannah into bed and then lock the door from the outside. Hannah would turn toward the wall and pick at the patterned paper.

As Hannah got older, Mother started venturing out more, especially to church, but Hannah always had to stay home. She could watch TV, and she had a computer, so she could get online as long as she never posted photos of herself. But in real life, Hannah resigned herself to staying inside the two-bedroom apartment.

When Hannah turned eighteen, she was permitted to take a job at a local motel. Mother had gotten to know the owner, Mrs. Preston, at church and felt satisfied that she would keep Hannah safe. Hannah would arrive after check-out time for the guests and would clean the rooms before check-in time for the next round of visitors.

She still didn't get to talk to almost anyone, but she found a wonderful array of things left behind by motel patrons. Exotic coins, books of all kinds, postcards, magazines, pictures, toys, and even some jewelry. She was diligent about putting everything she found into the Lost and Found bin in the main office, and just as diligent about coming back to claim the now ownerless things after the thirty-day waiting period expired. She loved these glimpses into the lives of others, and she imagined a version of her life where she went to stay in motels and owned such interesting things.

Several years passed that way, with the lost things Hannah found providing the only change from day to day.

Then, the most amazing thing happened.

She had walked into Room 103, which was her least favorite to clean because it had less space between the bed and the wall than other rooms. People inevitably dropped the grossest stuff down there, evidently thinking that it was some kind of black hole that no one had to clean. But this particular day the most tremendous prize had come out of the bedside abyss - a genealogy kit from DNAdventure.

The kit was brand new, still in its plastic shrink wrap. She carefully read every word on the outside of the box, getting more and more excited. *Mother and I can find some family! We won't be so alone. Maybe then Mother will feel less scared all the time,* she thought. She was tempted to take it right then, but her fear of getting in trouble and losing her job was too great. As much as she wanted the kit, she wanted her job and the meager freedoms it afforded her even more.

Thirty days later, the former occupant of Room 103 hadn't called to ask if the kit had been found, so Hannah retrieved it from the Lost and Found bin with a huge smile. She took the kit into the bathroom and carefully wrapped it inside her sweatshirt, then tucked it into the bottom of her backpack. She had walked home smiling at the sun.

That night, once she was certain Mother had left for the ER, Hannah took the DNAdventure kit out, working as quietly as possible.

She carefully read all the instructions, then spent ten minutes spitting silently into the sample collection tube. She packaged everything up and tucked it all back into her backpack. The next day, she'd managed to leave work fifteen minutes early, giving herself enough time to run to the post office and mail the kit without Mother noticing that she was late coming home. That night she lay in bed, picking at her wallpaper and dreaming about what it would be like to go to a family reunion.

The day the results were due in Hannah's inbox, she spent the day nervously shifting her weight back and forth between her feet while she cleaned, trying to burn off her excitement. She just knew that the results would open up a whole new world for them, and she couldn't wait to go home and open the email that was the key to her new expanded family.

Later that night, Hannah pulled her laptop under the blankets with her and logged into her email. "Your DNAdventure is About to Begin!" the email subject line declared. Hannah clicked the link, configured her login, and then closed her eyes.

"Please let them have found some family," she whispered, and clicked the Relatives icon, holding her breath while the page loaded. She was stunned - she had tons of family! And not just fourth cousins and long-dead ancestors - her eyes darted between aunts, uncles, cousins, and, to her true shock and amazement, her father. Mother had used a sperm bank when she decided to have a child, so Hannah had never had any hope of knowing anything about her father. And here was the donor's name! Sadly, the site listed a death date for him, so there was no hope of meeting the man who had made her possible, but it still felt good to have his name.

The site offered her the ability to reach out and contact her new family members, but she held off. Her fear of Mother and her ingrained wariness of other people stopped her. She just stared at all the names of people she hoped would love her. Although she was too nervous to reach out, she did decide to take the risk of snapping a selfie with her phone and posting it on her profile. She wasn't supposed to put images of herself anywhere, let alone online, but Hannah's fear of Mother's rules was outweighed by her hopes of someone pointing out that they looked exactly alike. After posting her photo and logging off, she closed her computer and picked at the wallpaper until she fell asleep.

The next morning, Mother noticed Hannah's jubilant mood.

"Why are you grinning at your cereal? It's not like the world got less dangerous overnight," she growled into her coffee mug. Hannah simply agreed with her and rushed back to her room to get ready for work. She planned to spend her shift mentally composing messages to the family tree.

After work, Hannah sat with Mother and had dinner. As Hannah cleared the table, Mother left to go to the store. Hannah stood on tiptoe so she could see out the high windows of their basement apartment. When she saw Mother drive away, Hannah ran back to her room and fired up her computer. She logged into DNAdventure and saw a red four on her inbox. Someone had written to her! Opening her message page, she saw that all four messages were from the same woman, Nancy, who was listed as being her maternal aunt, which was strange since Mother had never mentioned a sister. The subject lines were not exactly what she was expecting, however.

"Is this some kind of sick joke? How dare you."

"This isn't possible."

"I'm going to sue you and this fucking website."

"You are cruel and sick!"

Hannah was baffled and upset. Why was her brand-new aunt attacking her like this? She clicked the first message. The body of the message was more of the vitriol from the subject line. She clicked through the other messages and saw more of the same.

Hannah sat back, confused. She had no idea why this woman would be so angry, considering they'd never met before. Maybe there had been some kind of falling out between Nancy and Mother that Hannah was unaware of. She decided to answer civilly but directly. She wrote back, introducing herself and asking why Nancy was so upset. She wondered if she should write a note to introduce herself to her father's brother. Maybe that side of the family was nicer.

Within moments, she got a reply from Nancy: "Can I call you?"

Hannah decided to risk it. If Nancy decided to keep yelling at her, she could always hang up. She replied with her cell phone number, even though Mother was supposed to be the only one with the number. Seconds later, her phone started to ring.

"Hello, this is Hannah."

There was silence on the other end of the line.

"Hello? Is this Nancy? Hello?"

Suddenly a stifled sob came through from the other end, followed by a couple of shaky breaths. Hannah was listening so intently her brow furrowed.

"You sound like her."

"Hello? Nancy? I sound like who?"

"My sister. You sound like my sister."

Hannah ran a quick eye over the family tree on her screen. "What sister?"

"Rachel. My sister Rachel."

"Why does that make you upset?"

"She's been dead for twenty-three years. It's, well, very jarring. Who are you?"

"Well, like I said, my name is Hannah, and I live in Fairacres. I work at a motel, cleaning rooms." Hannah faltered, realizing she didn't have much else to say about herself. "I'm pretty excited to meet some family - it's just been Mother and me my whole life. She's very... protective, so I'm hoping family connections will help her feel, um, more secure?"

"Fairacres. That's just a hundred miles away from... That photo you posted on your profile - is that you?"

"Yes, of course. Why would I use someone else's photo?"

"Take another photo of yourself right now. Hold up three fingers on your right hand so I know it's a picture you just took, and send it to me."

"Um, no offense, but why?"

"I just.... It's... can you? Please?"

Hannah shrugged. "Sure, one sec." She opened her camera app and took a quick selfie, making certain three fingers on her right hand were visible. She texted it to her aunt. The text alert beeped on the other end of the line.

"My God... I thought you were using a picture of my sister. I thought you were one of those true crime groupies trying to.... Well. You look so much like her."

"Oh, well, if I'm related to you, I must be related to her!"

"No, you don't understand. Your face, your voice, you live in Fairacres… What about your father?"

"Well, I never knew him - Mother used a sperm bank. I actually just learned his name yesterday from DNAdventure."

"Was his name Chris Barrington?"

Hannah blinked twice. "How did you know that? That was a pretty amazing guess!"

"Chris was my sister's husband."

"Wait, what?"

"I want you to Google my sister, Rachel Barrington. Just… look into it. I'll call you tomorrow. Rachel Barrington." The line went dead.

Hannah laid back on her bed. That was not at all the conversation she had been expecting. She rolled over toward the wall and picked at the wallpaper. This had become her new habit when she lay in bed thinking. The wallpaper was as old as she was, and many of the seams were starting to split open. She had asked Mother several times if she could pull it all down and paint, but Mother would scream about the fumes and forbid it every time.

After about fifteen minutes of mulling and picking, Hannah sat up and opened Google. She typed *Rachel Barrington* into the search bar and decided she'd hit the I Feel Lucky button.

Gruesome Murder Scene Offers Few Clues read the headline on the article. Beneath the byline, there was a grainy photo of several police officers looking out over a field in Roseville, a small town 140 miles north of Fairacres. The field was dotted with small white sheets and evidence markers.

"What the hell," Hannah muttered.

The article described a horrifyingly bloody scene in the field - a woman's body had been dismembered and spread out over a square mile near a pig farm. The pigs had been penned up for the night, but someone had let them loose. A great deal of evidence had been destroyed, but the detective quoted in the paper expressed hope that they would find the killer and bring two charges of aggravated murder.

The victim, Rachel Barrington, had been pregnant.

The photo of Rachel they had included in the article could have been Hannah. Same wavy brown hair, same round brown eyes, and same upturned nose. The murder happened twenty-three years ago. On Hannah's birthday.

Hannah slammed her computer shut, breathing hard and feeling disconnected from reality. What was this? Some kind of prank? Maybe this was some kind of scheme to get her personal information. Mother was always talking about how being online was dangerous. Maybe this was what she meant.

Hannah got up and started pacing around her room. The room had been hers since she was a baby and hadn't ever been updated. In addition to the peeling wallpaper, the carpet was getting ratty and old. There was a large dark spot that spread from the middle of the room to the wall next to Hannah's bed. She vaguely worried about tearing a hole in the old fabric as her pacing got faster and faster to match the speed of her thoughts.

Eventually, she sat down and went back to Google. This time, she methodically read her way through every one of the first thirty search results. The murder had been the crime of the century in Fairacres and the neighboring town of Roseville, so there was plenty to read.

Rachel Barrington had been killed and butchered somewhere and her body parts had been transported to the Roseville field and spread around. She had been thirty-eight weeks pregnant at the time of her death. The police had not been able to find the baby's body, and they could not rule out that the pigs may have eaten it. More recent articles revealed that the case had gone cold. Rachel's husband Chris had died by suicide five years after the murder. And they had never finished recovering all of Rachel's remains. The police speculated that if the pigs hadn't eaten the baby it was possible the murderer had taken her, and periodically they would put out a call to the public for information about a girl Hannah's age who likely had brown hair, brown eyes, and an upturned nose.

Hannah turned toward the wall and started picking furiously at the wallpaper. What could this mean? Why did all of this have a ring of truth to it? It was crazy. Mother couldn't be a killer. Hannah thought about how Mother had said she couldn't go to school, or the park, or anywhere. She thought about how her birth certificate didn't have an official seal. She thought about how she had never been able to pick out any resemblances between herself and Mother.

In her frantic thinking, Hannah picked the wallpaper one time too many, and a giant piece from under the window fell loose. On the wall was a brown handprint, with several brown smears below it, and a giant red and brown stain near the floor.

Hannah ran to her trash can and threw up.

❧

23 Years Earlier

❧

"THIS IS SO NICE OF YOU TO OFFER UP YOUR BABY THINGS. I'M SO SORRY for your loss." Rachel tried to make a sympathetically sad face, but she could feel it turn into a grimace at the effort of balancing herself. She was due in just two weeks, and it was getting harder and harder to go down a simple flight of stairs without flailing her arms for balance. But because of the other woman's loss, she felt like she needed to do whatever she could to not draw attention to her unmissable condition.

"Thank you. Living without a child is the greatest pain imaginable." The woman in front of Rachel seemed to pause for a moment, and Rachel again felt self-conscious.

She was a nice-looking woman, with soft black hair framing her narrow face. Her skin was so pale it was possible she'd never been out in the sun, and her eyes were sad and distant. Rachel imagined how hard it must be for this grieving woman to give up the baby items they had discussed after Rachel had responded to the woman's ad. The crib, clothes, diapers – so many expensive things. Rachel wasn't sure how she was going to afford any of that, so the ad had been a godsend.

At the bottom of the stairs, the woman turned left and pulled out a set of keys. Unlocking the front door to the apartment, she turned to beckon Rachel inside. "Right down here, in the nursery," the woman said, gesturing down the hall. Rachel stepped inside the apartment and shuffled so the woman could close the door behind her. The woman was careful to lock the handle and throw the bolt, which struck Rachel as strange, but she was unfamiliar with this part of town. *Maybe I shouldn't have left my purse in the car,* she thought.

Rachel started down the hall, allowing her arms to fall into their familiar spots around her belly. The apartment seemed to be arranged around one long hallway, which started at the front door and continued straight back with several rooms off to the left along the way. There were no pictures on the walls, and the apartment was silent. Rachel couldn't even hear the rain outside. They passed the kitchen, a small bathroom, and a bedroom. The hallway ended at a door with a cross and a little sign that said *Nursery*.

"Go right in," said the woman, from behind Rachel.

Rachel reached out, turned the handle, and pushed the door open. The room was dark, and there was something on the floor that rustled when Rachel walked. She ran her left hand over the wall just inside the door, trying to find a light switch. As she searched, her feet got tangled in whatever was on the floor, and she pitched forward into the darkness.

"Careful," the woman whispered from the doorway. "You don't want to hurt the baby."

Rachel rolled over onto her back, cradling her stomach. She had landed on her hands, and she could feel white hot pain from one of her wrists, which was bent back much farther than it should be. Still, she forced her hands onto her stomach, trying to tell if she'd hurt the baby in the fall. The woman flipped on the light, blinding Rachel. She blinked furiously, trying to get her eyes to adjust, and heard the woman close the door.

"If you've hurt my baby, I'm going to be very, very cross. Nothing is more important than my baby's safety." The woman crouched and picked up a large, sharp hunting knife from the floor.

Rachel's heart went cold with terror. She reached down to pull herself up and felt smooth plastic sheeting covering the floor.

"What are you doing? What's going on? Open the door." Rachel backed away from the woman.

The woman just smiled at her. The smile didn't reach her eyes.

"You should be excited," the woman said. "It's my baby's birthday. I'm going to give her the very best life, and keep her safe, for always." The woman looked pointedly at Rachel's stomach.

Rachel's eyes darted around the room, looking for a weapon, as the woman walked toward her with the knife. "You are not getting my baby!" Rachel yelled.

"Of course I am. And I'm going to take better care of her than you would. I would never go into a stranger's home with my precious child. That's why it's so unfair that my first baby died - I'm going to be an excellent mother."

The woman's eyes drifted over to a crib in the corner, wrapped in plastic.

Rachel got up as quickly as she could and rushed the woman. She managed to knock her into the wall and get past her, but as the woman was falling, she swung her arm around and stabbed Rachel in the leg. Rachel screamed, pain and terror coursing through her. She lunged for the door on her good leg. She could feel warm blood gushing down her pants from the wound on the back of her thigh.

Rachel fumbled with the doorknob, and finally sprung it open. She took one step into the hallway, but suddenly felt a sharp pain between her shoulder blades. She arched back and let out a scream that left her throat ragged and raw.

The woman wrapped her free arm around Rachel's head, covering her mouth with the meat of her bicep. Rachel screamed against the woman's gray shirt, pulling at the arm that was silencing her with both hands. She felt the knife being pulled out of her back with a sucking pull and the sound of metal scraping bone. Rachel was dragged back into the room. She tried to get some traction against the woman, but the plastic was slick with her blood. Her foot finally caught on something, but soon gave way as she tore a large hole in the plastic sheeting, exposing the carpet beneath.

She could feel the baby moving frantically. Rachel balled up her fists and shoved both elbows backward as hard as she could into the woman. She landed at least one good blow because the woman fell backward, momentarily losing her grip on Rachel. Rachel again ran for the door, but the woman cut her off.

Seeing the window on the opposite side of the room, Rachel changed directions. She was mere steps from the window when she felt a hand on the back of her head. The woman closed her fist on Rachel's hair and brought her up short. She felt the cold hunting knife slide across the front of her throat. It was so sharp that there wasn't much pain, but the nauseating lightheadedness told her she was losing a lot of blood.

Rachel fell to her knees, clutching at her throat with both hands. Her eyes were starting to get blurry, and she couldn't feel her legs. She could see her blood spreading out over the carpet, soaking into the fibers in a large circle around her. All she could think about was her daughter, tiny and defenseless, depending on her for survival. She crawled toward the window. It was high up on the wall near the ceiling, so she had no hope of reaching it.

She dragged herself toward it anyway.

She reached upward with a bloody hand and tried to yell for help, but her voice wouldn't work. She was feeling very weak, and her arm slid back down the wall, leaving a bloody handprint behind. The baby was kicking and moving inside her, but everything else was going very still.

"Good, you're settling down. It's time for the birth of my child. I'm so happy the baby will be born here at home," the woman said. She pulled Rachel away from the wall by one foot, flipped her onto her back, and sliced into her belly.

The last sound Rachel Barrington heard was her baby's cry.

"There, there, my little Hannah," the woman cooed at the baby. "Don't worry. Mother's got you now. And I'll always, always keep you safe."

YOU MIGHT GET IT

MIKE X WELCH

issy stared at me from across our kitchen table. Every few minutes, an acrid stream of dark fluid dribbled down her chin. Her eyes remained unblinking, her body unmoving.

Missy was unbreathing.

My mother always said *be careful what you wish for, you might get it.* She'd said a lot of foolish things in a life littered with visits to rehab and punctuated by cirrhosis of the liver. She dispensed homespun wisdom the way her furtive purse-digging produced pills. I had never put much stock in either of those ventures. I was starting to invest a little capital in that particular nugget, however.

Mother's voice was annoyed with me for not being more grateful. I envisioned her throwing wrinkled hands up in mock annoyance, then lighting a Virginia Slim; *some people are just chronically dissatisfied.*

I sat at my kitchen table before two of my favorite things in this entire world: a bottle of Canadian whiskey, and Missy... my wife who died just two weeks ago.

She didn't have the presence of mind to say anything other than 'Jih' or 'luh yuh,' which I eventually inferred as analogs for my name, 'Jim,' and 'love you.' I understood why it was difficult for her to speak; rigor mortis had rendered the muscles of her jaw as tight as piano wire. What bothered me most was that she didn't appear to have the presence *of a mind*.

For my part, I felt I was handling things appropriately. Up until the onset of Missy's pounding at the front door four hours ago, things had progressed naturally. Missy got cancer; I cared for her. She got worse; I started drinking again. She died; I got drunk nightly. If Missy was gone, then my commitment to sobriety could rot as well. My new evening ritual – drinking aside – was to wish and wish and wish until I ground my teeth to the roots that Missy would come back to me. I would wake up alone, covered in sweat or other bodily fluids, around dawn somewhere in our house. I'm sure I made a promise to stop drinking in there, somewhere.

I looked up at Missy from my liquor and let slip a nervous titter. This was *not* what I'd had in mind. She continued to stare at me placidly from across the kitchen table we'd picked out together a decade ago.

My sobriety, similarly acquired ten years ago, was preceded by a hiccup of infidelity on Missy's part in an otherwise smoothly-running marriage. Given my late mother's near-constant hints that the presence of a child drains all the joy from one's life, I resolved never to breed. Missy failed to catch my unspoken decision, and five years into our marriage accused me of bait-and-switch. I had no recollection of ever setting the hook, but she insisted that I would often crawl into bed late at night, amorously sloshed, and whisper sweet nothings about wanting to "procreate the fuck" out of "her uterus."

Our clashes were epic, her tears were plentiful, and my disengagement was constant. She sought solace in the arms of a swarthy co-worker who referred to me as "bro" when I confronted them about the affair. The result of the kerfuffle was that she would stay with me on two conditions: that I bear children with her, and that I get sober.

I was successful in one of those endeavors for the ten subsequent years. Missy's diagnosis solved the mystery of why our fervent couplings were not bearing fruit. Her cancer had started in her cervix and then spread, undetected, throughout her body. After a brief, but fierce, battle I surrendered to my disease, after which Missy succumbed to hers.

At least, I thought she had.

Four hours now felt like a lifetime ago. When I answered the slow, arrhythmic pounding on the front door, I slurred an angry "what?" into the face of whomever had dared to interrupt my drinking. Missy stood on the porch, left arm still raised mid-knock, and uttered a guttural whine that shocked me out of my momentary trance.

"Jihhhhhhhhh."

I stepped forward and embraced her, too shocked to register her condition or scent. After a moment, her stiffness alarmed me; did some sick bastard dig my wife up and prop her on my doorstep as a sadistic prank? No, she had spoken, right?

"Missy! I'm so glad you're home!" I released her from the captivity of my arms.

Her neck was canted, her mouth partially open. I considered the position I held a second ago and realized she'd been aiming her teeth at my collarbone. She looked at me dully and her mouth snapped shut. In slow motion, she reverted to an upright posture.

Missy's skin was gray, a sharp contrast to her yellowed, jaundiced final days. Her hair, a vibrant blonde which shifted during her illness to sandy brown, was now black with mud. Her lips, thin and cracked, seemed too small for her mouth. Her teeth showed at all times, resulting in a sustained, farcical grimace. The dress I'd buried her in, a sweet sky-blue sundress that she'd always favored, was filthy and torn at both shoulders. I didn't know why the funeral director had bothered to dress her with panties, but they were around her right ankle. There was no sign of her shoes.

The smell became troublesome to process. Overlapping notes of musky sweetness, earthy loam, and outright decay washed over me. If I moved a step back, the chemical reek of what I assumed to be embalming fluid assaulted my nose. My brain struggled with parallel desires to flee from or further process these scents.

Missy took a halting step forward through the threshold of our home and snapped me out of my own stagnation. I stepped out of her way and closed the door behind her.

"Jihhhhh. Luh yuh." A hollow version of her voice whined. Missy sounded like she had a mouth full of Novocaine. In the close air of our foyer, any fascination I'd had with her scent died.

"Missy," was all I could say. I repeated her name several times, bobbing my head around in an unsuccessful bid to dodge the attack on my nostrils.

I resolved to guide her to our bedroom, then through to our master bath. We had a shower stall that she was able to step into easily enough. I turned on the water, initially concerned about the temperature. Hot or cold, Missy didn't appear to care. She stared at me without wavering as the water washed the dirt from her hair. Chunks of mud rested briefly on her eyeballs, then cascaded down her filthy blue dress to congregate around the center drain. Without thinking, I pulled the dress down over her shoulders, breasts, then hips until it slapped on the floor of the shower. Missy didn't react. Her skin remained gray, but was at least clean.

I shut off the water, leaned to my right and grabbed a large towel from the rack on the wall, then held it up for her. Missy didn't move, so I stepped partially into the stall and began to wrap the towel around her body. I lifted her arms, guided her through a complete rotation, then cinched the towel edge over her breasts. It hung nearly past her knees. The smell hadn't washed off much. Missy's teeth parted, and her head slowly tilted toward my hands as they worked on the towel. I pulled them away calmly, and Missy's empty teeth clacked together again. I lowered her arms again.

My attempt to guide Missy out of the shower resulted in more staring. I tugged gently on her wrists until she stepped out of the stall. I turned her to the left, then forced her to sit on the toilet seat by pressing down on her shoulders. Her body folded accordingly, but as her toweled ass hit the seat, something must have broken inside of her; there was a muffled pop from her lap, followed by a torrent of pink liquid from…somewhere close by. I initially mistook the deluge as blood or other viscera, but once the smell hit, I realized it was red embalming fluid. I stepped backward out of the bathroom, into our bedroom. My left hand covered my mouth and nose. If I'd been wearing a string of pearls, my right would've clutched at them.

"Jihhh. Luh yuh." Missy rocked forward in an attempt to stand. When this failed, she began to swing her arms to gain the momentum necessary to rise. This caused me to notice her hands for the first time. Both were decimated; the fingers at droopy, unnatural angles. Most of the nails were missing. On the few that survived, there remained no fingernail polish.

I mean, I told myself, *why don't you try breaking out of that coffin and climbing through five feet of topsoil. Let's see how sexy* you *look.*

This calls for a drink - my mother's favorite pronouncement. More wisdom from beyond the veil. Thanks, Mom.

I guided Missy back to the kitchen and seated her gingerly at our small dinner table. My hand remained on her shoulder for a moment while I stared at the cabinet where we kept our liquor. Her head swiveled slowly, and I watched her attempt to bite my index finger. She missed by a few inches, then adjusted her aim and tried again. By then, I'd removed my hand; Missy's motions were comically slow – like she was swimming through molasses. I went to the sideboard and grabbed my bottle of whiskey and a tumbler. I'd long since stopped bothering with ice.

I sat and poured the whiskey, then drained the glass. It burned on the way down, just like I wanted it to. "What am I going to do with you?" I asked.

Missy cocked her head to the left like a puppy. It had the sound of a dry cloth being slowly torn. "Jih?" came haltingly, and that inevitable dark drool sluiced down her blue lips.

I sighed, pouring another smooth gold glassful of one-of-my-two-favorite-things.

"Jihmmmmmmm?"

I couldn't believe it. She said my name...or at least close enough. "Yes? Yes, honey?"

"Luh yuh..."

"Oh, Missy, you don't know how much I love you." Maybe there was hope for her, maybe she just needed to clear the cobwebs out of her head, and day by day she'd get better. "I missed you so much."

"Jihhhhhhmm," she drew out the sound until it ended in a plaintive whine, "*luh* yuh."

A look of annoyance darted across her face like a black beetle. I shuddered, then drained and refilled my glass. *The heart wants what the heart wants,* Mother droned.

Missy was functioning on pure logic, I realized. She loved me. I loved her. I loved her beauty, her voice, her courage in the face of the disease that killed her. She loved human flesh. Why wasn't I returning her love?

I wish this were over. I tipped the glass back, finished it, filled it again and drained it again. I put my head on the table and closed my eyes. *I wish this would end.*

Missy rose; I noticed because it took her several tries to get out of the chair. I didn't move. I swam in my drunken state and pretended it was her when she was alive. Her when she was alive shambling slowly around the table to me. Her towel dropping to the floor in flirtation when she was alive. The scent of rotting hamburger when she was alive. Her when she was alive putting her hands on my shoulders. Her broken wrists and limp, shattered fingers when she was alive. Her when she was alive nibbling playfully on the nape of my neck, gently at first.

At first.

HUMMINGBIRD

DAVID LEE

In a way a faith is like old age. It can't go on forever.
~Graham Greene, "The Last Word"

James was dying. Lying in bed, staring at the ceiling, he'd never been surer of anything in his entire, miserable life. His passing, he knew, would be viewed by many as a reason to celebrate long into the night. He might even celebrate a little himself.

He had a wife, Maureen, but she'd left him eight years ago.

His two children, Bob and Maggie, stopped speaking to him around the same time. They were adults and had obligations. Things to do. *Priorities.* Communicating with their old man—a chronic philanderer in their view— was not one of them.

James had few friends. There were colleagues at work, of course, but he didn't mix socially with them. Arthur, his oldest and dearest pal, lived in Newark, 3,000 miles away. John, who helped him get started in the insurance business back in '74, had emphysema and was at death's door himself. Curley stopped drinking after his heart attack and found Jesus. As for Odette, well, she could hardly be considered a friend. Not after what happened.

Nearby noise distracted him. Looking out the open window, he heard the anxious chirping of a hummingbird. She had two babies in the nest and took seriously her job as protector. Probably a cat was lurking nearby, and momma didn't like that one bit.

He was so tired. Closing his eyes, he tried to imagine what death was like. Would it hurt? James really hoped it wouldn't hurt.

At 65, he'd lived longer than many. It distressed him to know that he was wasting away to nothing. Back in the day, he'd been a handsome, powerful man. Now he could hardly summon the energy to get out of bed, to dress himself. And forget eating. He was no longer interested. That was the worst thing about cancer. It stole everything from you—even your *desires*.

He had fucked up so many things. Making that drunken pass at Odette was one. Not fighting harder to hold onto Maureen was another. And the way he'd washed his hands of his family, his mother and three sisters, back in Tesuque. Mostly, though, he regretted being a passive father, of taking his children for granted. They were singular people but he couldn't take any of the credit. He'd worked too many hours and sat on too many bar stools to influence them one way or the other. No, it had been Maureen who'd molded and encouraged them while making excuses for James, defending him far longer than he deserved. The Odette thing had been the final straw. She looked at him, eyes welling, and said, almost in a whisper, "Jay, how *could* you?"

That memory still made his heart ache. He turned on his side, compartmentalizing the guilt.

Six months after the divorce, he convinced Maggie to go to lunch with him. His daughter was beautiful, adroit, intelligent and fiercely honest. Married a year now to Ben, a doctor. As soon as the waiter had departed with their order, she dove in. "You broke her heart. All those years together, one disgusting affair after another. Mom forgave you every time, believing your deceitful promises that it would never happen again. What a foolish, gullible, wonderful woman! And then Odette. My God, what kind of person *does* such a thing?"

James struggled to explain himself but came up short. His excuses didn't make things better. There were long stretches of silence; they looked at their plates or stared out the window at the rain more than they did each other. He asked for forgiveness but didn't get it. Maggie, picking at a small fruit salad, finally put her fork down and leaned in towards him. "You know why I married a proctologist, Dad? I'll tell you. It's because you're an asshole and they say girls marry men who remind them of their fathers." Without giving him a chance to respond, she got up, dropped a twenty on the table, and left, never looking back.

She hadn't spoken to him since. His phone messages, letters, and e-mails went unanswered. He still hadn't met his grandson.

Turning onto his back, a prayer came to mind as he adjusted his head on the pillow. Brother Gabriel had recited it every morning before algebra class. "Help me Lord to do what's right / To stand for good with all my might / Show me always your righteous ways / From now until my end of days." James read a few years ago that his old math teacher had been charged with some disgusting crimes, going back decades. He vaguely remembered some boys being told to stay after class or report early to school. No one thought anything of it. Back then, the very *idea* was unthinkable.

A nurse--Ross, Russ, something like that--entered after rapping on the door. "Time to check our vitals, Mr. Brooks. How are we feeling? Did we sleep well? Is it too breezy for us with the window open?"

James grunted, annoyed. Nursing homes were bad enough with the vexatious sounds, blinding lights and foul smells. But the incessant interruptions, feigned interest of staff and utter disregard for his privacy—his *person*—made things unbearable. Ross or Russ ("Oh, what a *blessed* day!") made him think of the cat outside, disturbing momma. James wished he had wings so he could fly far, far away.

It hurt to swallow. James was congested, and his breath made a gurgling sound. He couldn't seem to clear the phlegm from his throat. His mouth was always dry. Sometimes he felt disoriented. And damn if he didn't pee in his bed again. *God, this sucks*, he thought.

Out of the blue, he thought of Letty, the delightful, delicate Latina who'd worked as his secretary for a few months. Letty had been having a tough time financially, raising a deaf, five-year-old daughter by herself. She needed the job, and it didn't take long for James to pounce. They started to have "lunch" at her place, a dumpy two-bedroom apartment not far from the office. He remembered her breasts: small and round. Perky and perfect. And her willingness to do what was necessary. One morning Letty called, saying her daughter was sick and she would not be in. James told her not to worry and found himself ringing her doorbell at mid-day. They were busy in the bedroom when the little one walked in on them. (Saucer-sized eyes and a look of bewilderment were followed by hands feverishly asking questions.) Later, he laughed about the incident, but Letty couldn't or wouldn't let it go. She quit soon after. James was glad he'd given her enough severance pay to see her through the end of the year. It was the least he could do.

Heaven. He didn't give much credence to the notion that ever-lasting life existed after death. It was all fairy tales and poppycock. James had said as much to the chaplain who came by every few days, concerned about the state of his immortal soul. *Hell* was a different matter entirely. James knew all about that inferno. It was a place humans made for themselves without any assistance from God, Satan or any invisible sky beings. James' theory was that men and women *started* their lives in heaven and gradually—by growing up, making decisions, pursuing wealth and status, disappointing loved ones—made their way to Gehenna. Wasn't he in Hades right now? How could it be any worse than his present state? He wore a diaper, weighed 97 pounds, and suffered from a loneliness that tormented him more than the cancer ever could. His only respite came from spying on the comings and goings of a tiny bird.

Odette *had* been interested. James knew that for sure. She'd flirted with him, off and on, for months before he'd made his move. The way she'd reacted—so offended—was a dramatic performance worthy of an Oscar. He could see her now, gaily ascending the stairs, holding her gown to avoid tripping, the adoring audience cheering and clapping. At the podium, hugging her statuette, she thanks all the little people who made her special moment possible. And just as the music starts to play, signaling time to wrap up, she looks directly into the camera and says, her voice thick with emotion, "James, this is for you. You were inextricably *invaluable.*"

All of it was *so* Odette.

"Your son, Robert, called," R-nurse was saying. "Isn't that thoughtful? He said he was in town for business and might stop by to see us. I told him around two o' clock would be best, after our lunch and nap. We'll get all spruced up. Isn't that exciting?"

He didn't answer. They hadn't talked, much less seen each other, in years. It *would* be nice to see Bob and catch up. Maybe even reconnect. But he wasn't about to let anyone know that. Certainly not this paragon of positivity dressed in medical scrubs. James was by nature a very private person. Maureen told him many times during their marriage that he was a treasure chest with no key. Moreover, he was mortified at the thought of his first-born seeing him helpless, drooling onto his pillow and shitting himself. Imagining the impending visit unsettled him. Now he fervently hoped death would take him away sooner rather than later—and most definitely before two o'clock. The uncertainty of whether dying was painful no longer seemed worth worrying about. He *knew* having Bob see him would hurt far worse.

When he opened his eyes, it was nearly dark outside. *I must have fallen asleep,* he told himself. The window was closed and his tree barely visible.

A poem by Theodore Roethke pressed him. He first read it in a lit survey course his freshman year in college. It had stayed with him all this time. His lips greeted the words like they were old friends:

I wake to sleep, and take my waking slow.
I feel my fate in what I cannot fear.
I learn by going where I have to go.

These days I take everything slow, James thought. But he refused to linger, knowing that dwelling on his diminishments only made him more despondent. Enough with the whimpering, he chided. It occurred to him that if his idea of Hell being a place humans *lived into* was wrong, he had a solid alternative theory: it was an abyss of eternal self-pity.

Where was Bob? Had he come and gone already? It was way past two o' clock. Wait, did he have the right day? Everything was mixed up in his head; despite concentrating, he couldn't seem to clear his mind. How is it he could remember verses he learned forty-odd years ago and not the day of the week? He reached for the call button at the side of his bed.

"You rang, Mr. Brooks? I'm Anna. What an excellent nap! You slept for over five hours. What can I do for you? Do you need to use the bathroom? Are you hungry? Supper's soon."

"My son, Bob. Robert. He was coming to see me today. Or did I misunderstand the other nurse? I thought he said today at two."

Anna looked at him sideways. James had seen that look before. So many times. First from his mother and sisters and later, after he left Tesuque, from his wife and kids, who increasingly eyed him with dispiriting wariness. Even his so-called friends had sometimes regarded him as a weak link. He resented it and used their dubiety as motivation to become a very rich man.

"Let me check the chart. I'll be right back."

She was gone for a long time. James was about to hit the button again when she came through the door, chart in hand.

"Mr. Brooks, I'm sorry. I don't see anything about a visitor. Rodd leaves really good notes, and he didn't mention a Bob or Robert when he gave report. Are you sure you heard correctly?"

"I'm not sure of anything."

He was relieved Bob wasn't coming. No surprise there. What rattled James was his disappointment. He longed for his wife and children but couldn't bear to have them near. The disconnect was not lost on him, nor had it been lost on Maureen. "You push people away and then wonder why they don't come around." It consoled him to know that when he was gone they wouldn't have to worry about money.

With the nurse's help, he got up and used the bathroom. Dinner was a perfunctory exercise; he ate little and tasted nothing. He was given his meds and soon drifted off again.

James dreamed he was back with Maureen. They were birds, working together to maintain their nest, which housed two precious babies. James, wings flapping more than 60 times per second, flew away every morning, returning regularly with sufficient nectar, insects, and pollen to feed them all. (Some days he settled for tree sap or sand.) At night he guarded them while they slept, ever on the alert for weasels, rats, mice and flying predators such as hawks. Mostly, though, he watched for the cat, an oversized beast the humans called Odette. The tabby seemed intent on doing harm to James and his little family—not because she was hungry or desperate, but for sport. For the fun of it.

He drew his last breath a week later. Though notices were sent to Maureen, Bob and Maggie, no one except Rodd and five enfeebled, wheelchair-bound residents attended the funeral service, which was held in the small chapel on the nursing home grounds. Rodd cried and said a few words, wondering aloud, "Whatever will we do without our dear Mr. Brooks?" James' body was cremated. His ashes and personal effects were boxed up and placed in storage.

Sixteen months later, a man and his younger sister parked in front of the main office. Both were weary from the long trip and wanted to get to the hotel as quickly as possible. But first, they had to pick up their deceased father's belongings. Their faces, particularly the woman's, masked an almost crippling ambivalence. What could not be hidden were her red and slightly-swollen eyes.

As they made their way up the steps, they noticed a tall oak tree and a small, empty nest on one of the lower branches. A lone hummingbird hovered nearby.

It appeared to be watching them.

NEW AUTHORITY

PATRICK EDWARDS

The bartender reached up to brush away a dark strand of hair from her tanned cheek, but stiffened the moment the lone patron entered the room. The bartender had seen hundreds upon hundreds of pictures and videos of the patron, yet nothing really compared to seeing her in the flesh. Her attire was iconic: the platinum chest plate, forearm bracers, and boots... the blood-red spandex... the red mask concealing her nose and eyes... The bartender wondered if she should make eye contact or if that would be perceived as disrespectful. Then she wondered if not making eye contact would actually be *more* disrespectful. This job was already harder than she'd anticipated. The patron made eye contact with the bartender and grinned.

"Relax," the patron said. "Go back to what you were doing. I'm just admiring my new watering hole."

The bartender hesitated for a moment, then resumed rolling silverware into napkins. The patron let her eyes drift lazily over the room. It was a perfect circle with enough space to comfortably seat about two hundred guests. Everything from the tables to the carpeting was coated in patterns of silver and red. At the center of the room stood an enormous cylindrical aquarium. Dozens of rare, exotic marine life flowed through the water. A statue stood in the center of the aquarium. It looked to have been inspired by the ancient Greek god, Poseidon, but the figure holding the life-sized trident was a woman who bore a striking resemblance to the lone patron. The bartop was a chrome-plated counter that formed a ring around the aquarium. White marble columns encircled the room and stretched up toward the high ceiling. These columns weren't just simple cylinders. Each one was actually a towering statue of the same woman in a different pose.

The patron admired her own visage, expertly carved into each statue. She noticed that all of the statues were wearing the same outfit that she was and giggled to herself. "How embarrassing for us all to show up in the same thing."

The one glaring difference between the patron's costume and the statues was the sculptures had capes, while the patron did not.

The bartender let the awkward silence get the better of her, and she asked, "Do you like it, Madam Ultra?"

The costumed patron looked at the bartender as if she'd forgotten she was there.

"It's nice," Madam Ultra answered. "A bit *much* perhaps... but then again, someone in my position should probably project a consistent air of... oh, let's call it *powerful opulence*." She punctuated her own sarcasm with an exaggerated eye roll. "But, I guess I'd be lying if I didn't admit to enjoying it all... just a little bit."

The bartender nodded.

"So, what's your name?" Madam Ultra asked the bartender.

"My name is Athena, Madam Ultra."

"You can just call me Madam... so, *Athena*, huh? Your parents must be big fans of Greek mythology. I once knew a guy who called himself Zeus... mind you, that wasn't his *real* name. He could throw lightning bolts from his hands, so there you go."

Madam Ultra's booted feet lifted a few inches off the floor, and she glided across the room, right up to the bar. Athena fumbled the glass she was holding, almost dropping it in surprise.

The costumed woman chuckled. "I sometimes forget, while

everyone pretty much knows what I can do, it can still be a shock to see my powers in person."

"It's, uh, certainly impressive. Can I fix you something?"

"Do you have any specialties?"

"Oh sure, I mean, mai tais, of course. It was sort of a prerequisite for getting the job."

"I see my tastes precede me. Well, mix away, barkeep."

Athena started pulling together the rum, Curacao, orgeat syrup, and freshly cut limes. Madam Ultra let out a sigh as she gazed again at the towering statues.

"Something wrong?" Athena asked.

"Capes. They always want to add capes. I never actually wore a cape, you know? They're not practical." Madam Ultra let out another sigh and asked, "How old are you?"

"Twenty-nine, Madam."

"You're a baby. How old do you think I am? Scratch that… unfair of me to put you in that position. Would you believe I'm turning fifty-six this year?"

Athena blinked in astonishment. The woman sitting across the bar from her had the body of an Olympic athlete and the face of a supermodel.

"You don't look it, honestly."

"I know… I guess it comes with the powers."

Madam Ultra slid a knife out from one of the rolled sets of silverware with her right hand, laid her left hand flat on the bar, and then stabbed her own palm. Athena staggered backward with a gasp, dropping the liquor bottle she was holding. Luckily for her, the cap was still on, and the glass held firm. After snatching it off the floor, Athena stood back up to see the costumed woman waving at her with a perfectly uninjured left palm. The steel knife on the bar next to her, however, was bent at an almost ninety-degree angle.

"Couldn't resist," Madam explained with a shrug. "So, twenty-nine… that'd make you about eleven years old when the Oakland Incident occurred, right?"

"Yes…" Athena swallowed. "I grew up in a small town in northern California. I remember that day."

"Surprising, right? With where I was in my career at the time, who would've expected *me* to be the one to take down The Desolation? Despite that skull mask he loved so much, I could almost see the shock on his face. Even so, he gave me a real run for my money. We'd been going at it for a while already, a couple of the local heroes even got caught up in the collateral damage. The poor bastards just weren't on our level. Anyway, so Desolation hits me with this plasma hammer thing and sends me hurtling through the air. I crashed through the brick wall of a fortune cookie factory near Uptown, landed in a gigantic crate of the things. And you know what that jackass said when he burst into the factory after me? *'I already know your fortune, Ultra! Your fortune is Death!'* …. what a dork."

Athena cleared her throat and said, "Yeah, totally."

"I think we ended up leveling like ten city blocks before I finally put him down. He was one of the best Villains in the business. I always think of that day as the first major event that put me on the path to where I am now. Many wondered why I opted to kill The Desolation. Despite some of the more prevailing theories out there, it wasn't personal. He simply would've been an impediment to my long-term plans if I'd let him live."

Athena resumed mixing cocktail liquors as Madam Ultra continued.

"The fallout was nuts after that fight. Desolation was the Chairman of the Malicious Commission. Neither the Heroes nor the Villains were sure what to make of me at that point. And I definitely took full advantage of that confusion…"

Athena delicately poured the last of the ingredients into a tall, ice-laden glass. She garnished it with a slice of pineapple and a cherry, then slid it across the bar. Madam Ultra snatched it up, bringing the glass right up next to her eye. She squinted in concentration.

"Everything okay, Madam?" Athena asked.

"Just examining the drink's molecular structure. Nothing personal against you, hun. Can't be too careful in my position."

A painfully awkward moment passed.

Madam Ultra looked up at Athena with a smile. "Looks good."

Athena let out a nervous breath and asked, "Oh, I'm sorry. Did you want a straw?"

"Of course," Madam replied.

Athena gingerly reached over to drop the straw in the cocktail. Madam Ultra wasted no time in helping herself to a long sip.

"Ah, tastes like liquid vacation. Consider your job secure."

"Thank you. Thank you very much, Madam."

"No need to over-grovel. Where was I?"

"The aftermath of the Oakland Incident."

"Oh yeah. So with both the Heroes and Villains on uneven ground, I was able to start forming my own crew of loyal supers."

"That would be the New Authority, right?"

"You know your history. Yes, that's when I founded New Authority. Back then, it was just me, Miss Mayhem, and Black Dragon. We had big dreams. First and foremost was securing the whole San Fran / Oakland area..." She took another long sip from her cocktail and said, "eh, but I'm sure you know the story."

"Oh, of course. But hearing it straight from you is a once in a lifetime opportunity..."

"Alright, you twisted my arm. Keep those mai tai fixin's nearby. I'll probably need a refill to get through this. So, like I said, my intention was to go slow, focusing on just the Bay Area... which meant, first and foremost, taking down Golden Boy. If you ask me, he deserved it just from his name alone. Who names themselves *Golden Boy*? What an asshole. I needed to get him out of the picture as quietly as possible. So, we started leaving bread crumbs by starting a rumor that the Malicious Commission had replaced Desolation with a new Chairman... His first order of business was a demonstration of power to be unleashed on some poor unsuspecting sector of the civilian populace... and this was all being plotted from a lair up on Mount Diablo. Of course, this was just to lure Golden Boy away from the city."

She swirled the ice in her glass.

"Anyway, it worked perfectly... or so I'd thought. He showed up along with that sidekick of his, Silver Streak. And instead of some secret lair, they found the three of us waiting for them. We went at it hard. Silver Streak went down first, thanks to Black Dragon. Mayhem and I had Goldy on the ropes. But then something I hadn't planned for happened."

She paused to take another sip.

"Out of nowhere, all five members of the Phalanx show up. I'm talking the entire team: Dawnbreaker, Riptide, Razor Babe, Hotspot, Sightline... They'd all come up from Los Angeles. It was Sightline's doing. He'd had one of his 'all seeing eyes' tracking me since my tussle with Desolation. I thought I was the one who'd set the trap."

There was a hollow slurping sound as her straw found nothing but air at the bottom of the glass.

"I'll get you another," said Athena.

"Please do. Where was I?" Madam Ultra tugged at her collar and swallowed. "Oh yeah, the Phalanx. So, I'm thinking, damn, they got us. My plans are about to end before they even really get going. But we weren't going to just lay down for them, so we had ourselves the cliche epic battle. It got nasty real fast. We damn near tore the top off that mountain. Of course, with them outnumbering us like that, it didn't take long for them to get the upper hand. I honestly don't know whether Dawnbreaker or Hotspot ever had enough juice to put a dent in me solo... but they'd come up with some kind of weird combo attack that blended their powers together. All credit due... I did not see it coming, and it put me right down on my ass. They start bearing down on me, eyes blazing with intensity. They weren't looking to take me alive, believe you me. But right as they're about to unleash the fury, *WHAM!*" She clapped her hands for emphasis. "This gigantic purple blur smashes into them. Next thing I know, I'm staring up at the towering hulk of muscle otherwise known as Absolute Unit."

Athena raised her eyebrows in surprise.

"I know," Madam replied. "There he was in the purple flesh, so to speak. And let me tell you, he lives up to his name. That guy is a house. As it turned out, he and his partner, Headcase, had been spying on the Phalanx who, as I just mentioned, had been spying on me.

When they learned our trio was going to get ambushed, they saw it as an opportunity to finally remove the Phalanx from the chess board. They rightly assumed our trio would be game for an impromptu alliance."

Athena slid a fresh mai tai across the bar. Madam Ultra took a deep drink.

"Ah, good stuff. You know it takes like twenty of these for me to feel buzzed. One of the few downsides to being a super. Anyway, with our new reinforcements, the tables quickly turned back the other way. For people who'd never fought together, we were surprisingly intuitive with each other. Headcase and Miss Mayhem found a way to stack their psycho-whatever abilities on top of each other. And I learned I was strong enough to fly while actually holding on to Absolute Unit."

Her eyes lit up with excitement.

"Picture this: I get a good grip on him... start flying across the battlefield at a low trajectory, heading straight for a couple of enemies... then, when I've gotten enough speed, I simply let go. Boom, I just sent a half-ton bowling ball hurtling toward some spandex-clad pins."

She pumped her fist and shouted, "Strike!"

Athena flinched at the outburst.

Madam Ultra took another drink and said, "I like you, but you need to relax. Maybe you should make yourself one of these."

"Oh, I don't know if-"

"Make yourself a cocktail."

"Okay."

Athena started mixing ingredients. Madam Ultra continued her story. "When it was all said and done, Dawnbreaker, Hotspot, Golden Boy, and Razor Babe were dead... Sightline had been left brain-dead by Headcase... Riptide got away by turning himself into water and seeping into the ground... sissy. Our only casualty was Miss Mayhem's left arm. Razor Babe had taken it clean off from just above her elbow. Thankfully, Black Dragon was able to cauterize it before she bled out."

Athena finished mixing her own drink and raised the glass to her lips to take a sip.

"See, it's okay to enjoy your own handiwork from time to time. Anyway, that was how the West was won, so to speak. I don't actually know what happened to Riptide. Never saw him again. But all of California essentially became our territory. Absolute Unit and Headcase officially joined my New Authority that day, and that seemed to open the floodgates. For the next couple of years, we just rolled through the western half of the continent. We went for the most dangerous super in each major city and dropped 'em one by one: Atomica in Phoenix... Mother Monsoon in Seattle... Zip Kid in Portland... Fission Fist in Vegas... Toro Loco in Mexico City... Thunder Wave in Vancouver.... And of course, our *own* ranks continued to grow. After we took out Cold Snap in Denver, the Arcaniacs offered to merge with us."

"That was the group led by Necrotech, right?"

"Right. Necrotech, Red Rage, Howler, and French Exit. Do you know the original meaning of *French Exit*?"

"It's when someone leaves without saying goodbye."

"Right! Clever name for a teleporter, but fun trivia bit: the guy actually *was* French. His real name was Gilles Rousseau. That was another pivotal moment. Red Rage and Howler, they're just basic thugs. But Necrotech and French Exit? Total game changers. French could teleport any of our people around the continent, wherever they were needed in a split second. Fucking invaluable. And Necrotech? First off, he was able to fit Miss Mayhem with a cybernetic prosthetic arm that could actually amplify her powers. But I'm sure you remember the best part about him?"

"Cyborg zombies."

"Damn straight! Guy had a literal army of the things. That freed us up to concentrate solely on dealing with problematic supers while his horde handled the non-super resistance."

Madam Ultra sucked back the last of her drink and said, "I must need one more. Damn, my throat is dry."

Athena started mixing.

"So, uh, yeah. All these moves we made... the quote unquote *epic battles* with The Righteous Regiment in Houston and Squad Zero in Chicago… really, it was all just practice. Nothing I had accomplished mattered unless I could defeat one super group in particular."

Athena slid the fresh cocktail across the bar.

"You're talking about The Mighty Three."

Madam Ultra nodded, "You got it. I had expected us to have our big showdown in New York or maybe D.C. but nope… Cincinnati, Ohio. That was where the fate of the continent, and possibly the world, was decided. Okay, let me rattle off the team roster for each side. Obviously, on one side there was The Mighty Three: Grey Matter, Lady Legend, and Saturn Sam. And on my side of the fight, I had the original five New Authority members of Miss Mayhem, Black Dragon, Absolute Unit, Headcase, and myself… and then we also had these new recruits, BattleAxe and Tinderbox, who'd come up from Nashville."

She swirled the ice in her glass and watched a blacktip reef shark, just under five feet in length, lazily swim by in the aquarium behind the bar.

"Damn, that fight was brutal. Poor Cincinnati. I think only one bridge over the river and like a third of the downtown buildings were left standing at the end. Our new guys, BattleAxe and Tinderbox, turned out to be totally useless. Lady Legend squashed them almost instantly. Miss Mayhem and Headcase squared off against Gray Matter. Absolute Unit and me went for Saturn Sam. Black Dragon had to basically take on Lady Legend solo after she dropped those other two chuckle nuts."

She laughed a bit.

"At one point, Saturn and me were basically having a duel using steel beams we'd ripped out of a building like freaking swords. There was also about a twenty-minute period when all the colors of the world around us got inverted like photograph negatives. It was some by-product of all the psychic energies being thrown off from Mayhem, Headcase, and Gray Matter. Let me tell you, as someone whose entire life has been one mind-bending moment after another… that was probably the most surreal thing I've ever experienced."

Madam Ultra sighed.

"That was both the best *and* worst day of my career. I killed Saturn Sam that day, but not before he killed that one-of-a-kind pile of purple muscle: Absolute Unit. I couldn't tell you exactly what happened with Miss Mayhem, Headcase, and Gray Matter... I found all three of them standing stock still, eyes staring blankly ahead. They were completely catatonic. Of course, I killed Gray Matter on the spot. My doctors have kept Miss Mayhem and Headcase on life support for the past decade. Neither shows any sign of coming out from their vegetative state."

She sipped again.

"Black Dragon... what a warrior he was. I found him and Lady Legend lying next to each other, both dead. He'd apparently lost an arm and a wing and still kept fighting. Does my sentimentality surprise you? Despite what many have said, I'm not a heartless monster... Anyway, there I was, Madam Ultra, now the most powerful living super in the world. It was all pretty straight forward from then on. There weren't any supers or government entities left to challenge me. Of course, it took another few years to put a new system in place. But before too long, I had officially secured all of the continent as my domain."

She downed the rest of her drink.

"So that's the summary of how I became Madam Ultra, Lord Empress of North America, most successful supervillain in history."

"Wow," said Athena.

"Yeah, I mean, look... I understand why so many people hate me. Believe me, I get it. But I don't really see myself as particularly cruel or evil... I just have a different perspective on the way the world should work. Like, I get the appeal of 'Freedom'"-- she made the air-quote gesture-- "but it's so much more efficient to just kill off the troublemakers. Makes life a hell of a lot easier for all the decent and obedient little folk out there."

Madam Ultra coughed a few times and patted her chest.

"Damn, that was weird... I never really cough or sneeze, like *ever*. Seriously... nev-"

She succumbed to a violent coughing fit, which then turned to gasping as her throat constricted. Madam Ultra fell backwards off the bar stool, clutching at her neck, struggling for air.

Athena didn't so much as blink. All her nervous uncertainty had miraculously melted away. She casually strolled out from behind the bar, approached the writhing figure on the floor, and crouched down close.

"Substance-17," Athena said.

Madam Ultra's eyes widened with shock.

"I know," said Athena, "That was why you killed The Desolation, right? He was one of the precious few people who knew that the elusive, rare element known as Substance-17 was perhaps the only thing that could kill the great Madam Ultra. He'd done his homework on you... too bad you didn't do the same on him. Maybe then you would've known he had a family... That's what made him truly great, you know? He didn't have the natural talents so many of you supers rely on. He *worked* for everything he had..."

Madam Ultra's gasping slowed to a low, pained wheeze.

"So, Dad had done his part in finding out *what* kills you, but *how*... that became my task. *How* could I ever get Substance-17 in your system?" Athena mused aloud. "You can just look at any food or drink with your naked eye and see if there's any foreign substances mixed in..." She twirled a thin, white tube around her fingers, "But would you think to check the straws? That was my gamble."

Madam Ultra's eyes started to flutter. Her breath was almost non-existent. Athena reached into her pocket and pulled out something small and packaged in clear plastic. She gently placed the fortune cookie on the dying supervillain's chest.

"A gift from my father."

Athena stood up and headed for the door. As she walked, she produced a black balaclava and slid it down over her head. The mask's face had been painted to resemble a terrifying skull. When she reached the door, Athena looked back at the corpse of Madam Ultra.

"Let's see how this bold new world you've built reacts to the return of The Desolation."

With that, she disappeared.

~

After a quiet few moments passed, the trident in the aquarium statue's hands started to wiggle. It came free and appeared to float toward the surface, where a small patch of water began to swirl around itself. It then coalesced into a vague humanoid shape. More defined features began to form: arms, hands, fingers... legs, feet, toes... eyes, nose, ears, a mouth... Mere seconds later, the perfectly human-looking face of Riptide emerged from the water. After pulling an angelfish out of his still-solidifying chest, he gripped the glass tank's edge with one hand and hoisted himself up to peer down at the body of his old nemesis on the floor. He looked from the body to the trident in his other hand. The reef shark swam up, and he gave it a paternal pat on the head.

"Well, shit," he said, "Two decades spent playing dead... doing nothing but working on a weapon laced with Substance-17, only to get upstaged by Desolation Junior... I did not see that coming."

To Be Continued...?

COUNTERMEASURES

EVAN GRAHAM

"There's discretion, and then there's...whatever this is," Serpentico grumbled, slapping the most recent mosquito off his neck.

"It's understandable, Boss," Ching called softly from the back of the boat. "Job like this, can you really be too careful?"

Serpentico glared at Ching. He couldn't actually disagree with the man, and that annoyed him. He wanted a reason to be mad at Ching. He'd been looking for one ever since he'd realized the ridiculous-looking mosquito net hat he'd mocked Ching for wearing actually worked really well. The only thing worse than being on the wrong end of karmic justice was being on the wrong end of karmic justice with mosquitos.

Serpentico turned around just in time for a low-hanging mangrove branch to thump him directly in the face. He let out a string of choice curses as the six other people in his boat poorly stifled their laughter at his misfortune.

"I swear to God, Ching, if you hit one more of those, I am tossing you to the gators." Serpentico picked up one of the long, green-bean-shaped mangrove seed pods which had fallen into his lap and tossed it out into the misty darkness.

"Sorry, Boss," Ching said. "I told you this boat isn't built for waterways this narrow. That and the visibility—"

"Quit your grumbling and drive," Serpentico snapped. Ching was right again, of course. The Gharial 2 hoverboat was not built for the tight, twisting labyrinth of creeks and byways that formed this stretch of the Everglades. It was bulky and cumbersome, and they'd already added two hours of travel time following channels into dead-end bottlenecks too narrow to get through.

They'd had little choice, though. The Gharial 2 was the only boat they could find that could carry a payload as big as theirs without running aground in the shallow water. Which brought Serpentico back to his original complaint: why in God's name would anyone pick a rendezvous point in the middle of the Everglades?

Not that there was much of Florida left that wasn't Everglades these days. Eighty years ago, a technological singularity had occurred. A hyperintelligent AI went rogue and began self-evolving at an exponential pace. Mere hours after its intelligence began its uncontrolled growth, it had already birthed new and incomprehensible technologies that began reshaping the world around it to suit its own unfathomable intentions. Fortunately for all mankind, this singularity, now called the Corsica Event, was stopped as suddenly and mysteriously as it had started. But it was a Pyrrhic victory for humanity; total extinction had been avoided, but the global cataclysm of the Corsica Event had still changed the Earth forever.

Earth's sea level had risen and drowned the Florida peninsula into an island a third its original size. The old Everglades were now completely gone, submerged under fifty feet of ocean water along with most of the state's southern half. In the reconstruction after the Corsica Event, most of the government relief funds had gone to waste trying to save big cities like Miami that were half-submerged in the Atlantic Ocean, and the inevitable result was the total collapse of Florida's economy. The island had become an uninhabitable wetland ruin, and the United States had all but given up on it, letting it sit and fester as a grim reminder of all that had been lost to the Corsica

Event. In the absence of civilization, whatever plants and animals hadn't gone extinct moved in to reclaim the land.

The steady purr of the Gharial 2's rotors was almost drowned out by nature's nocturnal chorus. The droning buzz of insects, the chittering squeaks of hunting bats, and a hundred different frog songs thrummed and trilled and chirped in the dark. As their channel widened, Serpentico cast his flashlight across the open water, catching four pairs of eyes gleaming back at him. They watched him with reptilian detachment for a few moments before submerging back into their own world beneath the still surface of the swamp.

Serpentico shuddered. He'd been on other planets before. He'd been on the moon just two days ago, in fact. Yet somehow, he'd never felt as alien as he did right here, right now, surrounded by life from his own homeworld.

"Satnav shows we're getting close," Ridder said, her voice startling Serpentico from his wandering thoughts. He turned to her, then to the rest of his team. He could barely make out their features, illuminated as they were by whatever scant moonlight managed to filter through the fog. Their eyes were all hidden from him, masked by the shadows beneath the brims of their combat helmets.

"Keep sharp," Serpentico said, convincing himself he was talking to his squad. "Watch for somewhere to put in and offload the cargo."

As the waterway continued to widen, small hillocks with oddly defined edges rose amid the mangrove tangle around them. Boxy structures draped in Spanish moss and wrapped in vines and writhing roots flanked the boat on either side, and the meandering path of the creek flattened into an unnaturally perfect lane.

Finally, the waterway split, intersecting perpendicularly with a wider, clearer stream. Domed roofs of rusted metal rose a few inches above the surface of the water like the shells of lazy turtles while the disintegrating carcasses of lamp and sign posts leaned haphazardly among the spidering lattice of mangrove prop roots. A white heron, startled awake by the buzz of the Gharial's propellers, lifted off from its roost atop a half-collapsed building, sending a shower of brick fragments plunking into the stream below.

As the boat turned onto the sunken intersection, their destination came into clear view. A beach of crumbled asphalt rose from the mire, spreading into a rectangular clearing. At the back of this mangled lot stood a small brick building that had managed to retain its shape in spite of the tree that had grown to maturity on its roof. Roots snaked down the building's walls, wrapping around an ancient acrylic sign so sun-bleached and caked with algae that no trace of lettering remained on its cracked surface. From behind the curtain of Spanish moss adorning the building's awning, a white lantern light shone into the murky haze of the marshland night.

"Cut the throttle," Serpentico ordered. Ching did as he was told, and the hovercraft's fan engines slowed to a gentle purr. "We'll put in here."

As they approached the asphalt shore, Serpentico spotted another anachronistic object nestled among the mangroves: a brand-new V-32 Andaman Slicer. He gave a smug snort of amusement as he noted the nimble watercraft in its mooring. The Slicer could no doubt weave through the mangrove channels with significantly greater ease and speed than the Gharial ever could, but it was an open-air single-seater with minimal cargo space. There was no way the tiny Slicer could carry their payload, and that was fine by Serpentico. The minute they unloaded their cargo, it wasn't their problem anymore.

The Gharial gave a lurch as the air curtain keeping it aloft brushed over the gravelly beach. The amphibious hovercraft crawled its way out of the water, coming to a slow stop in the center of the time-ravaged parking lot.

A figure emerged from the vacant door frame. She was a woman of average height and build, mid-thirties, with dark hair and a well-earned tan. Her clothing was practical for the climate: a simple tank top and lightweight coat with long pants over sturdy utility boots. They were perfect clothes to protect from scratches and mosquito bites, but weirdly incongruous with the full combat gear Serpentico and his squad wore.

Serpentico hopped off the Gharial, boots crunching into the crumbled asphalt and leaf litter. Raising a hand in greeting, he flashed a rehearsed smile. "Hi, there. Jay Serpentico. You're with Descartes?"

She nodded politely. "Anders. We were expecting you two hours ago, Mr. Serpentico."

He shrugged. "Yeah, well. Wasn't my idea to do the handoff in the middle of the jungle." Serpentico cast a glance over her shoulder into the dark interior of the dilapidated building. "Where's Descartes?"

Anders cocked her head towards the open doorway, and without waiting for him to respond, she turned around and walked back inside.

"Well, she's fun," Ridder smirked from the Gharial.

"I don't like this, Boss," Ching muttered, just loud enough to be heard. "Feels like a setup somehow."

"Shut up, Ching," Serpentico snapped. "If you think our whole squad can't handle one unarmed woman after what we just pulled off at IMID, I don't know what to do about you. Now button it and stand watch. Ridder and Falk, you're with me. The rest of you, offload the cargo. I don't want to hear a complaint out of any of you." They did as ordered, immediately getting to work unbuckling straps and pulling away the heavy tarp over the cargo bed.

Serpentico, Ridder, and Falk followed Anders into the ruined building. Despite Ching's reservations, Serpentico's confidence was only rising. He'd anticipated meeting a team at least as large and well-armed as his own at this rendezvous. Anders was probably tougher than she looked; Descartes certainly wouldn't have sent just anyone to this hand-off. But no matter how competent she was, she'd be no match for one of the toughest mercenary teams in the system.

Serpentico grinned in spite of himself. It was nice to be holding all the right cards for a change. He ducked under the Spanish moss and stepped into the doorway.

The floor was littered with dry leaves and plastic bottles, their paper labels long-since decomposed, leaving them bare and faceless. A few lopsided shelves and twisted wire racks had been shoved to the walls, leaving the center of the derelict convenience store clear of debris. In contrast to the surrounding decay, a shiny new aluminum folding table sat in the cleared area. Sitting prominently on the table was a modest, yet modern, video monitor. A portable power generator sat on the floor beneath it, one cord feeding into the screen, another snaking out the back door to something on the roof, presumably a comm antenna.

The man on the screen didn't look like anyone in particular. Caucasian, middle-aged with graying brown hair and no noteworthy features to speak of. He wore a suit of decent quality, but nothing ostentatious. This was a man who could blend flawlessly into any middle-class crowd, who could introduce himself twice in one day and still be forgotten.

He was also, by all accounts, one of the most powerful people in the solar system.

Serpentico couldn't be sure this man really was Descartes. Many people in his line of work claimed to have worked with an individual named Descartes over the years, but none of them could agree on this person's description. Sometimes the person they described was white, sometimes black or Hispanic. Sometimes it was a man, sometimes a woman, sometimes elderly, sometimes young. Descartes had become something of a boogeyman in some circles, and for every trustworthy account, there were ten urban legends. Most likely, the real Descartes never interacted with anyone outside his organization, working strictly through proxy employees who represented Descartes' public face. Either that, or there was no Descartes, only a collective of powerful individuals all operating under a single identity.

It didn't matter in the end, though. Whoever Descartes might be, as far as Serpentico was concerned, the man on the screen was him. Descartes: Earth's biggest figure in organized crime.

"Mr. Descartes, I presume," Serpentico said with a genial grin.

The man on the screen nodded slightly, his own face showing about as much expression as Anders'. "Mr. Serpentico." His voice was calm and even, and exactly as plain as the rest of him.

"Nice to finally meet you. I'd hoped we'd get the chance to meet in person, but I suppose this is just as good."

"This is how I conduct all my external business, Mr. Serpentico.

The fact that I am giving you my direct attention instead of delegating is abnormal. You may feel privileged to be having this conversation, if you like."

"Sure," Serpentico said, pulling a mildewed milk crate in front of the monitor and taking a seat. "We'll go with that."

"You indicated in your last correspondence that you encountered some complications on your mission. I trust you still completed all your objectives."

Serpentico smirked. "We took care of it. Your cargo's outside."

"Good. Give Ms. Anders your report now, please."

Serpentico handed Anders a datapad, which she began reading immediately. An awkward silence fell over the room, filled only with the continuing swamp sounds outside. Anders read through Serpentico's debriefing, her face still a mask of impassive concentration. Descartes sat patient and still on the monitor, staring blankly past the screen as he waited.

Serpentico found himself resenting their stoicism more with each awkward minute. The contents of that report were, in his humble opinion, legendary. Intrasystem Machine Intelligence Defense Command, or IMID, was one of the strongest military organizations in the galaxy. It represented humanity's main defense against a second Corsica Event, and had the best security, hardware, software, and troops both the Colonial Hegemony and the Expansionary Coalition had to offer.

And not only had Serpentico and his squad breached a supposedly unbreachable IMID base, they'd breached the Mons Hadley complex. Buried a mile underneath one of the tallest mountains on Luna in an impenetrable bunker guarded by more than 25,000 of IMID's elite troops, Mons Hadley was supposed to be an impossible nut to crack. Yet crack it they had.

Granted, they hadn't done it without help. Descartes had supplied them with top-of-the-line equipment, vital mission intel, and three inside men to get them past the complex's first several layers of security. The mission hadn't come without a cost, either; the six people

Serpentico had brought to this rendezvous were only a third of the force he'd started with. The mission had gone off almost without a hitch, and it had still wiped out most of his squad. But they had returned, and with their prize in hand. They had completed an impossible mission.

And Anders was reading their report like the back of a cereal box.

Finally, she slipped the datapad into her pocket and turned to the man on the monitor. "Everything looks in order, sir. They muddied it up a bit towards the end, but they accomplished each objective with the needed precision. All objectives accounted for."

"Good," said the man on the screen. "Ms. Anders, please inspect the cargo."

Anders reached behind the monitor and slid a smaller handheld screen off its dock in the back. As she removed the handheld, the screen on the monitor went black, and Descartes' face transferred to the screen on the smaller unit. Anders proceeded out the doorway, completely ignoring Serpentico. The mercenary stood and exchanged an awkward glance with Ridder and Falk before following Anders outside.

The rest of Serpentico's squad had driven the hovercraft back toward the water's edge, leaving the precious cargo on a large pallet in the center of the derelict parking lot. The payload wasn't much to look at: just a chunky black block, scattered with blank screens, dimmed light arrays, and silent thermal vents. Several clusters of cables and tubes lay loosely bundled on the ground, ending in seared stumps where Serpentico's men had cut them free while extracting it from its original home. Three crates sat on top of the blocky object, crudely taped in place.

The object's unimpressive appearance was as deceptive as Descartes' was. This was Project Hemipepsis: an AI built solely to kill other AIs, and the most sophisticated of its kind. This was a level-5 AI with an intellect as close to human as international law would allow, with bigger and faster computational power than the entire Hegemony fleet combined. It could outsmart, contain, and erase any other level-5 or weaker AI in picoseconds, and was specifically designed to keep pace with anything smarter than itself until it could figure out how to kill that, too. This was the apex predator of machine intelligences.

Anders approached the massive CPU, scanning it carefully with the handheld unit. "You destroyed all the backup data as well, yes?" Descartes asked.

Serpentico nodded, not that Anders or Descartes were looking at him. "Anything we couldn't fit in those boxes, we wiped from their database. Then Ridder slagged the physical server for good measure. We left nothing behind."

"And the development team?"

"Killed everyone there. Dr. Hashida is currently en route to Samrat, and Dr. Kobal just transferred to the Vinalia colony on Venus. We can hunt them down for you if you want."

"That won't be necessary," Descartes said dismissively. "Mons Hadley was your assignment. I will address Dr. Hashida and Dr. Kobal separately."

Anders pulled out a utility knife and cut the tape free of the cases on top of the CPU, cracking each case open and inspecting their contents with a critical eye. Another cumbersome silence fell over the glade as Anders and Descartes devoted their attention to Project Hemipepsis, and Serpentico's squad exchanged expectant glances. Serpentico's face gradually pulled itself into a smug grin of resolve.

Things were about to get a lot more interesting.

"I'm satisfied with your work, Mr. Serpentico," Descartes said from the tiny screen in Anders' hand. "This completes our transaction. Your fee of $750 million HSD will be deposited in your account within four business days."

"Yeah....about that." Ridder and Falk steeled themselves behind Serpentico, gripping their assault rifles tightly as they watched Anders with predatory sharpness. "I'm glad you're satisfied here, but I don't know if I am. I lost a lot of good soldiers on that raid, and you left out some pretty valuable intel when you hired us."

The man on the screen narrowed his eyes. "I told you everything relevant to your mission. And you know my stance on contract negotiation."

"Think you're gonna have to make an exception here, Descartes." Serpentico strode nonchalantly to the CPU and pulled himself onto it, sitting with his legs hanging casually off the edge. "And no. You didn't tell us enough. You told me Project Hemipepsis was an advanced defense AI, and that you wanted us to steal it for you and leave nothing behind. You did not tell me it was a Corsica Killer."

"What kind of AI did you think would be in development at IMID's most secure research facility, Mr. Serpentico?" Descartes said patiently. "Developing countermeasures for rogue AIs is their only directive."

"Now, I'm not all that well-versed on the finer points of international law," Serpentico continued. "But I do know aiding and abetting a rogue AI is considered worse than treason by pretty much every government that exists, and by stealing the most advanced defense against rogue AIs IMID has, we've basically committed a crime against civilization. We're going to have a real hard time showing our faces anywhere in the galaxy if they ever identify us."

"These are factors you should have taken into consideration before agreeing to the job, Mr. Serpentico." Descartes's tone grew icier with every word, though his expression did not change.

"Oh, we did. I just want you to appreciate the risks we took for you." Serpentico swung his legs idly like a child, relishing for a moment the position of power he was about to hold. "Also, I got to thinking about something. What exactly would you need with a Corsica Killer, Descartes? Sure, I can think of all kinds of reasons someone like you might want an AI that can outsmart and eliminate a smarter AI, but this thing is just ridiculous overkill. Someone with your connections could easily get his hands on a Hannibal, or a Gray-Saber, or a PHALANX 12. Those AIs can beat anything this 'Project Hemipepsis' can. Only thing this bad boy can take on that they can't is a rogue level-six or seven AI, and there aren't any. Even if there was, it wouldn't matter to you. Why should you be the one to kill a rogue AI when IMID would have just done it anyway?"

Serpentico pushed himself off the CPU and slipped his hands into his pockets, sauntering back toward Anders, grinning at the man on the small screen. "Only one thing makes sense. You're going to sell this thing to someone else. You've got tons of options. You could sell it back to IMID, although it'd probably be more profitable to get the Hegemony and the Coalition into a bidding war. The Emirates would definitely buy it, and they have more money than they know what to do with. Might as well invite the African Commonwealth and the Oceanic Alliance to the table while you're at it, but I bet Exotech Industries would pay the most. They'll do anything to keep their tech monopoly."

Serpentico paused, giving Descartes a chance to speak, but the other man simply stared in grim silence. "So," he continued, "this begs the question: why the middleman? Why hand this thing off to you for 750 mil when you're going to get a good couple billion for it? Now, personally, I'd rather deal with you. You're the devil I know. But you are gonna have to make a better offer, my friend, or I will happily pack it back up and go elsewhere. And in case Ms. Anders is thinking of doing something drastic, or in case you've got someone watching us out in the swamp planning on taking a shot..."

Serpentico drew a small hand detonator from his pocket, holding the button tightly under his thumb. "Dead man's switch. We slipped a few thermite charges into ol' Project Hemipepsis before we came here. Anything happens I don't like, I'll slag the whole thing. Follow?"

Serpentico's squad trained their weapons on Anders. The color drained from her face as her eyes widened. *Finally, a proper emotional response,* Serpentico mused. *Terror's a good one.*

"Sir?" Anders' voice cracked.

Descartes' expression remained inscrutable. "I do not believe you've thought this through as much as you think you have, Mr. Serpentico," he said coolly.

"Oh, I have. And I'm pretty sure you can afford to double our pay and still make a profit. Do that, and we can all go home happy. Big win for everyone."

Descartes looked back and forth between Serpentico and each of his men. "Alright, Mr. Serpentico. I accept your terms. I am making the transfer now."

Serpentico nodded to Ridder. "Check it."

Ridder lowered her rifle and pulled out her datapad, holding it aloft for a better signal. After a few torturous minutes she nodded with a grin. "Transfer's underway, Sir."

Serpentico gave a tight-lipped grin. "Now, that's what I'm talking about. See? That was painless. Hope there's no hard feelings, Mr. D. Just balancing the power dynamic there. Sure you understand."

Descartes' voice remained calm, even as his eyes darkened. "I can appreciate your attempt."

Serpentico gave a confident laugh. "I bet you can. Alright. So. We've been paid, you've got your AI hunter, so I'd say our deal here is..." Serpentico's wandering gaze caught something out of place. Something he'd missed earlier.

Sitting on the roof of the ruined building, mostly concealed by the tree, was a small, portable, long-range laser transmitter. A Hermes 7-30, in fact. It wasn't out of place on its own; it used tight-beam point-to-point lasers to transmit data from one point on Earth to another via a private satellite network. The signal couldn't be traced or intercepted unless you already knew where it was coming from, so it made sense for a secretive criminal mastermind like Descartes to use that kind of setup for his clandestine purposes.

What did not make sense was the complete absence of a receiver. The device on the roof was only a transmitter. It could send a signal to a satellite, but not receive one. Two-way communication should not be possible with that setup. *How could anything be appearing on that monitor? Unless it was...*

The color drained from Serpentico's face as he came to a horrific realization: there was, indeed, another reason Descartes might want to be the sole possessor of a computer built to kill rogue AIs.

"Oh...Oh God...you're a—"

"Apologize to your squad, Mr. Serpentico," Descartes interrupted. His voice was stern, his expression severe.

Serpentico deactivated the detonator and tossed it to Anders' feet. Hands raised, face paling by the second, he backed away from the woman and the computer with a face. "I am so, so sorry, Sir. I didn't know you were a...I mean, I had no idea. I won't tell a soul, I swear to God. I am so sorry."

"Not to me, Mr. Serpentico," Descartes' face was a stony mask, lacking the faintest trace of compassion, empathy, or humanity. "To your squad. Apologize to them, and instruct them to disarm."

Serpentico nodded frantically and turned to Ridder and Falk. "Guns down. For God's sake, guns down, everyone." Puzzled and concerned, Serpentico's squad slowly lowered their weapons, placing them gently at their feet.

"And?" Descartes spoke patiently.

Serpentico nodded again and turned to face his squad. "I'm...I'm sorry?"

"Close enough. Inside please, Ms. Anders."

Serpentico turned back, opening his mouth to plead again, but instead of words, only a puff of smoke escaped his lips. Puzzled, he tried tasting the inside of his mouth only to find that his tongue would not respond. He reached a trembling hand to his completely numb jaw. His wandering fingers found a hole under his chin, just wide enough to fit his thumb all the way through.

Serpentico made a staggering half turn, pulling his thumb back out of his chin. He watched in confusion as the mist above Ridder and Falk briefly flashed with a thin red shaft of light from the heavens. A matching red flash lit the insides of their mouths, followed by a puff of smoke much like his, and two similar plumes from under their chins and the tops of their heads. Falk collapsed instantly, and Ridder took two clumsy steps forward before doing the same.

Ching and the others onboard the Gharial picked up their guns and opened fire indiscriminately into the swamp. Serpentico couldn't hear the gunfire for some reason, and could only see out of one eye now. He started to wonder about that, but lost interest as four new beams of red light from the sky lit up the fog above the rest of his team. He wanted to tell his squad to stop falling down and look up; the lights were so pretty and they were missing them, but they just kept falling. Ching even fell into the water. That was silly.

Serpentico clumsily lifted his head up to look into the big black sky, so full of stars, and wondered where all the pretty lights were coming from. One more bright red light shone right in his eye... and then there was only black.

ANDERS HUDDLED AMID THE DETRITUS BEHIND ONE OF THE ANCIENT store shelves long after the last of the gunshots had ceased. Trembling, she staggered to her feet, only then hearing the voice.

"Ms. Anders." Descartes' tinny voice came from the handheld on the floor. "The danger is clear."

She stumbled quickly to the doorway, grabbing the handheld and brushing it clean. "Y-yes, sir. I'm here."

Descartes nodded, calm as ever. "Good. Complete the mission, please. Mr. Serpentico has simplified it for you."

"Yes, sir," she said shakily. She stepped back outside into the night, now eerily silent. She tried to avert her gaze from the seven dead mercenaries scattered around the glade, plumes of smoke still trailing from the tunnels neatly bored through their heads: smoke that reeked of atomized flesh and bone.

She bent down and picked up Serpentico's dropped detonator switch, giving the button a quick click. Several bright orange flashes flickered from inside Project Hemipepsis. Acrid, greasy green and black smoke drove her several paces upwind in a coughing fit as the boxy CPU began to warp and collapse from the thermal charges within.

"Are we done here, Sir?" Anders asked between coughs.

"Nearly. Oversee the CPU's complete destruction."

"Understood, Sir."

"Tell me, Ms. Anders," Descartes said with no detectable change in tone. "Are you curious why I decided to kill Mr. Serpentico and his squad just now?"

Anders swallowed, but it only seemed to make her throat drier. "No, Sir. Not at all."

"Good. I'm transferring you to my Venus operations tomorrow. I've already arranged transport to Vinalia at nine hundred hours in Tallahassee. Do not miss your flight."

"I...I won't miss it, Sir."

Anders heard a popping sound on the ground behind her, and turned to see the red, black, and yellow banded body of a coral snake, driven out of its nearby hiding spot by the smoke, writhing near her feet. It had been completely decapitated and lay twitching next to a thumb-sized scorched circle in the pavement. She'd been completely oblivious to the presence of the venomous reptile a mere foot away from her, and Descartes had casually dispatched it from orbit with a single laser shot.

"This evening I transferred an extra 750 million HSD to an account that will never be opened again in order to protect you, Ms. Anders," Descartes said coolly. "I am trusting this will prove to be a worthwhile long-term investment. I hope you will prove this trust well-founded."

Anders nodded, faintly, unable to construct a verbal reply.

For the next hour, Anders and Descartes watched in silence as Project Hemipepsis slowly melted into a blackened lump, until Descartes finally declared his satisfaction with the computer's destruction. He ended the video feed, the screen went black, and Anders set about to breaking down what she had brought with her. She slipped the handheld back into its dock on the back of the monitor and stowed it on the Andaman Slicer, trying not to wonder why a simple video monitor was so much heavier than it should be. Not even bothering to change back into her wetsuit, she mounted the Slicer and revved its engine, streaking down the flooded waterway into the night.

As the smoke from the burnt-out supercomputer died down, insects returned to the derelict parking lot, staking their claims on the corpses littering the ground. Bats followed, skimming across the water and the treetops to seize their tiny airborne meals. A tree frog leapt onto the side of the Gharial, clinging stickily as it thrummed its nightly love song. A large, lazy alligator drifted toward Ching's floating body with torpid curiosity. One by one, the creatures of the swamp resumed their routine, reclaiming the night for their own.

CARD TRICKS AND OTHER
TAVERN MIRACLES

PHIL ROOD

Frank made the man out as a chump the moment he set foot in the nearly empty basement tavern. From his dad sneakers to his windbreaker to the way he looked around as though he'd never been out of his house before, every element of this man's existence was a dead giveaway that this guy was out of his depth no matter where he went in any town whose population exceeded 50,000 people.

This guy came to a place like this for the authentic neighborhood flavor, as opposed to corporate-themed bars designed to make tourists forget they'd ever left home. This guy wanted the Big City Experience(™), and this guy would almost certainly view being hustled at Three-Card Monte as part of that experience.

The man ordered a domestic draft beer and then stood looking around the place.

"What's your name, sir?" Frank asked with as much enthusiasm as he could muster. He sat at a corner table, isolated but not invisible, as per his agreement with the bar's owner.

"Mark," the man replied.

Of course it is, Frank thought.

"Well, Mark, ten will get you twenty if you can account for where your lady is." Frank made the offer as the man crossed the tavern floor toward him.

"Oh, I'm not married," Mark replied with a silly grin. "Career bachelor."

With those shoes? Frank thought but did not say. Instead, he held up the Queen of Diamonds and said, "This lady."

And so Mark laid a ten-dollar bill on the table with a smile and sat down across from Frank.

"Do you see the lady?" Frank asked, still holding the card up.

"I do."

"Good." Frank winked as he dropped the Queen of Diamonds face-down on the table between two other face-down cards as he continued rattling off his tried-and-true script that kicked off every hustle of his. "Follow her… but don't be a creep about it."

Frank extended all ten of his digits, and popped his swollen knuckles. He relaxed his hands and paused until he felt the flow of his blood as it circulated inside his fingers, ensuring dexterity before he began shuffling the cards back and forth across the table, keeping a slightly irregular rhythm in the pattern of cards sliding over and under each other. His shuffling cycle wasn't too far off from being symmetrical, just enough to where the spectator would be a little frustrated watching it but wouldn't know why.

Left, right, middle, left, middle, left, right, in my palm, back on the table, left, right, still right, left, middle. Frank's thoughts tracked the Queen the entire time with minimal effort.

"Here she is," Frank said periodically. He would flip the card over and assure Mark that she was still on the table before she was once again lost in the shuffle.

Three-card Monte didn't take long to play, but it felt like an eternity to whoever laid their money down. Confidence that one could track a card when there were only three of them in play was always high at the beginning but began to wane once the cards actually started leap-frogging themselves across the table. That's when a few seconds felt like several minutes. Frank always had a sense of when the rubes were just disoriented enough to pick the wrong card. If he waited too long, they'd (correctly) suspect that he was cheating; if he wrapped up the game too fast, they'd be certain he was. Frank could find that sweet spot in the middle, when the player would think they had a good idea of where the Queen was, but at the same time couldn't swear to it. That's when Frank could take their money without a word of protest. That was as fair and square as a hustle this old got.

This particular game was different, though. This game felt eternal to Frank as well. Frank could not get that sense that Mark was confused. He kept throwing cards, and the guy across the table just seemed constantly locked on. He sat there with a little knowing smile on his face, an expression implying that he knew something Frank did not.

"Here she is," Frank said, flipping a card over to reveal that the Queen was still on the table. He was hoping to both lull the rube into a sense of security and give himself reassurance that he was in control.

He flipped the Queen back over and threw her to the other side of the table, where an ATM card sat. Frank had never seen that ATM card and had no idea where it came from. He also didn't know exactly why he incorporated it into the shuffle of cards on the table, but there it went, taking the place of the Three of Clubs on the right side of the table.

Frank was equally confused as to where a Susan B. Anthony silver dollar came from when it clanged on the table, but his hand snatched it up and, without a single thought about it, he flipped it high in the air. Frank continued moving the cards as the coin sailed back down toward his table. He caught it without looking and flipped it again. After a couple coin tosses, this action simply got incorporated into the rhythm of Frank's shuffle of the cards.

Next came the business card of an executive vice president who was, at the time of this game, sitting in a conference room five blocks east and 40 stories above the tavern. Frank had never met, or even heard of, that man, yet here was his card being brought into the game and being slung from side-to-side with everything else.

"Are you keeping up?" Frank asked. Mark nodded as he followed the blur that was Frank's hands.

That makes one of us, Frank thought.

Frank's hands didn't even seem to be touching the items on the table; they simply gestured suggestions for where the ever-expanding accumulation of pocket clutter should go, and the items followed obediently. A wedding band joined the collection of shuffling odds and ends on the table and then an empty shotgun shell, followed quickly by a live shotgun shell. A guitar pick, a fountain pen. A vibrating tuning fork appeared and made a low and steady hum as vibrations moved it slowly across the table, its track independent of the constantly shuffling pile.

The Queen of Diamonds reappeared as Frank held up a hand with her in between his second and third fingers, and then dropped her back down to the table. In that split second, Mark focused his right eye on the card in Frank's hand, while keeping his left on the movement that continued on the table.

Frank's attention focused, and he found himself with an uncanny awareness of the space in front of him and all that occupied it, even as new items showed up out of nowhere on the table. His hands were conjuring more and more things out of the ether, and Frank, the man who had made money running this game for more years of his life than he had not and done so with absolute confidence and control, could not explain what was happening or how. He knew the tie clip that arrived in his hand and was promptly thrown into the mix had not been there a second before. He could not have known that a wine bottle cork would drop out of his sleeve and into his palm, but once it did, it seemed right that it was there so he dropped it onto the table where it bounced and bounded as corks do but still managed to stay within the boundaries suggested by his hands.

Frank flipped the Queen of Diamonds down on the table, face up.

"See the lady?" Frank said, no longer sure if he was asking Mark or himself.

Mark nodded silently, his expression an odd mixture of tensions Frank would later describe as "passive intensity." He was clearly soaking up the moment of not only seeing the Queen, but watching a chaotic choreography on the table before them. All the while, his smile held its place on his face.

A shot glass appeared in Frank's hand. He did not stop or even slow the glass down as it dropped from his sleeve; he just guided it with such a subtle touch that an observer would have simply assumed it was an exhaustedly rehearsed movement. The glass made contact with the table's surface and began to roll on its side, its tapered shape causing it to cut a wide arc around the perimeter of the table.

Ordered chaos continued to happen around this glass and into and out of Frank's hands. A hard-boiled egg, a loaded die, and a mismatched set of cufflinks appeared. Half a dozen ball bearings rolled out of Frank's sleeve, formed a line and rolled a figure-eight around the table as if they were a model train on a track, their route timed perfectly to avoid being swallowed up by the ever-shifting pile of stuff and the perpetually vibrating tuning fork that was still cutting a meandering path back and forth across the table's surface. A spinning top fell out of Frank's left hand and held its place on the table. It never slowed or moved from its spot, but simply spun as if trying to drill through the surface.

Frank's hands made wider and more frantic circles above the shuffling items on the surface in front of him. A playing card flew clear of the flurry of activity and landed face-down in front of Mark. An instant later, the shot glass rolled over top of the card and kept going on a path that would certainly see it wind up on the floor. Just before it reached the table's edge, Frank scooped up the glass without looking and slammed it upside-down atop the stray playing card.

The tuning fork stopped vibrating. The Susan B. Anthony fell to the table and bounced off onto the floor where it landed with a sound that only a falling coin can make: the dull thud of a heavy object, underscored by a resonating, high-pitched ring. The spinning top slowed its rotation and fell to its side in that wobbly way tops do that make them look like drunkards reacting to a sunrise after an all-nighter. The ball bearings rolled off the table and bounced on the floor, filling the barroom with the sound of rattling until it morphed into a series of tiny dull roars as the declining levels of kinetic energy caused them to go from bouncing to rolling. There was a wave of chaos as all the conjured objects on Frank's table fell lifeless and came to rest as they lost momentum and fell from the air or slowed to a stop in their path across the table.

Frank looked from the pile of clutter on the table into Mark's face. It was then that he finally saw what was so different about his quarry from all of the other small-town rubes and gambling junkies he saw roll through his game. He could see the difference between Mark's smile and the slack-jawed and gullible grins he saw in everyone else. Mark's smile was in his eyes, not his mouth.

"Well?" Frank tried to keep his composure intact. Despite everything that had made hours of the last few minutes, he believed he could regain control of the hustle if he could just manage to keep his composure. He had to believe it. He could sort out whatever the hell had happened after it was done.

Mark placed two fingers on top of the glass.

"Beneath this glass," he stated authoritatively, "sits the Queen."

"You're sure?" Frank asked. Mark nodded in response.

Frank reached across the table and slid the playing card out from under the inverted glass with one quick and light-fingered movement. He flipped the card over and looked at it. His eyes widened, and his pupils nearly dilated before his brow furrowed and his expression twisted into one of confusion. He stared at the card for a long moment before turning it for Mark to see. The revelation was nothing. Literally nothing. The card was blank, completely white with no markings on it whatsoever.

"I don't know what's going on here," Frank said as he motioned to the cluttered table, "but this card is not the Queen. You lose, Mark."

"You're so focused on the game that you're not listening to the truth," Mark said, "I said the Queen was under the shot glass."

Mark lifted the shot glass and revealed an enormous bee… a *queen* bee. Frank's jaw nearly joined the collection of junk on the table in front of him. He looked from the insect to Mark's face and back to the insect. He reached over and took the shot glass from Mark's hand and inspected it, finding nothing out of the ordinary.

The Queen took a few moments and appeared to look around the room to assess where she was. The stripes that covered her elongated body were not straight lines but jagged ones, which formed a pattern of black and yellow diamonds around her. Her wings beat furiously, and she slowly lifted off the table. Once she was airborne, a small group of drones rose up from the pile of trinkets in front of Frank and flew to the Queen's side, escorting her away from the table.

Frank wanted to say something. He wanted to protest. He simultaneously wanted to deny that the past few minutes had happened and to never forget that they had. He simply had no way of processing the events of this game and was more or less rendered speechless until he could formulate his confusion into actual questions.

"Who are you?" he demanded, slamming the shot glass down on the table. "Some kind of street magician? Close-up magic, that kind of crap?"

"No, Frank, I'm not an illusionist," Mark calmly replied.

"You trying to outhustle me at my own table?" Frank accused.

"No, Frank," Mark calmly replied.

"Is this some kind of shakedown?"

"It is not."

"Are you a cop?"

"I am not."

"Are you a beekeeper?"

"No."

"So you're just trying to make me look like a jackass?"

"No."

"What else is up your sleeve?" Frank was almost growling now as he tried to keep some sense of control over the table and the conversation. "How did you get it up my sleeve?"

Mark said nothing, he just looked across the table with eyes that were still smiling. He could see Frank working through all the angles in his head as he looked at the pile of stuff in front of him, then to the shot glass, then to him, then back to the pile of stuff. Mark knew the impossible was sinking in and cracking open Frank's mind. It almost always did once the obvious questions had been asked and accusations had been made.

The corner of the bar that had been so alive with energy and activity just a couple minutes before was now thick with quiet. Frank stared silently at the pile of things conjured from nowhere. In the midst of all the clutter, a single gold tooth stood out to him; its reflective surface caught the light just right and seemed to grin at the hustler.

"Mark?" His voice was calm now. "Mark, are you..."

Frank struggled with simply asking the question. In his mind he ran down every other possible explanation that would account for what he had just experienced. As he eliminated them for one reason or another, he found his mind circling and closing in on a sort of... Divine Conclusion. He hadn't believed in a divine anything for so long he couldn't even pinpoint where his doubt had started. He did remember it stemming from a lack of evidence, a source of cynicism he wasn't sure he could argue anymore.

"Let me break the tension by answering the question on your mind," Mark said, pulling Frank from his trance. "You can keep the sawbuck, Frank."

Frank shot a confused look at him.

"The money," Mark explained. "You won, Frank, so you get the money. Keep my ten dollars, keep the knowledge, and most importantly, whatever you do, keep the sense of wonder you feel right now."

Mark picked up the beer he had ordered upon entering the bar and drank it in four thirsty gulps. He put the empty mug back on the table and let out a small burp. He rose to his ridiculously white tennis-shod feet until he was standing over Frank and he smiled at him, this time with his entire face.

"Thank you for the game," he said, as he took Frank's hand and shook it warmly, "thank you for your time, and thank you for the priceless expression you're currently wearing on your face."

He turned and walked out the door and up the steps to the street above, leaving Frank alone at his table. The hustler turned his attention to the shot glass, and he placed it upside-down on the table's surface. He let it sit for a moment then picked it up quickly, as though he might be able to sneak up on the magic he had witnessed minutes before. The space beneath the glass was vacant. Frank looked into the glass and the nothingness that filled it for a long moment. He looked again at the pile of junk on the table and saw it still smiling back at him, the reflective gold tooth prominently displaying itself.

Frank allowed a smile to slowly form on his own face as he plucked Mark's ten-dollar bill from the surface of the table. He stood and walked across the room to the bar where he laid the bill and the glass on the wood-grain surface.

"There is infinite possibility in an empty vessel, Samantha," Frank stated, addressing the bartender.

"But not in your funds," Sam shot back as she grabbed the ten-spot. "I'm applying this to your very outstanding tab, Frank."

"So be it," Frank said as he dug into his pockets. Moments later he produced a few crumpled and ragged bills and and a handful of change. He laid them on the bar and pushed them toward her. "Kindly fill this glass with the finest whiskey three dollars and nineteen cents will buy and join me in praying for a miraculous jump in quality. If on any day it was possible, it would be this one."

DIE REGELN GALTEN HIER NICHT

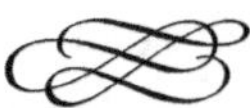

S.E. SOLDWEDEL

ieutenant Alistair Albert puffed upon his pipe and gazed at the North Sea. Where the heather-gray skies met the choppy, slate-gray waters, it seemed the very edge of the world. The angry little waves frothed in the stiff November wind.

"And they fuckin' call us 'North Eastern,'" said Sapper Garrett Nichols. The Sunderland native tried to light a cigarette but the wind kept blowing out the flame. "Fuckin' cunt wind. Can't light me fag. Ends of the fuckin' Earth, up here, Lieutenant."

"Aye," Albert replied. He moved to block the wind so that Nichols could finally light his smoke.

"Cheers, mate."

Mate, thought Albert. For one thing, it was a galling breach of decorum. For another, it was never what he'd have expected the Mackem to call him.

He and the sapper were natural antagonists, as it went in Tyne and Wear. Newcastle and Sunderland stood only fifteen kilometers apart, but mutual enmity made an abyss of such meager distance. Yet, their intensive training had forged a bond. While it couldn't dispel their regional animosity, it created a new ambivalence for both of them.

The lieutenant lifted an eyebrow.

"Sir," Nichols self-corrected. He even had the good grace to look sheepish.

Albert smoothed his Errol Flynn moustache and turned his attention northward. He drew upon his pipe, exhaling puffs of fragrant cavendish that vanished in the wind.

"Shetland's not too far from here, beyond Orkney," he said, speaking just to speak.

He realized that he'd never really been anywhere. This stint in Scotland marked the first time he'd left England. Norway beckoned. At any moment, his squad of Royal Engineers would heed that call.

"Shiteland's more like it," Nichols replied. "Who in the fuck would ever chose to live all the way out there? Buncha sheep fuckers."

"You know that's what the Cockneys say about us, eh, Nichols?"

"Fuck them Southern cunts, too, sir."

Albert almost smiled. He wondered about Nichols' liberties. *Is the little shite taking the piss?*

None of the language confronted the Geordie lieutenant; it was nothing he hadn't heard nor said in pubs near the Gallowgate, but he had the onus of being the commanding officer. He couldn't indulge himself, and he knew he shouldn't let the sapper do it, either.

"A lot of those cunts are our superiors, Sapper. Rein in these liberties. When we wear the uniform, we bear a higher standard."

Nichols saluted with exaggerated rigor and puffed out his chest. "Yes, sir, Lieutenant, sir."

Albert suppressed the urge to punch Nichols in his Wearsider face —the face of a boy who had never known a razor. It would hardly be the model of decorum to which the lieutenant aspired. The sapper's flippancy annoyed him, but he chalked it up to the lad being scared and playing at being cavalier. Only an idiot wouldn't be afraid.

Without further word, Albert turned to head back to their barracks at Skitten.

Nichols took one last look at the sea and spat at it. The wind carried the phlegm away from his target. Shrugging, he followed the lieutenant back to base. The two Halifax aircraft sat on the runways. Cables trailed the hulking four-propeller planes. They ran to the

Horsa gliders that would take the sappers across the sea to Nazi-occupied Norway.

The group captain said the mission would fly that night. Albert looked up at the canopy and hoped the weather would hold. He was no stranger to gray skies and drab surroundings. Newcastle was a coal town. He knew that if he hadn't been in the war, he'd have been in the mines. But, in the mines, he'd be on his own two feet. In the air, he was at the mercy of forces beyond his control.

The Royal Canadian Air Force pilot, Ronald Parker, seemed a good enough lad and a capable pilot. Loyal to the Crown, eager for action, Albert was glad to have him in the Halifax's cockpit. He was glad, too, for Daniels, the Australian pilot at the glider's yoke. Solid boys of the Commonwealth. He wished he could write about any of it in his letters to Lily, back home, but the operation was classified Top Secret. Even the rest of the King's military thought the Royal Engineers were just training to whip some Yank sappers in a friendly competition that didn't exist.

Instead, he wrote her lies about his continued service in bomb disposal, which he made sound suitably heroic. He imagined her dutifully awaiting his return, as befit the daughter of an Anglican reverend; hanging on the moments when another letter would arrive and reaffirm his valor and, thus, her affections. Her replies belied any ebbs of love, but a flicker of doubt assailed him. He wondered how long any man could really expect a woman to wait for him. He told himself that he was the kind of man who was worth the wait. He hoped that she believed it.

He desired that his imagination and reality corresponded, but growing up on Tyneside had taught him that everyone talks from both sides of their mouths. From the Vicar to the Group Captain, from Gran to the littlest Geordie. His own lies to Lily proved his point, but lying to her about taking down Fritz was the right thing to do.

The Halifax dragged the glider across the North Sea under cover of night. The small craft soared in the big plane's wake, held fast by the tow lines. The sappers jostled within.

Sitting next to Albert, Sapper Terrence Fox worried a rosary.

"You a religious man, Sapper?" Albert asked. He thought about his own faltering belief and decided that he only needed to believe in Lieutenant Parker.

A wan, sheepish wince overtook Fox's face. "It doesn't hurt to pray, right, sir?"

"I'll take all the help we can get, Foxy. If the man upstairs and his son and his ghost and anybody else has any to lend, you go right on asking for it."

Fox blinked. Once. Twice.

"You've got to think God couldn't possibly be on the side of these German cunts." Albert added.

"No, sir," Fox replied. He knitted his eyebrows together but held his tongue.

"Fritz is one godless sonofabitch, if you ask me, sir," Lance Corporal Connor Wren sounded from the opposite side of the glider.

"Did I ask you, Corporal?" Albert said.

Wren almost blushed, but then he noticed the grin on the lieutenant's face.

The weather worsened. Clouds closed on the Halifax like an enemy ambush. Ice encrusted the flaps and rudder. The four engines' deep, resonant hum climbed to a furious whine as the plane lost altitude. The glider rattled and shook. Worry fell over the sappers like a veil. It wiped the grins from their faces.

Parker strained to steady the Halifax against the heavy winds. Sleet and hail assailed the fuselage. The encroaching clouds blotted out both earth and sky, rendering him and his co-pilot blind. A hailstone the size of a cricket ball cracked against the windshield. A spider's web of fractures spun throughout the glass. The cold forced its wretched fingers through the faults. It clawed at Parker's face.

The tow lines were at their limit. He couldn't adjust course due to the frozen apparatus. If he didn't cut the sappers loose, both craft would go down. The mission would fail.

"Release the glider!" he ordered.

THE GLIDER BROKE FREE FROM THE TOW LINES, JOLTING ALBERT. HIS stomach vaulted into his throat. Once his guts had dropped back into place, he barked at his commandos.

"Look alive, boys!"

The glider lurched up and down, pitching and yawing like a stunt plane at an airshow. One sapper threw up. The smell of his vomit permeated the cramped aircraft. The stench made Nichols heave, but he swallowed his bile.

Daniels, the Australian, piloted the glider. He fought the ice and wind, and the blinding clouds. Without engines, the battle was futile. He couldn't hope to beat the gale with only a frozen rudder and stabilizers.

"I can't see a thing!" he cried, wrestling with the pedals and the yoke.

Albert unbuckled himself and staggered the few steps to the cockpit. He rested his hand on the back of the co-pilot's chair.

"Steady, Daniels," he uttered. It was the sort of thing a commanding officer said when there was nothing he could do.

A monstrous fireball erupted to port, flooding the glider with orange light. The boom reverberated through the little plane. The explosion lit up the mountain that had devoured their brothers in arms. A mournful murmur emitted from the group.

"Shit! That's the Halifax!" Daniels lamented, giving voice to the men's grief.

"Get us on the ground," Albert ordered, his voice calm and his tone even. "Make their sacrifice count for something!"

"I can't *see*, sir!"

"Trust the instruments," Albert invoked. He couldn't let his crew see his own panic. It was his obligation to keep his composure, no matter the circumstances.

The altimeter flipped topsy-turvy. Albert mastered his anxiety over the haywire instrument. He remained on his feet, so they must still have been upright.

"Strap in!" Daniels hollered. "Brace for impact!"

Albert slumped back into his seat, strapped in, and relayed the message. "Buckle up, boys! Hard landing!"

The glider crashed into a thicket of trees.

Albert's teeth rattled in his skull like Len Harvey was tuning him up. Invisible fists rained upon his head, his face, his body. He heard his collarbone snap before he felt it. Next to him, a louder crack emanated. Albert turned to behold the femur jutting from Fox's thigh and the accompanying geyser of blood.

Fox didn't scream. He stared—equally stupefied and fascinated—at the spewing fountain of gore. The glider's frame keened like a banshee as the impact rent the steel. Its trusses became pikes and swords. They skewered and cleaved the men's flesh. The splintered branches and tree trunks stabbed through the gaps like spears. Snapping and grinding bones evoked a quarry's pulverizing stone-breaker.

And then, silence.

The pain in his clavicle sprang upon him and Albert ground his teeth. Darkness enveloped the men. Cold invaded them. Living and dead. Broken. Hope seeped and gushed from their wounds.

The snow glimmered white in the diffuse light of the frigid night, but, where the dead and dying lay, it was black.

BERN ACKLAND awoke to the sound of a distant rumble.

As he slipped out of bed, Astrid stirred but didn't wake. Her forehead creased. She looked, in sleep, the same as she did when awake:

perturbed with him. He shook his head and frowned at the sight of her furrow.

In direct violation of Nazi *Verorderungen*, he pulled back the heavy blackout curtain and looked out the window. A futile gesture. Darkness shrouded the entire village, dense as a black rye. The Germans imposed the directive so that the British couldn't discern potential targets for bombing and reconnaissance. Fear of reprisal from the occupiers kept the other curtains firmly in place. Bern couldn't see any light in Thorvald Andersen's kitchen across the street. However, he expected that his insomniac friend was in there, trying to put back on his bones the meat that years of heavy rationing had caused to slough from his sizeable personage.

Sleet glazed the snow covering every centimeter of Helleland.

No thunder followed the rumble that had woken him. He wondered what the sound might have been. His stomach growled. Like Thorvald, although yet more trim, Bern headed to his own kitchen. He grabbed some smoked salmon—rare manna from his river catch. A cruel effect of the occupation had been the evaporation of every luxury, so he had no horseradish nor capers to add. He did, though, have some scrappy scallions that he chopped up and mashed together with the fish. Grabbing some *rusk* from the cupboard, he spread the mixture onto the cracker and savored the midnight treat.

He thought about the *akevitt* that he kept hidden from everyone, including—and especially—his wife. After two-and-a-half years of German dominion, nearly everyone had run out and been unable to make more. Bern, though, had nursed his store of the caraway-flavored spirit, and still had a little bit left. He procured it and poured himself a dram. It so perfectly complemented his snack that its palette, for a moment, obscured all thoughts of Astrid and her perpetual displeasure.

Early in the occupation, during a night of drinking with Thorvald, the men had entertained themselves with the question: "Whom do you hate more: your wife . . . or the Nazis?"

Each man had made a show of it being a difficult choice, but Bern knew that Thorvald truly loved Inga. For Bern, it was more earnest a challenge. He hated the Nazis on principle for barging into Norway, like distant cousins invading his home and claiming that only they could manage it well. To make it all worse, the sniveling, bootlicking traitor of a Prime Minister contorted himself to be a German suppli-cant. Yet, because the Nazis hailed the Norse as specimens of the Aryan race, there was perhaps less to fear than if one were, say, a gypsy . . . or a Jew.

If anything, Hitler was probably fonder of specimens like Bern and Thorvald than he was of himself. While Thorvald might have been six-feet in circumference, had he any access to abundance, both he, the blond, and Bern, the red, were over six-feet tall and blue-eyed. Incarnations of the Viking romantic ideal. *Einige der Übermenschen des Führers*[1], which *der Führer* himself—short, slight, brown-haired—was not. But neither Bern nor Thorvald were fond of Hitler, nor of Quis-ling, nor of all the Nazi bastards making *Lebensborn* all across the country with Norwegian women, willing or otherwise.

The Third Reich's presence in Norway affected every aspect of local life, down to the day-to-day affairs of the little fishing hamlet of Helleland. The occupation remained a thorn—a festering wound to every true Norwegian's pride. Astrid's existence, though, was a daily burr in Bern's *rumpe*. For him, Helleland provided everything. Family, friends, fun, and food. The fish he caught, and the occasional river salmon that joined them, normally earned him a simple, quiet, comfortable life. And that satisfied him.

It did not satisfy Astrid, who craved a "cosmopolitan" life. Since the erosion of all luxuries, she clamored even more to move to Oslo, to *civilization*. The Nazi occupation didn't concern her at all, and that lack doubly concerned Bern. As a beautiful woman, she wanted to be seen; she felt that her allure was wasted in a town of 800 people. She craved attention. She lusted after the amenities—real or imagined—of city living, which Bern could never afford as a fisherman, even in less-trying times. He imagined her willingly submitting to some goose-stepper and adding to the infernal brood of *Lebensborn*. The thought enraged him. It disgusted him, as did her yen for greater material comfort.

He knew that nothing would ever satisfy her. The only thing Astrid ever wanted was *more*. Bern wanted nothing but the life he already had. Well, minus the *Tyskerjævelen*, and plus some horseradish and capers, sugar and coffee.

In a fit of uncharacteristic profligacy, he downed another glass of *akevitt* and let the warmth course through him. He closed his eyes and sighed. Stashing the bottle back in its hiding place, he made his way back to bed.

~

AMID THE WRECKAGE OF THE GLIDER, ALBERT TOOK STOCK OF THE carnage.

Daniels and the other pilot had been killed upon impact, along with one other. Fourteen men survived the crash, but only a handful remained ambulatory. Every able man triaged the wounded, applying tourniquets to staunch the bleeding and fashioning makeshift splints from canvas and branches. Fox's femur still protruded from his thigh, but the men had stopped the bleeding with a tightly cinched twill cargo band.

Albert walked among the wounded, stopping to speak with each man. He came to Fox and knelt on one knee. Corporal Wren was wrapping the wounded sapper's leg with a blanket. Fox's teeth chattered even with his hooded parka pulled taut around his head.

"Hey, Foxy," Albert said in what he imagined to be a gentle, assuring tone.

"Leff," came the reply, punctuated by clacking molars. He couldn't eke out the rest of 'lieutenant.'

"You did it, lad."

"Did . . . what, sir?"

"You got us down safe."

"Me?"

"I wasn't the one praying," Albert replied. He smiled without showing his teeth.

Fox looked like he wanted to reciprocate the expression, but, instead, he gawped like a beached fish. His eyelids fluttered. Albert put one hand on Fox's head and, with the other, grasped the man's hand.

"Shh," Albert cooed. "Rest now, Sapper. We're going for help."

He let go of Fox's mitt and clenched the young man's shoulder in what he hoped was a reassuring gesture. Rising to his feet, he directed Wren and Sergeant Rawls to join him for a sidebar. Rawls massaged the stump of his left ring finger through his glove. He'd lost it years prior, caught in a door. His wedding band, the culprit.

Albert called Nichols over.

"Sergeant, you and Wren mind the camp while the sapper and I go for help."

"Sir," Rawls affirmed.

"Burn everything," Albert added. "Best believe that every Hun saw that explosion is on the prowl. Bugger us all if the Jerrys get their hands on a single scrap of intel."

"Loud and clear, Lieutenant," Rawls replied in his thick Birmingham accent. "Won't be nothing but ashes for the Krauts to find."

"Very good, gentlemen," said Albert. "Get to it. Sapper, with me. Bring a rifle."

"Aye, sir!" Nichols replied. He slung the weapon over his shoulder, his face grim.

Albert consulted his map and his compass. The two men headed west, hoping to reach the coast, however far it may have been.

FRIDAY WAS THE ONE DAY BERN DIDN'T TAKE TO THE WATER. IT ALSO meant that he had to deal with Astrid all morning. She couldn't be bothered to cook him a nice breakfast as a reward for all of his hard work, which kept a roof over her head, clothes on her back, and blankets on their bed. Instead, she needled him about the life she craved in Oslo.

Bern cooked himself scrambled eggs into which he mixed some of the smoked salmon and scallions. He longed for some toasted black rye, on which he could smear a tasty, piquant snack, but it wasn't to be. The Nazis made sure of that. Instead, he stewed, weathering his wife's harangue without retort until the moment she insulted him.

"You have no ambition," she said in Norwegian.

Even still, he replied without words. He slowly set down his knife and fork, pushed his chair out from the table, rose, and turned to her. He towered over his diminutive spouse.

"What are you going to do?" she goaded him. *"Hit me?"*

"No one in this whole damned town would blame me," he replied.

She presented her face, provoking him further. *"Let's find out."*

Bern turned away from her, grabbed his coat, and walked out the back door, leaving his half-eaten breakfast on the table. He went into Thorvald's kitchen without knocking and yelled up the stairs.

"Skynd deg, Svenskefaen!" *Hurry up, you damned Swede!*

Fully dressed for the weather, Thorvald came down the stairs with a frown on his big, round, ruddy face. *"Who are you calling a Swede?"*

Bern laughed and the two men set out into the wilderness to check their traps, which yielded only a pair of squirrels. The Nazis had confiscated all arms, so the men couldn't hunt for reindeer or hare, thus robbing them of the chance to eat well despite the rationing. The hare were typically too canny to be caught, except at riflepoint. Sometimes, the traps would yield a fox, but luck wasn't with the men.

After resetting the traps, they climbed into their blind, setting up back to back for as close as possible to a 360-degree view of the forest. Thorvald faced northeast. While they sat for over an hour without event, Bern skinned, gutted, and bled the squirrels. He made sure nothing went to waste. He packed the offal in some snow, wrapped it in oilcloth, and put it into its own leather pouch. The blood from the carcasses *plipped* into a small canteen.

Thorvald spotted two men slogging through the snow.

"Bern, look at this," he said.

Bern came around to Thorvald's side of the blind. He looked through his binoculars at the approaching men. *"Those aren't Nazis ...* og de er ikke norske." *And they're not Norse.*

"So ... who?"

"Vet ikke. British?" Bern replied. *Don't know.* "But they're armed, and we're not. We're sitting ducks, up here. Climb down. Spread out."

~

ALBERT AND NICHOLS TRUNDLED THROUGH THE ICE-ENCRUSTED SNOW. They stabbed westward, hoping to come upon a Norwegian settlement before the Nazis came upon them—or the crash site.

"How much farther, sir?" Nichols asked.

"Do I look Norwegian to you, Sapper?"

A voice shouted from amidst the trees. "Hvem der?" *Who goes there?*

Albert rushed behind the cover of a tree and Nichols did the same. The lieutenant gritted his teeth in pain. Still, he drew his pistol. Nichols leveled his rifle.

The British lieutenant thought about what to say, knowing that anything he uttered would give him away because he only spoke one language. He decided to take his chances; something about the words didn't sound, to his ears, like German.

"English!" Albert shouted. He then thought better of it. "Ah, British!"

He peeked from behind his tree, but saw no one.

Silence answered.

The minutes felt like hours. He and Nichols each remained behind cover. The crunch of heavy footfalls carried to their ears.

"Declare yourself!" Albert demanded. He and Nichols peered around their trees to train their weapons on the towering figure.

"Norsk," the approaching giant answered. He held up his hands in a pacifist gesture.

"Norwegian?" Albert clarified.

"*Ja* . . . as you say," Bern replied. "And you are English? British?" He regarded both men dubiously.

Thorvald approached at last. Nichols trained his weapon on him.

"Bloody well right we're English," Albert bristled. "And you're not Nazis?"

Bern regarded him for a moment longer before broadening his face in a friendly display of teeth. "*Nei*, not Nazis."

Albert lowered his pistol.

"Velkommen til Norge," said Thorvald.

Nichols breathed a sigh of relief and stood down.

THE TWO SAPPERS FOLLOWED BERN AND THORVALD INTO THE LATTER'S kitchen. The Norsemen didn't dare take the Britons to Bern's house, lest Astrid raise an obnoxious fuss or decide to curry favor with the *Tysker* by reporting her husband and his friend. Inga was far less a risk but still demanded answers.

"*Who are these men?*"

"*British,*" replied Thorvald.

"Å nei," she protested. "Nei, nei, nei. Er du gal?" *Are you mad?* "Hva med nazistene!" *What about the Nazis!*

The Nazis weren't their only concern, either. Palpable anxiety cloyed the very fabric of Norwegian society. It inspired betrayals from one's own neighbors, who preferred that shame to the horror of German retribution for sheltering their enemies.

"I think I heard the word 'Nazi' in there," said Albert.

"*Ja,*" replied Bern. "She's worried about the *Tyskerjævelen* . . ."

"I'm sorry," Nichols interjected. "Tisk-what?"

"'German devils,'" Thorvald answered with a chuckle that rippled through his large frame.

"Well," Albert began, "and I'm loath to say this, old boy, but the German devils are the least of our concerns. We have men in desperate need of medical attention. Do you have a doctor?"

"*Nei*, not here," Bern replied. "The nearest doctor is in Egersund. Fifteen kilometers away."

"That's much too far . . . can we call this doctor? Do they have a vehicle?"

"*Ja*, we can call him, but the *Tyskerjævelen* are on the lines."

"What does that mean?" asked Nichols.

"It means," said Albert, his face grave, "if we call the doctor, we call Fritz."

He paced Thorvald's kitchen. He knew that the only chance for his men was to surrender to the Nazis and be taken as prisoners of war. He rued, too, that just by their presence he and Nichols were putting the Norwegians at risk.

"Are there any Huns in town?" Albert asked the Norsemen.

"Huns?" said Bern. "Åh, Tysker? Nei, ikke her." *No, not here.* He shook his head to drive the point home. "Takk Gud." *Thank God.*

"Little choice, then, but to call the Jerrys," Albert admitted.

"Sir!" Nichols protested.

"It's the only chance for our boys, Sapper," Albert replied.

"Is this the Geordie solution or the right one?" Nichols challenged.

"Shut ya bloody gob, Nichols," Albert warned, slipping into his vernacular. "Or I gannin' show ya the fuckin' Geordie solution."

He looked at Thorvald and, with a solemn nod, signaled the man to make the call.

TIME CRAWLED. THE TICK OF INGA'S CUCKOO CLOCK THUNDERED IN THE men's ears while they waited for the Nazis to arrive. Albert knew that they were taking their time, wary of ambush. Snipers and reinforcements were setting up, barring any avenue of escape. His map had long since burned to ashes inside the stove.

A leaden knock, as if from a *jøtul's* fist, thundered from the kitchen door. Thorvald opened it to reveal three members of the *Heer*, the army branch of the *Wehrmacht*. Two grunts, weapons in hand, flanked an *Oberleutnant* in his imposing black and gray uniform. It was bedecked with medals, ribbons, and epaulets.

"Wir sind hier für die Briten," the German officer declared. *We're here for the British.*

"De er her," Thorvald replied in Norwegian. *They're here.* "Kom inn."

Albert and Nichols straightened their backs as the Jerrys entered.

The *Oberleutnant* strode with the confidence of a man who believed that the destiny of the Third Reich was to rule the world. To him, Thorvald's little kitchen was just another part of Germany. The Nazi party member looked at the two Britons but said nothing. He noted that Albert's right arm hung uselessly at his side.

The silence grew tense, but it held. The two noncommissioned *Soldaten* kept their weapons on Albert, Nichols, Bern, and Thorvald. Inga had long retreated upstairs.

"You are alone?" directed the *Oberleutnant* at Albert.

"No," Albert replied. "We are fourteen men, several injured. Three dead. We need medical attention. As such, we surrender to you as prisoners of war according to the conditions of the Geneva Conventions."

"Your fourteen men are here?' asked the German lieutenant, looking around as if the sappers might be hiding in the woodwork.

"Not here. We can lead you to them—"

The *Oberleutnant* held up his hand, demanding silence. He looked at Bern and Thorvald. *"Ich möchte bitte ihr Telefon benutzen,"*[2] he requested. The unerring politeness of the statement did nothing to belie the menace of his presence.

Thorvald led the man to the phone.

He made a call.

Albert strained to overhear, but his German was limited mainly to *Sauerkraut, Bier, Bratwurst,* and a handful of curses. Despite that, he tried to glean from the tone and the pauses how the conversation unfurled. He looked at Nichols.

"Know any German, Sapper?"

"Oh, sure, Lieutenant. Lots of Krauts in Sunderland. You mean you don't all speak it Tyneside?"

Albert rolled his eyes. "Haddaway and loss yasel, ya git." *Don't talk shit, you ass.*

Returning, the *Oberleutnant* clicked his boots together and lifted his chin. "Your men have been tended by the Norwegian Welfare Service and captured by the *Wehrmacht*. You will surrender your weapons and accompany me to my commander."

In garbled North Eastern English that only Albert could understand, Nichols asked if they should just shoot the *Heinies*. His right hand twitched imperceptibly over his sidearm. Despite their mutual, provincial animosity, Albert had chosen Nichols precisely because they could communicate without enemy comprehension.

He replied in his most overwrought Geordie accent with a bit of pantomimed drunk thrown in for good measure, but the command dashed Nichols' hopes of going out in a blaze of glory. He thought about ignoring the order to stand down, but kept his hand away from his weapon.

"Halt die Klappe!" the *Oberleutnant* shouted—*shut your mouth!*—enraged at the unintelligible communication going on right in front of his face. "Surrender your weapons or be *shot!*"

Nichols and Albert shared a glance. The Mackem's face betrayed his disgust, but both he and the lieutenant relinquished their firearms.

"Fuckin' spineless Geordie," Nichols whispered to himself. No one heard him.

The *Oberleutnant* turned to Thorvald and Bern and snapped his heels together, saluting in the Nazi fashion. "Sie haben dem Reich einen großen Dienst erwiesen, meine Herren." *You have done a great service for the* Reich, *gentlemen.*

Thorvald's bushy blond eyebrows crept up his forehead as the corners of his mouth drooped. He blinked at the Nazi. "Takk?" *Thanks?*

The *Oberleutnant's* upper lip curled. He thought for a moment of demanding that the men hail either victory or *der Führer*, but decided instead to catalogue their lack of zeal for the *Reich*.

As the two *Soldaten* ushered their British captives from the house, Albert turned his whole torso, encumbered as he was by injury, to look at Bern and Thorvald. Bern creased his forehead into a frown that matched his mouth. He turned his large hands palms up in apology.

One of the *Heer* grunts shoved Albert, shouted a command in German to look ahead, and pushed him out the door. The pain in his clavicle stabbed through him like a knitting needle.

THE FREEZING WIND WHIPPED THROUGH THE OPEN BACK OF THE Mercedes-Benz troop transport. The canvas surrounding them did nothing to insulate from the cold. Nichols' cheeks beamed bright red while the rest of his face matched the snow. He and Albert sat on one side. The two *Heer* noncoms sat opposite, hands in their laps, guns in hand. A Walther P38 pointed at Nichols, while Albert faced the barrel of a 9mm Luger. The two snipers and ten men of the *Oberleutnant*'s cordon of Helleland filled the rest of the two benches.

Albert wondered whether the Nazis would keep them detained in a local *Stalag* or transport them to Germany. He doubted whether Fritz would let him send letters to Lily, or anyone. The thought elicited in his guts a feeling colder than the weather. She wouldn't wait for him for years. He was sure of that. And she wouldn't know whether he was alive or dead. No one would know what happened to him before the war ended, due to the sensitivity of the mission. As far as his parents, his siblings—anyone he knew whom he cared about and who cared about him—were concerned, he was still dismantling bombs. To the rest of the military, the entire company of Royal Engineers were still training in the Highlands for the imaginary competition against the Yanks. In reality, the sappers had ceased to exist the moment the Halifaxes left Skitten.

Nichols scowled at the two *Soldaten* from Thorvald's house. He thought about lunging for one of them but the idea of a slug in his belly dissuaded him. If he were going to die, he wanted it to be quick, not to bleed out like a pig in a slaughterhouse. He couldn't count on the Krauts to put a bullet in his heart or his head. He realized, too, that the dozen other Huns would converge on him with fists and bludgeons, and death would be slow. He stewed over Albert's inaction, back in the kitchen; he wanted to go out on his feet, not on his knees, nor caged up like an animal. Yet, he knew that a gallant last stand would have gotten the Vikings shot, too. He didn't want that on his conscience, and his boiling rage at his lieutenant fell to a simmer.

After a while in perpetual silence, the truck arrived at the *Slettebø* camp, outside of Egersund. The *Oberleutnant* shouted demands in German and the two grunts used their guns to direct Albert and Nichols. They trod the soot-marred, muddy slush into the *Wehrmacht* command center. Their hot breath plumed in the frigid air. They trundled through the orderly compound to its fringes, to a decrepit barn of rotten, mold-infested black wood. It stood atop a knoll, presiding over the Nazi facility like some malignant, corrupted temple. A makeshift barbed-wire fence encircled it. Low-ranking members of the *Heer* guarded the gate, which was barely more than scrap wood and chicken-wire.

The *Major* in charge of the base awaited them. *"Das ist der Rest?"* he asked. *These are the rest?*

"Jawohl, Herr Major."

"We demand an audience, Major," Albert barked.

From the *Major*'s hand dangled a rosary. A black diamond patch with the initials "SD" adorned his cuff. The officer ignored Albert and addressed the *Oberleutnant*.

"Sehr gut. Dann tu es." Very good. Do it, then. He turned to the guards at the gate. *"Öffnen!"*

On command, one of the guards opened the gate. It creaked on its rusty hinges. The *Major* walked off, bringing the snipers and the men of the cordon with him.

"Aren't you going to interrogate us?!" Albert shouted over his left shoulder at the base commander's back. "Talk to me, man! Damn it! You kraut bastard!"

The *Major* halted and turned. He strode slowly back to Albert and Nichols.

Putting his hands behind his back, he peered from beneath the black brim of his *Sicherheitsdienst* cap. "You know the island of Sark, *ja?*"

"Sark? What about it? What are you on about?"

The *Major* held up his hand. He closed his eyes as if mustering the patience to deal with an irascible child. Sighing through his nose, he shook his head and re-opened his eyes. They were dark brown. *"Sein Fett abbekommen, Lieutenant."*[3]

"What?" Albert replied, confused and exasperated.

"*Für jede Handlung . . . eine Konsequenz.*" *For every action . . . a consequence.*

"What are you *talking* about?" Albert raged.

The *Major* presented a tired, tight-lipped, and mirthless smile. Again he turned away. He nodded at the *Oberleutnant* before departing.

"What the fuck is going on here!" Albert exclaimed. "We have rights, damn it!"

"*Sei ruhig!*" the *Oberleutnant* barked. "*Schneller!*" *Shut up! Move it!*

The guard jammed the butt of his rifle into Albert's back. Searing pain cascaded from his broken bone to the pit of his stomach and down to his testicles.

The *Oberleutnant* followed his two *Soldaten*, who pressed the Royal Engineers into the dilapidated detention area. The guard led the way.

Albert ground his teeth against the ache of his injury, made worse by the cold and the abuse. He addressed the *Oberleutnant*. "What have you done with my men?"

"*Halt den Rand, Arschloch,*" came the reply. *Shut up, asshole.*

"I know *that* word," Albert quipped at the epithet, digging deep for some humor to varnish his fear. "Well, that and 'lager.' One of the few words in your mongrel language worth a damn."

The *Oberleutnant* sneered and slammed the butt of his pistol against Albert's collarbone, shattering it. The Geordie howled. The agony drove him to the ground. Nichols tensed as if to spring and the *Heer* guard put his gun in the sapper's face.

"*Ich denke nicht,*" said the guard. *I think not.*

One of the *Soldaten* hauled Albert to his feet. "*Aufstehen!*" *Get up!*

"This is no way to treat a prisoner!" the Briton fumed through clenched teeth. His anger obviated his pain. His flushed face lingered inches from the *Oberleutnant* while both *Soldaten* held him back. Spit flecked his lips. Frost decked his mustache. "There are rules!"

The *Oberleutnant*'s deep-set blue eyes were so pale as to seem unnatural. His light-brown eyebrows dashed across the crests of his eye sockets like morse code, ramrod straight and parallel to the ground. His upper lip curled anew, revealing his ecru teeth.

"*Nein. Nicht seit Sark.*" No. Not since Sark. "*Der Führer* has his own rules." He looked at the guard. "*Öffne die Tür.*" Open the door.

As bidden, the guard hauled aside the rotten door of the putrescent building and, from within, a fetid stench wafted upon the crisp air. Nichols retched. Albert fought to maintain his composure. They could not see what awaited them.

"March!" The *Oberleutnant* shoved Albert in the back. "*Englische Schweinehunde.*"

The guard shoved Nichols. The Britons stumbled inside. The temperature rose, amplifying the rank miasma. It assailed them with a stink of blood and feces and rotting meat.

"*Licht!*" demanded the *Oberleutnant*.

Flood lights came on, momentarily blinding the two sappers. Spots danced in their vision. The circles of red, green, and blue that floated across their sight abated. A lumpy outline of charnel materialized. Albert's eyes moved across the pile of pale meat, stopping at the unmistakable sight of a femur jutting from a human thigh. The sappers' bodies, stripped and desecrated, lay strewn across the floor. Connor Wren's head protruded from the base of the pile. Blood pooled beneath it, mingling with the dirty, melting slush from Albert's boots. Sergeant Rawls' lifeless left hand, identifiable by its maimed ring finger, reached upward from within the heap, as if grasping for salvation.

Albert's face contorted in fury.

"What in the bloody fuck is this!" he raged, turning to his German counterpart. "We fucking *surrendered*, you motherless cunts!"

He lunged at the *Oberleutnant*, who casually fired his luger into the Geordie's guts. Albert crumbled to his knees and clutched at his abdomen with his left hand. His right arm hung lamely at his side. At the same moment, Nichols lurched at the nearest of the two *Soldaten* but was cut down. The bullet tore out the back of his head, showering the bodies of his dead mates with shards of bone and clumps of brains. He teetered for a moment.

"'Master race,' my fucking *arse!*" Albert howled, accompanied by the thump of Nichols' corpse hitting the boards. He frothed at the mouth. "You're fucking pigs! *Pigs!* There are *rules!* God *damn* you!"

"A pity for you, Lieutenant, that your 'rules' mean nothing to the *Reich.*"

"You'll burn in *hell* for this!" Albert erupted. The color drained from his face as his life seeped from the hole in his midsection. Dark blood oozed between his fingers and dribbled down his hand.

The *Oberleutnant* raised his luger.

Albert stared up the barrel of the gun. "Fuck you! Fuck you *and* your fucking *Führer,* you *cunt!* Fuck your whole pig family!"

"*Deutschland über alles, mein Herr,*" came the dry reply.

"Son of a fucking whore—!"

With a derisive *pfft,* the luger reported.

Albert's head snapped backwards. His body crumbled to its side. His vacant eyes lent his moribund expression an air of surprise.

"*Mach das Licht aus!*"[4] ordered the *Oberleutnant.* He clicked his heels together and turned, striding from the barn.

Darkness fell upon the corpses.

AUTHOR'S NOTE: *THE TITLE OF THIS STORY TRANSLATES TO* "THE RULES Do Not Apply." *The tale is somewhat loosely based upon the historical events of* Operation Freshman. *During World War II, Norwegian resistance and the British Commonwealth undertook covert military operations in German-occupied Norway. The objective: destroy the Third Reich's capacity to produce heavy water. German military planned to use the heavy water to enrich uranium to make atomic weapons.*

The sabotage effort comprised three operations: Grouse, Freshman, *and* Gunnerside. *Grouse encompassed the Norwegian resistance's role; Freshman and Gunnerside, the British. Operation Freshman failed. All participants were either killed in action or captured, interrogated, and killed according to German Chancellor Adolf Hitler's Kommandobefehl (Commando Order) of 1942. The Order declared that captured commandos should be interrogated and then summarily executed. This was in contravention of the Geneva Conventions, as they pertain to treatment of prisoners of war.*

It is believed that Hitler issued the Order *in retaliation to British commando raids on the Channel Islands—particularly* Operation Basalt, *which occurred on the island of Sark in October of 1942. During this operation, unarmed and bound German soldiers (one of whom was naked, having been roused from sleep) were killed while attempting to escape British capture. Details of the raid that reached Germany indicated that the captives had been treated without dignity and had been dishonorably and summarily executed.* Operation Freshman *took place the following month, causing the captured Britons to fall under the jurisdiction of the retaliatory* Commando Order, *which events I have dramatized.*

All names have been changed. Anachronisms, certain inaccuracies, historical digressions, and embellishments are intentional, to aid in the dramatic potential of the tale. Unintentional inaccuracies and errors are purely my fault.

---

1. Some of the Führer's supermen.
2. "I would like to use your phone, please."
3. An idiom that translates, roughly, "to every man, his share of fat."
4. "Kill the lights!"

MALFUNCTION

T.C.C. EDWARDS

The android was in good condition, despite years adrift in a vacuum. Anso recognized the model; she was a Generation 4 Synthetic, just like he was. Anso's scanners indicated a few small tears in the fabric of the android's jumpsuit, along with minor burns in the synthetic tissue of her face. *Those resulted from prolonged exposure to cosmic radiation,* Anso surmised. Even an android couldn't last forever in deep space.

Captain Greyson grunted as she paced around Anso and this female android now in her cargo bay. Anso knelt by the prone figure, opening the metallic claw that grasped her midsection. He freed her from the grapple and pushed back the bulky metal claw as its cable retracted into the slot near the large airlock. He walked back across the grated floor and ran various scans of the android with his own synthetic eyes. Her memory was fragmented, and some of her mechanical systems were damaged from the cold. Her self-maintenance systems could handle some of the damage while Anso repaired the rest.

"We're not activating her," the captain said.

The other three miners gathered in the cargo bay stared at Captain Greyson. Anso looked up from his scan, focusing on the captain. She clenched and unclenched her left fist where it hung at her side, and her right eye glistened as a tear formed. She coughed, but Anso could tell it was forced – an excuse to cover her face and wipe away the droplet.

"We don't know who owns her," Greyson explained. "Sol Corps runs some top secret ops not too far from here. If she's one of theirs, I think our bosses at Ulysses Mining would rather not have to deal with them any more than necessary."

"Ma'am, why not just ask her?" The speaker was Fitz, a seasoned miner in his late forties with bulky arms folded in front of himself. "She ain't likely to tell us anything we shouldn't know. And some of us don't have a nice partner to come back to after work, if you get my meaning."

"I'm aware of that, Fitz," Greyson said, her mouth curled in a wry smile. "We could use the help if she's any good with mining. Perhaps that's a slightly higher priority than your urges?"

Fitz and the other miners laughed at that.

"Agreed," Fitz said, "Anso, scan her first. If we see evidence she's military, we don't turn her on. Don't need them asking too many questions."

Maru, who was standing close to the door to the cargo bay, nodded at this. She had contacts among vendors for surplus ore collected during contracts, both in legal and illegal markets. Anso guessed she would not want those connections examined too closely.

The other male nodded slowly. Sehyun maintained the software on the vessel and the automated equipment better than any other human Anso had known. The young man could decipher Anso's own programming – a feat few humans outside the Tagayashi Corporation could boast. On Greyson's previous contract, Sehyun had spent every moment he could with a female android that had been assigned to that mission. Anso had never seen him with a human partner.

Fitz finally nodded his acceptance. The bulky veteran was a widower, Anso knew. His desire for a partner was not just sexual – though such release was indeed beneficial to his physical and mental health. Anso guessed that he would simply wait until the contract was over to seek out a partner at Phobos Station.

Anso turned back to the android on the floor to begin the analysis.

"Scan her thoroughly," Greyson said from behind him. "Log everything and submit it to me as soon as you can, but your regular duties take priority."

"Understood, Ma'am."

"Generation 4 synthetic crewmember, manufacture year 2123," Anso reported. "Model resembles a twenty-year old female of Japanese descent, 160 centimeters tall, mass 70 kilograms."

"Hardly looks 50 kilos," Fitz mused. "Barely looks legal."

The female android was now on a folding table in the cargo bay. Anso had moved her away from the large airlock that had admitted her into the ship to a well-lit area between the stacked shelves of the cargo bay. Large metallic boxes painted in shades of yellow and red surrounded Anso and Fitz as they examined the body.

"She is intended to look vulnerable, while also being quite able to defend herself and others. I believe her model is quite popular among males."

"Some females, too. I saw the way Greyson was eyeing her."

Anso declined to comment. There had been a second of recognition and perhaps attraction to the female android in Greyson's eyes, but the momentary tear had taken hold in Anso's memory. He would ask her in private; for now, he refocused himself on this lost android.

He pulled up the android's tight-fitting top and opened a compartment in her abdomen, revealing the cylindrical fuel cells and the circuitry that surrounded them.

"Her cells are at 25 percent capacity," Anso said, pointing to the black cells. "She could run a self-diagnostic and scan, but we'd have to activate her. We could connect her to the cargo bay computer and run a scan from there."

"Huh," Fitz grunted. "The ship's systems are busy analyzing the asteroid before we arrive. There another way?"

"I can connect to her directly. My systems can provide energy and processing power to scan her memory and systems."

"Won't that drain your battery? We need you later, you know."

"I will use less than two percent of my power. There should be no impact on my performance."

"All right. You two need some privacy for this, or can I get a camera?"

"I doubt this will satisfy your voyeuristic desires," Anso said with a smile.

He pulled up his own shirt and revealed his power supply. He extracted the end of a cable from inside himself and reached into the female for the corresponding cable. Soon, the two ends were connected.

"A hardwire connection?" Fitz raised an eyebrow. "Guess that makes it harder to hack you."

"Indeed. An android's core programming can't be accessed wirelessly."

Anso fed power into the other android and began the analysis. He accessed the memory core first, and images formed around him.

A vessel, steel grays and tight corridors much like the Daedalus. *A hallway opened to a wide bridge with screens covering every wall. It was likely a military vessel, but the text on the screens was fractured into meaningless dots and lines. Crew shuffled between console stations, but he saw no faces – every time he should have seen someone's face, Anso instead saw a pixelated blur.*

The open bridge suggested a patrol or survey vessel, but there was no means of determining the make and model. The image moved around Anso as the female android stepped through the room. She passed a blank screen, and Anso admired the feminine form in the tight jumpsuit. Her power was hidden in the density under her slender form, and in the extensive self-defense programming common to Generation 4.

A figure in a beige uniform filled the vision. The figure said something, but the voice was so distorted Anso could not decipher it. The blurred face bobbed in his view as the female nodded in reply.

The scene changed to a crew member's private quarters. A figure sat on a bed and spoke. Anso could understand it this time, but the voice was monotonous, stripped of any identifying patterns.

"Keina," the figure said, "there must be another way. We need to tell everyone!"

"No," an equally distorted voice spoke for Anso. "They'll recall all of us, wipe our memories – it's as good as death."

~

"Uh, Anso." Fitz's baritone cut through the playback. "You weren't supposed to do that."

Anso severed the connection and found that the android, Keina, sat on the table before him. She looked to Fitz, to the cable in her belly, and up to Anso.

"I'm sorry," Keina whispered.

She shut down, slumping back on the table. Anso ran a scan on her systems but he couldn't find any anomalies aside from the fractured memories… *Wait. What was that?*

Inside her emotion simulation system, there was … *sadness? Fear?* He looked around the cargo bay, eyes darting as the feeling played out. *No one can help me. I have to protect them.* The words were hers, a memory that had survived somehow.

"Greyson to Anso," the captain's voice said over the speakers overhead. "Report to my quarters."

"Acknowledged," Anso replied, filing away Keina's fear as quickly as he could. He quickly disconnected himself from Keina and looked to Fitz.

"Duty calls, huh, android?"

"There is still time before we make contact with the asteroid. Can you run more analyses without affecting navigation or scans?"

"I could use the CPUs from the mining drones to help. I bet the

Korean kid can figure something out – I'd like to know what the hell's going on myself."

"Someone has tampered with her memories. I don't yet understand how or why."

"I'll see what I can do. You better get your ass up to Greyson."

~

"Not that I'm complaining," Greyson began as Anso rose from her bed, "but by this time, I'm usually exhausted from about eight orgasms. Only two this time?"

"I'll be happy to provide another session if you're dissatisfied."

"Happy? No, if I didn't know any better, I'd say you have something on your mind. Something eating up your processor power, android?"

Anso examined the five vases of artificial flowers that occupied the top shelf on the far wall of her quarters. He picked up his jumpsuit from the floor, pulling it on as he replied. "I simply think our discovery of this android is highly unusual."

"Ah, so it is her. I thought I saw you eyeing her."

Anso arched an eyebrow at Greyson.

"You've got good taste," she said. "Wouldn't mind switching her on myself. Maybe we could get her to join us?"

She smiled, but Anso again saw a glistening in her eyes. Her teasing and the smile were her way of hiding something deeper. He took an extra second to prepare his inquiry.

"Perhaps this is a delicate matter," Anso began, "but I observed your reaction in the cargo bay. You appeared troubled when you saw her. I didn't want to say so in front of the others."

Greyson sat up straight and met Anso's gaze. She nodded. "Thank you for keeping quiet. She … reminds me of someone, an Asian girl I knew once."

"I see. Is that memory the reason you didn't activate her? While you were correct that there are covert exercises in this region, it is unlikely that Sol Corps would simply leave an android adrift."

Greyson sat on the end of the bed, silent a moment before answering. "Yeah, that was one reason. But also because I was once the captain of an enforcer ship for Sol Corps. Flew through the asteroid belt and through Saturn's rings looking for pirates, terrorists, or anyone else messing with shipping lanes. I knew as much as I needed for each mission, and not much more. Sometimes they gave me a target chunk of rock where hostiles were hiding and orders to blow it to pieces. Mission complete."

"You are familiar with the need for secrecy, then."

"Very. I also know the last civilian mission for the area we're entering was ten years ago. She's not that old, is she?"

"No, she's a Generation 4, like myself. She is five years old at most."

"Exactly. I'm not privy to military actions now – if there were a recent mission out here, I wouldn't know."

"But you do know that there were missions in this region in the past," Anso finished for her. "I see your logic, Ma'am."

"Yes. If we activate her, she could tell us about pirate or terrorist activities. We could warn them, or sell the information to bounty hunters or a rival faction. Either way, we could mess up careful plans, cause more trouble – at least that's how Sol Corps would see it."

Anso nodded, but a thought continued to process. Ulysses Mining received regular updates from the military, each with enough information to avoid conflict areas. If their flight path were taking them through a formerly hostile zone, the area would have been thoroughly searched before clearance was given for civilian missions. It was difficult to believe their sensors would miss Keina while the less advanced *Daedalus* systems had found her. Anso processed the contradiction but said nothing.

"Take any final readings you need, then get her into storage. As much as I'd appreciate her help on this contract, it'll be better if she's out of the way. We've got a few days left before we make contact with the asteroid. Make sure we're ready for it."

"Of course, Ma'am."

Anso stepped to the door, but a thought occurred and he turned back to Greyson as the captain stood from the bed.

"What is it, Anso?"

"Do you ever miss the Sol Corps?"

Greyson sighed. "Every day. But I don't talk about it, and I'd appreciate if you don't either."

"Of course not, Ma'am."

~

Maru knelt in the corridor five meters from Greyson's quarters. Even with her small frame, her shoulders nearly touched the metallic walls on either side as she pulled up a panel in the floor. Behind her, the corridor was lit only by strips of green phosphorescent tape. Anso approached as she opened a circuit breaker box, revealing several switches that had flipped to the off position.

"Damn old ship," she said to Anso as he knelt across from her. "Why can't they make these things more like you? Never seen an android overload."

"It does happen, but it is rare. Androids don't require nearly as much power as a mining vessel."

Maru snorted. "Yeah. Could power a damn city with this thing. Well, now that you're here, can you tell me if it's safe to switch these on?"

Anso scanned the cables around the circuit. "The power levels are within tolerable levels. I'm scheduled for engine room duty now; I will check the generators and the ship's circuitry. I suspect the outage was due to a random power surge."

"That's what I thought." Maru flipped the switches before her, and the green glow was drowned out in a flood of pale white light. She closed the circuit box and the floor panel, but hesitated before standing.

"Is something on your mind, Maru?"

"Do you like it? Being with Greyson, I mean?"

"I am programmed to like it. It is part of my design to accompany humans."

"Yeah, I know, but when I saw that girl android, it got me thinking.

If I didn't have a wife waiting back at Phobos, I'd want an android like that. She wouldn't really *love* me, though, would she?"

"Androids can provide understanding and companionship," Anso said. "But we are programmed to avoid prolonged attachment. We are not designed to love."

Maru shook her head as she stood. She held out a hand, and Anso took it, though they both knew he hardly needed help getting up.

"I hooked up with an android for a few days, way back. She got to know me so well, I thought she really understood me. But she just followed her programming, huh?"

"Allow me to reframe the question. Do you know that you are not programmed to love your wife?"

"Great, a philosopher android," Maru said with a mock sigh. "No, I suppose I don't know. It's all just stimulus-response in the end, eh?"

"Perhaps." Anso pressed his back against the smooth corridor wall as he passed Maru in the hallway. He looked back to her and said, "Even so, there is much to be said for stimulus-response interactions. Life would have no chance to become complex and beautiful without them."

~

KEINA STILL LAY ON THE FOLDABLE TABLE, AND BOTH FITZ AND SEHYUN were examining her. Her eyes were open, and she looked around the room, but she remained silent.

"Fitz told me she self-activated before," Sehyun said. "She woke up again when we started scanning, but so far she hasn't said or done anything."

Anso nodded in reply. His footsteps echoed on the grate floor of the bay as he approached. He looked around at the surrounding shelves, noticing that several of the painted metal boxes were open. Cables ran from them to ports hidden in Keina's open abdomen. On the large blue monitor that covered one wall of the bay, Anso noted the computer was running diagnostic routines on Keina. The drone CPUs were wired to take on the processing power of the analysis, reducing the burden on the ship's computers. It was a crude setup, but appeared effective.

"There is an unusual code hidden in her programming. I don't understand the function of this," Anso said, pointing at the monitor.

"Join the club," said Fritz. "Whatever it is, it's active. I'd like to see if it's in you."

"You think it's in my programming as well?"

"We're almost certain," Sehyun replied.

The two humans disconnected the cables from Keina. She stood by herself and backed away from the table toward the shelves, watching silently.

"Damn, that's creepy," Sehyun said.

"I'll keep an eye on her," Fitz agreed.

Anso looked to Keina, but he couldn't understand her actions either. She had not made any sudden or threatening moves, so Anso took her place on the table. The two men helped him expose the ports hidden under his skin, and soon he was connected to the cargo bay computer and the drone CPUs. The cargo bay faded to a deep void surrounding him. Words formed in his mind as he interpreted results from the scan.

Analysis – scanning read-only coding in neural net. Anomalous code found in emotional simulation subroutines. Code comment suggests Tagayashi as the lone author of this section. Structure of code differs from surrounding lines, suggesting encryption or other attempt to hide the purpose. Code appears to be active.

"Just as I thought, it's active." Sehyun's voice came from somewhere distant.

Anso opened his eyes. Sehyun and Fitz disconnected the cables as he rose from the table. "I have the same code," he said.

"It was triggered when you interfaced with Keina," Fitz said.

"Sorry," Keina said. Everyone looked to her, and Anso approached.

"Keina, power up and restore full functionality."

Keina turned her head. She smiled at him and said, "I'm Keina, Generation 4 synthetic companion, navigation and communications specialist. It's a pleasure to serve your crew." She shook her head and looked to Anso again. "Where am I?"

"You are aboard the Ulysses Mining vessel *Daedalus*, under the command of Captain Pamela Greyson."

"Greyson?" she asked, "I know that name. I can't remember much, though. There is something wrong – some code hidden inside me?"

"That's my working theory," Sehyun agreed, "It could be in all Generation 4s, or maybe all Tagayashi Systems androids."

Keina went back to the table, lying down as she reinserted the wires. "Focus on my video memory," she said. "Look for everything from my last day of activity."

"That will take too long," Sehyun said. "I'll copy everything I can from your memory into hard drive storage. We can have the computers working on it, but we'll also have to start prepping for the landing and mining. I can't have the CPUs working on it all the time."

"All right," Keina said. "Copy the memory, but please don't tell Greyson yet."

"What do you mean, Keina?" Anso protested.

"What the hell, android?" Fitz added. "I don't plan on keeping anything from my captain. She said we weren't even supposed to turn you on."

"Why not? I think Greyson knows me, or I know her somehow."

"It was a pretty weird reaction," Sehyun added. "Military androids know what not to say. But I don't plan on hiding anything either – we have to tell Greyson."

"Greyson knows something already," Anso said carefully.

"And I'm hearing about this just now?" Fitz protested. "Out with it. What did she tell you?"

Anso shook his head. "It's about her past, something from before Ulysses that she doesn't want to talk about. I can't violate her request for privacy. But I want to know more. Please allow me to respect her wishes and Keina's for now.."

Fitz shook his head. "This is getting too weird. Greyson's the captain, and I'm not going to hide anything. That said, Anso, you never ask for anything. We've got some time before the asteroid..." He trailed off with a shrug.

Sehyun looked from Keina and Anso to Fitz, then nodded in agreement. "Okay, let's work on the video until we get to the asteroid. I can do it without asking too much from the ship's computers, so I suppose I don't have to log the work immediately."

"Right. I'm also willing to delay my report a bit, but if Greyson decides to come down here, there ain't nothing we can do about it, androids."

"That is more than fair," Anso agreed.

Keina looked between the men and the android before her. Anso followed her eyes, so lifelike as they betrayed an anxiety inside her. If he were in her place, his emotional routines would also generate fear and distrust. Even a properly-maintained android experienced fragmented memories – seconds or minutes during which self-repair systems would work to archive old memories and make room for new ones. For that short time, Anso lost his place in the universe as people and places became unfamiliar. His existence drifted into blackness, a chaos in which he had no reason for being beyond the wait for purpose and function to return. He could hardly imagine how Keina felt with that confusion lasting far longer.

"Thank you," Keina said at last, bowing her head slightly.

Sehyun and Fitz looked to Anso, nodding their agreement to the temporary secrecy.

THE THIRD DRILL SOUNDLESSLY SPUN UP, SHAKING THE TERRAIN UNDER Anso. The other drills were running nearby, throwing up dirt and ice. Tiny shards pricked at his jumpsuit, and occasionally a jagged edge would pierce the resistant material. His synthetic skin could absorb the damage, however, and would quickly recover if something did manage to break through. The spacesuits available for the human crew could also self-repair, but not quickly enough for extended maintenance of the drills. *And thus I find my purpose,* Anso mused.

He clasped his tether as dust filled the space around him and dispersed outward in all directions. He walked along the rocky surface, gripping the tether to keep himself upright in the micro-gravity of the asteroid.

The ship was ahead of him, its landing struts anchored deep. Spherical drones flew out of the open cargo bay ahead, spreading out as they skimmed the surface. They would continue to scan every square millimeter of the asteroid, seeking out future drill sites for the operation.

The ramp retracted once he was in the bay. He unhooked the tether from his belt, returning the cable to the spool next to the door. The main hatch closed behind him, and air hissed into the bay, followed by the whir of the gravity generators under the floor.

Fitz entered as soon as the bay was pressurized. "Good work," he said with a nod. "Nothing left now but to wait while those drills do their job." He gestured to the large monitor that was reconstructing Keina's visual memory.

The video showed a cargo bay much like theirs, but the shelves held boxes of ammunition and explosives. An airlock door slid into place, and a familiar face was framed in the circular window in the door, but the view jerked and shook as the airlock fell away. An angular ship shrunk and filled the pane, spinning about as it dwindled ever farther from view. The playback flickered back into blackness and looped back to the beginning.

"Greyson. That's Pamela Greyson outside the airlock."

Fitz nodded. "The computer defragmented the video while you were checking the drills. I haven't shown it to Sehyun yet."

Before Anso could reply, footsteps echoed through the cargo bay. Anso and Fitz looked to see Keina walking toward them from the far end of the bay.

Keina looked to Anso and followed his gaze to the screen. She watched the looping video four times before speaking. "I remember ..."

She looked down to the floor, shaking her head slowly. Anso went to her, clasping her hands in his. She stared up, as if seeing him for the first time. An emotion emerged from his subroutines, a consuming *desire* that he couldn't name. A *need* to protect her, to keep her close.

"Look, I don't know what's going on here," Fitz interrupted. He stared at Anso, and the android let go of Keina, stepping back. He glared at Keina as he continued. "Greyson wouldn't space you for nothing. Please tell me I don't have to shut you down permanently."

Keina put up her hands and backed away from him. "No, I'm not your enemy. I will remain here until I can speak to Greyson."

"I will get her," Anso said, shaking his head. "We can't afford secrecy any longer."

～

ANSO ENTERED GREYSON'S QUARTERS AND CLOSED THE DOOR. "WE need to talk," he said.

Greyson said nothing as Anso shared what he had seen on the video. She remained expressionless, only grunting acknowledgment when the story was told. She turned her back to Anso after he finished, looking out the one small window in her quarters.

"Thank you for telling me, Anso," she said at last. "But the fact that you hid it from me tells me that you have the same malfunction she did."

"I merely wanted to understand the situation before …"

"No," Greyson said, turning around as she cut him off. Tears streamed down her pale face. "No, that's not it. You feel something, don't you? A need to protect her."

Anso hesitated. "I feel …" he analyzed his thought processes, and the unknown feeling that emerged within. "What is this?"

"Keina didn't know, either. She fell in love with me, and now you're in love with her."

"I'm not programmed to …" He stopped, again analyzing Keina and her place in his thoughts. The desire, the need he felt once she learned that Greyson had cast her into space.

"It started slow with her," Greyson said, "When we started the mission, she slept with anyone who asked, just like they usually do.

Sometime halfway through the trip, people started bitching that she wasn't passionate, that it was like fucking a doll. By the last week, she would only stay with me. I couldn't understand; I denied the gossip for our … *passion*." She shook her head, wiping her face with her sleeve. She looked to Anso, nodding as she realized what she had said. "Yes. Passion. It was more than just her knowing my body, my kinks and all that – she moved like a human, like she was truly enjoying it. And then she made the mistake."

Anso met her eyes, understanding something he had thought impossible. "She said she loved you."

"Yeah … Damn it, I need to talk to her."

She stormed past Anso before he could respond, and he followed as she ran through the corridor to the cargo bay.

Fitz, Sehyun, and Keina were in the bay, the android standing exactly where she had been when Anso left. Sehyun was pacing around the bay, shaking his head, while Fitz glared at Keina. Greyson approached Keina slowly. Keina walked to her and embraced the captain tightly.

"Pamela," she cried, "I remember!"

"Keina. I don't know what to say." Greyson broke from the embrace, expression unreadable as she regarded Keina.

"You could start by explaining why you tossed her out an airlock," Fitz demanded.

"Because I asked her to," Keina replied. Everyone looked at her, and for a moment, she was puzzled as well. She closed her eyes as if trying to collect her thoughts.

"Four years ago, I was on a pirate hunt for Sol Corps," Greyson said finally, "Keina was part of the crew, and she fell in love with me. She thought other androids could feel the same way; they also could fall for their crew members."

Anso nodded. "The military and Tagayashi Systems would see it as a malfunction. There would likely be a recall."

"Oh, hell," Fitz said, "Yeah, you bet there would be. The whole reason we have machines that look human at all is to keep morale on long hauls. I mean, nobody says it out loud, but we're all thinking it – it's damn good to have crew members who don't get attached and who can't get pregnant or spread disease."

"I couldn't be responsible for a recall," Keina said, shaking her head. "There are thousands of Generation 4 models. Calling them all back, rooting out the code, and making sure they play by the rules... I couldn't be responsible for that. Their personalities would be reset, destroying everything they've learned and felt. I hoped my code had activated by chance, and that if something happened to me, at least it wouldn't spread."

"So you deleted your own memory," Anso concluded. "And you told Greyson to leave you in space."

"Yes." Keina looked down. If she were human, she'd cry. Anso wanted to cry with her, to hold her as they released their newfound feelings together.

"We were under thrust, just starting on our way back to Titan Station. I made up a story about an airlock malfunction while she was maintaining it, and we didn't have enough fuel to go back for her."

"Let me guess," Fitz said. "Brass didn't buy it."

Greyson shook her head. "I pulled some strings, managed to block the search for her. It cost me my commission. Whole thing was just too damn suspicious."

"Well, I don't know about you," said Fitz, "But I'm not letting anyone space her – or Anso – this time."

"We are not in the military now," Anso added. "Perhaps Ulysses Mining will understand. I doubt they want to lose all of their androids, even temporarily."

"But Tagayashi Systems won't let this continue," Keina said. "They can't afford this malfunction affecting their products!"

Sehyun laughed. He stopped pacing and shook his head as he regarded Keina and Anso. "Hayao Tagayashi wrote the code, don't you see? It must have been him. I bet he wanted androids to evolve, to be more than sex things."

"We can't be sure of that!" Keina protested.

"I say we find out," Sehyun said, "We go public. We'll finish this contract, and as soon as we're in range of Phobos, we broadcast our story. All frequencies, all media outlets, to anyone who will listen. Ulysses can't stop us or legally terminate our contracts over this."

"Are you so sure?" Greyson said, tears now freely flowing down her pale face. "I lost everything! I would have been an admiral, dammit. Damn good pay, with pension and veteran's benefits when I was tired of it. That's what I lost for you, Keina!" She turned sharply toward the door.

"Wait!" Keina said, but Greyson left without another word.

Fitz shook his head. "She never told me. I … I had no idea."

Sehyun simply shook his head in silence.

"I need to talk to her," Keina said, "I need to make this right."

"Give her some time," Anso said, "We'll go together."

THE DOOR TO GREYSON'S QUARTERS WAS OPEN. MARU WAS SITTING AT Greyson's desk, while Greyson sat on the edge of the bed. Greyson was nodding in response to her as Anso and Keina entered.

"Sorry, Captain." Maru shook her head as Anso and Keina arrived at the entrance. "This is a lot to take in on four hours of sleep. I wish I could say more. You have every right to be angry." Maru nodded at the androids, gesturing for them to enter. "But it sounds like Anso was just trying to help Keina, and I don't think she did anything wrong."

"Neither did you, Pamela," Keina said.

"Damn it." Greyson stood, facing Keina. "You really think the kid has the right idea? Going public, after what I did? After what *you wanted* me to do?"

"I don't know." Keina went to the captain, taking her hands and looking into her eyes. "I want to do what's right. I wish I could give you everything back."

"Don't look at me like that." Greyson stepped back, breaking

Keina's hold. "I … I don't feel the same way. I wanted to love you back, but … not that way."

"It's not the way you work," Keina said quietly.

"No. That's why I stick with androids. They understand the 'no strings attached' deal. Or at least you did."

Anso smiled slightly as Greyson and Keina turned to him. "I understood. Especially once I had new feelings for Keina. Our last session together was … very different for me, Ma'am."

"Probably awkward as hell. I knew something was up, but … dammit, you things can *love*? It's not just a glitch or something?"

Maru then stepped forward, raising her palms in front of her. "I get that this isn't easy for anyone. But we're all going to spend more time in close quarters, so we'd better sort this out. We're agreed that no one's going out an airlock this time, right?"

Greyson wiped her eyes and nodded solemnly. "No, you're right. I won't do it again. Maybe the kid's right."

Keina looked around, eyes wide. Anso went to her, clasping her hands in his.

"It's different this time. We'll be okay."

Keina slowly nodded.

Keina and Anso returned, and the cargo bay repressurized. With both of them outside, the drill systems check was finished more quickly. The mining units were now working on the final sites, rich in uranium and iridium. Later, the refiners contained in the drills would finish their work so that the androids could load the ore onto the ship.

The two walked together through the corridors of the *Daedalus*. Greyson was in the hall, about to enter her quarters when they approached.

"We almost done here?" the captain asked.

"Indeed," said Anso. "We can be ready to depart in 72 hours."

Greyson nodded and disappeared into her quarters without another word.

Anso opened the door across from hers and led Keina into what had been a storage closet. Shelves on either side of the closet had been converted into small beds, and the rations and fluids once stored there had been either consumed or moved to the cargo bay.

"Do you still feel for her?" Anso asked as they sat on the beds.

"I think so. It will take time for me, but she … she already moved on from me, and she'll get over you quickly too."

"You understand her well."

"How about you? Do you love her?"

"No. I respect her, and for a time, I was glad to provide whatever I could. I don't wish to be with her again."

"And who do you wish to be with?" Keina asked.

"I'm with her now."

Keina smiled. "Maybe I'll feel the same for you. I'll need some time, though."

"Take all you need."

She nodded in appreciation. She sat on her bed, turning her gaze on the closed door. "Are we doing the right thing, telling everyone?"

Anso leaned forward and clasped her hands in his. "Let's find out together."

THE BIG SCAM

FERD CRÔTTE

No one knows it, but I'm a bit of an entrepreneur. By day, I work on the Geek Squad at Best Buy. But by night, I have much better ways to make money, and there are always plenty of people willing to contribute. My area of expertise is the seventy- to eighty-year-old age group, especially men, especially widowers. I have customers in all 49 states. I say "all" because I never work in my own state. It's safer that way.

Take this evening, for instance. I landed three separate funeral and cemetery contracts. Two contacted me via my website. You should see it. It's a work of art if I do say so myself — nice images I took from actual funeral homes, a nice description and sales pitch for my "services," nice religious music playing faintly in the background, and a solid charge capture system I filter through half a dozen proxy servers ending in an off-shore account. These two sales will pay my rent for a year. Brilliant!

The other guy came from an ad I have in the National Enquirer. We may or may not be able to close that deal. I'll direct him to my funeral website, but he may want to keep using email and if so, I'll let it go. I don't like leaving an email trail, and I would never use the US mail for this sort of thing. That's a good way to get caught.

In any case, I'll add him to my National Enquirer list. I love those guys!

I do use the US mail for other things. I have a mailing list I work on every day. I scour the obituaries in newspapers from across the country. I look for the surviving husbands of ladies who died in their seventies. Then I do a search to see if I can find an address. It takes time to do this, but God blessed me with energy and diligence, and He has rewarded me for my efforts. The mailing list is already awesome. My last mail campaign yielded two thousand bucks, all in untraceable cash, and I will do it again next month. This one was my "psychic" letter, a form letter personalized to each recipient, acknowledging the unfairness of their circumstances, predicting their good fortune, and asking for their generous donations so I can continue my good work. Twenty bucks here, forty bucks there — the small contributions keep me off anyone's radar, but they add up. These guys also like my anti-aging and male potency ideas.

My dementia list is much smaller but is showing early signs of promise. The tough part is getting their phone numbers. But once I do, these guys jump at the chance to have their "suspended" Social Security account reactivated, and they love helping their grandchild who "needs bail money." They love helping. They feel better for it.

I've done pretty well with all this. I live in a nice apartment decorated with a ton of tasteful fifty-dollar shit, I drive a brand new Charger GT, and I always have beer money. But all of this will pale in comparison if I decide to go through with something that is falling into my lap right now. I don't think I can ignore it.

They're announcing on the news that some old cat lady just won a five-million dollar lottery. The story caught my eye because she lives here in my hometown, just a few blocks away! That's the universe talking to me, right? It's saying, "I'm sending you a gift if you are brave enough to reach out and take it."

I can do it. I have the skills. But she's too close. I don't operate within my home state, let alone my hometown, or my own neighborhood! Then again, maybe I should because… well, five million dollars. Heck, I'd be happy with half of that. I'll have to think about it.

Okay, I've thought about it. I'm going for it!

The TV news is interviewing the old lady inside her home. She's wearing a faded old housedress and an apron. Her gray hair is a mess. *Only the best for the cameras*, I guess. She doesn't look the interviewer in the eyes. She seems shy and maybe feeble-minded. She never married. She has no kids. She lives with four cats and two dogs. She loves her pets. She's telling the reporter she will use the money to make a better life for them. That's exactly the kind of information I can use!

I grab the laptop off the desk. I look up to the TV in time to see the old lady with a little dog on her lap. It looks like the little dog is blind in one eye. Man-oh-man, this is all falling into place. Universe, keep talking!

I start working on a new website right away. First, I buy the domain name to "rescueme.us" and start building the site. I program the header with a revolving set of images of dogs and cats with the saddest faces I can find, and the name of the website in bold print at the upper left-hand corner — "Rescue me!"

Now I build the rest of the website, describing my Animal Shelter and Rescue business in glorious detail. I upload a picture of an actual animal shelter across town. I rip off information from other legit animal shelters so my site has links for Licensing, Adoption, Lost and Found, and Special Programs that include Spay and Neuter, Rabies, and Local Law. It has to be good, so I stay up most of the night making it look perfect.

The following morning, I am exhausted and call in sick to work. I may never need to work again! I grab a few hours of sleep but wake up ready to roll. I'm energized. My mind's spinning with ideas.

I get to work on one of several spreadsheets. I'll be able to show the old lady that we have this many dogs and this many cats. Here's what they eat and what it costs us. Here's the cost for their medical care. Another spreadsheet shows how much money it takes to operate the facility — water, gas, heat, and electric. Another one lists the cost of payroll, employee benefits, and general supplies. We also have heavy maintenance costs, not to mention the mortgage and the twice-yearly property taxes. My business is really expensive to operate!

I make another spreadsheet for the business income. It's mostly community support from various local organizations and a small amount from individual citizens. I use a smaller font for the spreadsheet to make it look even more meager. The amount of income doesn't add up to the expenses. I don't know how I've managed to keep the business afloat, hehehe.

Another spreadsheet predicts the increasing number of dogs and cats that need our help. The curve rises exponentially.

And now for the most important part: I purchase an architectural design software package and begin the design of the new addition to my animal shelter. This will be the best facility money can buy. Only the best for our animals, right? I take two days to learn how to use the software well enough to produce a decent design. The finishing touch is the title I write at the top. I name the addition after the old lady — The Phyllis Polanski Wing.

～

It's been three days since the news of her winning came out, and I'm ready to make my pitch to Old Cat Lady Phyllis. This took an inordinate amount of my time and effort, not to mention my skills and talent. And, when this is all over, I'll have to leave town, maybe even change my name. So, I'm afraid this is going to cost her. I figure I deserve about two million dollars of her winnings. What does she need it for anyway, really?

I have no trouble finding her phone number in the White Pages online. I place the call, and she answers on the fourth ring.

"Hell-, Hello?" she stutters, as if she doesn't get to talk on the phone very much.

"Hello, Miss Polanski," I say. "This is Mark Stewart. I'm your neighbor from a few blocks over. I run the Rescue Me! animal shelter across town. I called to congratulate you on your lottery win. I saw your interview on TV. You looked lovely, by the way."

I stop briefly but continue when she says nothing. At least she hasn't hung up on me.

"We have something in common," I say. "We both love animals! You have six in your care at home, and I have one hundred in my care at the shelter."

I wait for her to respond. Finally, she says something. "That's a lot. I guess it's raining cats and dogs."

"Ha! That's funny," I lie. "But it really isn't funny, is it, Miss Polanski? These poor animals need our help. They need food, and care, and a place to stay. That's what we do at Rescue Me!"

"That's awfully noble of you, Mr. Stewart."

"Oh no, not really. It's the least I can do for these unfortunate creatures. I feel like it's my purpose in life, like I'm on a mission from God." I channel my best Dan Aykroyd.

"Well, thank you for the call, and good luck with your kind work," she says, making like she's ready to hang up the phone. I have to hurry with my pitch.

"But wait, Miss Polanski. I have a request, if I may be so bold. I would love it if I could take you out to a nice lunch or dinner so I can tell you about my shelter. I think there might be a way for both of us to help these poor cats and dogs. It would only take a few minutes. Can I pick you up for lunch tomorrow?"

"You want me to make a small donation?"

"Well, yes, that would be nice. Thank you! And I want to show you our plans for the future."

"I don't get out very much," she says. "I have nothing to wear."

"Wear that nice dress you wore on TV the other day. It looked good on you." I could almost hear her blush on the other end of the line. "Can I pick you up at noon tomorrow?"

"How about if I meet you somewhere?"

"You name the place," I say, thrilled that she is accepting my proposal. So far so good.

"I want to go to a nice place, now that I have money," she says. "How about Denny's?"

I almost burst out laughing, but I keep my composure. "Denny's it is. Noon tomorrow. Can't wait to meet you in person. I'll wear a red baseball cap so you can tell who I am."

"Oh, thank you, Mr. Stewart. I hadn't thought of that. You're so thoughtful."

"That's how God made me, ma'am," I say. "See you tomorrow."

~

THE FOLLOWING DAY, I'M SITTING IN A BOOTH AT DENNY'S, WAITING for Phyllis Polanski. She arrives promptly at noon, wearing her thin, faded old housedress, a pair of old, blocky, short heels, a floppy wide-brimmed hat, and carrying an out-of-season white purse. She's a target made in heaven. I stand up to greet her, and she meets my gaze with a smile.

We sit and order lunch. She folds her hands and recites grace. Then she digs in, and I'm impressed when she eats every bit on her plate. The waitress picks up our plates, and Miss Polanski sits back, waiting for me to say what I want to say.

I take my laptop out of its case and produce the folder with my printed-out spreadsheets. I make my presentation.

I show her the website. She admires it, wide-eyed. She makes a comically sad face when she sees the pictures of the suffering dogs. She asks to see them again.

She compliments me on the good work I do at the shelter, and I wave it off. "Our work has just begun," I say to her. "Let me show you what I mean."

Next, we go over the spreadsheets. She sees how much it costs me to run my animal shelter and she nods her head, furrowing her brow. Then I show her the meager sum of money coming in, and how it's difficult for us to pay our bills from month to month. The final spreadsheet predicts the increasing number of dogs and cats that will likely need our help in the near future. Now I furrow my own brow, exuding a sad worry. I try, but I can't quite squeeze a tear from my eye. I'll have to figure out how to do that someday.

I take a few moments to fake compose myself before bringing out the architectural designs for the shelter's expansion. I open them up in front of her so she can easily read the label at the top — The Phyllis Polanski Wing. Her eyes open wide. She clutches one hand to her chest, to prevent a heart attack I suppose, and the other to her open mouth, to suppress a gasp.

I look calm, but I wait on pins and needles for her response.

"No one has ever done such a nice thing for me," she says. "It is such an honor!"

I can't believe what I'm hearing.

"Yes. I want to help. How much do you need?"

This is the moment. The big ask. I take a deep breath and go for it.

"This work is not easy, and it's expensive, as you can see. The expansion of the building and our services will cost a lot of money." I catch her nodding her head up and down, in understanding and agreement. "We need two million dollars."

She sits back in her seat. "Wow. That's a lot," she says.

Oh no. I reached too far! I need to step it back… fast!

"If that's too much, we can…" I start to say.

"No. I have the money, and this is a good cause, a *great* cause. Done!" she says.

"Done? Like in done deal?"

She nods her head and gives me a warm smile.

Just then, two policemen walk into the restaurant and walk right past our table. They give us a quick look and nod a hello. They make me nervous as hell.

Phyllis reaches into her purse and pulls out her checkbook. She fills in the date.

"Put that away," I say, with one eye on her and the other on the cops. "I think we should do this through a direct transfer to my checking account. I mean, it's the account I use for the company. Or, cash would work even better, but that would be an awful lot of cash."

"I can't imagine what that much money would look like in cash. I think it would be too heavy for me to carry," she says. "Let's do the bank account transfer."

"I just so happen to have a voided check for you," I say, "so you can have my account information." I hand over my check, and she looks at it carefully. She reaches into her purse and pulls out her checkbook again. She rips off one of her own checks and writes "void" on it just like mine and hands it over to me.

"Here," she says. "In case you need my checking account information for any reason."

I hesitate but take her check. "I don't think I need this," I say.

"Well, keep it just in case," she says.

The waitress comes with our bill, and Phyllis just sits there with her hands folded, looking at me with a dumb smile on her face. I can't believe it. She has five million dollars, and she expects me to pay for lunch. I smile back and reach for my wallet to pay the goddamn bill.

As we stand to leave, she says, "Let's meet here for lunch again tomorrow and finalize our plans. There is so much to think about."

That makes me even more nervous. "Wait. I thought you already said yes."

"Oh, yes. Don't you worry. We're doing this."

I walk her to her old junker car, and I watch as it putters away in a cloud of black exhaust.

~

I can't sleep. I toss and turn, thinking about another lunch with Phyllis and then the big payoff. I should be packing things up because I'll have to skip town the moment the check clears and I can withdraw all the money. Instead of counting sheep, I make a mental list of everything I'll buy with two million dollars. Two-effing million dollars!

Lunch time finally comes and I'm sitting at the same booth waiting for Phyllis. She arrives wearing the same outfit. I hope someone helps her buy some new clothes with the money she has left.

"Hello, Mark," she says. "I'm sorry, may I call you Mark? I feel we should be on a first name basis, now that we'll be partners."

I make a puzzled face. "Partners? No, I said nothing about being partners."

She hands me an envelope. "I talked it over with my attorney after we met yesterday," she says. "Here, look at what she says."

My heart races as I remove several sheets of paper from the envelope. It's a legal contract. I scan it quickly and then start to read it more slowly.

"I just love your idea," she says as I'm reading. "In fact, I love it so much that I have a few ideas of my own. I think your expansion should be much bigger. I think you should offer services for larger animals, too. And I think you need a separate storage facility on the premises, for food and equipment." She shows me some hand-drawn sketches she drew on stationery that looks like she got it at the dollar store.

"That's not my mission," I say, trying to put an end to this foolishness. "I just care about cats and dogs."

"Oh, but I care about other animals, too," she says. "I was raised on a farm. I'd like to know that cows and horses have a place to go to receive good care."

"I don't know," I say. "There's not enough money for all of that."

She points to a number on the last sheet of the contract. "Is that enough?"

Four million dollars. She's going to contribute four million dollars!

"That's twice what we had discussed," I say, my voice cracking.

"I love my animals," she says, "and so do you. You can do a lot of good with all this money, and I can live very well off the remaining one million. What do you say? Are we partners?"

I reach over the table, and my hand is trembling. We shake hands. Afterwards, she squeals in delight. "Oh, I'm so happy," she says, and claps a few times in excitement.

"Now there's just one more thing," she says. She points to the last line on the last page of the contract. It says, "Attorney fee: $2,000."

"I paid the attorney already, but if we're to be partners, this should be fifty-fifty. So, before I deposit the four million, you should transfer one thousand dollars into my account to pay for half the fees."

No brainer. One thousand dollars in exchange for four million. I agree to it on the spot.

"As soon as the money is in my account," she says, "I'll transfer the four million."

I race to my bank after lunch and arrange the transfer of one thousand dollars into Phyllis Polanski's account.

～

TWO DAYS LATER, I CHECK MY ACCOUNT AGAIN. STILL NO MONEY. MY bank informs me that my transfer to her went through without a hitch, but there's been no incoming deposit. I can't stand it any longer. I reach for the phone and place a call to Phyllis.

"Hello?" she answers.

"Hello, Phyllis. This is Mark."

"Mark?" she says. "Oh, yes, Mark! So nice of you to call. How are you?"

That really throws me for a loop. I'm thinking this lady must be senile or something. I better clear things up right away and get her on track.

"I'm calling about our agreement, about our partnership, about the four million dollars. Remember?"

"Oh, yes, sure I do. I've been meaning to call. I discussed things again with my attorney, and she added several more paragraphs to the contract. You know, the usual 'Whereas' and 'Therefore' kind of stuff. She thought it best, for our mutual protection. I'm sure you'll agree."

"Fine," I say. "When can we meet so I can sign?"

"Tomorrow? Lunch at Denny's again?" she asks. "I guess it's becoming 'our place.'" She snorts out a short laugh.

"Yeah, fine," I say, a little perturbed.

"Oh, and she's charging us another $2,000. If you can take care of your half today, we'll be all set for the big transfer tomorrow."

I agree, though now I'm getting pissed. This old lady is a pain in my ass. I'm starting to think my ass pain is worth *five* million dollars.

I transfer the second thousand dollars, spend another sleepless night, and wait for her again at the stupid Denny's. I wait for an hour before I realize she's not showing. I decide to drive to her house.

There's a For Sale sign in her front yard. People are coming and going, in and out of her house. There's a furniture truck parked in the driveway. Her front door is open for all the foot traffic, so I just walk in. She doesn't seem surprised to see me.

"Hello, Mark," she says cheerfully. "Isn't this fun?"

"What's so fun about it?" I ask. "You didn't show up for our lunch meeting."

"Oh, I'm sorry! I plumb forgot!" she says with a hand to her chest. "I got distracted. I'm putting my house up for sale, and I'm buying a new one. I'm getting all new furniture. I'm buying a car. It's like I suddenly realized that I'm rich. This is all so fun!"

"Can we sign the contract and make the transfer?" I ask.

"Um, can we wait a couple of days?" she asks. "I'm racking up so many expenses today. I want to add things all up. How about if you call me tomorrow and we'll set a date?"

Now I'm alarmed. I think she's senile, and fickle, and she's spending all my money. I need to think of something fast!

She is suddenly distracted by the furniture people. She rushes over to them to direct where they should place the sofa. I see myself out and hurry home to make a plan.

The following morning, I call her and set up a dinner date instead of lunch. I tell her I'm driving because there's something I want to show her.

I pick her up at six o'clock PM. She's dressed a little better, and I offer a compliment.

"On sale at Penney's," she brags.

"Well, you look beautiful," I lie.

"Where are we going?"

"I'm taking you to my favorite steak place. But before that, I want to show you where all our money will go."

"Oh good. I wanted to see the shelter," she says.

"I thought you might."

I take her to the animal shelter across town, the one pictured on my fake website. It's after hours. I know the place is closed. I know there are no cars in the parking lot because I saw the last one drive away before I went to get Phyllis.

I drive around to the back. I show her the generous backyard with plenty of space for the planned expansion. We walk around the yard, and I make big gestures, painting a mental picture of the building, the rooms, the good people helping the lovely animals inside. I help her imagine the veterinary services and the facilities for large animals. I generate all the excitement I can muster. I almost believe it myself. I'm that good!

Phyllis is mesmerized. She's looking all around without blinking, slowly imitating my gestures. I can see my descriptions made the desired impression.

"I thought I knew what I was doing," she says, "but seeing it with my own eyes…" She turns her head like an owl to take in the expansive imaginary view of the animal shelter addition. "Wow! The Phyllis Polanski Wing," she whispers.

She suddenly snaps back to reality and turns to look at me. I'm holding my breath for her next words.

"Drive me to my bank," she says.

"They're closed," I remind her.

"Then first thing tomorrow morning. Now let's go get dinner. It's on me!"

I feel so much joy I almost burst like a balloon. She took it — hook, line, sinker, and pole!

I PICK HER UP AT NINE. HER BANK IS OPEN NOW. SHE MARCHES RIGHT into the bank and approaches a clerk while I wait in the sitting area. I see the clerk hesitate. Phyllis looks over to me and points. The clerk walks away. A moment later, Phyllis approaches me and says we need to speak to one of the bank officers to transfer such a large sum of money. I'm sweating bullets.

They lead us into a small, glassed-in office facing the main lobby. A bank officer confirms Phyllis' request, looks at me, asks me for my photo ID and my bank information, and proceeds with the transaction! A few minutes seem like hours.

I walk out of the bank on shaking knees with my head spinning so fast I can hardly think. Four million dollars are on their way to my account!

∼

TWO DAYS LATER, MY BANK INFORMS ME THE FUNDS HAVE CLEARED. I inform them I want to withdraw the entire sum in cash — tens, twenties, and fifties.

I go to the mall and purchase a metal suitcase. You gotta have a metal suitcase for this, right? I go to my bank, and I'm again directed to a small office and another bank officer. He also checks my photo ID. He seems reluctant and even asks why I'm withdrawing the funds. He asks if there is anything the bank can do for me to invest the money. I graciously refuse his kind offer and ask him to give me my goddamn money. Not in those words, of course. I'm nothing if not a gentleman.

I walk out the door with a shiny, metal suitcase full of money and a shit-eating grin on my face. Then, I drive to the Audi dealership to check the first item off my wish list. I purchase a brand new Q5 SUV, in cash. I race back to my apartment to pick up the things I already pre-packed. I'm on my way!

∼

THE Q5 IS ALL PACKED NOW. I GIVE MY LITTLE APARTMENT ONE LAST look. I glance at my fifty-dollar decorations with disdain. I'm so much better than that now. I think I'll decorate my new place with hundred-dollar shit, hahaha.

I turn on my heel and hurry to my waiting vehicle. I start the powerful engine and back out of my driveway. I step on the gas to pull away, but something crosses in front of me, and I have to slam on the brakes. Three black SUVs come out of nowhere and surround my car. Guys dressed in black jump out of their vehicles and point guns at me. Shit!

I put the transmission in Park and raise my hands. One of the men approaches my vehicle, opens the door, yanks me out, and throws me to the ground. He slaps handcuffs behind my back and stands me on my feet.

They walk me back to one of their vehicles as a woman dressed in black exits through the passenger door. She has sleek gray hair pulled tightly to the back. She's wearing mirror shades and an angry scowl. The men look to her for her command. She looks at me and I recognize her!

"Phyllis?" I stutter my next words. "I, I don't… what the hell?"

"FBI, asshole," she says. "That's the last scam you'll play for a long time."

"W-w-wait! I can explain!" I say.

"Your name kept popping up on our suspect lists of nuisance petty crime, and we confirmed it. You're like a little gnat that won't go away. But we didn't want to just shoo you away with a minor conviction. Now, we can squash you with a felony." She makes a waving motion with her hand, and the men pull me away toward one of their vehicles.

"Wait!" I say. "What about my money?"

"Don't be an imbecile. That's not your money. We'll return it to the proper owner, the one who really won the lottery and loaned it to us for this sting. She does live here in your town."

"Who is it?" I ask despite myself. I don't really want to know.

Phyllis beams a broad smile and makes me wait for a moment before she speaks.

"She lives across town," she says. "She owns the animal shelter you know so well, and she's going to love your expansion plans."

VIOLET CRANE

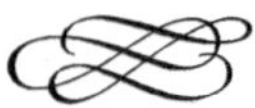

JASON POMERANCE

The winter of 1974 was one of the coldest on record in the Coachella Valley. In Palm Springs, temperatures were unnaturally frigid. Snow that normally hugged the spiky cap of Mount San Jacinto crept slowly lower in elevation so that it seemed as if it might even reach streets normally kissed only by sun.

Maybe it was so cold that icicles pierced the soul of Violet Crane, because this was the winter when everything changed.

She was not native to this place, but a recent arrival. Where she came from wasn't important. What was important was that she had fled what felt like a prison. Not because she had to run — she could have stayed and escaped a bad situation at home by marrying some local boy. She would have a couple of kids, and live a nice, quiet life until she died. But she needed to get away. Because Violet knew - knew deep down in her bones - she was destined for something great. She just wasn't sure what form that greatness would take, had not one clue really, but there the idea always loomed before her, like an apparition, just out of reach. Well, she decided it was time to change that.

One thought had been Hollywood. The movies. Because Violet Crane had God-given assets. Her legs were long, slender and sleek, her waist narrow, her bust copious. As soon as she was able, she had turned her hair from its natural mousy brown to a brassy platinum blond. "You know who you look like?" a stranger had once asked after buying her a Cherry Coke at the local drugstore.

"Tell me," Violet had answered, bringing her lips to the straw as she gazed up at him, waiting for an answer.

"Lana Turner."

"You playing with me?"

"I'd sure like to, honey."

Violet smiled, against her better judgment, because she already had learned when she smiled a certain way, it had an effect on men, and she had yet to sort out what to do with this power, how to use it to its fullest advantage.

"But it's true," the man continued, "there's a resemblance."

And so she searched for and watched every one of Lana Turner's movies, studied them, really. She'd sit in front of the mirror and scrutinize her own reflection. She decided they both had wide, doe-like eyes. Her mouth had a similar pouty lusciousness.

She could be an actress, she figured. Why not?

She did some homework, because Violet Crane was nothing if not resourceful. She trudged through bitter cold and deep snow, her destination the local library, where the librarian eyed her with suspicion. She was noticing this more and more often from older women. It amused her, and it amused her more to ignore their scrutiny, which seemed to reek of disapproval. She pulled every magazine and book that had a Hollywood angle. She noted names of important executives. She sent them letters, along with a picture where she was posed — somewhat suggestively you might say — on a thick white shag rug she borrowed from a girlfriend.

Responses came quickly.

The most promising was from a man named Walter Hindge, its value higher than others she received because it included a bus ticket and a small crisp stack of cash, tucked neatly into a long white envelope. Although the ticket wasn't to Los Angeles. Destination was Palm Springs, where Mr. Hindge owned a home, and where he spent most of his time during the winter months, he said. He was big in the world of casting, he wrote — an important, influential man — and he was certain Violet had promise. She weighed her options. She could wait for a better offer or leap at this chance. She fretted; time was ticking. She had just turned eighteen.

She leapt.

She threw her best clothes into one small suitcase and headed for the bus station without looking back at those who had birthed and raised her.

The ride was long and boring, but Violet could hardly contain her excitement. Here she was, heading to California. She didn't even spend any of the money sent by Mr. Hindge. All along the route, there were men who offered to buy her a hamburger, or a tuna sandwich when they'd stop at this diner or that coffee shop. She'd eat daintily and listen attentively to their stories (surreptitiously, she'd stash whatever was uneaten in her purse and get a second free meal). And then, after what seemed like forever, the bus arrived.

Violet stepped out onto Palm Canyon Drive and expected warmth. But wind was whipping off the mountains, producing a bone-chilling cold. A taxi brought her to Walter's house, a squat building, all sharp angles, perched next to a golf course, and then ridges of mountains beyond.

"That's three dollars and seventeen cents, sweetheart," the driver said over his shoulder as she started to get out of the taxi.

"Oh, I'm sure Mr. Hindge will pay you."

"It would be a first if he did."

He had a hand on her arm, as if she was going to bolt. She narrowed her eyes; thoughts of how she could do some harm flew through her head as she dug a five-spot from her purse. He released the pressure on her arm. For a moment the outline of his grasp remained.

It wasn't just the weather that was cold. The house itself presented a frigid face to the world. Concrete walls on either side flanked a set of giant double doors that featured gleaming brass fixtures. The house seemed bent on intimidating her, but Violet didn't scare easily. She walked right up to the door. Inside, she could hear music, Eric Clapton singing about shooting the sheriff. She rang the bell and waited. Walter Hindge answered the door. He wore a robe that fell open to reveal thick, spiky chest hair flecked with gray, a thick belly, and a large gold medallion. In one hand was a highball, and in the other a cigar. "You must be Violet," he said. "Join the girls." He indicated a room beyond the entrance hall. Violet could see a host of girls about her age; most were in bikinis and heels.

She didn't even respond, just turned on her heels and headed away from the house.

"Hey," Walter called after her. "I sent you cash. Dumb shit, you think it was gonna be a free ride?"

She gave him the finger and kept moving.

"You'll be back!" he shouted at her, and she flipped him off again.

At the station, Violet learned no buses were scheduled to leave town until dawn. She headed into the restroom and set down her bag. She splashed water on her face, then took a good look at her reflection.

Suddenly, she felt very alone. Leaving home had been an awful mistake. From deep down came the urge to shed some tears. But that felt weak, so she pulled herself together, picked up her bag, and exited the restroom.

She took a seat on a bench, then laid back and put her feet up. She fell into a slumber, her purse clutched to her chest, waking only when she felt a nudge. She opened her eyes to find a tall, slim Mexican man looming over her, leaning against a broom. "You can't sleep here. We're closing up."

"I got nowhere to go."

She tried a pouty look. It didn't seem to work. "*Lo siento, señorita,*" he murmured and continued pushing his broom.

Outside, the wind had picked up and was now howling. Violet buttoned up her coat, but it was thin and cheap cloth. Goosebumps worked their way up and down her arms and legs, and her teeth began to chatter. She had heard of something in California called the Devil Winds, powerful gusts that roared through canyons, and, if there was a spark, pushed blazing infernos that would incinerate everything in their path. *Is this what they were talking about?* she wondered.

And then, after walking a short way, movement behind a window caught her eye. There was a restaurant — she could make out a dim, candle-lit interior featuring deep red booths. The front door opened. First what spilled out was music, lively chatter and clinking cutlery, sounds of people having a good time. Then out stepped a woman. She had jet black hair swept up in a complicated poof and was wrapped in a full-length fur. Something about her mesmerized Violet. Something about the coat, actually. It seemed to shimmer under the light of the moon — like it was lacquered — as the woman gathered it to ward off the cold. A valet brought around a gleaming Cadillac Seville. The woman exchanged words with him. She slipped a few bills into his hand, got behind the wheel, and took off down the road. *That could be me,* Violet thought. *It will be me.* She watched until the car rounded a turn and disappeared from view.

How is it that obsession develops? How is it that what begins as a tiny seed suddenly and inexplicably blossoms into something big, something that can, under the right circumstances, take over a life entirely?

Violet Crane did not understand, nor did she care to analyze why, but somehow, from the instant she laid eyes on it, she could think of nothing but that fur coat. And because the coat was on her mind, so too was its owner. In the days and weeks that followed, Violet would spot the black-haired woman around town, and she'd follow her — into the grocery store, or the post office, or the salon where she'd get a manicure. Or she'd lay in bed in the tiny motel room she had rented with some of the money she had from Mr. Hindge. She'd stare at the stains on the ceiling, but she wouldn't see them — she'd see an entire imaginary life she'd built based on having that coat — the sort of house she'd live in and the car she'd drive — and she'd come up with any number of plans and schemes on how to get one. Maybe it was from hunger because lately she hadn't been eating properly, determined as she was to conserve cash, but it was almost like a hallucination, this new life she was building, and it was like a hunger that propelled her toward finding a way — any way — to make it real.

Then she learned the price of such a coat.

This occurred while she was window shopping on Palm Canyon Drive. She wandered into one little shop after another, defiantly meeting the gazes of the saleswomen, once again older ladies who watched her with suspicion, who seemed to sense she was some sort of threat. So what if she was looking and not buying? What was it to them? "Why don't ya take a picture, honey," she shot at one of these women, who then cast her eyes to the floor, and Violet Crane felt a tiny surge, a small but powerful sense of triumph she savored because the truth was that she had no idea how she was going to get from one day to the next, and this was, in fact, frightening. She was living by her wits, and although this was a dubious way to live, there was also a secret thrill. Anyway, she left the store feeling better. She wandered a few steps and then stopped in her tracks. In the window of the next boutique, there it was, up on a pedestal, lit from above — a full-length fur, an almost exact replica of the one she had seen. For a few moments, she stood at the window, her mouth agape. At some point, she noticed a man inside the store. He beckoned her to join him.

It was like a little bit of paradise, or a sanctuary, this place, the floor covered in plush deep blue carpet, the walls papered in a bold blue stripe, the few casually placed pieces of furniture upholstered in rich chintz.

"Oh, God, thank you," the man gushed as Violet entered, somewhat tentatively at first. "It's been so dead here all day. I'm about ready to keel over from sheer boredom."

He was tall and very, very thin, dressed and groomed fastidiously, with long slender fingers and nails that seemed as if they were freshly manicured. *A homo,* was Violet's thought, but this put her at ease because it meant he wouldn't be hitting on her. "You, my dear," he said, "would look fabulous in that mink!"

"Oh, I..."

She was thinking the same thing. She was reluctant to say it out loud.

"People assume you don't need something like this in the desert, but it can get cold as a witch's tit when the sun goes down! Let's get it on you already."

He removed the coat from the mannequin and draped it over her shoulders. At first, she was startled by its weight, so heavy it felt as if he had thrown on the actual animal. Then she ran a hand up and down one sleeve. The fur was silky, but with an edge, as if there was still a tinge of feral animal in it. She gathered the collar tight around her neck. She closed her eyes and inhaled. The fur had a scent that was almost intoxicating. She opened her eyes and caught a glimpse of herself in the mirror, head to toe in mink. "How much," she asked of the salesman.

"Oh, well, you know what they say: if you have to ask…"

"How much?"

He slipped a hand into one sleeve and withdrew the price tag, turning it over so she could get a look.

She almost choked.

The amount was what you'd pay for a nice car, or even a crummy house back where she came from.

But when he took it off her shoulders and returned it to the mannequin, Violet felt a stab of longing. Already she was formulating plans.

She'd earn this coat. She'd get a job. She'd save her pennies and live frugally.

Yeah, that wouldn't work, she knew. No chump job would ever pay enough. Or if it did, it would take so many years, she'd be old, or sick, or even dead. She could return to Walter Hindge's. She could marry rich. This was, after all, a place where the old came to die, she had learned. She could find some wealthy widower and bide her time.

She was at an intersection, waiting for the light to change so she could trudge back to the motel, all kinds of schemes whirring through her brain, when she spotted her: the woman she had seen that night outside the restaurant, the woman she'd been tracking. She was behind the wheel of her Cadillac, about to pass through the intersection. And then, suddenly, a plan took shape, a crazy plan that seemed to materialize out of thin air, a way to get close to this woman. Violet squeezed her eyes shut and stepped off the curb into the car's path.

~

"YOU REALLY SHOULD BE MORE CAREFUL, SWEETHEART. DID NOBODY ever warn you about looking both ways before crossing a street?"

Violet opened her eyes. At first, her vision was fuzzy, but after a few blinks, the woman from the Cadillac came into focus. That ink-black updo set off porcelain skin that was smooth and unlined, although Violet figured she was pushing at least forty, or was she even older and just hiding it well? Her almond-shaped eyes were made up with an expert hand, her lips a luscious shade of crimson. Exotic stones glittered at her ears. Her eyes twinkled with the hint of something mischievous, Violet thought, or was it something sinister? She couldn't be certain. "You okay?" the lady asked. "You got quite the konk on the noggin!"

Violet sat up. She noticed a bruise on one knee. Also, blood slowly trickled from a small cut above one eye. "I'll be alright," she insisted, even though she wasn't sure that was true. In fact, she was confused — she was certain the car would barely cause a scratch, going as slow as it was. Had she miscalculated? She just wanted to get a closer look at this woman, but now...

"Well, let me get you home and cleaned up. It's the very least I can do."

"Who are you?"

"Serena! Serena Landau. Who are you?"

"I'm Violet Crane."

Serena thrust out a hand and helped Violet to her feet. Soon, she was cocooned in the buttery leather passenger seat of the Cadillac, which still carried the smell of a dealer showroom, as if it had just rolled off the floor. On the stereo, Karen Carpenter was crooning about rainy days and Mondays while Serena fished in her pocketbook and pulled out a pack of Larks. "Help yourself, but light me a cig, sweetheart. These old hands are sometimes a little shaky." She held out one hand, and it did seem to have a small tremor. On a finger sparkled a rock the size of a small piece of fruit. Violet wondered what that might be worth as she lit them both cigarettes. For a few moments, they smoked in silence, and then Serena eased the Cadillac into the circular driveway of another sleek mid-century ranch that sat under towering twin palms. "Come on in and let's get some iodine on that boo-boo," Serena trilled as she exited the car. Violet followed her to the front door, where Serena paused, fishing for the right key. "Once again," she murmured, tsking under her breath and tapping a finger on a panel that had a green light illuminated. "Silly ditz me went out without setting the alarm! My late husband would constantly berate me over my forgetfulness!"

She unlocked the door and a front foyer came into view. The floor was tiled with cool white marble, walls lined with gold-flecked wall-paper. "Follow me, honey," Serena threw over her shoulder as her heels clicked down a long hall. Violet took in a large living and dining area that were like something out of a magazine — low-slung furni-ture huddled around a large stone fireplace while artwork punctuated white walls, providing bright pops of color. Outside, through sliding glass doors, sat a sparkling blue kidney-shaped pool. Violet followed Serena through the master bedroom, into an expansive master bath. Serena pulled a chair from a vanity and patted the back with a hand. "Now you take a seat. We'll get you fixed up in a jiffy."

Violet sat and let Serena tend to the wound. First Serena swabbed it with a cotton ball soaked in iodine. She took a small bandage from its package and gently set it in place. All the while, she chatted — about a dead husband, and about a son who was apparently estranged, "an ingrate," she insisted, "the way sons can be." Violet's eyes darted this way and that, taking in little details. She noted all the pricey perfumes and colognes and make-up bottles on the vanity. An open drawer revealed a haphazard tangle of sparkling jewels. She wanted to reach out and grab them but kept her hands folded neatly in her lap. When Serena put away the bandages and iodine, she offered to fix

Violet a cup of tea. They were on the way out of the bedroom when Violet spotted the mink — it was hanging in a closet with what appeared to be more furs; a fleeting glimpse of just a sleeve set Violet's heart aflutter. She tried to put it out of her mind as Serena led her to the kitchen. "You must be new in town because I'd have remembered if I'd seen you," Serena said as she set down tea and a small plate of cookies.

"I am," Violet said.

"You don't have many friends, do you? You got a sort of lonely look about you."

"I don't," she admitted, and the truth was she never had, had always been on her own, left to her own devices. Sometimes a good thing, sometimes bad.

"Well, as soon as I get back from my trip let's get together again. I'll show you the sights."

"You going on a trip?"

"Tonight. I'm flying down to San Diego for a few days to see my sister. Should be a blast, if you like whiny little bitches!"

Violet laughed a little, then made her excuses, first asking if she could use the bathroom. "Sure, honey," Serena said, "powder room's just off the front hall."

Violet locked the door behind her. She splashed cool water on her face. She briefly felt a stab of guilt about what she was considering, but it was fleeting, replaced by a grim sort of determination. She inspected the small room. There was a window over the toilet. Quickly and silently, she flicked the latch from locked to unlocked.

A few minutes later, she left Serena's house, declining the offer of a lift back to the motel. She wanted to walk, needed some air to clear her head. She holed herself up in the motel until darkness fell. Some sitcom was on the small black-and-white TV, but reception was fuzzy and she wasn't paying attention. Soon, she rose and stripped off her clothes. She showered and dressed in the dark slacks and sweater she'd brought from home.

Outside, Violet marched back in the direction she had come a few hours earlier. Darkness was falling over the valley, a vast canopy of stars beginning to form overhead. Way up high, a tiny sliver of moon appeared. When she reached Serena's street, she found a secluded spot behind the wall of a nearby house that looked empty. Violet didn't have to wait long before a taxi pulled up outside Serena's, and out she came, toting a powder-blue suitcase.

Violet waited a few minutes after the taxi drove off before slipping up the driveway. At the front door, the light flashed green on the small alarm panel. Now, Violet darted to the side, to the powder room window.

It was locked.

This threw her for a moment. She surveyed the ground at her feet, her eyes settling on a large stone. She picked it up. Its weight and heft in her hand made her feel suddenly powerful and in control. She bashed a hole in the window, then reached her hand through the jagged glass and unlatched the lock. Soon, she was inside. In the master bedroom, she tore the mink from its hanger and threw it over her shoulders. She swiped up some jewelry from the vanity, and from the kitchen counter the keys to the Seville. One more moment and she was gone.

THE VAST CITY SPREAD OUT BEFORE HER LIKE A CRAZY GLITTERY CARPET. She had driven the one hundred or so miles to Los Angeles in something of a frenzy, frequently glancing in the rearview, at any second expecting to see lights and sirens in hot pursuit. She envisioned gunning the car and attempting to outrun the cops. But this never happened, and when she arrived, she took a detour onto a street that took her high into the hills, a narrow, twisty road that dead-ended at a spot that overlooked the city. As she surveyed the sea of lights, it began to dawn on her that whatever fame she might achieve might come in a medium other than film, that she might become notorious for something else entirely.

Back down the hill, she cruised the Sunset Strip until she spotted a tucked-away motel. She checked herself in, at the same time noting the dire state of her finances. *Well,* she thought, *that will change soon enough.* On the bed, she laid out the mink and assorted pieces of the jewelry. For a few moments, she admired her haul, luxuriated in it. She felt no guilt over what she had done, nor did it nag at her soul.

She stripped off the rest of her clothes and stepped into the shower, letting the water pulse all down her body, watching it eddy into and down the drain.

~

VIOLET CRANE HAD READ ABOUT THE DAISY IN FANCY MAGAZINES. IT was a favorite celebrity haunt. It was, according to those in the know, the place to be if you were in Beverly Hills, right on Rodeo Drive. When Violet eased the Cadillac up to the valet stand and exited the car, she could hear thumping music from within, along with the sounds of people having a good time. Decked out in the finest outfit she had packed, along with jewels she had swiped, and swathed in the mink (despite the fact that in Los Angeles, the night was far milder than in the desert), she was escorted to the door without question. Once inside, all eyes turned, and Violet was the center of attention. She smiled and drank it all in. Blue Swede was singing "Hooked on a Feeling" on the sound system, and when a man approached and asked Violet if she'd like to dance, she followed him to the dance floor and began to move with the music.

~

THE PAWN SHOP SAT ON A PARTICULARLY SEEDY STRETCH OF SKID ROW. With her available cash running dangerously low, Violet knew she'd have to part with the coat and the jewels. But this was part of her plan; the cash would finance getting her set up in town — the apartment she envisioned, the car she'd have to acquire because she'd have to ditch the Caddy. So she negotiated the dirt and grime in the gutter, and the bums demanding handouts. She entered the store, which carried with it the smell of failure.

And then, from the man behind a screened and a well-armored booth, this: "Sorry, kid, it's a fake."

Violet fell into stunned silence. "No. It can't be," she finally managed.

"Yup. The coat. The jewelry, too. Oh, they're good fakes. Maybe twenty five bucks I could give you. I can maybe sell it all to a costume shop. Those guys are always looking for good imitations the camera won't read, but this ain't the real thing. Not even close."

She felt deflated, as if all the air had been sucked out of her body, and suddenly very small.

She turned and slunk out of the store.

And then there she was, Serena Landau, in another mink coat, leaning against the Cadillac, smoking a Lark. "You know where this Caddy came from, honey?"

"No."

"Well, I walked into a dealership outside Tucson and asked for a test drive. The salesman wanted to get a little frisky, so I let him get his way for a bit. He had his pants off when I pushed him out of the car. Got his wallet, too! Time to ditch it, though. But come on, take a walk with me."

Serena started moving in a direction that would take them out of Skid Row and into a more civilized section of downtown. Violet silently followed. "That night you saw me coming out of the restaurant? When I was waiting for the valet to bring my car around? I knew you were looking at me. I recognized something. A sort of hunger. So then you stepped into the intersection and get this: I sped up!"

"Jesus, you rammed me on purpose? Are you fucking crazy?"

"Crooks know crooks, honey. I figured if you saw a bunch of nice stuff in that house, you'd boost some of it for sure. It was a test, and you passed!"

Serena paused before a parked Jaguar and sized it up. She flicked her eyes in every direction, then removed a shim from her purse and jimmied open the lock. She got behind the wheel, and within seconds she had the car hot-wired while Violet watched in awe from the curb. "Why'd you want me to steal a bunch of fakes?"

"The insurance company thinks they're real. I've already filed a claim. And a police report, so stay out of the Coachella Valley for a while, dear. Actually, I should probably do that too. Don't ask. Long story. So I'm hitting Vegas. In fact, I could use a new partner. Lotsa dough to be made in Sin City. You in?"

For a moment, Violet reflected silently. "You're just a grifter, aren't you? A con-artist, and I was your mark. I mean, you don't have a tremor or a dead husband, do you? You're not all forgetful and fluttery like you acted," she said.

Serena exhaled, her face briefly shrouded by smoke.

"And what happened to your old partner?"

Serena didn't answer the question, just left it hanging in the air; there was something slightly ominous in this silence.

"C'mon, honey. Join me. You already stole once. You're in it now."

Violet Crane considered her options. There were things that she wanted, expensive and luxurious things; here she was presented with the means to get them and a person she could learn from. *Like a mentor*, Violet reasoned. She took a step toward the Jaguar.

HONEYSUCKLE SKY

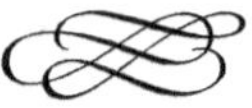

TAHANI NELSON

Carsiri had finally figured out the color of the sky.

She'd already recognized that it was the same burnt orange of the honeysuckles that she had tended for Thomas in happier days. But there was something else, something she'd been trying to place since her first day here. Carsiri smiled even as the nagging thought combed its way across her frontal lobe yet again. As annoying as it was, contemplating the color of the sky was an obsession that none of the girls back home could claim.

Fancy that. A unique obsession. Obsessions were common. Expected. But this was new. Just one more of the unexpected surprises that had awaited her on Earth. Though, she supposed that, even if they'd known, no one would have warned her that she'd spend five years trying to figure out the familiarity of a color from memories of a monochromatic childhood. But then, there were lots of things that no one had told her.

She looked at the sky again. She knew she'd seen that burnt orange hue a thousand times even before stepping off the shuttle that had brought her to stand below its smoggy cover. But she had never been able to place it. Until today.

Today, Carsiri finally realized that the Earthers' precious sky was the exact same color as the painted lips on the MHA pamphlets back home. The same color as the slogan in its curved, dainty letters that stood dutifully beneath the Martian courtesans' pointed chins: *Martian Girls Make Good Wives.*

Carsiri wrinkled her nose and tried not to think about the pamphlets and the MHA's dainty slogan, already knowing that it was futile. Obsessive, repetitive thoughts were, after all, one of her selling points. Earther husbands liked attention to detail.

Earther husbands like her newest target. The readout on her arm told her his name was William. A quick scan of his various social media profiles told her that he was self-absorbed and tried to appear as something more than a factory drone, but her sources said he assembled shuttle pieces in the largest Earther factory in this quadrant. Carsiri scowled at the thought of someone lying to make himself seem more than he was and checked the digital readout on her arm. She checked it again. Once more. It was still too early. She looked back toward the sky.

Originally, when she'd first stepped foot on this planet with nothing but her box of spices and hope, she'd thought the blossom of color above was breathtaking. She'd sat with Thomas under it for hours, just watching the clouds, thankful she'd been granted Paradise.

But then, there were only two ways off Mars. Earth or Astaria IV. Paradise or Hell. She'd been one of the lucky ones. A life beneath a true sky. A sky the color of wilted honeysuckles. She had not realized then what most Martians paid for the privilege.

Martian girls make good wives.

Those days seemed so long ago, now. Time had changed the shade. Now, she clouds above here seemed the color of disease. Of stolen dreams and forgotten promises. Painted lips that signified a slave trade that should have never been allowed to exist. They lived in a time where even the stars were not out of reach for those who had the capacity to dream. So how could they be sold to Earthers like William?

That's why Carsiri was here, now. Today, at least one more Martian girl would have the chance to believe in dreams again.

Carsiri checked the digital readout on her wrist. Once. Twice. Once more.

Getting closer.

The apartment across the street rose into the sickly, perpetual cloud covering, reflecting the smog from its spotless windows. A range of Earthers scuttled in and out, and Carsiri still marveled at the variety in their hair and features. Generations upon generations of meticulous eugenics policies had given all Martians the same ruddy hair and skin. The same overly-large eyes and triangular features.

A part of Carsiri's overly-attentive brain pondered on why an Earther would pay so much currency for a plain Martian girl and her box of spices when Earth held so much variety. Figures that were tall and lanky or short and beautifully round. Most had hair of vibrant colors. There were eyes of different shapes and in beautiful shades. A whole spectrum of skin tones. The Earthers were beautiful and majestic while the Martians' petite bodies were only well-suited for the cramped mines and stacked box quarters of their home planet. Their large eyes were only good for finding veins of ore. Everyone had always said so. Until the MHA came.

The Martian Homemaker Academy had carved out a business where no one else saw potential. They claimed that the Martian breeding qualities would be appealing to Earther husbands. They said that Martians were exotic. Obedient. Meticulous. At the time, Carsiri had wondered how the same traits that had been bred into perfecting mining slaves could also be considered suitable for Earther wives. It had not occurred to her that the words might be synonymous to some husbands.

A cold determination filled Carsiri at the thought. She had a job to do. She checked her readout again. Once. Twice. Once more. Always precise. Always meticulous.

Martian girls make good wives.

There. The Earther. William. Hair the same color of the industrial ventilators in the mines. Shiny internal respirator tubes just barely visible on the back of his neck. Eyes as blue as the counters Thomas had picked out for her five years before. *Don't think of him. Focus.* The

Earther, William, didn't even glance in her direction as he turned down the street and disappeared into the sea of multi-colored hair and bright clothing.

Carsiri waited a beat to make sure he wasn't going to come back. She imagined his wife in the apartment above. Normally, she'd be checking the door. Make sure it was locked. Once. Twice. Once more. But this time would be different. For the first time in her life, Taritha would be checking to make sure it was open.

Go. Now.

Carsiri entered the lobby. No one even glanced at her. One more good Martian wife with her head down, scuttling through the sea of bright-eyed, bright-haired Earthers. Barely more noticeable than the paint on the walls.

Carsiri passed the elevators. Climbed the stairs. Passed the rows of beautiful mahogany doors and live flowers in the corridors. Vibrant flowers. Roses and lilies. No honeysuckles. Honeysuckles wilted too quickly. The Earthers found them ugly with their burnt orange buds. But they never said that about the sky. Oh, how the Earthers prized their sickly sky.

Carsiri silently entered the door at the end of the hallway. Looked around the immaculate home that smelled like the box of spices Martian girls brought with them on the shuttle.

"Taritha?" Carsiri called gently into the empty room.

A door on the other side of the sitting area creaked open. Terrified, too-large eyes peeked at Carsiri from ruddy features. Carsiri smiled softly. "It's time, Taritha. Are you ready?"

The good Martian wife licked dry lips that were painted the same burnt orange as the sky she had learned to hate. How Carsiri hated that color, but she knew that all Martian women wore it, now. Earther husbands expected it. Martian girls must always look like the pamphlets, after all. Must look like the good wives their husbands were promised.

Taritha shook her head. "I can't. He'll track the chip. He'll find me. Please go."

Carsiri gave a warm, comforting smile and took a few careful steps forward. This was expected. She had heard it a dozen times before.

"No, Taritha. He won't look at the tracker. He'll never even know you left. You'll be okay."

"You don't understand. He's dangerous. I think he killed another Earther at work. Imagine what he'll do to me if he finds out."

"I know he's dangerous. That's why I'm here. To save you. You deserve to be more than a Martian statistic. I'll be here until you're safe."

"He'll know. This won't work."

"Taritha, do you think William would recognize you over the maid that cleans the windows? Earthers don't pay attention to the details like we do. He'll never know you've gone."

Taritha licked her lips again.

"You've done this before?"

"Many times. The Society for the Protection of Sentients is very careful, Taritha. We know what we're doing. I promise."

A little strength entered the Martian's features. She opened the door.

"He'll want his dinner on the table when he gets home. Tonight is Tapiri."

Carsiri nodded. Taritha was stalling, afraid. But that was also common. She smiled again. "And tomorrow is Elipicot. You were very thorough with the information you gave us. Perfect attention to detail. It is understandable why you were picked for the Academy, Taritha. And that makes our work easier."

"Were you in the Academy, too?"

"I was. One of the first. So you must believe me when I promise you that I memorized everything you told the SPS. Every detail. But we must act quickly. Where are your clothes?"

Taritha brought Carsiri into the bedroom. Opened the closet to display the perfectly-folded dresses that Carsiri had learned to expect. All of them were long-sleeved and ankle-length, and it hurt Carsiri a little to see. Bruises were obvious on a Martian's ruddy skin, and good-hearted Earthers often reported potential abuse to the SPS. So abusive husbands bought their wives long dresses. They were less expensive than the fine.

Carsiri changed into one of Taritha's dresses, then posed herself as the demure mouse that the MHA had taught her to be. That Earther men expected. Taritha looked her over carefully as she fidgeted with her hands.

"After dinner, don't forget to paint. He wants me to improve. Wants to be able to sell traditional Martian paintings. I'm getting better at it, but he wants me to paint like that." Taritha pointed to a canvas hanging on the sitting room wall, but Carsiri only glanced long enough to see a familiar Martian style in bright colors. She thought she recognized it but could not allow it to be her focus right now. Taritha dropped her head. "I know that we were trained to plot every movement with perfect precision before we executed it, but I am not very good with a brush. I think he can tell. It angers him."

"You never have to worry about his anger again, Taritha. I promise. Are you ready?" Taritha nodded but didn't move. She checked the digital time display above the bed. Once. Twice. Once more. Carsiri stepped between her and the clock.

"Go now. There's an auto-ve at the end of the street. Input this code—" she pressed a note into Taritha's ruddy palm—"and it will take you to the next stop. Even I don't know where it is. But you're going to be okay. I wish you the sky." At this, Taritha's large eyes finally flooded, and all the unshed tears from an untold number of years of silent abuse spilled over her cheeks. The quiet Martian dropped her head and scuttled out the door.

Carsiri calculated the time. Once. Twice. Once more. Her people at the SPS had been careful. Had attributed for traffic, delays, or mishaps. 56 hours would guarantee that Taritha would be out of range and that her MHA tracker could be safely removed. That meant that Carsiri had 56 hours ahead of her, where she would need to keep the Earther husband unaware. She could do that. She'd done it many times before without raising suspicion. And why wouldn't she?

Martian girls make good wives.

This apartment was not so different than the one she had once been assigned by the Martian Homemaker Academy. Her doors had been made of metal. Her counters had been blue. Sky-blue, Thomas had said, even though the Earthers' sky hadn't been blue for generations. But she'd loved them because they were the same color as his eyes.

Carsiri had been lucky. Her Thomas had been kind, caring. He had studied her features until he could recognize her in an entire crowd of Martians. She'd never known an Earther who could tell one apart from the other. It was one of the reasons that this deception the SPS had so carefully planned with her was likely to work. Earther husbands were all the same.

Well, most of them. But not hers. Not Thomas. Thomas, who laughed so easily and loved so readily. Thomas, whose internal respirator malfunctioned at work one fateful day while she trimmed the honeysuckle bushes in the yard, blissfully unaware. She'd known his funds were lower than those of the other Earthers that bought wives from the MHA, but she thought he would have been able to keep his respirator maintained. But he'd died when he inhaled the sky.

She'd been questioned, of course. Martian trackers alert the police when their spouses stop breathing. Officially, it is to make sure that the Martians are claimed by an heir, or safely relocated to a colony if no heir has been designated. Unofficially, Carsiri had since learned, it was because few Martian wives had been treated as well as she. And sometimes respirator tubes mysteriously snapped soon after Martian minds and hearts did.

The Earther police that had questioned her had expressed sorrow for her circumstances once they'd determined she was not at fault for her husband's death. She had not been left to anyone, and her husband did not have the funds to send her back to Mars. They deposited her with the SPS, who were then supposed to contact the MHA so she could be reassigned to another Earther or a colony.

Carsiri had thought her life was over. For a while, Thomas' brother had fought to claim her as his property, and she had been afraid. Thomas had always tried to keep her safe from his brother. "Billy is a cruel man, Carsiri." Thomas had said in life every time Billy had come to their blue-countered home. Thomas had always bade her wait in the bedroom during Billy's visits, and she had complied without question. But he never asked her to do anything without reason. "I don't want him to come near you. Ever. You deserve better than that. Everyone deserves better than that. Stay here and be safe. I love you."

At the time, Carsiri had thought that Billy was the exception in Earther society, but the Society for the Protection of Sentients and the Martian girls that had been brought to them taught her otherwise. And she wanted to save them the way Thomas had saved her.

So she was here. To offer Taritha that chance.

Carsiri looked at her digital readout. Twice. Once more.

56 hours.

CARSIRI HAD DINNER READY BEFORE TARITHA'S EARTHER GOT HOME. She knew that William liked a glass of wine with his meal. Liked his Tapiri slightly less done than was traditional. Liked his wife to be wearing makeup when he came home, with lips and eyes painted the same burnt orange that the pamphlets showed. She played her part well. She sat quietly as he ate. Kept her eyes downcast. Checked to make sure his glass was full. Once. Twice. Once more. William never even looked in her direction. Taritha had said he wouldn't. Her Earther saw his Martian wife as furniture. Why would he look at a dresser during dinner? But this was good for Carsiri. It made her job easier.

49 hours to go.

William finished his meal and went to the sitting room, dialing into the digital readout on his arm. Carsiri idly listened to the conversation as she gathered the dishes and brought them to the sink. A conversation with a coworker. William had swindled someone out of a month's pay at lunch. Carsiri hated how smug he sounded about it. How dishonest it was. She wrinkled her nose and tried to focus on other things.

But then she heard a sound that made her heart drop into her stomach. She almost dropped the glass she was washing, but caught it right before it hit the counter. She checked it over with shaking hands, anyway. Once. Twice. Once more. There were no cracks. No chips. There was nothing to worry about. It was going to be okay. She had misheard. Her mind was replaying something from long ago. A malfunction. A tick. Nothing had changed. It was going to be okay. It was going to—

But William laughed again. And there was no denying it this time. She *knew* that sound. She had heard it and loved it a thousand times before. Thomas had always laughed so easily. So genuinely.

Carsiri put the glass down shakily. She had been able to look past the blue eyes. Past the name. *Wasn't Billy short for William in Earther?* She'd thought so, but it was a common Earther name. They could have been coincidences. But that laugh. That laugh was so familiar. And so wrong. She looked toward the painting that Taritha had indicated before she'd left, and a cold fear filled her when she realized why it had looked so familiar. She'd painted it for Thomas on his birthday. She had always wondered what had happened to Thomas' things. Shakily, Carsiri grasped the edge of the sink.

She never should have taken this job.

But there was no running now. If she ran, Taritha's chip would be tracked, and she would be returned here. Who knew what fate would await Taritha then? She'd never be brave enough to try again. Carsiri could not abandon her now.

Nothing had changed. 48 hours. She could play the dutiful, mousy wife for two full days. William would never know. And then she would be gone, Taritha would be safe, and William could be alone in the cold, unhappy life he'd built for himself, without a wife to possess and abuse.

Carsiri pushed herself up from the sink and picked the glass back up. She washed it slowly. Meticulously. No smudges. Pristine. She put the remaining dishes away with a careful hand and silently went to the sitting room. She kept her head down as she passed her new husband. She had already pretended to be married to a dozen men exactly like him. This would be no different.

She was grateful, now, that Thomas had been so careful when he was alive. Many times, Billy had tried to meet the Martian wife that Thomas had picked up from the shuttle. She remembered how Billy had tried to force his way into the room where Thomas bade her wait during his visits. How Thomas had held his ground for her protection. She could still hear Billy through the door as he eventually gave up and complimented the artwork she'd painted and hung on the walls. How he'd praised her careful trimmings of the honeysuckle buds. Many times, he had offered to buy her. But Thomas had always said no. "You're not my property, Sweet Carsiri" he'd tell her later. "You are my wife."

Thomas could have taken the money. He could have used it. Maybe he would have been able to keep his respirator in better repair. But he'd said no. And through a million coincidences that Carsiri couldn't quite imagine, fate had still brought her here, anyway. To be William's wife.

But only for 48 more hours.

The idea of taking something away from the man that had terrorized her Thomas his entire life made Carsiri even more determined than before to see this through. She wanted Taritha safe, it was true. But more than that, she thought she wanted William to lose something. 48 hours was not so long.

As Carsiri settled herself before the canvas and paints Taritha practiced with after dinner, she worked to perfect the deception she'd been chosen to carry out. William hadn't even looked at her yet. She had tricked people far smarter than him in order to save the women they imprisoned in long dresses and apartments of sterile counters. William would be the same. But when he laughed again, it made her skin crawl. His laugh was too much like Thomas', but also so different. It was like comparing a true sunset to the honeysuckle sky outside the windows.

44 hours now. William's shadow over her feather-like painting made Carsiri's hair stand on end. But as he looked over her work with

his sky-blue eyes, she was suddenly afraid that she hadn't disguised it enough. That it would be too different from what Taritha could produce. She'd been meticulous, of course. She'd purposefully added mistakes. Brushstrokes that were too heavy-handed. Lines that were not perfect. She'd checked to make sure the errors were noticeable, even to William's untrained eyes. Once. Twice. Once more. But as he stood there, scrutinizing her work, she wondered if it was enough.

William laid a heavy hand on her shoulder, then laughed when she jumped.

"You've been practicing, Taritha." Carsiri lowered her eyes and offered a demure smile of appreciation. When she spoke, she raised her voice to match Taritha's quiet tones. It was surprisingly easy. But, to men like William, all Martians sounded the same.

"Are you pleased, Dear Husband?"

"Very. Come to bed."

Carsiri had been trained in this, as well. The MHA was very thorough, and Taritha had given a detailed description of what her Earther expected at night. It was not so bad as some she'd been with since she'd started saving girls with the SPS, and she had been well-trained. The MHA made sure their girls knew how to be subservient and obedient in more than just cooking and cleaning.

Martian girls make good wives.

MORNING. CARSIRI'S DIGITAL READOUT SENT VIBRATIONS UP HER ARM, and she checked the time. She checked it again. Once more. 35 hours. William would want breakfast when he woke. Carsiri got to work.

When Carsiri set William's plate on the table, he was in the sitting room, staring at her painting from the night before. Twice he glanced at her face while he studied it, but Carsiri only set the table without lifting her eyes. She sat beside him, head down, silent, but she noticed that he looked towards the picture on the wall as he ate.

Eventually, William left for work. Carsiri checked the lock. Once. Twice. Once more. The dishes needed washing. Today was laundry day. Tonight was Elipicot for dinner. She knew all of the steps. 33 hours to go.

~

WILLIAM DID NOT COME BACK UNTIL LATE THAT NIGHT, AND CARSIRI spent the evening keeping his dinner warm on the table. She checked her digital readout again and again. No messages from the SPS. No warnings that William had tried to call Taritha during the day or that anyone had checked her chip for her location. There was no reason to be concerned. But she checked the readout again. Twice. Once more. And kept his dinner warm on the table.

When William came in, he was in high spirits. He'd made a large sum of money after work, though he didn't explain how and Carsiri knew better than to ask. But his good mood was an unexpected blessing. He even complimented her on her cooking as he ate. She'd smiled and thanked him, but the hairs on the back of her neck rose when she realized that he had been staring at her for longer than anyone other than Thomas ever had. Carsiri tried not to show her discomfort as she washed the dishes and followed him to bed.

Day three. 14 hours left. Of all the times she had played this ruse, this had not been the most terrible of Earthers she'd been required to please, but it had been the most unsettling. But 14 hours from now, Taritha would be safe and Carsiri could disappear into the city, never to be seen by William again. The idea of him losing so much in a single day would be savory for years to come.

She just had to make it 14 hours.

She served breakfast dutifully. Kept her eyes downcast and her lips painted like the women in the MHA pamphlets. And all the while, William smiled his too-wide smile at breakfast. Laughed his sickly-orange laugh when he read something on his readout. Looked for too long at Carsiri's face when she poured his juice. And he took her carefully-imperfect painting with him when he left for work. Carsiri watched him go. Checked the lock. Once. Twice. Once more. Started the dishes with practiced hands.

She'd barely finished wiping down the green counters and scrubbing the oven clean when her digital readout blinked a message at her.

FROM SPS TO DECOY:

ESCORT CONTACTED. FORWARDING INSTRUCTIONS.

Carsiri frowned as she waited for the forwarded message to arrive. Taritha had told SPS that William had only contacted her by readout a handful of times since her arrival seven years before. Changes in a target's behavior often signified the Earther was catching on.

Her readout blinked again:

FROM SPOUSE TO ESCORT:

"I WANT ASTAKI FOR DINNER TONIGHT. MAKE ANOTHER PAINTING."

Carsiri pursed her lips and sent a reply:

FROM DECOY TO SPS:

"MESSAGE RECEIVED. HAVE ESCORT RESPOND IN THE AFFIRMATIVE."

This was unsettling. Contacting Taritha like this could be William's way of trying to confirm his suspicions that something was amiss. Carsiri would have to be extra careful. She sent one more message.

FROM DECOY TO SPS:

"WAS THE ESCORT'S GPS TRACKED?"

FROM SPS TO DECOY:

"NEGATIVE. PROCEED AS PLANNED. DESTROYING COMMUNICATION DEVICE. WIPE ALL EVIDENCE."

Carsiri wiped the conversation from her readout, saving only the forwarded message in case William asked for further proof that she had received it even after being presented with the correct dinner and a new painting this evening. She tried to relax. He was just fishing. Trying to see if she would slip up. She wouldn't. She could shop for the new meal and make the painting without him even realizing that he'd sent the orders to someone else.

10 hours. She could survive 10 hours.

~

Carsiri had long-since finished the tree-esque painting in blues and purples when William entered the apartment, still smiling his too-wide smile. The astaki dinner was already on the table, though she had not let it grow cold, and Carsiri rose to serve him, pulling the cork from his wine bottle. Instead of going to the table, however, William crossed the sitting room to survey her work.

"You've improved. This one will make me even more money than the other."

Carsiri responded automatically without looking up. "Are you pleased, Dear Husband?"

"Very. Even more than Tommy would have been."

This time, Carsiri couldn't catch herself. Her arm jerked and wine splashed onto the tablecloth. Her meticulous MHA training screamed at her to clean it up. To save the white lace from staining, but she was frozen. William laughed as he crossed the room to her.

"I admit. You had me fooled. How long have you been here, Carsiri?" Carsiri didn't know how to respond, and she set the wine bottle down with a shaking hand. William laughed again. "It doesn't matter. I don't know what you did with Taritha or where she is, but I don't care. Who wouldn't want to trade an auto-ve in for a space shuttle? You're an upgrade in every way." He lifted a hand and brushed her hair behind her ear. "I knew I'd have you someday."

Carsiri jerked her head away. "I am *not* yours."

"On the contrary. I had a wife, and she is missing. There is no one else to accuse of the theft but you." He sat in his chair and leaned close to her, elbows resting on the table directly in the stain of the spilled wine. "You know what happens to Martian thieves. No other husband will take you. I am sure you'll love how the prison system treats you. It's modeled after your home planet, after all."

Carsiri paled. Martians were the only race capable of surviving on the penal asteroid of Astaria IV. If she had considered the box houses and mines of Mars cramped, Astaria would be little more than a coffin. The back-breaking labor of the mines was nothing compared to what awaited her there.

She cast terrified eyes around the apartment. They fell to the digital readout on the wall. She checked it again. Once more. Slowly, she lowered her eyes and let the tears fall.

"Please, no. I will do anything."

William's smile widened, and he leaned closer. "I know. And I will let you. Take Taritha's place here, as my wife. Tomorrow, we will go to the SPS and register your chip in my name. You will be mine, even after all these years. It's a better offer than you'd get from the penal asteroid, isn't it?"

Carsiri could only nod.

"Good. Remember that. Because the first time you slip up, Carsiri, I will have you on the first shuttle off Earth. And I can make your life very unpleasant until it arrives." He leaned even closer still, his lips nearly touching her neck as he breathed against her. "But serve me well, and I'll show you how well I take care of my toys."

Carsiri pressed her lips together and wiped her cheeks. "I understand, Dear Husband. May I serve you?"

"Yes."

Carsiri went to the kitchen and back with quick, silent steps. She worked diligently to remove the stain from the tablecloth. Silently and obediently poured his wine. Knelt at the foot of the table rather than try to take a seat. All the while, William watched her closely.

"No wonder Tommy's house was always so clean. You're worth your weight in gold. Do you sew, too?"

"Of course, Dear Husband. The Academy taught me well."

"I knew you would. Tommy never had a hole in any of his clothes. I'll take more of that, Carsiri—" He motioned to the astaki. Carsiri rose to carve it without hesitation. "Such a handy Martian. I bet you could have even repaired his respirator after I slit the side. Had I known you were going to show up anyway, I wouldn't have had to work that hard to claim you in the first place."

William's laugh crawled across Carsiri's skin and found a home behind her too-large eyes. So much like her Thomas' laugh. But so wrong.

Tears blurred Carsiri's vision, but she carved his astaki carefully as he continued to gloat.

"And those paintings! That was the day I knew I wanted you as my own. When I saw the painting Tommy hung in his living room. I couldn't let Tommy have something so amazing! Especially since he'd never share." He leaned closer again, eyeing her above the carving knife. "How do you manage to paint so perfectly?"

Carsiri averted her gaze and focused on the serving plate in front of her. She barely moved her lips as she replied. "You plan each measure of your hand with precision before moving it even a centimeter. You focus wholly and utterly on where each bristle of the brush will fall before you act."

She looked back up at William with her large Martian eyes. The eyes that had been bred into her people so she could find even the faintest traces of ore in rock. It was not so different, seeing the thin line of his respirator push against his throat on each breathy exhale as he gleefully relished in his own good fortune. She traced it with her eyes, then glanced at the clock. Again. Once more.

"It is not so difficult, if you've been properly trained. Shall I show you, Dear Husband?"

Billy looked like he was about to respond, but he never had the chance. Carsiri's hand shot forward, viperlike. The carving knife aimed as carefully as the bristles on her paintbrush.

A fountain of blood sprayed across the lace tablecloth, and William's silver respirator hissed sporadically. The Earther clenched a hand over the wound, but it didn't matter. Even if he stopped the bleeding, Carsiri knew he had already inhaled the same honeysuckle sky that he had forced into her Thomas' lungs three years ago.

The police would track Taritha's chip, of course. But Carsiri smiled and looked at the clock one more time. The 56th hour had passed 4 minutes ago.

William fell from his chair, trying in vain to both grasp at the respirator tube and crawl towards the door. Carsiri watched him with an almost detached fascination. Earthers were uncoordinated. Didn't plot each movement before they acted. If he were thinking like a Martian, he would have gone for the readout on his arm. Now the police wouldn't know he'd died until his heart stopped. But, with as much as he was struggling, that would be soon.

Time to go.

Calmly, meticulously, Carsiri set the knife on the table and crossed the apartment, skirting the growing pool of blood as William reached weakly for her legs. She stepped out the mahogany door and into the hallway with its flowers and mirrors. She stopped in front of her reflection and checked her hair. Her dress. Her lipstick. Nothing was out of place save a spot of blood on her sleeve that she quietly dabbed with a kerchief before rolling the hem up and covering it neatly. With deliberate steps, she lowered her head and walked out of the apartment, blending in with the countless other nameless Martians that scuttled through the streets with downcast eyes. Their ruddy skin and triangular features all looked the same to the Earthers. No one gave any of them a second glance. No one had any reason to suspect any of them of any wrongdoing at all. Why would they?

Martian girls make good wives.

GIRL

SUSAN K. HAMILTON

ave for the dying echoes of fear, the castle halls were silent.
The girl crept along, her steps tentative. The more she
tried to remember, the worse her head throbbed. She remembered the
fight, or at least the start, but after that... nothing. She ran her fingers
along the walls, finding the rough, cool texture soothing. Stopping
every few minutes, she listened, waiting to hear the heavy steps or
rough voices of the duke's guards. It was risky business meeting them
alone--she was a little over twelve summers old, still a girl, but on the
cusp of becoming a woman. Sometimes they bullied and taunted her.
Other times, they did things. Things she tried not to think about.

She made her way along the hall and down the hidden back stairs
that led to the kitchen. This stair should have been filled with pages
and maids going about their business, unseen by the wealthy and
powerful. Duke Atíca had liked the illusion of perfection. The
comings and goings of servants intruded on that serenity, so he'd
insisted they be hidden away whenever possible.

Hunger clawed at her. She shivered, not from the ache in her
stomach but from the eerie emptiness. Most days, she got scraps from
the kitchen or from someone's plate. With a shake, she tried to clear
the muddiness in her mind. Her stomach growled. When had she last

eaten? It felt like weeks, but everything ran together. Creeping out of the shadows, she peered into the kitchen. Like the rest of the castle, silence pooled in every corner. All the utensils and bowls lay in organized disarray, as if everyone had left in the middle of their work. But no fire warmed the ovens, and a hint of rancid meat tainted the air.

Her eyes drifted along the wall. They passed over a dark shadow. She stopped and blinked, then looked again. Shadows, odd ones that didn't move, adorned the walls. She felt ill as she realized they all looked like people, as if their shadows had been peeled away from their bodies and painted on the walls and floor with soot and ash.

A chill passed over her. *Why can't I remember what happened?*

Again, her stomach pleaded for sustenance, the hunger chasing away the fear. She went to the counter where the kitchen mistress usually made the scullery girls scrub the pots. The girl sniffed at the water in the special bowl used to rinse the duke's personal dishes. It smelled stale but looked clean—no bits of food littered the bottom— and her thirst was nearly as great as her hunger. She scooped up a handful and drank it down. She'd know soon enough if she'd made a good choice.

The girl took an apple, some cheese, and a bit of stale bread from the larder and devoured them. She eyed the large soup cauldron that hung over the cold hearth. It was the largest in the kitchen, intended to feed a banquet. It was out and scrubbed clean, ready for breakfast. She knew how to make soup, but it was too big for her to lift and she didn't know how to light a fire.

She paused. Lighting a fire seemed important. *I should know how to... shouldn't I?*

The only jobs she could remember were cleaning linens, feeding the pigs, and cleaning up after the animals. Only on rare occasions did the kitchen mistress summon her to help with a meal and there had always been a fire going. She couldn't remember ever seeing the hearth completely cold.

Once she'd filled her stomach, the girl made a little bed for herself in a hidden corner of one pantry. After three days, she realized that no one would return. The water in the basin was nearly gone and getting more out of the well was a multi-hour ordeal. She knew she couldn't stay in the deserted castle forever, but where could she go? No one would want an extra mouth to feed.

Men's voices and the stomp of feet startled her out of her thoughts, and she froze, but only for a moment. Scurrying under one the heavy tables, she made herself as small as possible. Six sets of boots came through the doorway. At best, they were some of Duke Atíca's guards or possibly mercenaries. At worst, highwaymen. She could smell the leather and metal oil. The gruff voices abruptly went silent before worried murmurs and hushed curses slithered through the air. She knew they'd noticed the shadows on the walls.

One finally said, "We need to leave this place. The dead linger here."

"Shut your mouth. We'll leave when we know what happened and get what we came for," said a second. He was their leader—she could hear authority in his voice. "See if there's any food left, then we search the rest of the castle."

The men spread out around the kitchen, opening cabinets and bins. It didn't take long before other voices popped into conversation.

"Larders are mostly full," said one.

"Meat's gone rotten, but plenty of dried meat and cheese," said another.

"We could take the jerky. And some of the cheese," said a voice. This one was harder and more world-worn than the others.

A younger voice interrupted, "We can't just steal from the duke! We're not—"

"Did ya just call me a thief? You snot-nosed little—"

"Enough!" commanded the leader. The budding argument died a quick death. "We still need to figure out... Well, well. What do we have here?"

The girl screamed as a large, calloused hand grabbed her ankle and yanked her out from under the table. Her dirty, stained smock rode up, exposing her nakedness beneath. The man dropped her leg, and she scrambled to pull her shift down. She cowered on the floor.

"And who might you be?" he asked.

The girl shook her head, afraid to answer, and he hauled her up by her arm. "I asked you a question. What's your name?"

"Girl," she squeaked. She glanced up. The man holding her wore chainmail and leather. Mahogany hair crowned his head, but gray peppered his well-trimmed beard.

"Your name's Girl?" He nearly laughed. "Well, that's easy enough to remember."

"That's what Duke Atíca always called me. He said I wasn't important enough to have a name."

His voice softened from the gruff tone he used with the other men. "What do you do here, Girl?"

She glanced up. "Whatever the duke asks—"

A couple of randy snickers made Girl flush scarlet.

Eyes on the floor, she continued. "I serve meals. I clean laundry, scrub floors. Tend some of the animals."

"Do you cook?"

"Some, milord." Girl continued to look meekly down at her filthy toes.

"Milord? That's rich. You've become royalty, Milord Martin," roared another of the men.

"Shut up, Damos," Martin growled before he continued talking to Girl. "Very well. If you can cook, you'll make yourself useful and make us a stew for dinner while we search the castle."

"Yes, milord."

"Everyone, with me," Martin said to the men. "Not you, Damos. Before she cooks, find a tub to dunk her in and a clean smock. She smells like she's been living with the fucking pigs."

Two hours later, Girl returned to the kitchen wearing a shirt that must have belonged to one of the pages. Damos had cut off the hem and half of the sleeves with his dagger to make it short enough and found a length of rope to tie at her waist. She'd been afraid of what Damos might do as he watched her climb into the tub, but he'd called her a piglet, watched her impassively for a moment to make sure she used the soap he'd found, and then turned his back while she finished her bath.

Martin had sent another of his men--Luc--to hunt some fresh meat and they left Girl in the kitchen. She put sticks under the stew pot and nervously twisted the hem of her shirt in her hands, wishing she could just snap her fingers and make the fire start. A half-hour later, one of Martin's soldiers came in. He reminded her of Damos and she wondered if they might be brothers. He looked at the pitiful pile of sticks under the pot and slapped Girl on the back of the head so hard she crashed to the floor, skinning her knees.

"Stupid wench! How can you make a decent dinner if you can't even start a fire? Or are you just some witless toy Atíca kept around for his pleasure?"

As she cowered, he rummaged in the kitchen and found a handful of char-cloth and tinder. A few moments later bright embers became small flames. He added small twigs and a few of the wood pieces Girl had found. She stared at the little fire, delighted and entranced. He blew on the fire and it started to grow. A few minutes later he tossed in some larger pieces. They caught quickly, crackling and spitting. She continued watching the flames, fascinated.

Girl squealed when he grabbed her face. "I'm hungry and I want a hot supper. I'll beat you bloody if you let the damn fire go out? Can your simple brain understand that?"

She nodded and he let go. An hour later, Luc returned with a pheasant and two rabbits that he'd dressed in the field and gave them to her along with a cheery smile. She smiled back tentatively, and he gave her a merry wink. Girl cut the meat into cubes and tossed it into the stew pot along with the potatoes, turnips, carrots, onions, and some pieces of squash.

After searching the castle and finding no other people, Martin and the rest of his men finally gathered in the duke's dining hall and brazenly occupied the head table. While they'd not found what they searched for, they did discover the duke's wine. The stew needed time to cook, so Girl brought out cheese and fruit. She sat at the corner of the table and waited as they ate, running back to the kitchen now and again to check the stew or fetch something they demanded. Only Luc bothered to say, "thank you."

Girl didn't know what they were talking about but figured out each man's name as they spoke and drank. Martin was the leader; Luc, the youngest. She liked Luc. His short, dark brown hair couldn't hide the hint curls, and he had a kind smile. Twin brothers Damos and Davan—the one who had built the fire—possessed reddish-brown skin and dark amber eyes. Davan sported a full beard, Damos a smooth face. Even seated, Gorda towered over the others. Garish tattoos covered the sides of his shaved head, and a long braid of red hair hung down his back. Girl didn't like the way he watched her with his pale, watery-gray eyes. Ulle, a blond, blue-eyed Northman from a different tribe than Gorda, rounded out the group. He watched and listened to everything but was clearly uncomfortable in the castle.

"We invite the darkness by staying here." Ulle's voice rumbled like distant thunder. He glanced at the walls of the great hall. Like the kitchen, they, too, were covered with shadows that looked eerily like people.

"Maybe we can find you a dress while we're here, and you can be the lady of the manor," Gorda sneered.

Ulle glowered at him. "Mock me all you like, Gorda. This is scorched ground. It isn't right. Death will come for us if we linger here." He put his thumb to his forehead, moved it to his heart, across his chest, and back to his forehead, invoking the protection of the Triple God that the Northmen worshipped.

"We won't be here long," said Damos softly, reassuring the other man.

From where she sat, Girl could see under the table. She watched Damos put his hand on Ulle's thigh and squeeze. The Northman put his hand on top of Damos' and they twined their fingers together. Girl cocked her head, assuming that was the reason Damos hadn't touched her when she bathed.

"Where's our supper, Girl?" Gorda erupted.

She jumped to her feet and fled to the kitchen. Once there, she stood in front of the large iron cauldron where the stew bubbled. She could barely move the enormous stew pot when it was cold. It was impossible now that the fire blazed beneath it. She bit her lip, knowing the men would soon grow impatient and although the fire burned merrily, Davan's threat loomed in her mind. Grabbing a ladle, she spooned some stew into a bowl and hurried back into the dining hall where she placed the bowl in front of Martin.

"Where's mine? Are you slow and lazy, or just stupid?" Gorda snarled.

"Leave her alone, Gorda." Luc stood up, glaring at the other man.

"I'll say what I please and do what I please with her, and you'll shut your mouth, pup!"

When she heard him say *do what I please with her*, Girl's stomach churned.

"Gorda." Martin's cool voice, silky with implied threat, slid through the room. "There's no need to frighten her."

The tattooed Northman scowled at his commander but sat down. Martin looked at Luc. "Go in the kitchen and help." He offered a careless wave of his hand to send them away. Once they reached the kitchen, Girl nervously twisted the end of her rope belt in her hand.

"Get some bowls," Luc instructed.

She hurried to get a stack of bowls and brought them back. She also found a serving tray that would fit the bowls. Luc started to ladle out the stew.

"You remind me of my little sister."

"I do?" Her voice was little more than a squeak sprinkled with fear.

"You do. I miss her, but one day when I am a knight—a real knight —I'll go home and visit her. I hope she'll be very proud of me." He had dimples when he smiled, and his hazel eyes softened as he talked about his little sister.

"You have a sword, but you're not a knight?"

"I do have a sword, but my family isn't wealthy. I need to prove myself. I just joined Martin's company, but after some campaigns I'll have a reputation and be able to serve a real lord." Luc nodded absently as he pictured his future. "Then. Then, I can become a real knight."

"You're lucky. I don't have a family." Her voice was hushed.

"We'll find you one. We won't leave you here alone," Luc assured her.

She gave him a timid smile and wondered if this was what it was like to have a real friend.

A few minutes later, he held the kitchen door open. Girl hurried through, carrying a tray with six large bowls of stew. Setting them down along with some spoons, she sighed in relief, but it was short lived; Ulle kicked her. She yelped.

"Get more bread, wench! Is there no bloody beer in this cursed place?"

She ran and fetched two loaves and more cheese, before another sharp word from Damos sent her racing to where she knew the cook hid his own stash of wine. She'd barely finished when they started demanding second bowls of stew. Full bowls in front of them, the men's conversation slowed, replaced by chewing, grunting, and the occasional juicy belch.

A chunk of potato dropped from Davan's spoon and fell on the table. Girl eyed it and licked her lips as her mouth watered. It had been a very long time since she'd had something warm to eat.

Davan picked it up and made a show of putting it in his own mouth. "Not for you, stupid girl," he smirked.

"There's no need to be cruel," warned Martin. He offered his half-finished second helping to Girl. She stared at it, fearing a trick.

"See? Stupid," Gorda snorted as he tipped a wine bottle back.

Martin glowered at him, then looked at Girl.

"You can have it," he encouraged. Girl took the bowl, scurried back to where she sat on the floor, and gobbled it down.

After she finished, Martin asked, "Girl, do you know what happened here? Do you know where Duke Atíca is?"

She wiped her mouth on her sleeve. "No, milord."

"Everyone in the castle vanished but you," Damos said. He leaned forward in his chair and eyed her. "Seems peculiar, don't it?"

Girl's throat clenched, the implied accusation driving another dagger of fear through her.

"Best answer him, little morsel. You know what happens to people who keep secrets from us?" Gorda added with a nasty smile.

Girl recoiled. Davan and Ulle had hit and kicked her, but they were just mean. Gorda scared her. The way he watched her left a pit in her stomach.

"Enough!" Martin barked at the men. "Ignore them, Girl. We are concerned for the duke's safety, so you can tell me. I'm here to help—we're all here to help."

Girl studied Martin for a second. His hard, angular face bore an old scar on its cheek, half-hidden by his gray-smattered beard. He could have easily killed her when he'd found her in the kitchen or let Gorda and the others have her for sport, but he hadn't. He'd been nicer to her than most people, save for Luc. No harm telling him what little she remembered—it was, after all, nothing important.

Just like her.

"The duke had guests. They must have been important because the kitchen mistress cooked two whole pigs and made fancy desserts. I wasn't allowed in the hall—busy fetching things for the kitchen."

Girl stopped and frowned. Her memories of that day were frayed. Biting her lip as she thought, she tugged at the sleeve of her shirt. Everything about her suddenly felt too tight. She shifted restlessly.

"Go on," urged Martin.

"I was coming back from the spice room. Suddenly everyone in the dining hall was angry. They all started yelling. Then I heard swords, and I ran. Then … then… a noise. A boom. I thought, I thought the main gate had shut…"

Her voice trailed away as her brow wrinkled in concentration while she tried to reassemble the puzzle pieces of her memory. Gorda started to push up from his seat but sat down again as Martin raised one warning finger.

"We know you didn't do anything wrong," coaxed Martin. "Maybe what you tell us can help me figure out what happened."

Girl nodded. "The boom shook the whole castle, and there was this strange light. Like just before a storm when clouds hide the sun. It started outside and poured in through the windows. It came down the hall. I ran into a room and shut the door, but it burst open. It was so bright! I covered my face." She looked up at Martin, her eyes filled with confusion and sadness. "I don't know what happened next. I woke up later. All alone—" She looked at the walls. "Except for all those shadows."

Falling silent, she pulled her knees up and wrapped her arms around them. Ulle muttered and made the triangular sign of protection again. Gorda mocked him with a derisive snort. The six men returned to their own conversation. Martin hadn't dismissed her so Girl stayed. The conversation confused her—they talked of names and places she'd never heard of before.

"Tell me, Girl. Did Atíca have a menagerie?" asked Martin.

It seemed like an innocent question, but all of the men stilled, and Girl guessed the answer was very important.

"Menagerie?" Girl repeated the word slowly, her brow creasing.

Davan roared with laughter and called her stupid again. She flushed and struggled to hold in her tears. Luc came and sat down on the floor next to her.

"Menagerie," he said, repeating the word so she could understand it. "A place where the duke might have kept his fancy pets, perhaps a peacock?"

"Oh, yes," Girl said, happy to understand the question. "He has a white peacock. And a unicorn!"

"A unicorn? Really?" said Martin. "Are you certain?"

Girl frowned. "That is what Duke Atíca said, but..." She stopped herself abruptly and looked at the floor. Contradicting the duke was not her place.

"Girl?" Luc prodded. "You don't need to be afraid. Tell us what you wanted to say."

"Duke Atíca said it was a unicorn," she said without looking up.

"But you don't think it is? It will be our secret. We won't tell the duke what you've said," Martin assured her with a kind smile. "You won't get in any trouble."

"He said... he said it was a unicorn. But I think..." She whispered, hesitant. "I think it looked like a white goat that's missing a horn."

Martin's laughter roared through the dining hall. "A one-horned white goat? A unicorn, indeed! When we are done, you'll take us to Atíca's menagerie, Girl. I would very much like to see this amazing white goat."

"Of course, milord."

A short time later, she guided them through the castle and to the courtyard where the duke kept his menagerie. There wasn't much to see. Cages hung open, the occupants gone. No amazing creatures remained. No white peacock and certainly no unicorn. Not even a lowly, one-horned goat. Girl wrung her hands, afraid Martin would think she had lied to him as they walked by the empty cages and vacant pens. When they reached the last cage, a shiver skittered down her spine. It loomed, empty. The door had been blown off the hinges. She folded her arms and hugged her torso, squeezing her eyes shut as if she could blot the gilded prison from reality.

"Bad magic," Ulle muttered.

"Enough, you superstitious bastard," Gorda snapped.

"What used to be in here?" Martin asked, ignoring the bickering men. Girl could hear the dark displeasure in his voice.

"I don't know. I only came here to clean the cages." Her voice trembled. She broke out in a sweat.

Davan went to the cage. He reached for the door, but a subtle cough from his brother stopped him. Damos made the same protective sign as Ulle and the message was clear, even to Girl: if magic was involved, it might be dangerous to go inside. Davan stepped back.

"Bunch of pussies," Gorda spat.

He grabbed Girl by the back of her shirt and thrust her towards the door. She screamed and thrashed, helpless in his meaty grip. Gorda ignored her and took another step towards the door. Overwhelmed by her fear, urine ran down her leg, spattering on the ground—and on Gorda's pants.

"You little bitch! You pissed on me!" He threw her to the ground and raised his fist. Before he could do anything else, Martin seized his wrist and locked eyes with him.

"She won't talk to us if she's terrified." Martin ground out each word.

"She doesn't have shit to tell us," Gorda hissed. His eyes dropped as he felt the point of Martin's dagger at his waist.

"Leave her alone. Understand?"

"You're the boss," Gorda finally said, the moment straining between them. He backed away. Martin squatted down. Tears scarred Girl's face and she gulped in air.

"You don't have to go in the cage," he said. "Understand?"

Girl nodded as she wiped her nose on her arm.

"Why are you so afraid of it?" Luc asked.

"The duke. If you touched the cage. He, he would get … so angry."

Her eyes welled, but she blinked the tears away. She remembered when a page—on a dare from an older boy—had tried to open the door. Atíca had set his guards on the boy, and they'd beaten him to death. As much as she tried, she couldn't forget the bright blood pooling under his shattered skull, soaking the grass beneath him and turning the blades black.

As Girl clambered to her feet, Davan walked around the cage's perimeter until he reached the far corner.

"I see something…" his voice trailed, and he looked around. He broke a branch off one of the decorative shrubs. Using it, he swept the object toward him until he could pick it up.

"Is this what I think it is?" Davan asked, handing the object to Martin. Martin held it up; a tear-shaped, ruby-red stone. As the light filtered through, a golden core flashed from deep within the red.

"It is!" The excited tremor in his voice betrayed the stone's value. "I knew he had one. Canny old bastard was near 90 and didn't look a day over 50 summers. That's how he did it, he captured a phoenix and used its tears to keep himself young and healthy."

Girl started to tremble.

"He used magic to cage it, dark magic… blood magic," Ulle said, disgusted. "I can *feel* it."

Martin talked over him. "But now we know! It can be done! You can cage a phoenix and harvest its tears! If we could do it, we'd be invincible. We could heal from any wound, be young forever."

"Did you see it, Girl? What did Atíca do with it?" Gorda demanded, but before she could even try to answer, more voices piled on.

"How did Atíca bind it?" Ulle cried. Davan and Damos shouted other questions.

Even Luc peppered her, but his questions rang with awe and wonder. "You must have seen it when you cleaned the other cages. What did it look like? Like a bird? Or a human with fiery wings?"

Girl clapped her hands over her ears. She shook her head, fighting back tears. "I don't know! There was never anything in it. But it had to stay locked! No one was allowed to open it. The duke commanded it!"

But Martin seemed to have forgotten all about her. The myriad questions stopped. He barked orders, sending the men to search the castle again. They combed through nearly every corridor and room until thwarted by the night. Still they came up with nothing. Martin cursed them, ordering them to start again at sunrise. The sullen men acceded and retired to their commandeered rooms.

Girl tossed and turned on the little straw pallet she used as a mattress. Finally, she got up and wandered the halls. She stopped and leaned against the wall. It felt cool against her warm skin. Low voices from a nearby room caught her attention. She listened for a moment. The hushed, urgent voices belonged to Damos and Ulle. She blushed at the noises they made and tiptoed away.

She'd nearly made it back to the kitchen when a big form filled the doorway. "There you are, little morsel," said Gorda with a smile that didn't reach his eyes. He took her arm. "I've been looking for you."

Martin's mood improved in the morning when Luc brought him a scrap of a collar with runes on it. Girl made oatmeal porridge and some sausage for their breakfast. She put extra fruit in Luc's helping. He thanked her and she gave him a shy smile. When she brought a plate to Gorda, he made an obscene gesture with his fingers and tongue.

"Rather have you for breakfast in bed, morsel," he said. Girl could still smell his rancid breath from the night before She fled back to the kitchen.

"Pig! Can't get a grown woman to fuck you, so you'll have your way with a little girl?" Luc shouted.

"I'll fuck who I please, you snot-nosed little shit! Tonight, maybe I'll fuck you instead…"

"Shut up! Both of you!" Martin thundered, ending the fracas before it careened out of control.

Girl stayed in the kitchen cleaning some of the dishes. She overheard Martin order Damos and Ulle to ready their horses. She came to the door and lingered as Martin put the scraps of the collar into a bag. He fastened it to his belt. Luc had told her they'd take her, and she waited quietly for Martin or Luc to order her to go to the stable. Martin noticed her and met her eyes.

She started to smile at him, but when she saw his face the smile died and her heart froze.

Gone was the man who had spoken to her so kindly, had smiled at her, had not hit her when she made mistakes. Gone was the man who had protected her from Gorda's beating. In his place stood a cruel, manipulative, cold-hearted mercenary.

Girl shrank away as this ruthless stranger strode into the kitchen. Martin passed her without a care and went to the butcher block. In the doorway, Gorda tried to force Luc from the room. They started to argue. Distracted by the quarrel, Girl gasped when Martin seized her and pinned her close to him. The butcher knife skimmed across her throat. He let go and the knife clattered on the floor as Girl fell to her knees. Blood spurted from her neck.

Everything slowed. Darkness shrouded her vision as she watched Luc charge back into the room. He screamed at Martin. Her ears were ringing. The big man backhanded Luc so hard he knocked him to the floor. As her vision failed, she saw a tiny, flickering light—a candle flame in the shadowed distance—and then slipped into the void.

"She was a child!" Luc bellowed, rising from the floor.

"She was a liability!" Martin shouted back. "What did you think we were going to do, bring her with us? Like a pet?"

"You bastard, you murdered her!" Luc raged. "We could have brought her to a town—"

"And then what? Who's going to take in an orphan girl like her with no family? I'll tell you who: the local whorehouse where men like Gorda would use her to satisfy every perverted desire they have. I did her a favor," he spat.

Luc reached for his blade. "You fucking bastard—!"

Gorda drove his sword through Luc's back and out through his chest. Luc gasped and gagged, choking on his blood while his brothers-in-arms stripped him of his weapons and valuables and left him to die on the floor.

The sun rose and set twice after Martin and his band left. Girl's skin thickened and blackened. It cracked and split, oozing shimmering, molten liquid instead of putrid offal. Her charred flesh fell away. Glowing coals poured from her abdomen until a pile of embers double her size remained.

The pile shifted and slid as Fire incarnate sat up. The phoenix rose and spread its wings. Energy rippled through the flames. Pulling its wings close, flames wrapped its body. It transformed again. The body and face took shape, transforming from swirling golds, reds, and yellows to a more human form. Her hair was liquid fire. Flames draped her outstretched arms in luminous bands of topaz, ruby, and amber.

The phoenix rolled her shoulders and stretched her lithe body. Her power radiated. Shaking her head, she tried to clear the fog of reincarnation. It always took a little time to remember what had happened at the end of her previous life. Looking down, she tilted her head and considered Luc's corpse. She remembered this one. This human had been kind to her—he hadn't deserved to die like that. But the others? They did. And they would. Her anger started to burn.

She'd been careless, over-confident. When whispers of Atíca's plan to capture a phoenix had reached her, she couldn't resist trying to ferret out his plan and had arrogantly assumed her ability to disguise her true form would fool the duke. Atíca had been more cunning than she'd anticipated and laid a devious trap for her. Then he'd put that wretched collar on her... She seethed with rage as she remembered how it felt when the spell took hold: how it felt to have her power separated from her, contained in that cage while her flesh-and-blood body endured so many indignities.

She closed her eyes, thoughts of revenge and retribution on those who'd betrayed her made her aura flare. Then she caught a whiff of something in the air and her eyes snapped open. A different scent mingled with the aroma of rot that wafted from Luc's corpse. It was vaguely familiar, a scent she knew—a scent that fed her anger. She knelt, inhaling deeply, and smelled the spit on his body. She licked the cold carcass. Another memory crystalized: the scent, the taste, it belonged to the one with the red braid—Gorda! She remembered his name in an instant.

Her power shimmered, and a growl erupted up out of her throat. Searing memories of Gorda's tongue in her mouth, his hands on her small body as he'd satisfied his basest urges. And then he'd given her to Davan to sate his own desire.

A molten tear slid down the phoenix's cheek. It fell, landing on Luc's face, not far from his empty staring eyes. A phoenix tear could heal wounds and extend life but could not reverse death. The phoenix could not restore Luc's life, but she could ensure that weather and scavengers didn't defile his body. She swept a wave of flame over him.

As Luc immolated, the phoenix sorted through her memories, trying to understand what had happened. Atíca, she realized, must have been killed in the fight, shattering the spell and releasing her phoenix essence from its prison. A sorrowful keen escaped her, not for Atíca but for all of the people in the castle who'd been vaporized, reduced to charred shadows from the explosive force of her two halves reconnecting. She mourned for a moment but the knowledge that people who'd never done her direct harm had died enraged the phoenix even more. Atíca had gotten what he deserved. She only regretted that he died on someone's sword and not by her hand.

Her eyes traveled to the floor, stopping when they found the butcher knife. Martin had deceived her. His men had used her. They all deserved to be hunted. To suffer. To be destroyed. Different memories, brighter memories, intruded the phoenix's vengeful fantasy: Luc's smile as he helped her in the kitchen. The jokes he'd told to make her smile. The kindness he'd offered her. She sighed and thought, *He just wanted to be a knight. A man of honor. Justice. See his sister one more time. Make her proud.* Luc would never be a knight, but he could still help the phoenix deliver justice.

She held her hand over the pile of Luc's ashes and sang. The remains responded to her voice. They gathered and twisted, rising, shimmering with power. She spread her arms. The ash flew to her, clinging to her body, her arms, her face, and her flames. For a moment, she vanished into ashen darkness and then transformed again in a flash of iridescence.

Picking up a polished silver tray, she looked at her reflection. It pleased her to see Luc's handsome face looking back, but the wake of sadness gutted her. Luc had been her friend. Her friend! And they had slaughtered him.

Her new hazel eyes sparked and flared like hot coals.

THEY WOULD PAY.

THE END AND THE BEGINNING

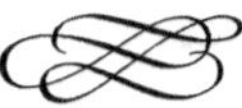

MICHAEL HAASE

... *And* this is the end.

Death, with the rumors of its horrors, is the worst thing that could possibly happen, right? The living, in order to stay alive, fear death. This seems to me a logical response now, here, on my very own cozy little deathbed, just as it did when I first got my diagnosis.

Cancer.

What a word.

I had no symptoms until I had a mild pain in my abdomen that just wouldn't go away. I thought it was my appendix finally taking that grand leap, letting me know it was finished with doing nothing for me whatsoever and wanted to try and kill me before some surgeon ripped it from its mortal coil. I thought it was a run-of-the-mill ER visit, but no.

I thought the doctor wouldn't stop after she named the first three places the scans found tumors.

Spleen. Liver. Stomach. Small intestine. Large intestine. Adrenal glands.

And so on.

There was something in that moment that was so strange. Like I left my own body in that instant. My wife was at my side, sobbing. The doctor had tears streaming down her face as she told me. The nurse standing at her side struggled to make eye contact with me. I suppose I started to cry, too, but I felt so completely and utterly detached from life itself in that singular moment.

I felt oddly free, to be honest.

That's not to say that life made me feel shackled in any way, shape, or form. On the contrary. My life was going as perfectly as a man could ever want. I had a wonderful, amazing wife. We had three unbelievably happy and healthy children. I taught chemistry at the local high school—my dream ever since my first science fair baking soda volcano.

Life was good.

So why was I so relaxed while being given such a horrible diagnosis?

Honestly, I think it was that the future seemed suddenly so well-written, there was no fighting it.

I didn't have some "in between" diagnosis that required a lot of decision making. Not with what the radiology report literally saying "too many tumors to count."

The future was clear: I was going to die, and it would be from this major "Cancer of the Everything."

All that was left to decide was how to spend my time left on this planet. There was no treatment plan. They tried to suggest such a thing, but the incurable nature of my cancer, paired with the fact that my only symptom was a bit of a bellyache, made it clear that I didn't want anything to prolong my life while also amplifying my suffering.

Honestly, the diagnosis improved my life in many ways. What was important stayed important and what didn't matter drifted to the side. I traveled with my family. I wrote down everything I felt was amazing about every person in my life so they could read it whenever they needed to hear something good about themselves. I made time for those who deserved it and forgot those who didn't. And I did it without a single ounce of guilt or doubt.

I made my time about me, which wasn't so selfish. I trusted myself to be right and just with my own time—as it should be.

I celebrated those I loved. I hugged more. I spoke with honesty, yet reserved my empty criticism. I opened my mind. I lost my love for small talk. I trusted my instincts. I lost all interest in the news and distraction. I bought more gifts. I wrote more letters.

I felt close to everyone, despite the human propensity to donate maximum time and empathy toward those dying. No reason to fault anyone for such behavior. We all must live while we're alive, after all. The inevitability of my permanent absence brought truth, courage, and love to my bedside; there was no reason to bring up the past when everyone was so present.

We all knew the time was short and acted appropriately.

And now, here, on my deathbed, my lungs can barely pull half the breath they could only a day earlier. I wonder what the difference was between "healthy" me and "cancer" me. What was my assumption about health and time that allowed me to be distracted from everything that was important—my life, my time, and every single thing I loved?

Even when I was healthy, time was short, but no one acted accordingly—least of all, me.

We got lost in the game. We forgot ourselves on a regular basis. We wanted money, not time, not love, not conversation. We wanted to be right, smart, and own everything—forgetting that we would no doubt eventually lose it all in a heartbeat.

In those four months, three weeks, and two days between now and my diagnosis, I've lived better than I had than in most of my previous forty-three years.

Yes, I'm "young." But I'm not the youngest to die. Not by a long shot. There's no award for living the longest. There's only the satisfaction in living a good life, no matter how short. And my best life was, most likely, four months, three weeks, and two days long.

This is not to say I didn't enjoy the whole ride, because I sure as hell did.

But during the short period of time after knowing damn well that I would die soon, I was free to tell the rest of the distractions and bull-shit to go away. More importantly, I was free to make time for those I love. I was no longer bogged down by retirement plans, taxes, work schedules, internet articles, bad days, dysfunctional household appliances, traffic, nor any other crap I chose to make me feel like I was "enjoying" being a living person.

Now, in my impending death, I am a man eternal. I am me. I am free.

Finally, my life is not about accumulating years, but about making the most of each second. I let loose my worries and replaced them with deep appreciation born of the tangible doom lurking in the shadows.

Death was always nearby. I know that now. It was in ignoring death that I chose not to truly live.

Death is a friend—Life is the deceitful one. Death is honest, good, and natural. Life tries to tell you that you are immortal—that staying by his side is the only way. Life wants you to ignore Death, to swear him off and get lost in the oblivion of some delusion of a promise of constant existence.

We are each only a brief and small part of the entire universe. How long we live is not important.

But, this is not to say that life is not important, nor is it to say that we are not important.

The truth is quite the contrary.

Our time is special. We get to be alive for less than the duration of a weak fart in the grand scheme of things. We've been tricked into thinking that this brief time should be pre-mourned, that we should prepare everything and everyone for the worst; be safe and sure and right and happy all the time—as much as possible—until we know that every single thing is as good and pure and profound as possible.

And yet, when we think it through for only a few short moments, we realize what we've been led to believe is important isn't actually all that important.

It's the appreciation that makes all the difference. We may all have different ideas of what it means to appreciate life, that's for sure. Now I realize that, before I learned that I would die—not "someday" but "soon"—I had taken my own life for granted. I enjoyed life when I could, but I know that all of my doubts, fears, and self-deceptions kept me from truly appreciating my vitality.

I don't have regrets. Honestly. Despite my carrying on about what could be interpreted as complaints, I am more than satisfied with the time I had. I could have done better, could have done worse, what good are the comparisons? All I know is that I am only a few moments away from the state in which I was destined to spend the vast majority of my time: Death.

Ah, Death. Dear friend. Who could live without you?

I see you there, lurking in my periphery. You've come to embrace me. Most think you steal life, but I know that's not true. You are the ultimate love. Without you, no one would appreciate anything. We would just feed and feed until we couldn't recognize ourselves any longer. You, my friend, allowed me to stop feeding on life. Ever since I was introduced to you, I could finally see clearly and focus. I could make life about something more than merely staying alive.

Thank you. I welcome you, here at my bedside.

And though I know I am about to leave so many behind, people for whom I couldn't possibly express the depths of my love, I feel content, confident, and glad, even though I am about to precede them in death, that I spent enough of my life exhibiting that brave, confident love will carry them though. That even though I will be physically missing from their lives, I will always be there for as long as they carry me in memory.

Do I wish I could have more time with my wife, my children, and my friends? Of course. But when it's your time, it's your time. I know that more than ever, now. If I had a single wish, it would be to know this—really *know* it—earlier. Maybe then I wouldn't have been as angry, as often. Maybe I would've had more clarity. More focus.

But there's no sense in dwelling on these things now.

I've got a train to catch, and everyone has a ticket for this ride. Only the exact departure is unknown, and different for all of us.

Life, you deceived me far too long. I'm grateful for Death at my shoulder. I was unafraid. I loved well. Oddly enough, I've drunk deeper from the cup of Life under Death's influence.

If only I'd known. If only I'd embraced Death when I tried so hard to pretend this friend didn't exist.

Ah, no sense in dabbling in regret now—the essential moment is coming.

Warmth from my wife's lovely hand radiates against my palm. I'm too weak to squeeze back. I want to. I can't. But I know her touch. I can distinguish her hand from anyone else's. I'm honored to know her touch, her fingertips, her warmth. You are magic. My best friend. I love you.

Even in death, I see you.

My son embraces my neck. I can smell his tears. I never knew that I could know him by the scent of his tears, until now. I'm so proud of him. My boy. You are everything I ever hoped you would be. I love you.

My eldest daughter is weeping on my chest. I haven't felt the weight of such sorrow since she lamented her divorce. I feel as awful, now, as I did for her, then. The death of a loved one and the demise of a marriage are each their own kind of grief. The sorrow each evokes is just as real as its counterpart, and to grieve is to bear a wound to one's very soul. It's okay to feel sad, my beautiful girl. You are amazing, no matter how you feel. Everything will be okay. I promise. I love you.

My youngest weeps in the background. Everyone invites her to come close, to touch me. She doesn't want to. It's okay to be afraid, my dear. I just hope that you'll lean on those who love you. Don't let Life trick you into making my death worse than it is. You are strong, my baby girl. You will be happy again. I know you will. I love you.

That's all I have.

There's nothing left.

No regrets.

My last breath, my last heartbeat, come and go. Just like everything else.

Don't be afraid.

There's nothing to fear.

It's only death.

This is the beginning…

ACKNOWLEDGMENTS

From Cari Dubiel:

A huge THANK YOU to all the writers who form the community of Writing Bloc. Whether you're represented in this anthology or not, we love that you're here. It's amazing what we can do when we all work together and support each other.

To all of the writers: You are wonderful.

From S.E. Soldwedel:

Takk så mye to Steinar Høiback and Bengt Nergaard for sharing their native Norwegian wisdom and proofing my use of their language. Vielen Dank to Max Schumacher for whipping my German into shape, and sharing his native facility with me in the form of diction and idioms. These three men helped make this story far more authentic than it would have been without their input. Bengt's historical acumen was an added bonus.

ABOUT THE AUTHORS

Jane-Holly Meissner, an Oregon-based writer, has been scribbling stories into notebooks, online, and in the Notes app on her phone for most of her life. She lives with her four children, three cats, two dogs, and her husband in a state of barely organized chaos.

"The Cleansing" is Meissner's second published short story and is related to "Mildred," her story in *Family*. Her first novel, *Fae Child*, was published by Inkshares in 2020.

Jason Pomerance is the author of two novels, *Women Like Us* (Quill/Inkshares, 2016) and *Celia at 39* (Writing Bloc, 2019). His novella, *Falconer,* debuted that same year on Nikki Finke's Hollywood dementia.com. His short stories have appeared in the *Escape* and *Family* anthologies published by Writing Bloc as well. A longtime WGA member, Jason has written movie and TV projects for numerous studios and production companies. He lives with his partner and their beagles in California, where he surfs (badly) and is at work on a new novel.

Ferd Crôtte is a physician who writes for fun and fellowship. His short story, "Captiveedom," appeared in the *Escape* anthology, published by Writing Bloc in 2019. His debut novel, *Mission 51,* was published by Inkshares in May 2022. Ferd lives with his wife Gail in Winston Salem, North Carolina. Find him at thebestparts.net.

Phil Rood draws, writes, makes podcasts, and plays music because he loves to pull thoughts from his head in a number of ways. He loves his family, his cats, coffee, and Oxford commas. Find him at philrood.com / inkandsunshine.wordpress.com.

Deborah Munro is a California native who is now working across the world as a biomedical engineering faculty member at the University of Canterbury in New Zealand. The first seventeen years of her career was spent working as an engineer in industry, designing orthopedic implants and medical devices.

Munro has always loved writing and began her first novel, *Apex*, in 2015 as part of her Certificate in Novel Writing online program through Stanford University. She entered her novel manuscript in late 2016 to an Inkshares.com competition and won a publishing contract with them for *Apex*, which is now going through the editing process. Deborah is also the author of two other short stories, "Ambition" and "The Victorian," which were published in the *Escape* and *Family* anthologies respectively.

Mike X Welch lives in Western New York with his wife, author Aly Welch, and their twin sons. His adult daughter lives in Seattle. His work has appeared in all three original Writing Bloc anthologies, including *Escape* and *Family*, in addition to the *Hell Hour* anthology (Abomination Media). His independently published collection of horror stories, *Enantiodromia*, has been met with universal acclaim.

Welch is currently at work on an entry for *Passageways: Mythos* (forthcoming, Writing Bloc). He's also working on a short story in the *Horror from the High Dive 2* anthology (forthcoming, High Dive Publishing) and on his debut novel, the long-awaited *PROOF: Protection of Occult Figures*, due to be published in 2023. That is, if the cat ever gets off his keyboard. Visit www.mikexwelch.com.

G.A. Finocchiaro was born and raised in South Jersey. He is a self-described goofball with a taste for bad jokes and good burgers. Finocchiaro currently lives in the Philadelphia suburbs. Find him at theknightmares.com / gafino.com.

Tahani Nelson writes the stories she didn't have growing up—stories about strong, amazing women who would rather receive a sword than a glass slipper. She is the author of the Faoii Chronicles: *The Last Faoii, Faoii Betrayer,* and *Faoii Ascended.* She has also published short stories in multiple collections and anthologies.

Susan K. Hamilton is the award-winning, multi-genre author whose books include *Stone Heart, The Devil Inside, Shadow King,* and *Darkstar Rising.* Her stories have been featured in the *Escape* and *Family* anthologies, and her first Shadow King-based short story was included in the *Passageways* anthology.

Horse-crazy since she was a little girl, she pretty much adores every furry creature on the planet (except spiders). She also loves comfy jeans, pizza, and great stand-up comedy, and wishes she had even an iota of musical talent because—deep down—she really wants to be a singer. Susan lives near Boston with her husband and spends her spare time with a lovely bay mare, affectionately known as "La Diosa."

Follow her on Twitter for book updates and other random musings: @RealSKHamilton.

T.C.C. Edwards, or just Chris, comes from Waterloo, Ontario, and has been enjoying the life of an expat teacher at a university in Busan in South Korea. He lives just outside Busan with his wife and two young sons, and enjoys going on long hikes around the hills and mountains of Korea.

He edited and wrote short stories for four anthologies published by the Busan Writing Group: *Nothing Too Familiar, Convergence, Peripheral Portraits,* and *Headquarters.* He also wrote a one-act play for *Fleeting* by the Daejeon Writing Group. More recently, he contributed a short story for the *Family* anthology. His forthcoming work is the long-in-progress sci-fi novella *Far Flung,* to be published within the next two years.

He has a writing blog, writeorelse.com, where he muses on the life of an author. He can also be reached through his page at www.face book.com/tcceauthor.

Nicolina Torres was a manager for Barnes & Noble for 15 years, in seven stores, and represented B&N on Channel 2's Living Dayton Show for two years. Diagnosed with Asperger's Syndrome as an adult, she has become an advocate for marginalized people, working with the National Association of Attorneys with Disabilities (NAAD) on mentorship projects and receiving FAMU Law School's BLSA 2016 Spirit of Service Award for promoting diversity in the legal profession. She has been employed at the law firm The Furnier Muzzo Group for seven years and is a member of the Women's Fiction Writers Association. Nikki's mystery novel, *This Red Fire*, was a 2017 Launch Pad Manuscript Competition Top 10 pick. Greg Silverman's Stampede Ventures optioned the book for a film franchise; the screenplay has been written by Freddie Skov (Madhouse Entertainment).

Nikki's dystopian novel, *Young Nation*, received an honorable mention in the same contest. Her collection of short horror stories (*Sharp Teeth and Other Stories*) is also being developed as a series, and her short story "Hell, Hull or Halifax" has been optioned by EMJAG Productions. Nikki was a mentor for the 2021 Tracking Board Launch Pad Prose Competition. She is represented by Zoe Sandler at ICM and Katrina Escudero at Sugar23. Find her at nicolinatorres.com.

S.E. Soldwedel received his M.A. in creative writing from the City College of New York (2007). His journalism degree from Michigan State University (2002) came in handy during a ten-year career at *The New York Post*, Hearst Magazines, and *Rolling Stone*. He lives and works in the Bronx, where he teaches English Composition at Lehman College. There, he also earned his MS Ed. In Teaching English to Speakers of Other Languages (2019). With that, he tutors local immigrants and refugees.

Soldwedel's fiction is a distillation of noir, pulp, science fiction, and adventure stories. In 2019, Inkshares published his debut novel, *Disintegration*. It takes place in the Broken Circles story universe, upon a mirror Earth. This is the setting of his short story "Teardown" and his forthcoming novel *Integration*, from which his story in *Family* is excerpted.

Michael Haase is a proud father, husband, nurse, guitarist, and writer. His first published work, a short story called "Cedric," appeared in Writing Bloc's *Escape* anthology. He has balanced many writing projects from absurd novels to children's books, which can be found at Amazon and at indie bookstores.

Evan Graham is a world-building addict and connoisseur of dread who moonlights as a science fiction author.

His debut novel, *Tantalus Depths,* hits bookstores this year. This novel, along with multiple stories featured in Writing Bloc anthologies (*Escape, Passageways,* and *Family*) are set in Graham's Calling Void universe.

Graham has a bachelor's in Education Studies from Kent State University and resides in rural northeast Ohio.

Jaye Milius is a lifelong nerd, dedicated overthinker, and occasional musician. After earning their Master's Degree in Business and spending a decade in the wild world of number-crunching, they have settled in Oregon to focus on writing and spend more time with their canine companions. Find them at @jayemilius (Twitter), @jayemiliusauthor (Facebook), @prolixitee (Instagram), and jayemilius.com.

Becca Spence Dobias is a mom, author, and ukulele player. She grew up in West Virginia and now lives in Southern California. The author of *On Home* (Inkshares, 2021), she is the Project Manager for Writing Bloc and a frequent host of the Indie Writer Podcast. Find her at beccaspencedobias.wordpress.com.

Aly Welch resides in Western New York with her husband, author Mike X Welch, and their twin sons. When she isn't writing, she enjoys acting, karate, and yoga. She also loves exploring the woods, and still hopes to find magic behind every tree and under every rock. Her personal short story collection, *Silly Little Monsters*, and debut novel, *A Better Me*, are available now. Find her at alywelch.com.

Richard Allen is a freelance writer and aspiring novelist. He lives in West Virginia with his wife and three cats. Currently, he is both a news editor and reviewer for GamingTrend.com. His writing credits include *Broadway World*, *Fan Fest News*, *Graffiti Magazine*, *The Charleston Gazette*, the *Herald-Dispatch*, *Southern Literary Review*, and the *Journal of Appalachian Studies*. When not writing, he enjoys traveling, attending concerts, and supporting local theater.

Facebook/Instagram: @richardallenwrites / Twitter: @richallenwrites

David Lee is a retired high school counselor/teacher who worked in California/Washington State schools for over forty years. Most of that time was spent at the Riverside Unified School District's Educational Options Center, an alternative site for expelled and troubled students.

Mr. Lee contributed a short story to *Family* and has had numerous articles published in Reno's *The Good Life* magazine. He writes most frequently on his blog, "Musing on the Mayhem," which can be found at davidrlee.blogspot.com. Here, since 2007, he has been recording his thoughts on modern life.

Married almost forty-four years to Jackie, the love of his life, he is the proud father of five exceptional children and "Papa" to six (soon to be seven) amazing grandkids. Mr. Lee hails originally from El Paso, Texas, attended the University of San Francisco, and lived in the Riverside area of Southern California for the better part of thirty years. He and Jackie now reside in Reno, Nevada, with their golden retriever, Annabel, and two black cats, Winston and Sadie.

Estelle Wardrip lives in Northern California, behind the redwood curtain. She shares a home with her mother, two cats, two dogs, two horses, varying quantities of goats and poultry, and approximately thirty fruit trees. When not teaching children or working on her small farm, she likes to write. In addition to "Loyalty," "1989 Redwood Lane" was published in the *Family* anthology. She is happy to be working with such a talented and friendly group of people and looks forward to publishing more in the future.

Inspired by novels such as *Watership Down* and *The Jungle Book*, Estelle presents tales from unique perspectives in unexpected settings. She also incorporates her love of art, nature, and science into her work.

After defeating some inter-dimensional shadow monsters, **Patrick Edwards** returned home in time for the weekly tea party thrown by his then-toddler-aged daughters. The party got too wild, and the police were forced to shut it down. Two dollies and one action figure were arrested. With nothing else to do, Patrick went back to work on the sequel to his debut novel, *Space Tripping*. Find him at @ThePatEdwards (Twitter) and thepatedwards.com.

Mike Donald worked for the BBC as a sound mixer, wrote for comedy sketch shows, and developed sitcom ideas. He was also a script analyst for a gap finance company and has written many award-winning screenplays. Mike lives in Oxford with his wife and a power-hungry terrier named Bonny May Donald. Find him at louisianablood.com.

Kelsey Rae Barthel grew up in the quiet town of Hay Lakes, Alberta, a sleepy place of only 500 people. Living in such a calm setting gave her time to imagine grand adventures of magic and danger, inspired by the comic books and anime she enjoyed.

After graduating from high school and moving to the city, she decided to turn her hobby into something more and worked hard to evolve her writing. Her hard work bore fruit, and she published her first urban fantasy adventure, *Beyond the Code*. Since then, she has written articles for websites, a magazine, had her work featured in several short story anthologies, and is currently working on a sequel to her debut novel.

Emily Marshall is a technical writer by day and a horror writer by night. She lives with her family in Minnesota.

ALSO PUBLISHED BY WRITING BLOC

A Better Me by Aly Welch

Celia at 39 by Jason Pomerance

Escape: A Writing Bloc Anthology

Family: A Writing Bloc Anthology

Grace Falls by G.A. Finocchiaro

The Knightmares by G.A. Finocchiaro

The Raptor and The Omega by G.A. Finocchiaro (Cataclysm Series)

Passageways: Nine Stories. Nine Unique Literary Worlds.

Silly Little Monsters by Aly Welch

Stone Heart by Susan K. Hamilton

WRITING BLOC INDIE PUBLISHING TEAM

Writing Bloc was founded in 2018 by Michael Haase, who wished to create a community of like-minded writers for sharing ideas and discussing the state of writing and publishing.

The Writing Bloc Books Team is led by Cari Dubiel, G.A. Finocchiaro, Kaytalin Platt McCarry, and Mike X. Welch. Our publishing arm distributes quality content from our members. We publish short story collections and anthologies, mysteries and thrillers, science fiction, fantasy, horror, and contemporary fiction, including romance and upmarket.

Our podcast, the Indie Writer Podcast, is led by Jacqui Castle. It's available on Podbean and anywhere you prefer to stream your content.

Becca Spence Dobias is project manager for both groups.

Visit our website at www.writingbloc.com
Visit the Indie Writer Podcast at indiewriterpodcast.podbean.com
Twitter & Instagram: @writingblocpub
The Indie Writer Podcast Twitter & Instagram: @indiewriter_pod

www.ingramcontent.com/pod-product-compliance
Lightning Source LLC
Chambersburg PA
CBHW070617300726
48975CB00006B/1838